SEALED
WITH
A TWIST

V. A. GIVENS

Ordering Information:
Quantity sales. Special discounts are available on quantity purchases by corporations, associations, and others. Orders by U.S. trade bookstores and wholesalers. For details, contact the publisher at the address above.

Editing by The Pro Book Editor
Book Cover Design by Damonza.com
Interior Design by IAPS.rocks (http://iaps.rocks)

ISBN: [978-0-9996492-0-6]

1. Main category—[Magical Realism]
2. Other category—[Diversity & Multicultural]

First Edition: January 2018

DEDICATION

To a family who planted the seed, friends who watered it, and a father who helped it grow. I could fill this page with all the help, support, encouragement, and advice given to bring my dream into reality, but it wouldn't be enough. You know what you did, and this book is for you.

I know, I know...it's about time.

PROLOGUE

AND SO THEY COME.

The old woman's eyes drifted to the tent's opening, taking in the line of jostling teenagers stretching toward the street. Their laughter filtered through the narrow split, blending into a surging hum that crashed against her thoughts.

Her eyes narrowed, a grin appearing on her thin lips. Shadows played about her face, transforming her into the Cheshire cat—escaped from Wonderland and sitting before a crystal ball, wearing a festive red muumuu and twenty pounds of gold-plated jewelry. But a flash of sunlight through the beaded voile curtains chased the darkness away, turning her back into a wizened gypsy.

Madame Celeste Dupre inhaled. She loved this town. Its energy fed her. And the money she raked in every year clothed her. In all her travels, she'd found no greater thrill than that of Willow coming alive when her fair rolled into its dreary borders, calling to its young to take control of the night.

With the sparking of one neon sign, homework fell victim to cotton candy, school buses took a bow to a lake ride through the Tunnel of Love, and chores grudgingly relinquished their thrones to hoop tosses and hammer throws. With a sweet siren's song, carnival music summoned herds of middle schoolers from the Tin Pin Bowling Alley and Ye Olde Antiques parking lot to the dusty fairgrounds. And she knew Willow Square Mall would be empty, abandoned by the more sophisticated teens who ritually staked their Friday claim on its domain.

She was the Pied Piper, watching every age, size, and color pour from all corners of Willow into the fair, filling the tents with screams of merriment, while filling the pockets of her friends with joy of another kind. Cars packed with screaming Kirby High students squealed through the parking lot, barely missing the mob of parents dropping their children at the gates before escaping home. And just when it seemed that no more kids could possibly be found in such a small city, it was time for the neighboring military base to empty its masses onto the grounds.

Little children were left at the carousel for hours, happily spinning themselves into oblivion to the tune of "It's a Small World." Love connections were made to be broken in the fun house. Rides were cheap, food was abundant, and parental supervision was scarce.

It was adolescent paradise.

"What more could a teenager ask for?" Madame Dupre inquired of the solemn girl sitting before her. "You have friends, yes?"

The girl shrank into the shadows. "Yes."

"I see no deformities needing to be erased. Your aura tells me you have no lack of friends or family. And you must have money, else you would not be able to pay my fee." She let out a dry laugh. "Yet you come to me with tears in your eyes and tell me your life is not complete. You have lived, what, eleven years?"

The girl scowled. "Fifteen."

"Fifteen years and you presume to know what life is? Much less how it is to be completed? Youth...you have it for such a short time and appreciate it only when you are too old to have it back."

The girl ducked her head and stared at the table.

The little one wants to play games. Madame's grin deepened. *I can wait. I have all the time in the world.*

Since the fair had first appeared in Willow, some thirty-odd years ago, Celeste Dupre had been there. As constant as the changing of the seasons, her crimson tent with the gold-brocade trimmings was always a much-welcomed fixture in the three-day celebration. Looking much the same as she had on her first visit to Willow, the sight of her pepper-gray beehive coif bobbing through the crowd was a thrill to any teenager. Before her rather generous frame could settle behind the famed Crystal Ball of Destiny, an anxious line of people would already have formed outside her tent, money in hand.

Madame Dupre, the Divine Diva of Destiny, she called herself. Proudly. And a master of destiny, many kids believed her to be.

Their requests never differed from year to year. Money, popularity, freedom from overbearing parents. And love. Always love, in some form or another—whether for the attention of the new boy at school or the deflowering of the frigid girlfriend, love was a constant in the minds of her customers. And as scornful as Celeste Dupre may have been of such fanciful notions of romance, desire, and—most tiresome of all—*soul mates*, she was never one to pass on a market ripe for financial exploitation.

So the years passed, while Celeste's pockets and bank accounts grew plumper off the trials and tribulations of adolescence. Her infamy also grew, a continuing answer to the hopes of teens in all towns she graced with her presence. A colorful possibility that where parents, teachers, and all self-proclaimed authority figures of the world fell short in understanding the dreams and aspirations of the young, a certain timeless gypsy would always be there to take up the slack.

For a small fee.

"I want love," the girl announced, her declaration not quite aimed at Madame Dupre but more toward the clawed feet of the table between them.

Madame held her features steady, never revealing she'd known what this snippet of a child had wanted before she'd even stepped into the tent. "Look at me," she commanded.

The girl's widened eyes rose to meet her gaze.

She took the girl's hands between her own painted talons. "Do you even know what love is?"

"No. I mean, I...I know what it is; I've just never experienced it. Well, I've experienced it, just not with another person..." The girl's voice trailed off in embarrassment.

Madame raised an eyebrow.

"I just want know what it's like to be loved back," the girl said. "I want someone to think I'm beautiful and smart and funny. Someone who'll take me on picnics, and we can feed ducks together and talk about our dreams and stuff." Her voice grew stronger. "I want my soul mate."

Madame cringed.

The girl whispered, "Everything would be perfect."

"How optimistic," Madame muttered. Sighing, she played the girl's words over in her mind, the voice changing to one that had come from her own mouth many years past. In her much younger and more idealistic days. Before too many wrong turns and dead ends had chased the stars from her eyes and replaced them with the earthly gift of practicality.

To the girl, she said, "Only once a lifetime, beginning with my own, have I ever seen that elusive emotion for which people search so hard. Real love in its truest form is a rare thing and so easy to miss. And miss it, we always do, because we never know what to look for." Bitterness crept into her voice. "Tell me. If I told you today that you would have your precious love, how would you even know when it found you?"

"I'd know when I looked into his eyes," the girl said without hesitation.

Madame snorted in response.

"No, I would," she insisted. "We'd make a connection."

"Ah, yes, the infamous connection." Another snort. "And how will this boy look? Will you know him upon sight, or will you be running around, staring into the eyes of every stranger you meet on the street?"

The girl's face softened, her eyes clouding over as she pictured the image known only to her heart. "He'll be a little taller than me. Skinny but not too skinny, and not too muscular. He'll have short hair and dimples in both cheeks. And a beautiful smile."

"Oh, so you have a face; you simply have not found the right set of *eyes* to connect with," Madame scoffed. "It is exactly as I thought—you don't even know what you are looking for. I would be much more productive to just give you a lollipop and send you on your way than to actually try to make sense of your rambling."

The girl opened her mouth in protest but was silenced with a rap on the knuckles.

"So you want for me to give you a...a soul mate. A boy who will fall as foolishly in love with you, on sight, as you have with him. He will do everything you want, think you are perfection incarnate, and you two will always be happy. Am I correct?"

The girl nodded, words of gratitude forming on her lips.

"Child, that is not love; that's a soap opera. Turn to channel six at noon if that is what you want. All I can give you is this." She placed her hands over the girl's knuckles, ignoring the look of alarm that contorted the young features. She gently tapped on each knuckle.

With each tap, the muscles in the smooth hand relaxed. The tension gradually eased from the girl's brow, and her eyes closed under the hypnotic rhythm. Background noise from the fair faded into silence. Finally, all that could be heard within the room was the rhythmic tap of her fingers.

"I have been a part of this world for many years," Madame said. "I have seen many places and experienced many dreams. I have looked into the eyes of a baby and seen the man he was to become, and I have touched the soul of a woman to grieve for what she would never be. I have walked the earth from one land to another, and never am I surprised by what I find beneath my feet. To a young one such as yourself, the word *love* is so easy to say but impossible to attain. For how can you win that which you do not understand?"

The tempo of her beat quickened upon the girl's knuckles. "What is your name, child?"

"Ricki."

"I like you, Ricki. You are me in a different time, and I see in you the chance to change what could never be undone. So listen closely to this gift that I give you:

"Only once in a blue moon is someone fortunate enough to find the path that leads her soul to its other half. And at that time, after you have waded through life's gathering of hearts to the one which was meant for you, open your eyes to what awaits you at the other end. See the reality, not the dream, or all you will find at the end of the path is a crushed spirit that will never be whole."

Releasing the girl's hands, Madame Dupre settled back into her chair.

Silent, the girl seemed to absorb her words. Nodding, she reached for her purse and rummaged inside.

Madame leaned forward with an indulgent smile, her hand extended. She waited patiently as the girl sifted through the bag's contents, her palm a suspended fixture beneath the girl's chin.

With a sigh of relief, the girl withdrew her hand from the bag, producing a pen and small notepad. She cleared her throat.

"Um…could you repeat that?"

CHAPTER ONE

ONLY A MOVIE COULD MAKE *death look romantic.*
Ricki Nichols considered this phenomenon as the
credits to *Titanic* rolled across her TV screen and Celine Dion
warbled the last passionate notes of her dedication to love,
reminding all who listened that while hypothermia and frozen
limbs might be a bit of an obstacle in any relationship, the
heart would always go on. *So a dead guy can get a date if he
waits long enough for his girlfriend to give up the ghost, but I
can't even get a live one to pay attention? Something is definitely
wrong with this picture.*

Sighing, she looked around the crowded bedroom, her
sanctuary against the outside world. Towering bookshelves
crammed with romance novels guarded its borders. Stuffed
unicorns lounged on several red beanbags, grateful to have
made it through her mother's latest spring cleaning frenzy.
Figurines of ballerinas posed in eternal plié on the headboard
above her bed, complemented by a host of comedy and tragedy
masks hanging in zigzag formation across every black wall in
her room.

The walls, she'd explained to her bewildered friends while
splashing the first drop of obsidian paint over her bedroom
door six months ago, symbolized the space of her inner mind,
and every object in the room reflected personality traits
that made up her individual psyche. They were, in essence,
standing inside her brain. Her friends had asked if the gray

ceiling represented the smoke she must've inhaled to come up with this decorative scheme, but she'd ignored them.

Unable to find a distraction from the familiar pull of loneliness, Ricki closed her eyes and allowed it to swell. She imagined a hole forming, creating an ache that traveled to her eyes and sent a small tear rolling down the side of her cheek.

"Get it together, girl," she whispered.

She rolled over and pulled a key from a slit in the bottom of her mattress. After using it to unlock her nightstand, she pulled out a small journal and skimmed its pages. Her eyes fell on a line written a few weeks earlier.

The prettiest flower doesn't always attract the most bees. It's the pollen that comes from inside the blossom that draws them, like moths to the heat of a flame.

Not quite what she was looking for, but it would do in a pinch. She started to close the journal when a more recent entry jumped off the page:

I think Aaron looked at me during lunch. I'll be shopping for a wedding dress tomorrow! YAY!!!!!!!

Beaming, she hugged the diary to her chest. Aaron Miller, the closest thing to perfection on this earth, and he'd actually looked at her...or at least looked in her general direction. Which wasn't a bad thing because it would've put her somewhere in his line of vision, and he *had* to have seen her at some point. Maybe...

She flipped to the next blank page and, with a poetic flourish, scribbled her new entry for the day.

Unrequited love sucks.

After reading the line several times, she returned the journal to the nightstand, locked the drawer, and slid the key back into its hiding spot. She turned off the lamp and settled into her sheets, then said her evening prayer in the hopes that this was the night she'd finally be heard and answered. She prayed for world peace, a cure for cancer, and Aaron Miller to talk to her someday soon.

Amen.

———— ✦⊰✶⊱✦ ————

When the alarm clock went off the next morning, the gloominess of the previous evening was a hazy memory. Yawning, Ricki summoned the willpower to open her eyes while listening to the sound of her big brother wreaking havoc in the downstairs kitchen. Once consciousness had wormed its way into her brain, she lumbered into the bathroom to get ready for Saturday drama rehearsal at school.

After taking one look at herself in the mirror, she moaned, "Oh gross," and almost crawled back into bed.

Her black hair, usually a coarse cascade of waves that fell just below her shoulders, had taken on a strangely geometrical appearance with tangled clumps of hair shooting in six different directions. And her skin... She ran her hand across a new colony of pimples taking up residence across her face and grimaced. Even though most of the bumps simmered just below the surface, one stalwart soldier had fought its way through her nightly benzoyl peroxide defense and now sat defiantly in the middle of her forehead.

"Great. Now I'm one of you." She glared through the bathroom door at the stuffed unicorns silently mocking her from their beanbag thrones.

Halfheartedly swiping an acne pad across her forehead and cheeks, she went to work on her appearance. Her dark-brown eyes, bloodshot from last night's movie marathon, were flooded with Visine until the bottle was almost empty. She mercilessly brushed and flossed her teeth to the point of her gums nearly bleeding. Then ten minutes were dedicated to cajoling, threatening, and torturing her hair into submission. It wasn't until she'd finished burying her face under a mask of foundation and powder no living organism could hope to survive that she felt presentable enough to face the world. *As long as the world is nearsighted and has stepped on its glasses.*

Okay, so she might not inspire poets to weep, and she could pretty much forget about sweeping sonnets devoted to countless ways of describing her loveliness, but she had to admit she was a far cry higher up the superficial scale of attractiveness than she'd been when first starting high school.

Her tongue slid across her teeth, relishing their smoothness without the braces that had distorted their surface for a good four years of her life. She could also suffer through a few red veins in her eyes if it meant not having to put on those two-inch thick bottle caps that used to sit on her face, giving her the appearance of a surprised owl. And no longer being mistaken for a little boy truly did do wonders for her self-esteem.

Ricki threw on a pair of jeans and a fitted T-shirt, then grabbed her play manuscript and headed downstairs. Her brother had just finished preparing his interpretation of bacon and pancakes when she ambled into the kitchen, grunted a greeting, and settled into the chair closest to the living room television. Grabbing the remote control, she surfed the channels while poking cautiously at what looked like a slab of caramelized beef jerky.

Michael snatched the remote from her. "Racquel Amanda Nichols," he huffed, "have some respect for the food I just slaved over, and at least take a bite before you ignore me."

Pushing the plate of food closer to her, he struck what she assumed was a parental pose.

"Mike, gimme," she whined, clawing for the remote. "*Pride and Prejudice* is on. I have just enough time to catch the end before you take me to practice."

"Who said I was taking you to practice?" He raised an eyebrow, flashing the platinum earring that sparkled at its edge—a recent declaration on his twentieth birthday of his individuality and artistic expression.

Her brother, the moderately rebellious one.

"Daddy," she said. "When I talked to him yesterday."

"Yeah, well, Daddy ain't here. And for the next month, while he and Mom are reliving their honeymoon days in the streets of Italy, all your travel needs are at the mercy of Mikey Ray's Park and Ride. So how much is it worth to you?" He placed the remote on top of the refrigerator, well beyond her five-foot-one reach, and leaned against the fridge to settle in for a healthy bout of negotiations.

She threw a piece of bacon at him. "One dollar."

He caught the slice and popped it in his mouth. "Twenty."

"Fifty cents."

"Thirty dollars."

"A quarter."

"Walking out the door..."

"No, wait! I'll walk Domino and won't tell your girlfriend that you were out gambling with your boys last weekend instead of studying."

"Sold!" He returned the remote to her and tugged her ponytail. "You got thirty minutes before I have to get to work. Get moving."

———— ◦✕◦ ————

It took Ricki ten of those thirty minutes to wrestle her rambunctious eighty-pound German shepherd back into the gates of the backyard. The other twenty minutes had been spent getting dragged through the neighborhood at breakneck speed while Domino chased phantom prey known only to his nose and chaotic mind. By the time she pulled her sneaker from the dog's frothing muzzle and escaped through the gate, locking it behind her and fleeing before his jaws clamped down on the hem of her jeans, she heard Mike gunning the car's engine in the driveway.

She limped up to the car and cringed at the image reflected in its window. Whatever small victory she'd achieved in her battle for beauty that morning had been overturned in one session with a hyperactive mutt. Her hair had snaked its way out of the ponytail to resume its hexagonal dance around her head. Liberated tendrils waved gleefully to the sky, a few sticking to her sweaty face. Her makeup had also melted away, leaving a pasty, almost corpse-like sheen to her skin. She tried to wipe away the sweat but instead left a smear of foundation and mascara streaking down the side of one cheek.

It's going to take the whole ride to school to fix this mess.

Mike rolled down the window and thrust an envelope at her. "We got some of the Marquez's mail again. Drop it off for me while the car's warming up."

Scowling, she obediently took the envelope and stomped across the yard to her next-door neighbor's house.

Enemy territory.

"Please don't let him be home," she muttered.

She warily surveyed the house, hoping to sneak the letter into the door's mail slot and leave. Just as her foot hit the front porch, the door flew open, and a group of seniors from her school's soccer team came pouring out. She froze midstep as Kirby High's finest headed her way. Guillermo Espinoza, twins Maurice and Marcus Greene, Victor Schultz. And Aaron Miller.

The earth paused midrotation. Time jumped off the clock and stood still. And Ricki's heart stopped beating and fell to the pit of her stomach.

Aaron Miller looked like he'd just stepped out of the pages of *Sports Illustrated*. The blue-and-gold Kirby soccer uniform hung from his frame like an Armani suit, and his closely cropped auburn hair reflected the sun's rays like molten lava.

Even the sun shines brighter for him, she thought.

He walked toward her in slow motion as she awaited his approach like a crippled deer staring into a set of oncoming headlights. She tried to think of something to say, but her brain had turned to sludge. She also seemed to have lost control of her motor skills because her mouth was stubbornly not heeding its instructions to smile and instead hung open like a dying fish.

She attempted to force a greeting from her throat, but all that emerged was a humming, "Hhhh…"

He acknowledged her with a polite nod of his head and kept walking. An aroma of spicy musk lingered behind to assault her senses.

You idiot! her mind screamed. *Say something. Say something!*

I'm not ready, she argued back. *I wasn't expecting to see him. I don't have anything planned.*

Her mind maintained its frenzied debate as his footsteps carried him farther down the driveway, each step taking her dream of claiming his heart with it. Brutally beating down her indecision, she thought to call out to him. Before she could form the words, another figure filled the open doorway—one just as impressive as the boy who'd come before it, but much, much less welcome.

Damian Marquez swaggered down the porch steps, his gym bag tossed casually over one shoulder and a sneer on his face. He looked like a pirate in a pair of gym shorts and soccer cleats. Silky black hair framed his olive skin in inky waves that fell around his pierced ears—the diamond studs threatening to blind anyone within five feet. The edge of an undefined tattoo peeked over the top of his jersey, stopping just short of his collarbone.

He stopped in front of Ricki, his six-foot-one frame blocking out the sun.

All thoughts of Aaron evaporated. Her spine stiffened, and eyes narrowed into an icy glare. Without a word, she held out the envelope.

Hooded eyes as dark as a moonless night swept over her in one long, critical appraisal. His sneer deepened.

In one horrified second, realization crashed down upon Ricki that her face was still smeared with makeup and sweat, her hair was undone, and she was missing a shoe. Mortified, she began desperately smoothing the unraveling bird's nest that was her hair while praying the earth would swallow her whole.

"Dang, Rocky," Damian drawled, using his own less than affectionate take on her nickname. "You actually leave the house looking like this? No wonder you can't get a man." He plucked the envelope from her rigid fingers and strutted down the driveway to an audience of laughter. "Mikey must've hit her with the ugly stick, again."

Her body flushed in embarrassment while her brain struggled not to imagine what Aaron thought of her.

The sound of Aaron's voice then joined in the laughter, and its amusement was more cutting to her heart than an actual blade. In fact, a knife would've been kinder.

She held her chin high and continued to face the house, waiting until Damian's Jeep Wrangler Rubicon pulled away from the driveway, all the while fighting against the bubbling river in her chest that threatened to escape from her eyes in a flood of tears. Taking deep breaths, she forced the humiliation into the back of her mind until it could be revisited at a later time. A time when her big brother wasn't waiting for her and she could be free to give the devastation of the moment the proper mourning it deserved.

As she limped back to Mike's car, she wiped the streaked makeup off her face with the underside of her T-shirt. If only she could start the day over.

Ricki had not always hated Damian Marquez.

In fact, it was love at first sight when he'd first strolled into George Washington Elementary School and straight into her six-year-old heart. But the love quickly faded after he pushed her face-first into a tree during an intense game of Superheroes, causing a nosebleed all over her new pink dress. Little Damian had laughed about her injury and hailed it as indisputable proof that Spiderman was far superior to Wonder Woman, who, after all, was just a crybaby girl. And when he then snatched Action Hero Chrissie from her scuffed arms and ripped off its head as a trophy of his victory, the love was truly gone.

Over the years, their disdain for each other blossomed, evolving from that schoolyard skirmish into full-blown war. Damian's teasing ran the course of most little boys with the typical buckets of sand in the hair, well-aimed spitballs, or blistering noogies, but as Ricki grew tired of his abuse and learned to retaliate in equally, if not more spiteful ways, their hostility took on a life of its own that manifested through insults, not-so-harmless pranks, and the occasional death threat.

Their parents tried to stay neutral, believing the conflict was just a youthful phase they would outgrow. As they got older, however, buckets of sand down pants became jars of fire ants and spitballs turned into pellet guns. When Ricki's parents found the book *The Artful Alchemist's Guide to Household Poisons* and a sack of rotting potatoes under her bed on the eve of her first day in high school, they knew it was time to put an end to the feuding, and an intervention was swiftly staged.

After an hour of lectures from Mr. and Mrs. Nichols on the recklessness of their behavior and another hour of counseling from Ms. Marquez on "healthier alternatives for releasing toxic emotions," three important things became clear to Ricki and Damian that night:

1. Their parents had lost all concept of what it meant to be young;

2. A sneak attack that draws less attention is much more effective than a full-frontal assault that can get you grounded; and

3. Never hide your ammunition under the bed where it can be found.

An unspoken agreement passed between the two—the war was still on, but it was time to move their battle under the parental radar.

Ricki and her best friend of almost six years, Denise Holmes, strolled through the nearly deserted halls of Ralph J. Kirby High on their way to rehearsal. With the exception of the drama students who made RJK Auditorium their second home every Saturday morning and the athletic teams getting in extra hours of practice, the school's blue floors were free of the traffic that stampeded through its two-story structure during the weekdays.

Ricki had managed to recover from the horror of that morning, having spent the ride to school repairing both her appearance and shattered outlook on life. She'd decided to cling to the belief that with enough time and brainwashing, she would be able to forget the first half of the day had ever taken place. Denial could be a beautiful place, and she planned on living there for a while.

"It couldn't have been *that* bad." Denise gave her shoulder a sympathetic squeeze.

"No, Denny," she replied. "It was worse. Way, way worse."

"So your hair was a little messy, and your makeup was a little smudged. Big woo. I'm sure you still rocked it." Denise tossed her own chestnut mane, which most certainly never had a strand dare to fall out of place, let alone go through such a mundane thing as a bad hair day.

"If *rocking it* means crawling under an actual rock and waiting to be put out of my misery, then yeah, I rocked it. Hard."

They stopped at their lockers to wait on the remaining members of their crew. Taking no more chances at being caught with her guard down, Ricki methodically examined her hair for flyaways in the locker mirror and did an inch-by-inch inspection of her makeup.

It hadn't been so long ago that her parents had forbidden the use of cosmetics, condemning her to a horrifically natural existence as her friends walked the line of glamorous artificial beauty. When she'd turned sixteen two months ago and was finally allowed to apply that first tube of Captive Coral lipstick to her barren lips, her friends had wasted no time in educating her on the fundamentals of transforming herself into a living work of art. Wielding her lip wand with the precision of Dali, she swiped a coat of gloss across her mouth.

"Ricki," Denise said, "I keep telling you: you're not just hair and makeup. Okay, yeah, the right hair and makeup can make anyone look good, but it's really all about being confident in yourself and owning it. You should be able to walk around in a potato sack and shower cap and still be the finest thing on two legs."

This coming from the girl who looked like Aphrodite's forbidden love child. Ricki sucked her teeth and applied a second coat of gloss.

Denise stopped her hand. "Look, you could have charcoal all over your face and a freaking mullet, and you'd still be beautiful. I mean, c'mon, one of our best friends has a Mohawk, and guys are all over her." She smoothed the edges of Ricki's ponytail. "Aaron would have to be an idiot to count you out because of a little dirt and sweat."

Ricki summoned a small smile. "It's easy for you to say that, Denise, but I'll never look like you."

Denise's mouth opened in mock horror. "God help you if you did. One of me is almost too much fabulousness for this dreary town as it is." Her azure eyes twinkled. "But seriously, you don't need to look like me. You only need to look like you. With some confidence."

Ricki shook her head and squinted at her reflection in the locker mirror. Was that another zit?

"Hey." Denise grabbed her chin. "I'm not saying this again, so listen hard. You're beautiful. You just need to believe it."

And this is why you're my best friend, Ricki acknowledged to herself. *Because you see things in me that no one else does. Including myself.*

Denise Holmes had first arrived in Willow five years ago when her father was stationed at its adjoining military base. George Washington Elementary was instantly held hostage by her charm. Within hours of her arrival, she had every member of the school faculty twisted around her adorable little finger. Within days, the playground had turned into a battleground for little boys competing for her attention. And within a week, every girl in her class had brought out claws they never knew they had, vying to become a part of her growing inner circle.

Ricki was the only person to not fall under her spell. A quiet girl, she saw through the dazzling façade that blinded her classmates and recognized a kindred spirit, having learned to cover her own shyness by avoiding the public eye. Except, instead of shirking attention, the new girl actually hid from the world by throwing herself into it, distracting everyone with a likeable character so the real Denise Holmes could remain buried away, safe from judgment.

One day in music class, Ricki had offered a piece of gum to Denise despite Mrs. Cavanaugh's strict rules against eating in the classroom.

Denise had looked questioningly at her.

"It's spearmint," she'd responded. "You don't have to chew it since it's not cherry. But I thought I'd give you something you *really* like, instead of something you just want other people to *think* you like."

They had been fast friends ever since.

"I'm running out of time." Ricki closed her locker, shutting her mirror image back into the darkness with the books and folders where it belonged. She looked at her friend. "My year is almost up, and I'm no closer to finding love than when I started. Correction, I've found love. It just doesn't want me."

Denise appeared to want to argue, but instead leaned against the lockers beside Ricki and waited for her to continue.

"I thought when I met Aaron, all of the questions were solved, y'know?" She tapped her toe against a crack in the cobalt pavement. "I knew it the minute I looked into his eyes—the way I always *knew* it would happen. But it's been so long, and he still doesn't know I'm alive. So what do I do?"

Denise let a few seconds pass before saying, "If he's the one, you shouldn't have to do anything."

Ricki considered Denise's words while examining the sprawling stain on her left shoe—a parting gift, courtesy of Domino's salivating maw. Instinct almost drew her back to the locker to recheck her makeup, but she stopped herself. Staring too closely at her pores for an extended period of time had given her a mild headache, and if she hadn't turned into a living work of art by now, it just wasn't going to happen. In any case, the genuine Picasso masterpiece already stood right next to her.

It had been almost a whole year since she'd sat in Madame Celeste Dupre's tent and received the riddle meant to lead her to her heart's greatest wish. True love. She had studied the riddle for months, dissecting each line for hidden meaning. Thinking "a path to lead her soul to its other half" meant she would meet her soul mate on a nature trail, she'd spent every weekend for two months going on hikes through Woodbury Park. And for a girl who believed bugs should only be seen under a broom or at the end of a stream of Raid, a sweaty trudge through bush and bramble just to run into a possibly nonexistent future boyfriend was pushing the limits of faith. When she came home one day with poison ivy in places where even the sun chose not to get too familiar, she was more than happy to kiss nature goodbye and move on to the next method of finding romance.

Wading through hearts. Also known as swimming lessons.

Her parents simply couldn't understand why their land-loving daughter—the one who screamed bloody murder if her hair was accidentally misted during a car wash—would pay to have herself thrown into the deep end of a pool every afternoon at the community center. Ricki couldn't quite understand it herself but faithfully subjected herself to days of plugged ears, red eyes, and a burning nose in hopes of meeting her "one." When the daily exposure to chlorine caused her hair to become brittle and start to break off, she decided maybe her interpretation of the riddle wasn't quite on the mark and retired her bathing suit to the far recesses of her closet.

After all, better to delay your meeting with destiny than run into it with a bald head.

Before she knew it, a full summer had passed, and she stepped into the line for sophomore registration just as single and lonely as the day she'd stepped foot into the gypsy's tent. She vowed she was done jumping through hoops over an impossible puzzle given to her by some geezer con artist. But as soon as the thought passed through her mind, a blast of wind from the school's lobby doors ripped a bunch of elective forms from her hands. She had followed the trail of fallen papers to the most beautiful pair of hazel eyes ever created, skin the color of buttered caramel, and a set of impossibly delectable lips. And the rest was history.

Ricki finished replaying the treasured scene in her head and returned her attention to Denise. "Do you know his first words to me were, 'Excuse me, you're in my way'?"

"Sounds like true love at its finest," Denise cracked.

She sighed. "Okay, I get it. If it's meant to be, he'll come to me." *Brave words. Now my heart just needs to believe it.*

Denise looked down the hall. A knowing grin spread across her face. "Maybe that's what he's doing right now."

Ricki followed Denise's gaze to a group of boys coming around the corner. They jostled and clowned their way through the corridor, their voices echoing off the walls to announce their arrival. Her heart quickened at the sight of a familiar head of dark ginger hair bobbing in the middle of the cluster and—much to her relief—an absence of Damian's dark one. Her mind sped through an audit of hair, clothing, and visage: ponytail in place and pulled neatly to the side; both shoes on feet, with doggy drool stain hidden against the locker; makeup freshly applied and no shine on forehead. Check, check, and check.

"Denise," she whispered, panic lacing her voice, "is he looking at me?"

"I can't tell. I only see the top of his head."

"What should I do?"

"Seize the moment. You might not get another chance. Quick, Marco Downing—yea or nay?"

Ricki tore her eyes away from the crown of her dreams to study the stocky redhead at the front of the group. He was in the process of punching a short boy with glasses on the shoulder and hooting with laughter whenever the wire frames almost fell from the boy's nose.

"Yea?" she answered.

"Yeah, I think so, too." Giving her hand a squeeze, Denise leisurely pulled away from the lockers to sashay across the hall to the water fountain. Seemingly ignorant of the cluster of unbridled testosterone making its way toward her, she ran her fingers through her hair, giving the glossy tresses a lazy shake as her fingertips reached their end. Sunlight pouring in from the nearby windows glinted off her natural gold highlights, illuminating each strand.

Cue singing birds and harp-wielding angels, Ricki observed in grudging admiration.

A hush fell across the corridor. Footsteps slowed as Denise lowered her head to the fountain and pursed her cherry lips against the flow of water. Her body created a perfect L with shoulders and chest thrust forward and butt straining against her form-fitting jeans.

Marco's fist paused midpunch and fell helplessly to his side.

After taking several slow sips from the fountain, she threw

her head back and unhurriedly wiped drops of water from
her mouth, her palm tugging gently at her bottom lip with
each swipe. As if noticing the crowd of mesmerized boys for
the first time, she feigned a look of surprise followed by a
blinding smile. Her eyes then fell upon the hypnotized statue
of Marco, and the smile was replaced with an expression of
annoyed indifference.

"Please keep on walking, Marco Downing," she said. "I'm
not speaking to you."

His face flushed a mottled shade of crimson. "Why?
What'd I do?"

"You didn't call me last night."

"But...but I don't even have your number," he protested.

A playful smile danced along the corners of her mouth.
"And whose fault is that?"

His eyes lit up in understanding. With a cocky grin, he
moved to join her at the fountain, giving Denise the opportunity to catch Ricki's attention and jerk her head in
Aaron's direction.

Ricki peeked at the group of boys lingering nearby. Aaron
stood conspicuously at the edge of the cluster, presiding over
his teammates from a short distance. She pushed back the
screaming doubts picking away at her resolve, knowing the
ideal moment to make Aaron's acquaintance had arrived—
while his running partner, Damian, was nowhere to be seen.
Smoothing a hand over her hair, she took a step forward.

Speak the devil's name, and he will appear. The dark
prince himself strutted around the corner, leaving the sound
of female giggles reverberating behind him.

Ricki watched Damian's approach with growing dread
and signaled to Denise to bring her flirtations to an end.
Unfortunately, her friend was too busy cooing over Marco's
flexed biceps to notice the frantic hand signs.

She whipped around to face her locker, rummaging inside

for an imaginary book. Maybe if he didn't see her, he would keep walking…

"Hey, Denise," she heard him call from the other end of the hallway, her shoulders slumping in resignation, "I heard your grandma was in town, but I had no idea you were gonna bring her to school today."

Ricki's jaw tensed.

"Oh, my bad," he amended, "it's just Rocky. Guess I wasn't too far off."

A couple of boys snickered.

Hot tingles shot through her spine. *I refuse to play your game, right now, Devil Boy.* She blinked repeatedly, trying to release the tension in her jaw.

"Give it a rest, Damian," Denise said.

"Yeah, D," Marco added. "I'll just be a minute, and we can roll out." Turning back to Denise, he resumed attempting to memorize her telephone number.

Ricki's head was still buried in her locker when the hairs at the base of her neck stood up. She felt the absence of warmth as a shadow replaced the sun's light on her back. Biting her lower lip, she accepted the inevitable fact that confrontation couldn't be avoided today. It never could be when it came to Damian. Shutting her locker, she turned around and looked up into his smug demeanor.

"Rocky," he greeted, using the nickname he'd given her in the third grade after a scarring bout of chicken pox had left her, as he charmingly put it, "looking like she'd been hit in the face one too many times."

"Satan Jr.," she hailed in return.

"I would've thought you'd fix yourself up a little since this morning." He reached into his gym bag and pulled out a brush. "I can't do anything for the face—you'll have to talk to God about that one—but maybe you can do something with this." Taking her resistant hand, he pressed the wooden bristles into her palm.

His cronies chuckled.

So much for hoping for peace. Snatching the brush from him, she stepped forward. "Look, Junior, I know you're on the way to your daily appointment to play with yourself, so please don't let me stop you." She looked pointedly at his gym shorts. "Better hurry. Doesn't look like there's much left."

A reluctant murmur of appreciation came from their biased audience. She looked at Aaron but couldn't read his expression. Denise gave her a thumbs-up.

"Besides," she continued, "don't you have something better to do than bother me? Like, I don't know, slaughter chickens or plan world domination or something? Maybe sacrifice a few virgins?"

He smirked and squinted at his watch. "Nah, virgin sacrifices aren't for another twenty years." He mockingly looked her up and down. "But don't worry, Rocks. I guarantee that you'll *still* be on the list."

Her cheeks grew warm as the kids around them sniggered.

Before she could retaliate, Damian pulled the brush from her hands and used it to motion to his buddies. "Let's bounce," he ordered. "Coach already got on us yesterday for being late." He turned and walked away, his teammates dutifully following.

Ricki released the breath she'd unconsciously been holding. She hadn't been able to talk to Aaron, but she'd at least held her own against Damian and still maintained a little of her dignity. Maybe it wasn't too late for her to impress him after all.

Damian paused in his departure and turned back to her. "Hey, could you come with us?" he asked. "We're out of space in the locker room, and I could really use that *huge*, flesh-eating zit on your forehead to hang my bag on." Holding his gym bag up to her face, he attempted to hook its straps over her brow.

With the exclusion of Denise and herself, everyone on the floor roared in laughter. Even Aaron.

Returning the bag to his shoulder, he gave her a demonic sneer. "No? Well, think about it and get back to me." With that, he and his gang disappeared down the hall.

Ricki drooped against the lockers. She put her face in her hands, running a finger over the cursed bump that had aided in her downfall.

Denise rushed to her side and gave her a tight hug.

"He got me, again," she mumbled through numb lips. "He ruined everything. He always ruins everything." Gently pushing away from Denise, she walked toward the auditorium.

Denise scribbled a quick note to their friends to meet them at practice and stuck it on her locker. Catching up to Ricki's dejected figure, she tried to distract her with chatter about their upcoming play.

Her words were a distant drone in Ricki's ears.

Nothing had gone right since getting out of bed that morning, and the end of her quest to win Aaron's heart was getting further and further away. Thanks to Damian. Once again, she felt the familiar stinging in her eyes as tears collected in the corners, burning the rims.

This time, she let them fall.

CHAPTER TWO

"I THINK MR. Q IS HEADED for another nervous breakdown."

Ricki and two other friends sitting in the dimmed auditorium observed the flailing hands of their drama teacher/play director, Julius Quincy, and nodded a unanimous agreement. If the veins throbbing along the edges of his receding hairline were any indication of his state of mind, the arrival of another unmarked van and mysterious "vacation" were undoubtedly in his foreseeable future.

Gripping the pages of a tattered script in one fist, he jabbed a trembling finger at the owner of the aforementioned Mohawk, Teresa Ma. She stood with arms crossed, her rolling eyes and barely suppressed giggles goading him to the verge of implosion. Nearby cast members, recognizing the warning signs, had drifted toward strategic positions behind furniture and large props.

"I hope he holds it together long enough for us to get through the play," the statuesque blonde seated to the left of Denise continued. "It would suck if this one got canceled like last year's, wouldn't it?" Lindsey Callahan turned to Ricki, waiting for a response.

Ricki dragged her thoughts away from the gloominess that was now her life and made an effort to join the conversation. "Um…yeah…"

"What're they fighting about this time?" Denise asked, stepping in to rescue her.

Lindsey grimaced. "Teresa's hair."

Julius Quincy had spent the past four years adapting Shakespeare's *A Midsummer Night's Dream* to fit his own vision of a modernized fairy tale. His creation, *An Evening's Reverie*, was a labor of love in which he had poured hours of blood, sweat, and uncontrollable tears during the moments he could find between teaching class, directing plays, and the occasional visit to the Knotty Pines Clinic for Mental Restoration and Recuperation in the nearby town of Hollowsbridge. He'd planned every facet of his play down to the tiniest of details, from cast assignment to set construction. And *nowhere* in the multitude of sketches, diagrams, and charts littering his office floor did Tatiana—Queen of the Fairies and an image of dignified, ethereal beauty—parade around his stage sporting a black Mohawk with electric pink tips flowing down the center of her head.

Denise watched the unscripted drama unfold onstage as she braided the hair of another member of their circle, Yolanda Matsi. "I don't get it. Terry always grows her hair out for plays. Why's she fighting Mr. Q, this time?"

"It's a protest because he didn't cast her as Puck," Lindsey said. "She claims Puck is the only character he didn't butcher, and she was born for the role."

"Uh, we've been working on this play all semester. She decides to protest *now*?"

Yolanda chimed in. "Her dad's check just cleared."

"Oh. That explains it, then."

Teresa came from one of the wealthiest families in Willow. With a real estate mogul for a father and a mother who was heiress to a nationwide chain of upscale outlet malls, she was accustomed to getting whatever her insatiable heart desired.

And its most recent acquisition was a spot in Kirby High's exclusive drama troupe.

Giving Yolanda's hair a finishing pat, Denise commented, "Well, she might want to bring it down a notch because Mr. Q is about to blow."

Lindsey and Yolanda flinched as Quincy threw his script on the ground and kicked it across the stage.

"Oh, wow," Lindsey breathed, "I think someone better get his pills."

"They're missing," Yolanda said. "He hasn't been able to find them since practice started."

Denise and Lindsey's mouths dropped open in matching O's of horror. The three girls looked back at the stage, dread stamped on each face.

Ricki half-listened to the discussion around her. Her friends' voices were dulled by the sound of Aaron's laugh as Damian used her face as a coatrack. She played the day's run-ins with Damian over in her mind like a movie stuck on replay, imagining countless versions of her day with different clothing, different routes to practice, and wittier comebacks. In every scenario, the outcome remained the same: the Dark Prince humiliated her.

"Guess it's my turn to return the favor," she mumbled.

Yolanda eyed her. "You okay?"

Teresa's voice rang out. "If you want long hair so bad, *you* wear a wig!"

All four heads whipped toward the stage.

"Oh no," Lindsey groaned. "We better get up there."

Yolanda and Lindsey hurried from their seats. As she walked away, Yolanda muttered, "It musta been one *big* check, that's all I gotta say."

Denise scooted into the seat next to Ricki. "It really wasn't that bad, y'know."

"What, Mr. Q's meltdown?" *What had they been talking about?*

"Come back to us," she joked. "No, I mean the whole thing with Damian." She prodded Ricki with her elbow. "Hey, at least you got Aaron's attention."

Scowling, Ricki slouched farther into her seat. "Not really the kind of attention I wanted."

"But at least it's a start. Before today, you couldn't pay Aaron to notice you. Now he knows your name, where you live, where your locker is, and that you've got a mean sense of humor."

Ricki nibbled on a thumbnail. "Okay, I'll give you that," she conceded, "but getting him to notice me doesn't really mean much if I'm looking like a joke. How do I turn *that* around?"

"With a pair of skintight lowriders and a smile," Denise teased. "Once he sees how tight you look at the party tonight, we'll have to scrape him off the floor."

She laughed. Teresa's parents were at a couples retreat until Sunday afternoon and blissfully unaware of the PG-13 debauchery about to go down in their peaceful home. "And this time, there won't be any Damian around to mess it up," she said. "God bless Teresa."

With a lighter heart, Ricki reached under the seat for her purse. Digging to the bottom of the bag, she pulled out a wrinkled piece of paper and smoothed it onto her lap. "Alright, I found the path at the beginning of the school year. If I finally made the connection today, what's next?"

"Looks like you need to wade through a gathering of hearts," Denise observed, peering over her shoulder. "What about the volleyball tournaments at the lake? There's always a bunch of guys there watching the college chicks bounce around in their bathing suits. Maybe you should go."

"Yeah, no," she said, shaking her head. "What're my chances of getting Aaron's attention with a bunch of big-chested amazons romping around in bikinis all around me? I might as well put a bag over my head, paint my skin camouflage, and wait to be ignored."

"Not if you're the one wearing the bikini."

"Huh-uh. I am not prancing around in a bikini every Saturday at the lake just for Aaron to look at me."

"You're seriously no fun." Denise sighed. "Well, I don't know what you're supposed to do—I've given you my best." She glanced down the aisle at a rapidly approaching figure. Casting a sly grin in Ricki's direction, she purred, "And here's someone else who wants to give you theirs."

Ricki hurriedly shoved the paper to the bottom of her purse just as Reginald Jacobs turned into their row to flop down beside Denise.

He brushed a lock of dirty-blond hair out of his eyes and groaned. "We're never getting out of here alive. Q is frothing at the mouth, and I swear he's cursing at Teresa in tongues." He looked at Ricki. "What's the word, Rick?"

She smiled. "The word is *fudge*. As in, you were supposed to bring some to practice, but my mouth is still strangely empty." Tilting her head to the side, she assumed a puppy-dog pout. "Don't you love me no more?"

He clutched at his heart and grimaced. "You wound me, Rick. O ye of little faith…" Reaching into his jacket pocket, he produced a small package and tossed it onto her lap. "Only for you."

"Thank you, Reggie," she sang. She ripped open the package and pulled out a chunk of marbled fudge. Breaking it in half, she tried to hand a piece to Denise, who'd suddenly become so absorbed in Teresa and Quincy's argument that she couldn't tear her eyes away from the stage. Shrugging, Ricki popped both pieces in her mouth and closed her eyes in contented bliss. "Your mom should be immortalized," she praised through a mouthful of chocolate.

Reggie laughed, his emerald-green eyes wrinkling at the corners.

Smacking her lips, she made a show of sucking nonexistent chocolate from each finger.

He swallowed. "With a response like that, I'll have to remember to bring the whole plate next time."

"This was the perfect thing to cheer me up," she said, wiping her hands on her jeans.

Reggie cocked his head to one side. A random curl fell over his eye, softening his angular features and giving Ricki the instant impression of a young Brad Pitt posing for his first photo shoot.

They'd first met in Dramatic Interpretation 101, immediately clicking over their passion for acting. When they were then inducted into Quincy's drama club midway through freshmen year, nobody could've been happier for them than they were for each other. Sophomore year had been a dream as they shared scenes during the production of *An Evening's Reverie.*

Ricki played Mia, Quincy's version of Shakespeare's Hermia—a young woman in love with one man but forced to marry another. Reggie played Darius, the man who loved Mia and attempted to marry her against her will. Because of their characters, Ricki took pleasure in teasing Reggie about secretly pining away for her, until he found a way to shut her up with offerings of his mother's fudge. He kept the bribes coming, she kept her cheerful abuse to herself, and a Saturday ritual was set.

Flipping the curl out of his eye, he leaned over Denise's back to whisper, "What's wrong?"

She tucked the errant curl behind his ear. "Everything. You ever have one of those days?"

"All the time," he said, leaning in closer. "But then I put my dad's bottle of Hennessy down, and it all goes away."

She giggled.

A yell shattered the muted atmosphere of the auditorium. "Darius!" Quincy bellowed. "Center stage, now!"

Their teacher stood at the foot of the stage, glaring in Reggie's direction. Lindsey, in the role of Elena—Mia's best friend who betrays her confidence to win Darius's love—lounged on a sofa, waiting to begin the scene. Teresa and Yolanda were nowhere to be seen.

"Gotta go," Reggie said. "Remember: stay off the hooch." Chucking a finger under Ricki's chin, he bounded from his seat and sprinted down the aisle.

Denise sat up, giving her a knowing look. "We're feeling better now, aren't we?" she asked coyly, her mouth pursed in a tight smirk.

Ricki stretched. "Yeah, I think I am."

The smirk dissolved into a wide grin.

"What?"

The grin faded. Shaking her head in disgust, Denise collapsed against the back of her chair. "You are *so* no fun."

Ricki reopened her purse. "Anyway," she said, her mind already moving on, "I checked out a few books on dream interpretation because of the whole 'see-the-reality-not-the-dream' thing, and it looks like I'm either about to come into some big money or—"

Her words were cut off by two manicured hands materializing behind her. They snaked around her neck and squeezed. Yelping in surprise, she yanked the hands from her throat and twisted violently in her chair.

Teresa sprang up from the floor and burst into a peal of

laughter. Ignoring the frown Quincy flashed her way, she hugged Ricki and cackled. "You're such an easy mark." Giving her an exaggerated smack on the cheek, she crawled over the seat and plopped down beside her.

Yolanda rounded the other end of the aisle and filled the spot vacated by Reggie.

"Whatcha doing?" Teresa sang. Her infamous Mohawk was feathered to one closely cut side, grazing the top of her perfectly arched eyebrows, which she wiggled at Ricki and Denise.

"We *were* watching you push Mr. Q one step closer to an early grave. Now we're just waiting on him to get there," Denise answered dryly.

"Yeah, you need to ease up," Ricki added. "I want to finish the play before he has another 'episode,' and you're not helping."

Yolanda cut her eyes sideways at Teresa and rolled them away in annoyance. "I tried telling her that already, but she's on a mission."

Teresa hummed happily to herself.

"A mission for what?" Denise asked.

Teresa raised a finger to her mouth, then stuck a hand into her jacket pocket, and with a vigorous shake, rattled an object that sounded suspiciously like a jar of pills.

The drama teacher stopped midway through his scene critique. His eyes darted furtively around the auditorium as he licked his lips. Pulling a faded handkerchief from the front of his shirt, he wiped a bead of sweat from his temple and shambled over to the podium at the foot of the stage.

"Okay, people," he shouted hoarsely into the microphone, "you have all worked hard and we're...um...well ahead of schedule."

Teresa sniggered, ducking into her seat when he squinted in her direction.

"So...everyone, go home, and I will see you all in class on Monday." Shoving the handkerchief back into his shirt, he clapped his hands in dismissal and rushed down the theater steps.

"C'mon, let's go," Teresa hissed, pulling the girls to their feet and herding them toward the auditorium's exit. When they got to the door, she stopped. Surveying the theater, she smirked with satisfaction at Quincy—now crouched in front of the aisle closest to the stage, searching under the seats and oblivious to the students scurrying by. With a flash of her hand, she pulled a white bottle from her pocket and placed it on the floor. Lightly tapping it with her toe, she rolled the bottle down the aisle and swiftly disappeared through the swinging exit doors, her Mohawk a bouncing flash as she skipped down the steps leading to the school grounds.

Denise, Yolanda, and Ricki shook their heads and followed her through the door.

Teresa waited for them at the bottom of the steps. "Hey," she chirped.

They eyed her with open suspicion.

She hooked her arm around Ricki's. "Isn't it great that we have the rest of the day to ourselves?" Inhaling, she beamed at their wary faces. "Now we'll have plenty of time to get ready for my party. But first, I got one stop to make. C'mon! Lindsey will catch up." Yanking on Ricki's arm, she began a determined march toward the soccer field.

Yolanda closed her eyes in exasperation and motioned to Denise to follow Teresa's lead. Strolling behind them, she mumbled under her breath, "Yeah, a *really* big check."

Ricki and Denise were serving a weeklong sentence of detention when Teresa Ma first made their acquaintance in the seventh grade.

Caught passing notes in Miss Thompson's English class, they'd been forced to sacrifice each afternoon in an unused classroom in the middle school's basement. Fortunately for them, whereas Miss Thompson was generous with the pink slips, she also had a short attention span and left students unattended for the majority of the time spent in their temporary holding cell.

In her absence, detention turned into an after-school social fest. Some kids took the opportunity to catch up on the latest gossip. Others smuggled in decks of cards and handheld game systems. A few enterprising students even brought in a stereo and created a makeshift dance floor at the back of the classroom, between the vintage film projector and mildewing coat closet. Ricki and Denise spent a good part of their sentence staging mock talk show appearances of the school's faculty members—the entire detention crew had agreed that Ricki's portrayal of Lunch Lady Sanderson Gone Wild was genius at its purest level.

When a young Teresa took a tardy but regal step into the bustling classroom one afternoon, she fully expected all activity to cease and attention to focus exclusively on her. Didn't it always for the girl who held the power of trips to Disney World and lavish sleepovers at the sprawling Ma estate in her privileged hands? That particular day, however, life as she knew it came to an unexpected end.

The Ma's substantial finances supplied little Teresa with an equally substantial flock of friends. Or, at least, people who showered her with adoration and agreed with every word she said, which, in her mind was close enough. And as long as everyone continued to cozy up to her with an open hand and a smile, she continued to believe that she was the funniest, smartest, most beloved girl to ever grace the halls of Willow Middle School—a girl who also thought rules were meant only for the homeless and those with bad credit. So when she entered her domain and found two intruders having fun on her turf who didn't even have the good manners to fall in line with insta-worship, she knew steps had to be taken.

First, she ignored them, taking immediate ownership of the detention hall and excluding Ricki and Denise. She became the queen of the dance floor, the hub of the gossip exchange, and even managed to throw an improvised comedy routine that had the room roaring in laughter. But the two girls chatting by the window didn't seem to notice they'd been shunned.

The next day, she tried intimidating them. As she single-mindedly burned a hole in each back with a cold stare, her entourage hovered at her shoulders and banded together for a synchronized group glare. But the girls never bothered to glance her way. They were too absorbed in their arm wrestling tournament with a group of recent defectors from Teresa's camp to see the daggers shooting from her eyes.

The day after that, she tried picking on them. With her cronies planted behind her, she began an onslaught of vicious jokes. She went after their clothing, hair, figures—anything she could think of that would reduce the two nobodies to tears and put them in their place. But she wasn't prepared for the comebacks they hurled in retaliation. Her opponents fed off each other, and their zingers were brutal. Before she knew it, she was floundering. And when the boys in the classroom began to rally behind the cute brunette—who looked like she was on the verge of turning their verbal battle into a more physical one—Teresa had no choice but to back down.

Finally, without realizing it, she began envying them.

The two girls shared a closeness that spoke to her heart and left it empty. They teased, argued, cried, and laughed—all in one conversation, without missing a beat in their friendship. People even enjoyed being around them, seeking their company without expecting something in return. She saw in them so many things she'd never experienced, even with her army of lackeys.

When Teresa at last shook her grasping followers from her hip and approached the girls to ask if she could join in their six-man game of strip poker, it was truly the smartest decision the overindulged little princess had ever made. Ricki and Denise accepted her into their world without a price tag attached, and in time, they did something for her that no one else had ever tried to do: they brought her back down to earth and introduced her to a wonderful new concept called *reality*. And it was then that she learned the real meaning of the word *friend*.

"Why are we here?" Ricki nervously scanned the soccer field from their hidden location in the bleachers.

The varsity team was in the middle of a skirmish—shirts versus skins, with Aaron on the side without clothing. Unfortunately, she wasn't sure if even the distant glimpse of his bare chest was worth the mild heart attack she was experiencing at the thought of getting caught.

Ralph J. Kirby was home of the Kangaroos, the perfect representative of the school's strongest sport—soccer. If there was one good thing to say about Kirby, it was that they might lose in almost every intramural sport known to mankind, but they knew how to play a mean game of soccer. The soccer players enjoyed an almost godlike status, with nothing too good for them. New uniforms were provided every year, along with luxury buses for away games; money was simply filtered out of the football and basketball funds. A separate wing had been built for their private gym. And a high GPA was practically guaranteed for anyone lucky enough to make it onto the varsity team. With only a few weeks left in the season, and every game a deciding factor between championship life or death against the Douglasville Ducks and Jefferson Jackrabbits, the soccer field was off-limits to spectators during practice. School security patrolled the grounds, and warning signs were posted along the stadium's perimeter to announce that anyone caught in the vicinity could kiss their high school freedom goodbye—along with their backsides, if Coach Jackson had anything to do with it.

Teresa, in the middle of a thorough cuticle inspection, picked at a hangnail and replied, "I just want to make sure the right people are coming to my party." She gave Ricki's hand a reassuring pat before resuming nail maintenance. "Don't worry, sweetie. You'll thank me for it."

"You couldn't do this later?" Denise asked.

"Nope, I'll be way too busy. Isn't it a good thing Q let us out early today?"

"Yeah," Yolanda said sarcastically. "Wonder what made him do that?"

The injured look of innocence on Teresa's face was so angelic it would have inspired the saints to weep. She then stuck out her tongue and went back to studying her metallic pink fingertips.

"Who all is coming?" Lindsey asked, her eyes glued to the field.

Ricki tried to follow the focus of her stare but only saw Damian's towering figure guarding the goal for the shirtless team. The sight was enough to almost bring up the chicken salad sandwich she'd eaten for lunch. Forcing it down, she redirected her view to Aaron.

"The whole school," Teresa said. "The cool part of it anyway."

"Considering the size of your house, they'd probably all fit," Yolanda quipped.

Teresa bit at the hangnail and pretended to spit it at Yolanda. "Whatever. Anyway, the only problem I'm having is convincing Granny Han to take Calvin. Even though *I'm* the one who got her the combination to Pop's safe, she swears she can't take an eleven-year-old into the casinos. She says leaving me alone without supervision is repayment enough. Again, whatever."

She broke from examining her nails to check her watch. Searching the field, she zoned in on a group of players gathered around the water cooler, then pulled a makeup compact from her purse, flipped it open, and placed it on the bench between herself and Ricki. Inch by inch, she rotated its mirror toward the sun.

Her tirade continued. "Now I'm stuck with the little snot, and I know he's going to invite all his middle school brat friends over. And I don't know about you guys, but just the thought of two dozen Calvins running amok during my party makes me…"

Lindsey turned away from Teresa's rant to nudge Ricki. "Do you think Mike will come?"

Ricki shook her head, watching Teresa's manipulation of the mirror and trying not to notice the disappointment on Lindsey's face. She never let on that she knew, but Ricki was well aware of the massive crush Lindsey had been nursing on her brother for as long as she'd known her.

Possibly even longer.

Even though he'd graduated two years ago, the legend of Mikey Ray Nichols lived on. He'd been Kirby High royalty—elected class president four years in a row, voted onto the

Homekoming Kanga Kourt each year until his senior year when he was finally eligible to be Kanga King, and made captain of the varsity soccer team when he was only a sophomore. He was the undisputed king of Kirby, making Ricki a reluctant princess by default.

Although she grudgingly accepted an elevated status at school thanks to her brother's legacy, she'd been somewhat taken aback when Lindsey Callahan had spoken to her out of the blue, freshman year in geometry class. The conversation was short but pleasant, and their talks grew longer and more personal each day. Eventually, they had their seats reassigned next to each other, and Ricki invited Lindsey to join her lunch crew. She fit in seamlessly with Denise, Teresa, and Yolanda to the point where none of the girls could remember her ever not being one of them.

They were as close as sisters by her first visit to Ricki's house. They had such a great time eating pizza and watching old movies that Ricki didn't even notice the unusual amount of attention her new friend paid to Mike's trophies and pictures. And after he arrived home from his evening classes, Ricki had spent the rest of the evening alone as Lindsey followed her brother around. Mike found it cute that his little sister's BFF had a crush on him, but Ricki couldn't help but wonder if Lindsey had only become her friend in the first place to get close to the legend who happened to be her brother.

Deep down, in a place she tried not to visit too often, she thought she knew the answer.

Her mind returned to their conversation. "Mike's in college and not interested in high school things," she stated, an edge to her voice. "So, no, he's not coming."

Continuing to observe Teresa with the mirror, Ricki deduced that a signal flashed to the players on the field whenever the sun hit the glass at a certain angle. After a few minutes, an answering flash returned from the ground. Two flickers, a pause, two more flickers. The team members then resumed their positions on the field, leaving a smug Teresa to return to scrutinizing her fingernails.

An idea formed in Ricki's mind.

Lindsey nudged her, again. "I tried to call you last night, but the phone kept ringing."

"Yeah, Mike was on the phone with his girlfriend," Ricki said airily. "I guess he didn't want to interrupt their nightly argument over who loves who more."

The light dimmed in Lindsey's eyes, and her lips folded into a pinched line.

"Girl, that's just wrong," Yolanda said. "When're your folks finally going to let you have a cell phone?"

"When I get a job to pay for one." Ricki slowly pulled her own pocket mirror from her purse and hid it between her knees. Careful not to draw any attention, she began fiddling with it.

Teresa looked up in mock horror. "What are they, Amish? That's just inhumane. Do they make you perform tricks for food, too?"

Ricki shrugged and continued to maneuver the glass into position.

Without warning, Denise stood up and slid over to the dim corridor of the stadium's stairwell. A shadowy outline looking suspiciously like Marco Downing detached from the wall. With a quick wave over her shoulder, she whispered, "Be right back," and vanished into the darkness.

The girls stared after her.

With everyone distracted, Ricki hastily wiggled the mirror, reflecting the sun off its surface and onto the soccer field...straight into the eyes of the star goalie. Satisfaction surged through her as Damian's arms flew up to block the blinding light, only to be beamed on the side of his head by an oncoming soccer ball.

Score! She shoved the mirror back into her purse and feigned nonchalance as the other girls turned away from the stairwell.

"And she's off," Yolanda huffed, her mocha complexion darkening to a new shade of burgundy. "With me about to follow, because I am too through. Teresa, you need to tell me why we're here, or I'm out."

"Okay, okay, Yogi," Teresa soothed. "I just needed to make sure the guys would be able to make it to my party. Coach Jackson's been threatening to put them on lockdown 'til next week's game, and I can't throw a party without the soccer team. That'd be like having a cookout with no meat, and I'm nothing if not prepared."

"You're nothing if not an itch in my backside," Yolanda grumbled. "So? Do you know now?"

"Yep! They're coming. No need to break out the big guns." Teresa threw up two fingers in a victory sign. "And as soon as Denise gets back from playtime, we can go."

Ricki felt as though a bucket of cold water had just splashed over her head. Gazing across the field, she asked in a casual tone, "The whole soccer team, huh?"

"Uh-huh," Teresa gushed. "My party's going to be the event of the decade."

"I guess that means Aaron is coming?"

"Of course! You know I'd get your man there for you."

She nodded, trying to relax the familiar tightness working its way through her jaw. "And Marco?"

"Most definitely."

She shut her eyes, taking a deep breath. "And Damian?"

Silence.

She opened her eyes and stared at Teresa, who had gone back

to inspecting her nails with such intensity, Ricki was surprised the polish didn't melt right off their tips. "And Damian?"

Teresa remained mute.

Ricki glanced at Yolanda and Lindsey, finding them mesmerized by the line of ants crawling on the ground between their feet. She exploded. "Teresa, how could you? After everything he's done to me, you invite him to your party?"

"Sweetie," Teresa protested, "he's captain of the team. How can I throw a party and not have the captain there?"

"But I'm your best friend," she argued. "You should be supporting *me*, not talking to him and inviting him to parties. With Aaron there, too? I can't believe you'd do this to me."

She started to get up, but Yolanda stopped her with a hand on the leg. "Hey, listen. You really think we'd let him bother you tonight?"

"Have you ever been able to stop him before?" Ricki shot back. "How about when he sold naked pictures of me? Did you stop him then?"

Damian had once sent his flavor-of-the-week to take pictures of her in the locker room shower, which he'd then blown up to poster size and put on sale. Ricki wasn't sure which angered her more—the fact that he sold the nude photos of her or that he only charged a nickel for each shot.

"But wasn't that payback for you calling his mom and pretending to be some girl he knocked up?" Teresa asked. "It took him months to convince her it was a lie. Nine, actually. He was really mad."

"No, I think he did it because of the 'Sleeping Dogs Lie' page she put up," Lindsey volunteered.

One of Ricki's most inspired ideas, the website had tracked Damian's "extracurricular activities," providing information about which girl he was with, at what time, and where, allowing other girls to log in and compare notes. It was a raging success until jilted females started going after each other instead of Damian, and the cafeteria turned into the WWF arena for catfights. In the interest of surviving one whole lunch period without dodging pudding bombs and baked potato missiles, Ricki finally had to shut the site down.

"You're both wrong," Yolanda said. "He did it 'cause of the fake STD test results she posted in the girls' bathrooms."

Teresa tapped a finger to her chin and nodded. "Yep, that was it."

"That's not the point," Ricki said.

"Yeah, it kinda is," Yolanda replied. "Girl, your hands ain't clean of the dirt that gets spread between y'all. And it gets kind of tiring sticking up for you and treating Damian like crap when it's real obvious you can stick up for yourself."

Ricki glowered at Yolanda, whose lips flapped on with a tiresome speech on how she should let bygones be bygones. She mentally stuck a pair of long pigtails on Yolanda's head in place of the braided crown, dirty denim overalls over the sleek gray minidress, and an assortment of scrapes and bruises onto her velvety brown knees and elbows. *There* was the Yolanda Matsi of the third grade who used to protect her from bullies on the playground. Where was she now?

When Yolanda's father was reassigned to an overseas station in the fourth grade, Ricki had been heartbroken to say goodbye to her playmate and protector. Throughout the years, they kept in touch with emails and weekly web chats. And four years later, when Colonel Matsi retired from the military and brought his family back home to Willow, there weren't enough tissues in town to hold the tears of joy the two girls shed.

Yolanda had left Willow a fearless, championing tomboy and came back a confident, practical young lady. Her sensible personality complemented the triangle of friendship Ricki had created in her absence. It toned down Denise's boy craziness, buffered Teresa's impulsive behavior, and challenged Ricki to step up when insecurities pushed her down. A solid quadrangle formed with Ricki being the common thread that held them all together.

She felt the thread unraveling.

Clearing the vision of an eight-year-old Yolanda from her mind, she tuned in to Teresa, who now had the floor.

"And he kind of put a bug in my ear, when we ran into him on the way to practice, that he thinks Lindsey is cute," she said. "So, if Aaron's going to be there for you, and Marco's going to be there for Denise, I think it's only fair to have Damian there for Lindsey." She ducked her head and inched closer to the exit.

Ricki gaped at Lindsey. "You'd actually date him?"

Lindsey blushed, twirling a piece of honey-blonde hair around her finger. "He's not a bad guy," she said, avoiding direct eye contact. "He's always been super sweet to us when you're not around, and he's really funny. And you've got to admit, he's gorgeous."

"Yeah, well, so was his father," Ricki snapped.

"You met his dad?" Lindsey's blue eyes widened with curiosity. "I thought he was raised by his mom?"

"No, I meant his other father. Wasn't Satan the most beautiful angel before the whole 'fiery pits of hell' thing messed up his pretty-boy looks?"

"That's horrible!" Lindsey exclaimed.

"Hey, I'm just saying. Don't eat the apple."

Yolanda rolled her eyes. "Girl, you need to stop. You know Lindsey's always thought Damian was cute. Well, it's more than that; she likes him. But she's kept it to herself, out of respect for you."

"Lindsey likes everyone," Ricki retorted.

Lindsey's creamy pink cheeks flushed bright red. "What's that supposed to mean?"

Ricki bit off the words about to escape from her mouth and instead offered a kinder version. "I'm just saying you tend to be interested in any guy who's interested in you." *And even some who aren't, like my brother.*

The hurt that flared in Lindsey's eyes drained the fight out of her.

"Lindz, I'm sorry," Ricki said, opting for a different approach, "but you're too good for Damian. He's shallow and evil. He's like a cockroach, only worse, because he won't go away when the lights come on. You can do better than someone like that."

"Better than Damian?" Lindsey scoffed. "He's totally the king of Kirby High. Almost every girl in this school would kill to get with him."

"Exactly," Ricki said. "He's like a dog in heat, and you'd just be one of his…you know. Do you want that?"

"A lot of girls like Aaron too," Yolanda pointed out. "Does that make *you* one of his 'you know'?"

"Aaron's not like that!"

"How do you know? Don't you think Lindsey should have the same chance to find out if Damian's a good guy, like how you want with Aaron?"

Ricki shook her head in disbelief and looked around at the faces of her oldest and dearest friends. It was like looking at a group of strangers. *First, he ruins things with my future boyfriend; now he ruins my friends.* "Do whatever you want," she choked out. "But don't come crying my way when Demon Spawn rips your heart out and uses it for toilet paper."

Knocking Yolanda's hand off her knee, she stood up and stormed into the stairwell, brushing past a disheveled Denise on her way out of the arena and away from the traitors she'd once considered friends.

CHAPTER THREE

"Is a pig tap dancing past the window?"

Denise almost looked at the window before catching herself. "Pigs are not flying by your window, Ricki."

"Then I'm not changing my mind." Ricki threw her purse onto the bed and plopped onto a crowded beanbag, crushing three helpless unicorns.

Denise folded her arms. "And why not? If you don't show up to your own best friend's party, what're people going to think?"

"That my best friend is consorting with the enemy and doesn't deserve my support. If Lindsey and Teresa love Damian so much, they can have him, but I refuse to drink the Kool-Aid." She pulled out a flattened unicorn and spitefully tugged on its horn.

"You're really losing it." Denise removed the abused toy from Ricki's grasp. She set it on top of the dresser, away from further harm. "I can't believe you'd actually miss out on a chance to hook up with Aaron just because Damian *might* be there."

Ricki produced another unicorn to torture. "It's not even about Demon Spawn being there. Okay, maybe it is. But it's also the fact they invited him in the first place. I mean, why bother getting closer to Aaron if the Evil One knocks me into a punch bowl as soon as I do?"

She burrowed deeper into the beanbag and stared at the

ceiling, rhythmically thumping the doll against the floor in time with the beating of her heart. *Maybe I should paint the walls red. That's the right color for betrayal.*

Denise pried the second victim from her hands and placed it alongside its fellow survivor. Before Ricki could grab the third unicorn, she was pulled from the beanbag and dragged over to the closet.

"Enough," Denise declared, jerking open the closet door. She rifled through a row of shirts with one hand while holding a struggling Ricki with the other. "The girls feel horrible about everything. They seriously thought you wouldn't even see Damian tonight. So just suck it up and put this frickin' outfit on so you can finally make Aaron fall madly in lust with you." Her grip loosened as she worked to pull a flimsy, off-white camisole from its hanger.

Ricki took advantage of the opening and nimbly spun out of her hold, executing a twirl so graceful the ceramic ballerinas on the mantle seemed to glow green with envy, and collapsed like a rag doll, facedown onto her bed. "I can't do it, Denise," she spat out through a mouthful of blanket. "Spawn's already made me look like an idiot in front of Aaron twice today. I'd be stupid to open myself up for strike number three. Just tell everyone I have a headache."

Which wasn't too far from the truth. The dull throb that had begun earlier in the day was spreading into every crevice of her brain and turning into a full-blown migraine.

"I'm not even trying to hear it," Denise said, wrestling the top from its hanger. She rummaged through piles of pants on the floor. "My mom has an entire pharmacy in her bathroom. A couple of her pills and a nap in the car, and you'll be fine." She finished picking through the first pile and dove into the mound next to it. "Voila!" she shouted, yanking a pair of brown capris belted with a silk paisley scarf from the bottom of the heap, then rounded on Ricki with a determined glint in her eye.

Rolling onto her back, Ricki threw a hand up to ward off her approach. "I've already made up my mind. All the stuff today has been like a warning or something. If I go to the party, it's going to be a disaster."

Denise tucked the bundle of clothing under one arm and seized a lone foot dangling from the end of the bed. She pulled at the sneaker. "Even if this is your last chance to talk to Aaron, you'll pass it up because your feelings got hurt?"

Ricki feebly kicked at the clutching hands. "Why're you trying to rush things? Even if me and Aaron hook up tonight, we still can't go out until my folks give the okay."

"Oh please," Denise retorted, dropping the liberated sneaker onto the floor and tackling the other waving foot. "I'd cover for you, and you know it, so come up with something better."

"Alright, then. I never told Mike I was going to a party. What if he sees me in that outfit and asks where I'm going?"

Denise freed the shoe with one solid heave. "We'll just tell him it's for the pep rally skit we're working on. Better yet, we won't tell him anything. He's your brother, not your parole officer." She pinned Ricki's wriggling feet together and began working her socks down each ankle.

"Denny, stop it! That tickles!" Ricki twisted her legs out of Denise's grip. Her mind latched onto a new excuse. "Look, I probably won't be able to fit into those pants anyway. It's that time of the month, and I'm all bloaty. You're just going to have to go without me."

Denise lowered her arms in defeat, dropping the clothes on the floor. "You want to talk about time of the month?" she huffed. "How about the amount of time left in the month before you have to go back to Madame Dupre and tell her you punked out on your last chance to snag your soul mate? How much time is that?"

Ricki gestured vaguely toward the wall calendar hanging beside the window and let her arm return limply to her side. "A day, a week, a month. What does it really matter if Damian's always around to get in the way? You realize once Lindsey starts dating him, we'll have to perform an exorcism just to get rid of him, don't you?" She flipped onto her stomach, burying her face in a pillow. "Stock up on holy water."

"Such a drama queen," Denise said in exasperation. She placed a finger on the calendar. "Okay...one, two, thr— Whoa, hold up." She squinted at the calendar. "Hey, did you realize 'blue moon' is listed on your calendar?"

An eye peeked out from the pillow. "What're you talking about?"

"Blue moon. Y'know, like how they put full moon, quarter moon, stuff like that? This day's got a blue moon."

"I didn't know there really *was* such a thing." Ricki rolled onto her side. "I thought it was just a saying or a song or something."

"Me too. I wonder what it is?" Denise went to the computer desk and flipped on the monitor. "What's your password?"

Ricki slid off the bed and joined Denise, her pulse quickening. She logged onto the computer, then ran a search on *blue moon*.

"The third full moon for a season that has four," the girls read in unison. They slowly turned to each other, an unspoken dialogue passing between them.

Ricki raced to the bed and snatched up her purse, dumping its contents onto the comforter. Plucking at the crumpled piece of notebook paper poking up from the clutter, she read aloud, "Only once in a blue moon is someone fortunate enough to find the path that leads her soul to its other half."

She waved the paper in the air and squealed. "A blue moon! The riddle says I'll unite with my soul mate on the night of a blue moon. When is it?"

Denise smirked. "Tonight."

Gnawing on her lower lip, Ricki glanced out the window toward the house across the yard. The window to Damian's bedroom directly faced hers. Her eyes strained to find movement behind the curtains, but his Royal Darkness didn't appear to be home. "Do you really think it'll happen at the party?" she asked.

"What else does the riddle say?"

She read the second line. "And at that time, after you have waded through life's gathering of hearts to the one which was meant for you, open your eyes to what awaits you at the other end."

Denise sauntered over to the discarded shirt and pants. "Sounds pretty obvy to me. What else could the gathering in 'gathering of hearts' *be* but a party?" She triumphantly held out the clothes.

Ricki stared at the bundle. A tiny smile appeared on her face, growing until it spread from ear to ear—all headache and bloating woes forgotten. Grabbing the outfit, she hurried toward the bathroom, then paused to look back at Denise.

"A quick shower and we're outta here. I've got a gathering of hearts to attend."

"Teresa's parents are going to kill her."

Ricki sat with Denise outside the Ma estate, gaping at the throng of cars jammed inside its courtyard. Swarms of teenagers weaved in and out of the metallic jungle in a single-minded trek toward the manor's main entrance. They surged onward, only to crash against another wave of partygoers already gathered at its mahogany doors. A separate horde surrounded the water fountain in the center of the courtyard, mingling at the base of its fifteen-foot stone mermaid and randomly tossing coins—and each other—into the pool of water at her feet. A line of small figures stealthily inched around the courtyard's perimeter toward the back of the house, carrying an assortment of buckets and shovels. They kept to the shadows, stopping only to pick up a fallen tool or throw a rock at the drunk who had somehow made a perch on the mermaid's shoulder and was now chucking beer cans at their heads. As the procession disappeared around the corner of the house, the last and shortest member, wearing an oversized baseball cap and a jersey two sizes too big for his little frame, threw up a middle finger at the beer-toting assailant and ran.

I guess Granny Han wouldn't take Calvin after all, Ricki thought.

"Servant's entrance," Denise announced, throwing her car into reverse. She eased through the main gate and headed toward a smaller, less noticeable gate half a block down the street.

"We could've gotten here before everyone else if we hadn't stopped for supplies," Ricki grumbled. She glanced at the back seat full of smuggled beer, wine coolers, and tequila.

"Gotta pay to play," Denise replied. "Besides, you're not the one whose phone is getting blown up by all those homely-looking GIs expecting to get laid just for getting us this stash. So, quit whining." She slammed on her brakes before mowing down a flock of teens racing up the street to get into the party before the main gates closed.

"But I don't even drink," Ricki muttered under her breath. A hint of her headache was reemerging.

When they pulled into the garage, the music filtering from the house was almost deafening. Bass thumped through the walls, reverberating off the ground and sending vibrations through the car floor. Denise jumped out of the car, adjusting her dress before tackling the case of beer in her back seat. Ricki grabbed a load of wine coolers and braced herself for the blast of noise about to assault her eardrums.

Denise fiddled with the doorknob leading into the kitchen. "It's locked." Shifting the beer in her arms, she kicked the door and began to shout.

Ricki screamed along with her until her arms went numb from the weight of the coolers. As she bent over to stack the bottles on the ground, the door opened.

"Well, well, well," a deep voice boomed from the doorway. "If it isn't Kirby High's own 'Ebony and Ivory.'"

Tiny needles tickled her neck. Awash with dread, she straightened and turned around. Damian, in all his sleazy glory, stared down at her. The migraine she'd fought all day erupted from its hiding place and flooded her head in one sweeping surge.

His sinful black eyes swept over Denise as he relieved her of her load. "Denise, beautiful as usual." His dark gaze then shifted to Ricki and lingered. It dropped to her sandaled feet and deliberately traced a lazy trail up her body.

Self-conscious, she pushed at the spaghetti straps sliding down her shoulders for the umpteenth time and tugged at the hem of her shirt, trying unsuccessfully to cover her belly button with its sheer fabric. Denise had insisted the top would make her look mature and sexy, but all it really did was make her feel exposed and trashy. She fidgeted in her capris—wistfully picturing the faded jeans and studded tank sitting at the top of her closet. Were the peek-a-boo chemise and butt-clinging stretch pants really worth all the trouble? Resisting the urge to pull the stretchy material out of her crotch, she decided the answer was a resounding "no."

Damian's inspection continued upward until it reached her narrowed eyes. "Rocky, the way you look tonight," he crooned. "Been sick, lately?"

Heat prickled her skin. "Only of your face." She brushed past him, shouldering him in the ribs and almost causing him to drop the box full of beer.

She stormed into the kitchen, startling a group of Kirby soccer players by the bar. Ignoring their leers, she took deep breaths to calm her nerves. It was time to push Damian out of her mind and focus on the task at hand: finding Aaron. Slowly exhaling, she followed Denise through a set of arched doors and entered a hot and sweaty world of writhing bodies dancing feverishly across the floor. What had once been the Ma living room was now an immense dancehall filled with a wall-to-wall sea of unstoppable limbs rising and falling in waves to the music's beat. A DJ skillfully controlled them like a puppet master, spinning music from the balcony encircling the great hall.

It took less than three seconds for her to realize that finding Aaron and cementing their eternal love might prove a bit more difficult than she'd anticipated. In fact, she'd have an easier time locating that elusive needle in the haystack so many people talked about. Even though Aaron was the "Waldo" of her world—the one person she could find in any crowd, anyplace, under any circumstances—she didn't think even her inner GPS could track him down in this crowd.

Only half of the people in the room were even from her school. The rest looked like a mix of Douglasville and Jefferson students forgetting all rivalries for one night of drunken bonding, kids from the nearby college, and undercover security guards trying to blend in with the crowd. There were even quite a few people who looked like they hadn't seen the inside of a high school in over twenty years. And was that her chemistry teacher doing the Cha Cha Slide down the center of the dance floor?

Denise guided her through the chaos. They kept to the wall, snaking past gyrating bodies as they made their way toward the staircase on the other side of the room.

"I can't believe the first person I see ends up being Demon Spawn," Ricki shouted as they elbowed their way up to the second floor. She fished a couple of extra-strength aspirin from her purse and forced them down her dry throat.

Denise brushed aside the hand of a gawky boy trying to draw her into a dance. "I know, right? But at least the worst is out of the way. It's all breezy from here on out." She politely removed another hand from her waist and hip-butted a necking couple who blocked the top of the stairwell.

Once they got upstairs to a quieter part of the house, Ricki said, "I guess I'm just cursed to see his face wherever I go. Maybe I ought to get some holy water, after all."

They strolled through the main wing with Ricki on the lookout for Aaron. Each room they came to offered different activities, from gambling to poetry readings. There was also a game room that boasted a pool table, foosball and pinball machines, dartboard, and fully stocked minibar. The combined attraction of games and easy-access booze had turned the room into the hottest spot on the floor for the male crowd, with a line to get inside extending halfway down the hall. The girls wormed their way through the traffic jam of testosterone, ignoring the blast of protests and catcalls that followed them. Inside, Ricki was disappointed to find Aaron's face missing from the group of soccer players playing pool. She turned to leave, only to discover Denise had vanished from her side and materialized in front of the pool table, becoming encircled by a pack of drooling jocks. She lounged shamelessly against the table, looking ready to settle in for the night.

Ricki stood dutifully to the side, allowing her friend time to bask in the mindless adoration. After several minutes, however, being invisible to every boy in the room soon took its toll, and she was ready to move on. With a few shoves and nicely veiled threats, she maneuvered Denise away from the salivating pack and strong-armed her to the next room.

The scarlet scarf draped across the doorknob gave them a moment's pause. Denise cracked the door open, cautiously poking her head inside. Soft music and the low sounds of whispering drifted from the room's smoky interior. Ricki moved to peek inside, but Denise abruptly jerked away from the door and slammed it shut. Her normally tanned complexion had turned beet red.

"You don't want to go in there," Denise sputtered. "It's… um, a different kind of game room. And what they're playing is a little too advanced. Even for me."

Three giggling girls from Kirby's cheer squad approached, hanging onto the arm of a Jefferson football player. With a wink at Ricki and a nasty smirk at Denise, they escorted the boy into the room and shut the door behind them.

Denise placed two fingers under Ricki's drooping jaw, snapping her mouth shut. "Let's go. I don't think there's anything we want in there."

The den across the hall was the perfect haven for the less-adventurous guests who wanted fun that didn't involve alcohol, dancing, or making out in dark corners. A sixty-inch flat-panel plasma screen aired a continuous stream of music videos, and kids lounged on sofas, chatting and eating appetizers. In the back of the room, girls leafed through piles of magazines and sipped virgin daiquiris.

Ricki floated into the room. *Welcome to heaven. I can't dance, I don't drink, and no boy has wanted to make out with me since that creepy Cousin Tony incident in the sixth grade. But there's even a place for the Uncool, like me, to call home.* She began to settle blissfully into a leather couch but was hauled away by Denise before her bottom hit the cushions.

When they finally reached the end of the hallway, two security guards barred their passage into the wing that housed the family rooms. "No guests beyond this point," the taller one barked.

"Is Teresa Ma back there?" Ricki asked.

"No guests beyond this point."

"I'm just ask—"

"No guests beyond this point." The short guard fingered the mace container hanging from his holster.

Pouting, Denise whipped out her cell phone. She typed a quick message, then stepped back, arms folded. Within seconds, the light on the guard's two-way radio blinked, and a muffled voice came through the speaker. After a quick conversation with the distorted voice and a few sideways glances at Ricki and Denise, he gestured for them to wait and resumed his stoic posturing.

"Hey, you guys!" Teresa's voice bounced off the walls behind them.

They turned around in time to see her tiny frame racing through the crowd.

Teresa leaped onto Ricki, locking her into a choking embrace. "I'm *so* glad you came! Now the night is *perfect!*" Still latched onto Ricki's neck, she said to the wooden-faced security guard, "You see these girls right here? They're family, so they go wherever they want. Got it?"

Ricki laughed, peeling the slender arms from her throat. She then accepted a less stifling hug from Lindsey, who appeared behind Teresa. Yolanda emerged, holding hands with her boyfriend of two years, Emille Hammerstead, and gave her a kiss on the cheek.

Ricki looked around at her friends, suddenly feeling like "Choice D" in a "Guess Which Object Doesn't Belong" puzzle.

Denise channeled the Greek goddess she'd obviously been in a past life, with her hair falling in loose waves around her tan shoulders and the gold tunic-style halter dress complimenting her voluptuous curves. Yolanda's smooth, dark skin contrasted stunningly with a white chiffon peasant blouse and pair of white low-rise dress pants, all accentuated with African costume jewelry, giving her the appearance of an exotic queen. Lindsey was angelic with her sun-kissed hair swept into a halo of soft curls atop her head, their tips settling against the shimmery satin of her baby-doll dress. And Teresa was the devilish counterpart to Lindsey, her formerly pink Mohawk tips now dyed a fiery red to match the dragon-print tube dress molded snugly around her elfin figure.

Ricki had always wondered if it was her blessing or curse to be surrounded with friends who, on a bad day, could put a pack of supermodels to shame. But maybe a curse could be a blessing if it let someone like her be included in such an amazing group of girls.

"I'm sorry I was being so difficult," she said, all grudges evaporating. "I'm glad I came."

They engulfed her in a group hug.

"So are we," Teresa said. "Sorry I didn't meet you guys at the door. Calvin and his little brat friends snuck past security, and now we can't find them. I'd put someone outside his bedroom, but they must've drugged the dude or something because we found him knocked out in the hall with an empty cup, and they were gone."

"I think I saw him and his crew heading into the backyard when we got here," Ricki said. "They had a bunch of shovels and stuff."

Teresa hurried over to the guards to relay the information.

The tall one issued a string of orders into his walkie-talkie. She then returned to the group, and they strolled back to the heart of the party.

"He's such a pain," she said. "Why couldn't I be the only child?"

"'Cause your parents were still trying to get it right," Yolanda answered.

"Ha-ha, Yogi." She jabbed her ruby fingernails toward Yolanda. Turning to Ricki and Denise, she asked, "What do you guys think of my party?"

"I'm thinking you'd better pick out a nice red coffin to match your hair," Denise said. "When your parents find out about this, your days among the living are numbered."

Teresa waved her hand dismissively. "Please. They'll have to find me first."

"Oh, and yeah," Denise added, her voice laced with disapproval, "we particularly got a kick out of the brothel you have going down the hall."

Teresa's step slowed. Her eyes darted to Ricki. "You looked in there?"

"Denise did," she replied.

Teresa stared guardedly at Denise, then shrugged. "Who am I to judge? People are here to have a good time. I'm their hostess, not their mother." She grinned impishly. "Marco's been bothering me all night, looking for you."

Denise looked around in surprise. "He's here? I didn't see him."

"Yeah, because he's been roaming the whole house trying to find you."

"Does that mean Aaron's here too?" Ricki asked. "Because I didn't see him either."

Teresa covertly studied Denise's face before responding. "Nope. Sorry, sweetie."

Ricki's heart dropped. "Are you sure? Could he maybe be at the swimming pool?"

"Pop's renovating, so that whole area is off-limits. No pool, no theater, nada. Anything going down goes down in this part of the house." Teresa put an arm around her waist and gave it a squeeze. "Don't worry about it. Just have fun, and he'll get here when he gets here."

Ricki's heart finished its plummeting descent into her gut. She'd been so certain he would be there. He was supposed to take one look at her from across a crowded room, ask her to dance, and the rest of the night would be history for them to tell their grandchildren about. They'd even invite Madame Dupre to their wedding, where passages from the riddle would be recited as part of the marriage vows. Pretty hard to get that life-altering dance with the future groom MIA, wasn't it?

They arrived at the stairs leading to the dance floor. She searched the sea of bobbing heads but couldn't find Aaron's. Swallowing the lump in her throat, she unenthusiastically followed her friends down the stairs to be swept up in the dancing horde.

There she was…left alone to hold up the wall.

As always.

Denise had disappeared with Marco shortly after they'd started dancing. Teresa had been called away by an urgent message from security. After shouting a few choice words about Calvin's rear end and the creative things she was going to do with it, she'd taken off. And Yolanda and Emille were caught up in their own little world somewhere in the middle of the dance floor. Ricki had been grateful to at least have Lindsey to keep her company for a little while—until Lindsey saw Damian watching them from the balcony and promptly abandoned her to go chase him down.

Ricki sighed. *I'm wearing an outfit that would barely cover a Barbie doll to come to a party Aaron's not even at, so I can stand by myself like a pathetic reject and watch other people have a good time. Too sad for words.*

A group of boys came toward her.

Her back straightened. Chin raised, she turned her head in the opposite direction and feigned nonchalance. Holding her breath, she stared at a fixed point on the other end of the room, trying not to panic when the boys slowed down to check her out. After a few seconds, they continued on their way.

She exhaled and slumped against the wall. *Too sad.*

Growing sick of her own company, she left her spot on the sidelines and headed upstairs. As she passed the game room, she glanced inside and saw a fresh crowd of soccer players gathered around the pool table. For one insane moment, she imagined Aaron had finally shown up to the party and was waiting for her to declare her undying love. When she squeezed through the crowd and instead saw Damian sneering at her over an extended pool stick, her dream was brutally dashed. Lindsey hovered at his elbow, eyes dripping with worship as she held his beer. She giddily waved at Ricki and motioned her over. Ricki considered joining her—if only to knock that beer down Damian's shirt—but then she noticed the wicked gleam in his eyes...and the direction of his next shot.

It didn't take a geometry wiz to realize that if he jumped the cue ball into the air, it'd smash into her ribcage instead of the nine-ball formation on the table. Her shoulder throbbed in memory of the last time he'd "accidentally" whacked her with a free-flying ball during a game of pool with Mike, in their basement. Knowing no good could come of her and

Damian being in the same room with improvised weaponry, she mouthed a hasty goodbye to Lindsey and fled.

Ricki wandered into the den and peeped out an empty loveseat in a corner of the room. She grabbed a soda and stack of finger sandwiches from the buffet table, then shuffled over to the couch and sank into its oversized pillows. Nibbling contentedly on the miniature sandwiches, she nestled in for the evening.

"I guess I see now how you keep your girlish figure."

She almost bit her tongue.

Reggie sat down beside Ricki, grabbed a sandwich from her plate, and popped it in his mouth. "'Cause there's no way you could get fat off these things," he said, chewing. "Where's the steak, the potatoes? Can I at least get a biscuit?" He took another sandwich, eating it in one bite. "What's the word, Rick?"

She smiled, glad to see a friendly face. "The word is *surprised*, as in, what are you doing here? I didn't think this was your kind of scene."

He moved to take another sandwich before she slapped his hand away. "It's about as much my kind of scene as it is yours, but here *you* are."

"I know, but it's kinda hard to say no to Teresa."

"Exactly. It was either come to her party or spend every rehearsal waiting for the stage lights to fall on me. I went with the less deadly choice." He settled back in the sofa and smiled. "Plus, I knew you'd be here, so how could I resist?"

"Oh, please," she scoffed. "Save your lines for that bunch of rabid fangirls who jump on you after practice every day. They don't work on me."

He held a hand to his chest and sighed dramatically. "You wound me."

She giggled. "If you had a heart, maybe I would."

The smile faded. Brushing his hair back, he turned away to watch some new hip-hop video playing on the jumbo television screen.

Ricki sipped her Coke, observing him over the soda can. He looked adorable. His sandy curls twirled around his temples, stubbornly fighting the hair gel he'd used to slick them down. She wondered if he was aware that most of the girls in the room were trying to get his attention.

"Why aren't you dancing?" she asked.

He peered down at her. "Real men don't dance."

"Does that mean you're going to hang out here all night?"

He stretched out an arm and casually rested it on the sofa behind her. "Will you be here all night?"

"Most likely. The crew has deserted me."

"Well, then, this is where I'll be."

A smile burst from her face. She laid her head on his shoulder. "You're the best, Reg."

His arm lowered to rest around her neck. "Yeah, that's what they tell me."

She leaned into him, allowing her insides to exhale. Maybe the night would end up okay, after all.

Reggie's arm jerked. "When did Lindsey start going out with Golden Boy?"

Ricki looked up. Lindsey had entered the room, leading Damian by the hand. The new couple found an empty seat—uncomfortably close to where she and Reggie sat—and began to snuggle.

Reggie looked down at her. "Are you okay with this?"

She scowled and nestled deeper into the crook of his arm, trying to block out the vision of her best friend being felt up by the enemy. "No, but it's not really my business, is it?"

"I thought *everything* having to do with Damian was your business."

"Well, apparently not when it comes to him screwing my friends," she bitterly responded. Cringing, she backtracked. "I shouldn't have said that. Lindsey's not doing anything with him."

"Are you sure?"

Poking her head up, she followed his gaze to Lindsey, who now sat on Damian's lap, engaged in a no-holds-barred tongue-wrestling match. The two were so wrapped up in the moment, they didn't seem to care that most of the room was watching them.

Ricki was taken aback. *Aren't they moving a little fast?* She toyed with the idea of storming over to them, snatching Lindsey from Damian's lap, and dunking her head in a toilet until she came to her senses and shook off her unnatural infatuation with the Unholy One. Two seconds more and she might actually have done it, but she realized Damian's eyes were open and alert. And he was staring straight at her.

He really is evil. He knows I hate the idea of him dating my best friend, so he's throwing it up in my face. That's just sick.

She stood up. "I am in no mood to deal with this crap, tonight," she said. Making a point of ignoring Damian's performance, she handed the plate of sandwiches to Reggie and marched out of the room. Alone.

As always.

With nowhere left to go that wouldn't make her feel like a friendless leper, Ricki headed to the one place in the house where she could escape from her troubles. The library. She entered scholastic heaven and proceeded to look for a nice, plump novel to occupy her time. Let the rest of the world indulge in alcohol-induced, sex-crazed madness without her.

"Psst!"

She looked up from the aged volume of Edgar Allan Poe tales and peeked around the corner of the bookshelf. Seeing no movement in the shadows, she assumed she was hearing things and went back to browsing the weathered pages.

"Psst!"

She shut the book and slid it onto the shelf, then walked to the end of the row and scanned her surroundings. Silence again settled across the room. She pulled the largest, heaviest book she could find from the nearest shelf and pretended to read, her ears now on alert.

"I *said*, 'Psst!'"

"Okay, who's there?" she demanded, slamming the book shut. She held it over her head, ready to start swinging.

"Up here!"

She squinted up at the ceiling. The vent above her head had been removed, and a collection of faces peered down at her through the hole.

She brushed a mist of plaster dust from her shoulder. "Calvin? Is that you?"

Calvin Ma poked his head through the vent's opening and grinned. "Hi, Ricki! Can you come up to my room for a sec? It's really important. Thank you!" His head withdrew, and the vent's cover slid into place. His voice drifted through the grill. "Oh, and don't tell my sister. Thank you!"

The guard stationed outside Calvin's bedroom looked as though he had seen better days. As Ricki passed, he whispered, "Word of advice, girlie. If they offer you something to eat, don't take it."

Nodding her thanks, Ricki edged past him. Whatever the poor man had gone through in his duties to watch over Calvin that night she decided was best left between him and his therapist. She stepped into the bedroom and was greeted by the sight of seven sixth graders standing in the middle of the room, watching her with varying degrees of suspicion.

Calvin stepped forward, his hands behind his back.

Smaller than average for his age, he was a few inches away from being the shortest member of his group. They ranged in height from a gangly five-foot-six acne-ridden boy who licked his chapped lips and gave Ricki his laughably bad version of a sexy "come hither" look, to a four-foot redhead with a face full of freckles who glared at her from underneath his poorly fitting baseball cap. Large, wire-rimmed glasses covered most of Calvin's small, oval face. Straight black hair encircled his head in the shape of an upside-down sugar bowl. The other boys waited respectfully for him to speak, making it clear that size didn't dictate leadership in their group.

"Okay, I'm here," she said. "What's up?"

"First, you have to promise not to tell anybody."

"Uh, sure." Their stares were making her nervous. Especially the one from the redhead.

Calvin's hands emerged from around his back, producing a vial of clear liquid. "We need you to open this."

Her mouth fell open. "You called me in here to open a bottle when there's a guy right outside the door? Is this a joke?" She looked around the room in bemusement.

"I told you she wouldn't help us," a small voice grumbled.

"We don't need her anyways," another one chimed.

"Yeah, she's just like your sister, Cal."

"Whoa!" she exclaimed, unnerved by the sudden hostility. "Chill, okay? Give it here."

She took the glass vial from Calvin. It was cut flawlessly in the shape of a pentagon with a round opening at the tip. A crystal cork inscribed with curious symbols sealed it shut. Light from the ceiling lamp reflected off the bottle, producing a kaleidoscope of colors that leaped from the cork's symbols.

Feeling herself being drawn into the glowing inscription, Ricki closed her eyes to break its hypnotic effect. "Where did you guys get this?" she breathed.

"The base of the pecan tree in my mom's garden. We were digging for buried treasure and found it. So you'd better not tell anyone, or I'll get busted for digging up Mom's garden." Calvin took the vial from her and yanked on the cork. "We tried to open it, but the stopper is too tight. You try."

She attempted to pull the cork out. Every time it started to give, some force seemed to draw it back in. When she removed her hand, her palm was bright red and throbbed painfully.

"How long have you guys had it?" she asked.

"We just found it tonight."

She stopped breathing.

"There was some weird, old map in some of my dad's stuff, and the instructions took us to the tree. It said if we dug there under a blue moon, we'd find a 'treasure of the heart.' But all we found was this stupid thing." He wrenched the bottle from Ricki's death grip and shook it.

She wanted to pass out from excitement. The answer to Madame Dupre's riddle *had* to be in that little bottle. "I've got an idea," she began, her mind whirling. "Since none of us can get the bottle open, and you don't want anyone to know how you got it, why don't you let me take it to Mildred's Curio Shop over on 5th Street? I'll see if she can do anything with it." She avoided eye contact with Calvin, hoping he didn't catch the hunger in her gaze.

A voice piped up. "How do we know we can trust you?"

"If you don't trust me, I can leave right now," she replied. "I don't have to be here, you know." She continued to stare innocently at Calvin's right ear.

"Conference," Calvin ordered, and the boys convened in the farthest corner of the room.

All Ricki could hear were a few hushed whispers. Occasionally, a boy would turn to cast a doubtful glance her way. It took everything within her not to knock them all down, grab the bottle, and make a mad dash for the door.

They eventually returned, with Calvin again stepping forward as the spokesperson. "Here's the deal. We'll let you have the bottle until Tuesday. But if you don't bring it back by Tuesday afternoon, we'll be forced to send Tom after you."

The belligerent redhead lifted the baseball cap from his face with one freckled hand and glowered meaningfully at her.

Concealing her excitement, Ricki nodded. She shook hands with Calvin to seal the deal and took temporary ownership of the vial. In that single moment, everything she'd gone through that night was worth it. Damian, Lindsey, feeling like an outcast—she would do it all again because she now held in her hands the answer to the gypsy's riddle and the key to her future.

And Aaron Miller will soon be mine!

CHAPTER FOUR

"**Y**OU KNOW THERE'S A LAW against dumping stuff in people's drinks to make them love you, right?"

Ricki laughed, gleefully tossing the vial into the air. "Think about it, Denise—a mysterious liquid found on the night of a blue moon, called a 'treasure of the heart?' Sounds like a love potion to me, and love potions are meant to be drank."

The two girls walked through the private wing on their way back to the party. Denise had tracked her down minutes earlier with news of an Aaron sighting, sending Ricki's flight to cloud nine soaring from the runway into the skies. Now, with vial in hand, all she needed to do was find him, put the potion to its intended use, and live her remaining days in Happily Ever After.

"How much do I use?" she mused. "A few drops or the whole thing? Do I have to be the first person he sees after he drinks it? I wish Madame Dupre had given instructions." She again pitched the vial toward the ceiling, admiring the prisms of color flashing from its surface.

Denise eyed her. "So you're gonna roofie him."

"No," she said firmly. "It is not a roofie."

"Oh, my bad. What would you call it?"

"I'd call it the hand of fate finally coming my way for a change and giving things a little push."

"In a liquid that you'll drop in his drink?"

Ricki hesitated. "Yeah."

"And then he'll be yours for the taking?"

She stopped walking and turned to Denise. "Yeah. So what?"

"Like I said, you're gonna roofie him."

"This is about love, not sex," she insisted. "There's no comparison."

"If a guy's got to use a roofie to make a girl sleep with him, odds are pretty big it wasn't meant to be," Denise said. "If you've got to use a love potion to force a guy to love you—"

"Why are you trying to ruin my high?" Ricki asked. "I won't be forcing Aaron to do anything. This'll just open his eyes to what's already there. I'm the one for him; he just doesn't know it yet."

"Same difference," Denise said, tossing her head. "If he doesn't know he wants you just by looking at you, then maybe he's not the one. You shouldn't have to use gypsy drugs on him."

"That's so easy for you to say because you have no idea what it's like to not be *you*," Ricki said. "To not even have to do anything but breathe, and every single guy falls all over you. Like Marco. You smiled at him this morning, and tonight he's stalking you." She clasped the vial against her side. "Boys don't ever look at me like that, no matter what. I wear the tightest, skimpiest outfit I can find, and I'm still invisible."

The vial's edges cut into her palms. "For the first time in forever, I've actually got some kind of hope that a guy will finally *see* me. And maybe he'll even think I'm beautiful. I'm never going to have what you have, so what's wrong with a little divine intervention stepping in to help me?" Her voice broke. "Maybe it's all I'll ever get."

"Ricki, how long is it going to take for you to see what everybody else does?" Denise said. "You don't need stupid fortune-tellers, or magic, or anything except some confidence in yourself. I wish you'd understand that. But if this is what you think you need…" She gingerly touched the vial. "Marco saw Aaron near the game room. You check it out, and I'll tell the rest of the girls to be on the lookout." Stepping back, she squared her shoulders. "Tonight, we'll make sure he sees you."

Okay, I've got my potion…now where is my guy?

Aaron wasn't in the game room. He wasn't in the kitchen. Den, dance floor, backyard—nothing. As a last resort, Ricki had even staked out every bathroom on the first floor. No success, but she at least had the comfort of knowing she'd left no stones unturned and no corners unexplored—even the ones that could benefit from an extra roll of toilet paper and a good dose of air freshener.

Her second sweep of the house was proving as unsuccessful as the first, and the vial had even begun to give her a hard time. The glass seemed to be getting progressively warmer, making it more difficult to hold. Every few minutes, she had to switch hands to keep her palms from burning.

She was in the middle of playing hot potato with the bottle and had just lobbed it into the air as she passed another bathroom. Distracted, she missed the opening door and collided with an unyielding body. "Excuse me!" she cried, stumbling backward.

The vial missed her hands and bounced onto her shoulder. It settled in the crook of her neck for one heart-stopping second before sliding down her arm. Fumbling to grab it, she couldn't stop it from propelling off her elbow and tumbling toward the hardwood floor.

A hand whizzed past her nose, scooping the bottle up before it smashed to pieces.

"Quick reflexes," she said in relief. "I'm sorry I'm such

a klutz." She extended a hand, words of gratitude forming on her lips, but the vial was jerked away and lifted beyond her reach.

"What the—" Her focus shifted from the vial to the face of the boy now holding it above her head. A familiar sneer and black eyes twinkling with malicious delight greeted her.

"Is that the only thing you're sorry for?" Damian said, his amusement growing at the alarm in her eyes. "'Cause I can think of at least ten things off the rip that deserve an apology. That face, those clothes, breathing..."

"Give me that," she barked, the stern command betrayed by the quiver in her voice.

"What, this?" Damian lowered the vial to her outstretched hands, then jerked it away just as it touched her fingers. He laughed.

"Junior, give it back. I'm serious."

He leaned against the wall, arm extended toward the ceiling. "Say please."

"Is that a joke? What are we, in kindergarten?"

His gaze dropped to her chest. He squinted. "Looks like it. Now, say please."

She clawed at the vial dangling just within reach. Latching onto his arm, she pulled at his hand with all of her strength. It was like trying to bend a steel beam. Fuming, she stepped back. Why was she born to be short? Out of the corner of her eye, she noticed an audience forming and struggled to curb her growing hysteria.

Her eyes darted around the corridor, seeking out sharp or heavy objects. With the exception of a few empty beer bottles and crumpled potato chip bags, she was out of luck. Teresa would kill her if she got bloody glass all over the floor, and she doubted the threat of death by Pringles bag would frighten Damian into submission.

"Prick," she ground out between clenched teeth.

"See, there you go again, Rocks. Showing how little you know about the birds and the bees. A prick isn't anywhere close to a please. And that's why you're not getting this back." He tried to sidestep her, but she shifted to block him. Chuckling, he slid the vial into the pocket of his varsity jacket.

More people had formed a semicircle around them. She searched their faces, desperate for help, but they were placing bets on who would walk away with bottle. And most of them were betting against her.

Her voice boomed across the hallway. "Please."

Damian pulled the vial from his pocket, holding it up to examine. She lunged forward, but he slid to the side, leaving her to clutch at the air as he said, "What is this stuff? What'd you plan on doing with it?"

"Something that's none of your business," she snapped.

"Interesting word choice." He nodded thoughtfully. "None of my business. You mean like how you thought it would be cute to flash a light in my eyes during practice, messing up *my* business?"

Looking into his eyes, she saw any hope she'd had of reclaiming the vial wave farewell.

"I know where you and your friends were sitting," he said, a tiny vein popping up along the side of his temple. "And I know no one else would be stupid enough to jack with me. So tell me, was it really any of *your* business to play kiddie games while I was trying to handle *mine*?"

She bit her lip, mind racing.

"Exactly." He waved the vial under her nose, spinning away when she grabbed for it. "I think this makes us even." He again moved to pass her, but she pushed him back.

"You owe, Junior," she hissed.

"I owe?" His voice lowered into a rumble. "You thinking of using this stuff as payback?"

She leaned forward, matching his tone. "After all your crap from this morning, you'd do best to just give me my vial back and leave me alone."

"Tell me what you planned on doing with this stuff, and I'll think about it."

"Get the wax out of your ears. It's none...of...your...business."

He lowered his head, grazing her earlobe with his lips. "In that case, you should thank me for taking it off your hands. I just saved your life. Because if the stuff in this bottle somehow made it into my drink tonight, even Mike wouldn't be able to keep me from you."

They glared at each other in a contest of wills—him trying to intimidate her; her mentally cussing him out. Their surrounding audience faded to the background of the wordless battle. Ricki was about to kick him in the shins—a favored takedown mastered in the third grade when Damian had stolen her seat at a neighborhood block party—when he glanced away from her to stare at the ceiling. His free hand brushed at his shoulder.

Seizing the opening, Ricki snatched at the vial.

Damian placed a palm against her forehead and nudged her back. He brushed again at his shoulders, frowning at the vent above his head, then swiped a hand across his face. "You'd think the Mas could afford better," he murmured, shaking something out of his hair. "This place is falling apart."

Ricki pulled back a hand to sucker punch him, but his attention swiveled back to her. He grinned and slid the vial back into his pocket. The smile widened, a daring invitation playing across his lips. Ricki's fist dropped to her side.

A slender figure nudged its way through the crowd,

detached from the pack, and strolled to Ricki's side. Speaking just loud enough for Damian to hear, Lindsey announced, "Ricki, we found Aaron for you. He's in the kitchen."

Mortified, Ricki frowned at Lindsey, who stared back with wide-eyed innocence.

Damian burst into laughter. "Little Rocky has a thing for my boy, Aaron? Talk about reaching for the impossible." He took Lindsey's hand and strutted past Ricky. "Trust me, you don't want to go that route, Rocks. You're not up to speed for it. Stick with the drama queer—I mean queen—you were laid up under earlier. He's more your level." Still chuckling, he walked away.

Taking her vial with him.

Ricki's head buzzed. The world became grainy, its edges growing hazier. Damian's retreating back was the only clear object in her narrowing field of vision. After almost a year of driving herself crazy, fate had finally dropped the key to claiming her soul mate into her hands.

And, once again, *he* was in the way.

Fists clenched, she rushed at his back. "Give it back, Demon Spawn!"

He whirled around, pushing Lindsey out of the way.

"Ricki, what are you doing?" Lindsey cried.

Just as she was about to land on his chest, two wiry arms swept around her waist and spun her through the air, away from Damian.

"What's going on?" Reggie demanded. Setting Ricki on her feet, he was careful to keep a tight hold on her squirming body.

She strained against his arms.

Damian watched her struggle with a smug smirk on his face. Placing a hand on the pocket with the vial, he gave it a small pat and winked.

"Spawn took something from me and won't give it back!" she shouted.

"I don't have a clue what she's talking about." He puffed up with injured righteousness. "I was just coming out of the bathroom when the girl jumps on me and starts acting crazy."

"That's *such* a lie," Ricki protested. "Everyone saw you take it from me."

He looked around the hallway. "Anyone know what she's talking about?"

She was disappointed but not surprised to see all heads shake a unified no.

"Search his pockets," she insisted.

Sighing, he stuck both hands into his jacket pockets. "You really have lost it." His hands withdrew, pulling the pockets inside out. A few quarters and a packet of breath mints fell to the floor, but the vial was missing. Slowly spinning around, he displayed his empty pockets to their audience.

She gasped. "What did you do with it?"

"That's enough," Reggie said. Letting go of her waist, he walked up to Damian and held out his hand. "If Rick says you took something from her, then you took something from her. Give it back."

Damian's eyes went flat. "How sweet, Rocky. Your little fairy champion is flitting up on his wings of chivalry to defend your honor." He took a menacing step toward Reggie. "Best to put a leash on him before he gets squashed."

"Reg, it's okay," she anxiously called out. "Spawn's just being Spawn. You don't need to get involved."

Reggie's hands balled into two rigid fists. "That's the problem, Rick. No one ever gets involved with Golden Boy. Maybe if someone did, he would stop stalking you and get a life."

The crowd muttered among themselves, backing away and whipping out cell phones as the two boys squared off. Bets were now being placed on how many bones in Reggie's body would be broken before security showed up to pull Damian off him.

"Rein your puppy in, Rocky," Damian said, his voice deceptively soft.

Reggie took another step toward him. "Don't you talk to her," he said. "Just give her back what you took and leave." He poked Damian twice in the chest for emphasis.

Damian didn't reply.

Emboldened, Reggie took his life into his hands and landed a third poke.

The tension drained from Damian's muscles. His weight shifted to one foot, his shoulders dropping unobtrusively into a slight hunch. He looked away from Reggie in cool disinterest.

His body language was clear to Ricki. Like a lion preparing for the attack, he was about to pounce. No words would be spoken. He would let his fists continue the conversation. Fear for Reggie crept through her. In the theater, the brave hero who challenges the evil villain to protect the damsel in distress always wins. In the real world, the five-foot-seven, 140-pound drama geek who goes up against the six-foot-one, 180-pound jock usually gets his face ripped off and used to wipe the floor. The actress in her knew Reggie pictured himself as the fair, sinewy David bringing justice down on Damian's swarthy, rippling Goliath. The poor fool didn't realize he was about to be choked to death with his own slingshot.

Her mind whispered a heartbroken goodbye to the vial, knowing it was time to leave before Damian decided to use her friend as a human mop. She placed a hand on Reggie's arm. "Let's go." Before he could object, she steered him toward the wall of spectators.

Damian mouthed, "It's on," as she glared at him on the way past.

Ignoring him, Ricki escaped into the crowd.

"Pretty boys aren't meant to fight roughnecks, Reggie. Deal with it."

Ricki sat with Reggie on a porch swing in the backyard, staring at the stars and trying to ignore the free-for-all belching contest held by a group of drunken basketball players on the other side of the patio. They had almost been chased away minutes earlier by the group's spitting tournament. Almost getting beamed in the face with a long-distance loogie had been a bit much for Ricki's delicate sensibilities, but she wasn't ready for Reggie to go back into the house and risk another encounter with Damian.

The boys now proudly burped their way through the alphabet, with the lead contender putting his own personal spin on the letter *Q*. With nowhere to go after *Z*, she had already decided that if air started blowing out of other body openings, Reggie might have to fend for himself.

"Golden Boy is not a roughneck," Reggie said. "He's just a puffed-up meathead who gets off on messing with you. It's almost psychotic."

She nodded. "I agree. But he's still rough enough to break your neck, and that's all that matters."

"Thanks for the faith in me," he grumbled.

"I've got nothing but faith in you. I just also have faith in Satan Jr. to be a sadistic bully, and you're not evil enough to fight him on his level. You don't have the horns yet."

Reggie chuckled, smoothing a handful of curls from his forehead. "You and him have been at it the whole time I've known you. How long have you guys hated each other?"

Wrinkling her brow, she stared at the sky. Minutes passed as she mentally ran through the years of her life, clicking backward in time through her unending battle with Damian until she reached its birth. Her thoughts were broken by the winner of the burping contest dropping his pants and streaking down the grassy hill of the backyard, cheered on by his companions bellowing out an off-key rendition of "We are the Champions."

"Forever," she responded.

"That's a long time to hate someone."

"Maybe," she allowed, "but we do it well."

"Why? What started it?"

Her thoughts floated through the sky, pulling days long forgotten from her past to the forefront of her mind. "Because he made me cry," she said. "I don't really remember the details, like what he did or why. But I remember crying and Mike holding my hand, trying to make me laugh. But I didn't want to laugh; I just wanted to find a way to make Damian cry, like he'd done to me. And so I did." She frowned at the memory. "Then he made me cry harder."

"Sounds like the start of a beautiful friendship," Reggie joked.

"It was the start of *something*, and it probably won't end until I kill him. Or he graduates and goes away to college." She shrugged. "Whichever comes first."

"Hey, at least you don't have much longer to go."

"No, I don't. And I'd really like to make it through the next couple months without any casualties of war." She tugged on a loose curl to grab his attention. "Please don't ever try to take him on again because of me. Promise?"

"But, Rick," he objected, "it doesn't hurt to have someone in your corner, does it?"

"No, but it would hurt if something happened to you because of me." She smiled, her eyes reflecting the moonlight into Reggie's. "You're a wonderful friend, Reg. Just keep being that, and that's all the support I need."

Smiling back, he pulled her head down to rest on his shoulder. They swung in silence, taking in the stars and listening to the sounds of the party. It was an odd mixture of hip-hop music drifting from the house, howls of pain from the basketball players rolling each other down the hill in their underwear, and dry heaves from the former belching champion. He had left his clothes, dinner, and dignity at the bottom of the hill and now had his head stuck in a rosebush at the far end of the porch.

Reggie cleared his throat. "I'm having a really good time, Rick. I'm glad I came tonight."

She stared at the full moon hanging fat in the sky and thought wistfully of the vial sitting in Damian's pocket. Somehow, someway, she'd get it back. "So am I."

He ran a shaky hand through his hair. "And, uh, I've been meaning to tell you how nice you look."

"You think so?" she asked in surprise. "I feel like I should be standing on a street corner or something." She self-consciously covered her exposed stomach with an arm. "This is what happens when I let Denise dress me. She forgets I can't pull stuff off the way she can. She makes anything look good."

"So do you," he muttered. Louder, he said, "Can I tell you something?"

"Sure, what's up?"

"It's just that—"

"Ricki?" One word spoken from the opposite end of the patio by a figure concealed in the shadows.

No more than a whisper to anyone able to hear it over the house-rattling music and drunken shouts, it was loud enough to freeze Ricki's world, deafening her to all sounds beyond that single voice echoing in her ears. Her stomach flipped. She was aware of Reggie's mouth moving but unable to process anything coming from it. Her eyes remained glued to the spot where the shadowy figure stood, straining to see if he was real or a product of her imagination running rampant.

Stepping out of the darkness, the hazy silhouette solidified into an Adonis-like body holding two drinks. It smiled a lopsided grin so enticing that her heart almost raced from her chest and passed out on the pavement. The night had just taken another unexpected turn.

Aaron Miller stood at the edge of the patio and was staring straight at her.

Was she dreaming? Had she fallen asleep at some point in her conversation with Reggie and conjured him up? It had to be a dream because Aaron had never looked at her in her waking moments the way he looked at her now.

Like she existed.

Ricki fought to control the unsteady pounding of her heart. She watched through a love-struck haze as he came toward her, his eyes drilling into hers and cutting straight to her soul.

He stopped in front of her. "Hello," he said.

She blinked twice and almost fainted to find him still standing there. "Hi," she croaked in reply.

Reggie studied her face, then scowled at Aaron in displeasure. "Hey," he said sourly.

Aaron's chin cocked in Reggie's direction, but he continued to look at Ricki. "You're a hard lady to find."

Her jaw slackened. "Excuse me?"

"Yeah," he said, moving in closer. "I've been looking for you since word got out about D's behavior."

She blinked. "Huh?"

"Me and the fellas felt bad about him messing with you and getting in a fight with your friend." He gestured curtly at a sullen Reggie, not breaking eye contact with her. "Stuff like that gives the 'Roos a bad rep. One person's actions reflect on the whole team, and we don't want to give off the wrong image." He motioned to the basketball player sprawled in an undignified, naked heap beneath the rosebush. "I rest my case."

He held out a cup. The harsh tang of liquor wafted up from the red liquid. "On behalf of the soccer team, I bring a peace offering."

"She doesn't drink," Reggie gruffly cut in.

"No, it's okay, Reg." She nervously accepted the cup, her head swimming in a surreal fog of bliss.

Only Aaron could make a pair of tattered jeans and a Polo shirt look so sophisticated and sexy. He put James Bond to shame with his blue-and-gold Kirby High letter jacket looking as elegant on him as any tuxedo ever could. In a delirium, she looked at her drink, wondering if it had been shaken, not stirred.

"I'm Aaron, by the way," he said, extending his hand.

She almost dropped the drink.

She had this boy's name scribbled on the cover of every book in her locker. Five pages of her journal were dedicated to the different ways of saying *Mr. and Mrs. Aaron Miller*. Her notebook was filled with creative games designed to predict their future relationship (the last one affirmed they would have two children and a cat within the next six years). And he was actually introducing himself to her like she didn't already know who he was?

"Nice to meet you," she squeaked. She shook his hand, almost expiring from the thrill of touching him for the first time.

"I'm Reggie," Reggie offered belligerently.

Aaron appeared startled. "Oh, my bad. How you doing?"

Shaking Reggie's hand, he took a sip from his drink. "You do plays, right?"

"I'm in the theater, yes." Reggie's face was pinched in displeasure.

"Right, I knew you looked familiar." He smiled, his perfect teeth gleaming in the darkness of the patio. "You're good."

"Uh…thanks," Reggie said. The frown that had been on his face since Aaron's appearance showed signs of relaxing. "That game you guys had with Douglasville was pretty close…"

The two boys proceeded to discuss the soccer match, giving Ricki time to calm her pounding heart. She wanted to join in the conversation, but her mind had turned to sludge. Droplets of sweat trickled from her underarms, gluing her sheer camisole to her body.

Why can't I think of anything to say?

Static drowned out her thoughts. She racked her brain for something clever to say but only succeeded in making herself more nervous. The cool evening breeze swept against her sweat-drenched top, giving her goose bumps.

You're blowing it.

Her nerves grew tighter, stretching thin like string about to snap. *Would it be possible to escape from this swing, dodge through that horde of athletes passed out on the hill, and flee into the night like a frightened jackrabbit without Aaron thinking something's wrong?*

In one swift, unplanned movement, she brought the drink to her mouth and gulped it down. It tasted like a bad batch of fruit punch made with spoiled pineapples. The bitter liquid burned its way down her throat, lighting a trail of fire through her body until it landed in the pit of her stomach to softly simmer. As tears shot to her eyes, she hunched over in a fit of coughing.

Aaron and Reggie stopped talking to stare at her. Moving

into action, Reggie yanked her arm into the air and thumped on her back.

"For someone who doesn't drink, you sure know how to drop it like a soldier," Aaron said, taking the cup from her. "Need some water?"

"No, I'll be fine," she choked out. "I must've swallowed wrong." *Great. First, you were a brain-dead dummy who couldn't talk. Now you're a wannabe alkie who can't hold your liquor.*

Setting the cups on the ground, he held out his hand. "Maybe a dance will make you feel better."

The frown reappeared on Reggie's face.

Her next cough was forgotten. She looked up at Aaron and caught her breath. He was so magnificent, standing in front of her with the moon hanging round and luminous above his head.

The blue moon.

The liquid courage still burning a hole in her intestines helped her to reply, "I'd love to dance."

Reggie's eyes fell to the ground.

Aaron pulled her from the swing, took a step back, and admired her in the moonlight. "You look...*wow*."

"Thank you," she murmured, tugging at a strap that had worked its way down her shoulder.

His arm slid through hers, and they walked toward the house. When they reached the door, she stopped. Excusing herself, she ran back to Reggie.

"Thanks for everything, Reg," she whispered, squeezing his hand. "You're the best."

He offered her a small smile. "You're welcome, Rick. Have a good time."

In a daze, she followed Aaron onto the dance floor. The DJ switched to a slow song, cementing her belief that a divine power was in control that night. She melted into Aaron's arms as they slowly swayed to the music. She looked up at his chiseled face through her ecstatic stupor, tempted to run her fingers along his jaw. He twirled a lock of her hair through his fingers and stared boldly into her eyes. Her body became a steaming puddle.

Was it just her or was the room slightly lopsided?

His hands slipped from her hair and rubbed slow circles into the back of her neck. Electrified tingles shot up her spine, nearly exploding in her head. She tried to concentrate on the moment, wanting to freeze it forever in her mind, but she couldn't quite focus.

His face lowered, inching closer to hers.

She stopped breathing.

Right before his lips touched hers, his mouth moved to her ear.

"Aaron?" she said, trying to collect her scattered thoughts.

His breath caressed her face. "Do you want to go somewhere a little more quiet?"

She tried to answer, but her tongue had doubled in size. She suddenly found herself staring into twenty pairs of hazel eyes. The room became stifling, and her body started to sizzle. She struggled to stay upright on wobbly legs as weak as Jell-O.

Aaron looked at her in alarm. "Are you okay?"

She couldn't speak. Her head swam, and the room spun in a sickening circle around her. "Help," she moaned.

Her eyes rolled in their sockets, and the world went black.

CHAPTER FIVE

WHEN RICKI OPENED HER EYES, *Damian's face was the last thing she wanted to see.*

He stood by the pool table, surrounded by a circle of groupies and preening with self-importance. Lindsey was suctioned to his side, leading the worshipping pack as they hung on his every word like it was the gospel passed down from the heavens.

She tried to look away but couldn't.

A familiar head of closely cut auburn hair bobbed past the edge of her vision. Instinct instructed her eyes to follow it, but they refused. Aaron's voice drifted back to her, followed by a girl's twittering response. Who was he talking to? The muscles in her neck strained ineffectively.

She continued to watch Damian.

He was bragging about his big shutout in the latest game against Douglasville. He'd just reached the story's climax—he'd blocked his nineteenth goal of the game and cemented his MVP title for the school year—when his words trailed off. He looked over his shoulder. A pack of freshmen huddling behind him stared back with open devotion. He nodded politely, eliciting a new round of giggles, and resumed his story.

Why couldn't she move?

Her body floated weightlessly in place, hovering unnoticed at the edge of the room. A set designer from the drama troupe walked toward her. She opened her mouth to say hello, but no words came out. The girl came closer, closer, until she was a hair's breadth away. Then she was gone.

Damian picked up a pool stick and strutted around the table, ready to demonstrate how the skills that made him a god among athletes weren't limited to a patch of grass. He chalked the end of the pool stick with exaggerated twists, boasting that the world was his soccer field and the pool table just another goal to be conquered. Leaning into the table, he drew his arm back for the first shot.

He froze.

She watched him again glance over his shoulder, then look around the game room, his eyes warily taking in each face. Aaron called out for him to stop grandstanding and make the shot. Releasing a strained laugh, he hit the cue ball with impressive force, knocking four balls into the pockets and provoking a fluent string of profanity from Jonas Rogers on the other end of the table. As the frenzied crowd chanted his name, he thrust his stick into the air and bowed, then turned back to the table and positioned the stick for the next shot.

It didn't come.

Seconds ticked by with him leaning over the table, his arms braced against the pool stick. Anyone else would think he was concentrating, but she could see that his eyes weren't on the game. They, instead, jumped furtively around the room.

A bead of sweat formed on his temple. Wiping it away with a shaky hand, he leaned his stick against the table and called for a break. He ignored the crowd's grumbling and brushed the groupies away, asking for air.

She watched his eyes bounce restlessly from face to face, corner to corner. He closed them, propping his hands against the pool table and taking in deep but unsteady breaths. He stayed there, inhaling, exhaling, until his muscles visibly relaxed. His eyes then opened, fixing on a spot across the table and seeming to see with sudden clarity what no one else in the room did.

He was looking straight at her...

The telephone woke Ricki.

It rang so loudly, her heart almost stopped beating from fright before her brain even had a chance to reach consciousness. Her eyes creaked open, trying to find the source of her coronary troubles, but the glare of sunlight through a nearby window proved fatal to her corneas.

"My head," she whimpered, flinching as her voice ricocheted like bullets through the caverns of her brain.

The ringing stopped.

She wallowed in the silence. Weak, she attempted to roll onto her side, causing her head to swim. Sickening waves of motion swirled through her stomach and bubbled dangerously in her gut. Her eyes throbbed with aching force against her eyelids.

Struggling to sit up, her hand fell onto a pile of soft objects. She ran her fingers along their fuzzy outlines until she reached the stiff, smooth cylinders protruding at the ends. Unicorns?

Peeping open an eye, she risked a quick look around before the sunlight resumed its assault on her pupils. A wall of comedy and tragedy masks leered back at her.

How did I get home?

The phone began to ring again. She buried her head under a pillow to block out the sound, but six inches of feather down didn't quite make for a good buffer. Each ring pounded like a sledgehammer against her skull.

"Must...stop...the pain." She slid from the bed and stumbled blindly toward the trilling bells. After knocking over several stacks of books and nearly twisting her ankle on a pair of misplaced sneakers, she finally reached the source of her misery. "Hello?" she whispered into the receiver.

Two sharp stabs raced through her temples. The churning in her stomach kicked up to the next level of queasiness.

"Rocky?" a boy's voice said.

"Junior?"

"Yeah. I heard you got kind of sick last night, so I wanted to see how you're doing."

"In what universe?" She tried to wrap her mind around the concept of Damian ever caring whether she lived or died. Maybe it was the hangover, but she couldn't quite grasp the plausibility.

"Pleasant as ever," he said dryly. "Guess it means you're feeling okay after all."

She cautiously tested her eyes against the light. "Whatever. You couldn't care less about me being sick; you just called to rub it in."

He gave a deep chuckle.

"Thought so. Go find some bunnies to torture and leave me alone." She prepared to slam the phone down, but his next words stopped her.

"Aaron said he really enjoyed you last night."

The fog in her mind evaporated. "What?"

Silence.

"What did you say?" she demanded.

"I said Aaron really enjoyed dancing with you last night."

"That is *not* what you said."

"Isn't it?" Another chuckle. "I gotta say, you two kids made such a cute couple. Him holding you close. You passed out in his arms." He paused. "Y'know, they say the sleeping ones are the best kind."

She squeezed her eyes shut, urging her sluggish thoughts to remember what had taken place at the party. Images flashed at her. Aaron smiling, offering her a drink. Aaron rubbing her neck, his lips against her ear. Aaron asking if she wanted to go someplace more private...

The urge to throw up rushed over her, now for a different reason.

"What are you trying to tell me, Junior?" she asked in a panic.

"Wait, hold up," he said, his tone changing, "don't get all serious. You know I'm just messing with you. I only called because—"

"Okay, you can quit talking now," she snapped, furious at herself for falling into his trap. "I should know Aaron would never try to take advantage of me. You, on the other hand, are a sick freak with too much time on your hands. Kick rocks and don't call back."

After dropping the phone in its cradle, she collapsed onto a nearby beanbag.

Why couldn't she remember anything beyond dancing with Aaron? As she lay there fighting to get past the black wall blocking her memories, her head became lighter, and her thoughts scattered. Her vision blurred, and she folded into an unconscious heap among the pile of stuffed animals...

There he was again.

Damian sat on his bed, talking heatedly over the phone. He barked one final word to the person on the other end and hung up, tossing the cell across the room.

He looked at his watch. Getting up, he walked to his desk and picked up a bottle of water sitting beside the computer. He unscrewed the top and lifted the bottle to his mouth. He stopped. Looked around. He set the water down and cracked his thumb knuckles. Rolling his shoulders in wide circles, he walked into the bathroom and turned on the shower. Steaming water poured from the showerhead. He ducked his head under the stream of hot water, vigorously scrubbing at his face before reentering the bedroom. He lifted his shirt, pulling it over his dripping head.

She recoiled in horror, trying in vain to will herself away from the scene in front of her. How could she make it stop?

Unzipping his pants, he started to pull them down when he again paused to look around. He dropped to his knees and peered under his bed before crawling over to the desk. His hands skillfully ran along its corners and the bottom of each drawer before his attention turned to the ceiling vent. He spent almost a minute staring into its grill, examining every dark crevice beyond the metal slits. Rubbing his neck, he gave one last sweeping look around his bedroom. Shaking his head, he dropped his pants and reached for his underwear.

She felt herself about to hyperventilate. What horrible thing had she ever done to make the universe repay her with a striptease from her archenemy?

He stopped. Frowning, he walked over to the window and looked across the yard to the window facing his bedroom.

Her window.

As he stared at her house, her eyes unwillingly dropped to his shoulders, broad and rippling with lean muscles. They traveled down his chiseled back to his waist. Before they could continue their journey, she forced them back up to his black mop of hair. If they had dropped any lower, she might've gone blind.

Running a hand across the back of his neck, he turned away from the window and reached for his boxers. His thumbs hooked into the lining. He pulled...

The phone rang, dragging Ricki from sleep.

This time, Mike answered. She heard his voice down the hall and tried to figure out when he'd gotten home.

"Racquel, the phone!" he bellowed.

She pushed herself up from the beanbag. The pain in her head had vanished during the nap, and a civil war no longer raged in her bowels. Too bad the dizziness was still in full effect. She crawled toward the phone and gingerly picked it up. "Hello?"

"Hey, sweetie, how're you feeling?"

She shuffled over to her bed, relieved not to hear Damian's voice. "Terry, my friend," she said, lying down. "I feel like crap nuked in a broken microwave and left out to rot."

"My poor baby," Teresa cooed. "We've been calling you all day. Denise and Yogi even stopped by your house a couple of times, but no one came to the door. Are you sure you're okay?"

She clutched her head, on the verge of floating away from her body. "What time is it?"

"Almost four o'clock."

"In the afternoon?" Her eyes shot to the alarm clock beside her bed. "I've been asleep *all day*?"

"Hey, that's what happens when you play with the big boys. How much did you drink last night?"

She sifted through her jumbled thoughts to one of her last coherent memories of the evening. "I only had one drink, I swear."

"Only one? Then it must've hit you really hard, because you passed out in the middle of the dance floor. Someone had to carry you up to my bedroom."

"Was I knocked out the whole night?"

"Pretty much. You woke up a few times, rambling about some weird dreams you were having, and then you'd fall back asleep. But you got up right before the party ended, and you seemed fine, so Denise took you home."

"I don't remember any of that." She closed her eyes, hoping it would stop the sensation of the room revolving around her. "Do you think the alcohol hit me so hard because of the headache medicine I took earlier?"

"So naïve," Teresa sighed. "Not only did you down a cup

of the soccer team's infamous witches' brew, but you mixed it with meds too? That's a pretty lethal combination. Sweetie, if you're gonna bark with the big dogs, at least have one of us around to show you how to howl. Don't go off doing stuff on your own."

"Don't worry," Ricki groaned. "It'll be a long, long time before I touch another drop of alcohol. I don't even want to smell it."

"Good. You're just not ready for the chaotic world of sex, drugs, and alcoholism. Leave that to me and Denise." Teresa giggled. "I'll tell the girls you're feeling better. Get some more rest, and we'll see you at school tomorrow."

"Thanks. See you." She started to hang up.

"Oh, one more thing," Teresa said. "Calvin wanted me to tell you 'the treasure is back in safe hands.' And he's willing to make a new deal with you, if you're interested. Whatever that means."

It took Ricki's pickled brain a few seconds to decipher the message. The vial. Her whole purpose for even being at the party in the first place, and she'd totally forgotten about it. But it hadn't brought Aaron to her, had it? That gift had been true magic, courtesy of the gypsy's prophecy and a blue moon.

"Tell Calvin I appreciate his offer," she said, "but I'll have to pass on the deal. I found my own treasure after all."

⊷⊶⬦⊷⊶

Her eyes opened to a dark room, illuminated only by green neon numbers glowing the time from across the room. She thought the numbers on her alarm clock had always been red, but her mind was too fuzzy to remember. And she didn't know when she had moved the clock from its usual spot beside her bed to the other side of the room.

Where was her dinner? Mike had let her eat in her room

since she wasn't feeling well. She'd taken about three bites of undercooked lasagna before succumbing to the heaviness in her head.

It was 4:16 AM.

It would be time to get up for school in a few hours, and she hadn't even picked out an outfit. She struggled to sit up, but the weight of her body pulled her back down to the bed. Her head swam, and she drifted back to sleep.

⟶ ⟞⟠⟝ ⟵

Monday morning, Ricki was in second period Algebra II class when the hairs on the back of her neck stood up.

Mr. Kirkpatrick had just written a complex equation on the board, giving the class five minutes to complete it. The first five people to solve the problem would get an extra ten points on their final exams, but any incorrect answers would result in a ten-point deduction. Ricki, in sore need of those extra points to bolster her floundering math grades, quickly got to work on finding the correct answer before the twenty other students in the room beat her to it.

She tried to focus on the problem, but her thoughts were too muddled. Every time she closed her eyes, she thought of the weird dreams that had plagued her sleep. Dreaming about Damian? Only in her nightmares. Realizing her mind had wandered off again, she reenergized herself with a light slap on the cheek and shifted her attention back to the equation. She was almost finished when a sense of uneasiness stole over her. A trail of goose bumps formed on her neck, each fine hair standing on end.

Someone was watching her.

She looked up expecting to find Mr. Kirkpatrick standing over her. No one was there. The teacher was still at the front of the classroom, glowering darkly at Kai Spencer, who'd just arrived late to class with a written excuse. The note, forged in his mother's handwriting, asked the teacher to please excuse her son's tardiness on account of a rabid dog attacking his scooter at a stoplight and running off with its tires. Something on the teacher's face said he wasn't buying it. She glanced over her shoulder, thinking to catch Cheri Dearling in the act of copying off her paper. Wrong again. Cheri's head was buried in her own work, and she looked up to give Ricki an annoyed frown before going back to it.

The sensation grew stronger.

She looked around. Every head was bent in concentration, pencils scribbling furiously against paper as the five-minute time limit neared its end. She looked again to Mr. Kirkpatrick, but he was preoccupied with comparing the writing on Kai's tardy note against a Spencer family Christmas card he'd pulled from his desk. Mrs. Spencer herself had sent the card hoping to smooth the way to a passing grade for her son—little did she know it would now be used as evidence to put the final nail in Kai's failing coffin.

Shaking off the strange feeling, Ricki redirected her attention to the math problem. No one was breathing over her; it was just a draft from the open window. She brushed at her neck. Tapping her pencil against the desk, she stared blindly at the piece of paper in front of her.

The person now stood beside her.

Her eyes closed. There was a density in the air around her, hovering at her shoulders. She bit the inside of her cheek. *Stay calm.* Opening her eyes, she peeked around the room— hoping to find someone, anyone, looking back at her.

Nobody.

She squirmed in her seat. The oppressive weight of the hidden eyes pressed down on her, their presence enveloping her body and tightening its embrace until she almost couldn't breathe. She smoothed the hairs on her neck down with a damp palm and struggled to keep from freaking out.

Doesn't anyone else in the room sense it?

Just when she couldn't endure the smothering feeling any longer and was on the verge of screaming, the unseen presence disappeared, leaving the room as suddenly as it had arrived.

She gulped in several breaths of air. *What* was *that?*

"Time's up!" Mr. Kirkpatrick announced.

She looked at the unfinished equation, the solution now obvious to her. She quickly jotted down the answer.

Mr. Kirkpatrick made his way up the aisle, taking an extra moment to study her paper before moving on to the next student.

"Good job, Miss Nichols," he said over his shoulder. "Too bad you didn't finish in the top five. Maybe next time."

She nodded, laying her head on the cool steel desk. Maybe it had been a panic attack. Finals were getting closer and her algebra grade was teetering on the edge of failure, so she'd probably psyched herself out over missing the problem. No phantom boogeyman had been watching her from the shadows. The pressure had been too much for her; that was all.

And when she could finally make herself believe that, she would feel so much better.

———◦✦◦———

Fourth period Spanish class was going about as well as her other classes had that morning.

Ricki couldn't focus on a thing Señora Torres was saying, and it didn't help that all of it was said in another language. The teacher breezed through the world of verb conjugations, informing the class of the different ways to say they were opening the window. Or they *had* opened the window. Or they *were going to* open the window. But all Ricki heard was a humming drone of rolling *R*s, gently lapping against her eardrums in hypnotic waves that lulled her to sleep.

Catching herself as her chin slid off her fist, she shook herself back to consciousness.

Señora Torres was oblivious to the glazed over expressions on the faces of more than half the class. She had moved on from opening the window to closing the window, and all Ricki wanted to do was throw herself through that window. Switching her chin to her other fist, she followed along in the textbook as Señora ran through the list of verbs.

The letters on the page blurred…

She sat in a steamy locker room surrounded by half-naked boys wrapped in white towels. Her body was slumped on a bench, her back propped against a row of lockers and her chin resting on her chest. She slowly lifted her heavy head, blinking through clouds of steam at the boys who passed by on their way to the showers. A parade of prized Kirby High flesh marched past in equal parts scandalous, yet thrilling. She didn't know whether to shut her eyes or keep staring.

"Man, I'm still hung over from Saturday."

She looked at the boy who had spoken. Victor Schulz stood in front of a mirror, examining the effects of an all-night drinking binge on his belly. It wasn't a pretty sight.

Johnny Davidson laughed and punched him in the ribs. "Yeah, well, nobody told you to drink so much. Were you trying to win a prize?"

"Hey, there were worse than me." He let out a loud guffaw. "Dude, what about that one chick who passed out on Aaron?"

She willed herself to wake up. What kind of dream was this turning into?

"Man, that was classic. He was all ready for her, and she just fell out, right on top of him."

"Talk about perfect timing," Victor quipped. "What's that thing you say about the sleeping ones, Aaron?"

The locker room burst into rowdy laughter.

She was stunned at the sight of Aaron coming around the corner with a towel draped loosely around his hips. "No comment," he mumbled. He wrapped another towel around his head, ignoring the round of boos from his locker buddies.

"Aw, don't be mad 'cause D threw salt in your game," Johnny teased. "He probably wanted a piece for himself. Right, D?"

Everyone turned to stare at Ricki.

She jerked in surprise. "Huh?"

Her veins ran cold at the sound of a boy's voice coming from her throat...

"Very impressive, Señorita Nichols." Señora Torres stood in front of Ricki's desk, arms folded.

"Huh?" Ricki yelped. Her heart raced erratically. She was embarrassed to find all eyes in the classroom on her.

"I'm glad to see you've been doing your homework." The severe frown on the Spanish teacher's face contradicted the pleasant words coming from her mouth. "You answered correctly, and your accent was flawless."

Confused, she gawked at the teacher.

Señora Torres slammed a hand down on the desk, causing Ricki to jump in her seat and nearly bite off her tongue. "But that's still no excuse for sleeping in my class. Since you know so much that you feel the need to nap through the lesson, you can spend your lunch conjugating verbs from chapters twenty-two and twenty-three."

"But we're only on chapter twenty-one," Ricki protested through tears of pain.

"A genius like you should be kept challenged," Señora replied. "We wouldn't want you to get bored and fall asleep again, would we?" Her steely glare was enough to glue

Ricki's mouth shut. "Right. Now, back to where we left off before Señorita Nichols graced us with her ladylike snores." Imparting one last hard look, she returned to the front of the classroom.

Ricki ducked her head and opened her Spanish book, then buried her face in its pages. Her tongue was on fire. Her head was a buzzing mass of turmoil and paranoid delusions. And now her lunch would be spent at the mercy of an irate Spanish teacher instead of talking to her friends.

As God was her witness, she would never drink alcohol again.

Ricki wasn't prepared to run into Aaron on the way to eighth-period drama class, but there he was, strolling through the Lane, when he should've been on his way to class in the Alley.

Unofficially dubbed "Sophomore Lane," the upper level of Kirby's north wing was home base for its tenth graders. It housed their homeroom classes and lockers as well as the majority of sophomore-level language and science classes. The other grades had their own headquarters: ninth graders ran rampant in Freshman Landing on the west end of the building; eleventh graders occupied Junior Run on the east side; and twelfth graders reigned supreme from Senior Alley at the southern tip of the school. The four factions came together at the base of their sections' stairwells, which formed the main lobby of the school, also known as the Junction.

Upperclassmen rarely demeaned themselves by slumming it in lower-class property except to use it as a shortcut to the stadium. But Ricki knew Aaron's schedule by heart—it was a responsibility she held with pride and had helped her on many an occasion to "randomly" pass him in crowded halls and stairwells. She knew it was time for his physics class, not soccer practice. And having him on the wrong side of the school put an unwelcome twist on an already insanely crooked day.

She still felt—and no doubt looked—like death warmed over. What had started as a miserable morning had continued on to be a miserable afternoon. After suffering through an excruciatingly tedious lunch period under Señora Torres's watchful eye—translating in Spanish an unending list of verbs she would never use in English (honestly, what were the odds of her ever economizing anything?)—her dwindling energy reserves had dropped to empty and stayed there. The only thing she wanted now was to go home and sleep until her eighteenth birthday, and then sleep some more. She was nowhere near ready to face Aaron, but time marched onward with each step bringing him closer.

She wished desperately for time to freeze, just long enough for her to comb her hair and maybe swipe a blotting sheet or two over her T-zone. She'd even will away her firstborn child in exchange for a mirror. Quickly rubbing her eyes, she attempted to make herself look more awake than she felt and ducked her head as she passed him.

"Hey," he said, reaching out a hand to stop her.

The cobwebs receded from her brain. Her senses zoned in on the feel of his hand touching her skin.

"You really know how to play hard to get," he said, his eyes twinkling. "I get one dance with you and never see you again."

Were the hallucinations starting up again? Had she slipped into another dream? She carefully tested her teeth against her bruised tongue. *Ouch!* Okay, definitely not a dream.

"How're you doing?" he asked. "I've been worried about you since Saturday night."

"You have?"

"Of course." He backed against the wall, pulling her out of the way of an oncoming pack of sophomores.

The feel of his arms around her made her so high, she swore she saw a passing cloud.

"I wanted to check on you," he said, "but D said your brother might trip if I called the house, so he offered to look in on you for me."

Her high crashed to the ground. "Damian did what?"

"Yeah, when I talked to him yesterday. He told me you were doing alright, but I still had to see for myself." He looked her over. "Well, you certainly do look fine."

Her cheeks warmed. "Thank you," she murmured, her delight over his concern almost overshadowed by her irritation with Damian.

An awkward moment of silence passed. She fished through her vacant mind for something to say, finally settling on, "So, um, how'd you know where to find me?"

"I didn't. I'm on my way to practice. It was just my luck running into you."

"But you have physics this period," she blurted. She heard the words leave her mouth right as her brain kicked in to stop them. *Can we say 'stalker'?*

"Yeah, I do," he said, giving her a strange look. "But Coach wanted us to get some extra practice time in before our game with Jefferson, so we're excused from class."

"Wow, that's really great," she gushed.

She received a blank stare in response.

"Because extra practice will help you guys win," she stammered, looking down at her hands. *Magic words to start this conversation over would really come in handy right about now.*

"Uh, right." He looked as though he wanted to say more, but the warning bell rang.

The sound let Ricki know she had exactly two minutes to get to drama class, which happened to be five minutes away from where she stood. If she ran and cut through the cafeteria, she could still make it on time, but she didn't want to leave that spot as long as Aaron shared it with her. Let Quincy be mad—she'd miss every class for the rest of her life if it meant being near Aaron.

"I'd better get going," he said. "Coach'll bench me if I'm late." He put a hand under her chin, lifting her face until their eyes met. "I'm glad you're doing good. Now that I found the girl of my dreams, I don't want to lose her before I even get the chance to get to know her."

With those words, he disappeared down the hall, taking a chunk of Ricki's heart with him.

Her spirits soared into the highest corners of the building's vaulted ceilings. She touched her fingers to her face, lightly brushing the spot where his hand had been. It was really happening. The gypsy's words had been true. She had figured out the riddle and gotten her soul mate.

With a smile that threatened to outshine the sun, she spun around on her toes and dashed through the hall toward drama rehearsal. The world was now a perfect place.

As long as she could stay awake in it.

CHAPTER SIX

" LINE!"

It was the fourth time Ricki had forgotten her lines. The dark clouds brewing on Julius Quincy's face informed her there'd better not be a fifth. She looked in apology at the other actors on stage and tried to concentrate.

"No, Demetrius," Duane Ellis shouted to her. "As long as blood flows through these veins, my heart will beat only for Xander."

She repeated the line in her head and turned to face Reggie. Feebly pushing against him, she cried, "No, Demetrius! Only as long as these veins flow through Xander's blood will my heart beat."

Silence fell across the auditorium.

Reggie's face turned red as he tried to hold in his laughter.

Oblivious, she continued. "Forget about me and find love with Mia. She will love you better than—"

"Cut!" Quincy bellowed.

Her mouth went dry.

The drama teacher stomped up the stairs to the stage, each footstep sending a thunderous echo across the auditorium. "Racquel Nichols!" he boomed. "It is shameful enough to not know your lines, but to not even have the right character name is inexcusable."

"I...I don't know what you mean."

"How, pray tell, is Demetrius to go find love with Mia when *you* are Mia?"

She looked to Reggie, who offered a weak smile in return.

"I would cry if we had enough time," Quincy sighed. "I would tear this script into a million pieces and weep in shame over its tattered shreds if we did not have just *three and a half weeks* before opening night." His voice hardened. "Tell me, if I do not even have the time to mourn the utter disrespect you have given my script, what makes you think you have time to make a mockery of this production?"

Her gaze fell. What could she say? That five minutes after getting on stage, she'd again felt someone watching her, and *that* was the reason she couldn't focus? She would sound ridiculous—the whole drama troupe was watching her.

His hand slashed diagonally through the air, inches from her nose. "No more, Miss Nichols! You will sit rehearsal out for the rest of the day. Possibly even tomorrow if I have not yet forgotten this amateur hour you've put on for us today." Without giving her the chance to respond, he shouted, "Miss Matsi! Front and center!"

Yolanda, her understudy, took her place on the stage.

Tears welled in Ricki's eyes. Quickly bowing her head, she let her hair fall across her face to hide the tiny rivulets trickling down her cheeks. Avoiding eye contact with Reggie, she brushed the tears away under the guise of fixing her hair and fled into the audience. She hurried to an empty seat, seeking refuge from the pitying looks of the cast. The day had been a roller coaster of weirdness, and instead of getting better after talking to Aaron, it had just hit rock bottom. Why did life insist on lifting her up only to knock her back down and tap-dance on her broken remains?

"It's just for today, y'know." Denise scooted into the seat

beside her, Lindsey sliding in next. "Q must be PMSing or something. You'll be back on stage tomorrow. No worries."

Grimacing, she slouched farther into her seat. "It's not his fault I screwed up. My mind just isn't acting right today."

"Still tired from this weekend?" Lindsey asked.

Tired was an understatement. The bouts of paranoia were taking their toll on her mental health, which was already battered from the freaky dreams plaguing her brief moments of sleep. She was literally two steps away from becoming a walking zombie. It was a wonder she hadn't fallen asleep in the middle of her scene, not just forgotten her lines.

"A little," she answered.

Lindsey cut her eyes in Ricki's direction. "We heard about what happened in Spanish class. During lunch, we stopped by Damian's table to say hi, and Aaron asked about you."

She shot up in her seat. "He did?"

"Yep. Then a guy from your class told everyone about you falling asleep and how you had to spend lunch doing work."

She slumped back down. "Too embarrassing." She frowned. "You're still talking to Damian?"

"Ricki," Denise warned.

"I'm just asking," she protested. "I just would've thought she'd be done with him after what happened at the party."

"You mean when you tried to jump him?" Lindsey said. She ignored the answering snort. "He was so upset that he took off right after you and Reggie left. I didn't even get the chance to dance with him."

Ricki stared in petulance at the stage. "Whatever. Well, I guess all is now bright and shiny in the underworld of Damian and Lindsey. My condolences."

"Thank you," Lindsey snidely accepted.

Denise groaned. "Unclench, you guys. No boy is worth twisting your panties over, so just stop."

"Bygones," Ricki mumbled. "Just try not to get hurt, okay?"

"Whatever," Lindsey said. She glanced at the stage. "My scene's coming up. Got to go." She rushed down the aisle just as Quincy shouted her name through the microphone.

Denise eyed Ricki. "They have your blessing, huh?"

"I wouldn't bless a diseased rodent to be with Damian," she said, her face scrunched in disgust. "But I figure if I stay out of it, it won't take long for Demon Spawn to show his true colors and Lindsey to kick his trifling butt to the curb where it belongs." A nasty smile appeared on her lips. "And if an opportunity happens to arise to help things along, I'll be there to jump on it."

The air around her shifted. She peered over her shoulder. Did something just blow on her?

Laying her head on Denise's lap, she closed her eyes. "I really feel like I'm losing my mind today."

Denise stroked her head in sympathy and began braiding the hair around her temple. "What's up?"

"Nothing, I guess. I don't know. Maybe I'm just tired." Eyes still closed, Ricki lost herself in the soothing feel of Denise's fingers massaging her scalp.

She half-listened as Denise talked about upcoming plans with Marco, nodding whenever a response was required. As the nods were needed less frequently, she let her mind drift into the dark world behind her eyelids. Denise's voice grew fainter as the darkness intensified...

The bright light of the sun shining on her face came as a shock to her senses. One minute, she'd been resting in a dim auditorium, listening to her friend plot an after-curfew rendezvous; the next, she was lying under a blazing sun, watching a herd of soccer players stampede across an open field. Squinting, she watched through bleary eyes as they descended upon the goal at the far end of the field. Her body was sprawled across a bench. Rubbing her cheek against its scratchy surface, she pushed herself onto her elbows. Her head swam, almost causing her to lie back down. Resisting the wave of lightheadedness, she sat up.

"Hey!"

She looked around.

Aaron stood in the middle of the field, bouncing a soccer ball on his knee. "You gonna sleep through the whole practice?" he yelled. "Get your lazy butt up and show these punk momma's boys how it should be done."

Her heart skipped. Her dreams were finally pointing in the right direction. She had no clue what Aaron was talking about, but at least the right boy now played the starring role.

She prayed not to wake up.

Except...the dream didn't feel as dreamlike as it should. As the haziness in her head cleared, things were becoming a little too...focused. Ignoring the alarms going off in the back of her mind, she stood up and walked toward Aaron.

Why did her body feel so heavy? Why was it so hard to move her legs?

She started to look down at her feet when a soccer ball whizzed through the air and collided with the side of her face...

"Ouch!" Ricki leaped from her seat, startling Denise. It took several seconds for her to realize where she was: back in the theater, away from the scorching sun and killer soccer balls. She looked frantically around the auditorium, her heart pounding through her chest.

It had all felt so real. She touched her face, expecting soreness in the spot where she had been struck. Nothing.

"Miss Nichols!" Quincy glared down at her from the stage, hands on his hips.

She then realized how quiet it was. Everyone in the theater had stopped talking. Even the actors on the stage had halted midscene, every eye fixed on her.

"Did I just scream out loud?" she murmured to Denise.

"Big time."

"Crap." Bracing herself, she tried not to flinch as Quincy grabbed the microphone to roar out his next directive.

"Out!"

Ricki sat outside of the school, waiting for Mike to pick her up. She stared across the parking lot, letting the day's events parade through her mind. She didn't know which was ruining her life most: the extreme sleepiness, the imaginary stalkers, or the twisted dreams. In the end, it didn't really matter—they were all doing a great job of driving her crazy.

The school doors banged open, and a mass of footsteps pounded toward her. She didn't turn around.

"How's it going?"

Her head flew up at the sound of Aaron's voice. He stood over her, still wearing his soccer uniform, with a half-zipped gym bag slung over his shoulder. A handful of his teammates gathered at the end of the sidewalk, waiting for the rest of the players.

Flashing a crooked grin, he sat beside her on the curb. "What're you doing out here all by yourself?"

"I, um, I'm waiting for my ride." She chanced a peek at him before self-consciousness drew her eyes back to the ground.

"I could take you home if you want," he offered.

"That's really sweet of you," she wheezed, her breath catching in her throat, "but my brother's already on his way."

"Call him." His head lowered toward hers. "Tell him you found a friend to ride with." The smoothness of his voice was intoxicating.

A shadow fell over them. Looking up, she was surprised

to see an impassive Damian staring down at her. Her body tensed for battle.

"Dude, I'm hungry," he said to Aaron. "Let's go." Without saying anything further, he walked away.

She was thrown. No tasteless insult? No tacky threats? Things never went that easily with Damian. If nothing else, he was at least good for his infamous sneer. She stared after him.

Damian stepped into the street, out of the school's shadow. Sunlight illuminated his left cheek, which appeared puffy and almost purplish in color. She tried to get a better look, but his back turned to her as he headed toward his car.

Aaron frowned after him. "We're heading over to Sheckie's for some burgers. I could drop you off at home if you want to come."

Any response that might have entered her dazed mind was drowned out by the squeal of tires from Mike's Honda Civic tearing across the parking lot.

She covered her disappointment with a bright smile. "Looks like my ride is here."

"Too bad," he said, standing.

He pulled her to her feet and held her backpack while she brushed dirt from her pants, then placed it over her shoulder. She glowed inwardly as he took extra time to adjust the straps on her arms, his fingers inadvertently caressing her neck.

Her heartfelt words of thanks were interrupted by a blaring car horn.

"Racquel! You see me sitting here, right?" The Civic sat at the curb, softly sputtering and emitting cottony puffs of black smoke into the ozone. Mike had rolled the passenger window down to glare at them. "I got stuff to do, so tell that boy to back up off you and get your tail in the car." He locked eyes with Aaron and grimly nodded in greeting.

"Okay, I'm coming," she hissed. She turned to apologize

to Aaron but found he had placed a good two yards between them and was now studying the cracks on the sidewalk with fierce intensity.

Stupid Mike.

As Mike sped away, she watched Aaron's figure in the side mirror until it was nothing more than a speck in the distance. And even after it had disappeared from sight, the image of his face looking into hers was still reflected in her heart.

———◦✕◦———

Stupid Mike.

Their parents had put him in charge of the house, not her personal life. Big whoopin' deal if he was a sophomore in college—that didn't mean his word was law. He was nothing but a smothering, power-tripping tyrant with a god complex. And things were going to change…as soon as Ricki got up the nerve to tell him.

The car ride home had been a chilly one, with most of the heat coming from Mike's mouth as he lectured her on the evils of the opposite sex. Apparently, she only had one thing they wanted. He was vague about what that one thing was, but her standing outside the school with some "shifty-looking boy" was somehow the first step on the road to giving it up. After a few blocks of listening to a bunch of warnings that made little to no sense, she'd fazed him out and let her cold shoulder do the rest of the talking.

She hated it when he kicked into overprotective big-brother mode. He was worse than their father. At least with her dad, she could bat her eyelashes, squeeze out a crocodile tear, and bend him to her will. If she batted her lashes at Mike, he'd just ask if dirt was in her eye, then put her in a headlock and drown her in Visine.

When they got home, she made a point to ignore him

for the rest of the afternoon, opting to stay in her bedroom on a five-way phone conference. Discussion centered around practice. Lindsey was shocked Quincy had actually made Ricki leave rehearsal. Yolanda was sorry for having to take her place. Denise was sympathetic but more concerned about her strange naptime behavior (she couldn't exactly put her finger on it, but something about Ricki nuzzling her chest hadn't seemed quite right). And Teresa was already plotting an elaborate retaliation scheme to be executed at the end of the school year, when her father would be out of the country on a business trip.

At that point, Ricki had hurried off the phone before hearing any incriminating details that could make her an accessory.

Denise's comments bothered her. First, she'd spoken Spanish, and now she was molesting her best friend? What was happening to her when she fell asleep?

The question plagued her into the night. It drew her eyes open every time she started to nod off and had her poring through old romance novels she'd already read a million times. Anything to keep from going to bed. At one point, it even felt as if her invisible boogeyman had returned, peeping over her shoulder and reading along with her through the steamy love scene between the enslaved heroine and noble pirate. She ignored the feeling, refusing to be sucked into her mind's irrational games. After a few minutes, the presence went away.

Her eyes grew heavier.

Maybe it'd be okay to fall asleep. Maybe she'd actually sleep through the night, and the weird dreams would leave her alone. Maybe...

The lights were off.

She must've fallen asleep, and Mike had come in to turn

them off. He was so anal about conserving energy. She needed to shower and change into her nightclothes, but the warmth of the sheets felt so good, she couldn't bring herself to leave the bed. Just a few more minutes, and she would get up. She burrowed deeper into the silky nest, and then froze.

She didn't remember getting into bed.

Was she sleepwalking now? She doubted Mike had gotten so carried away in his substitute father role that he'd actually picked her up from the beanbag and tucked her in. If so, they were going to have a serious talk about boundaries in the morning.

She opened her eyes, waiting for them to adjust to the darkness. The sound system mounted on the wall across the room flashed the time at her; their green numbers read 11:34 PM. Her body tingled as cold fear worked its way through her veins.

This wasn't her room.

She panicked, her breaths coming out in short gasps until she almost couldn't breathe. She was about to scream for Mike when her mind shut down and retreated into the safe haven of denial. It was another dream, just like the other ones. There was no other explanation for it. A voice in the back of her head tried to argue, but she immediately squelched it. Giving any legitimacy to that voice could lead to insanity, and she wasn't ready to take that step.

The telephone beside the bed rang.

She looked at it in horror. It sounded so clear in the silence of the night. So sharp. In a world that should've been hazy and ethereal, that one cutting sound turned her dream into a nightmare.

It rang again.

She reached out a trembling hand and lifted the phone from the nightstand. She put it to her ear, almost expecting a monstrous tongue to emerge from the receiver, wrap around her neck, and *drag her through the phone and into the telecommunications netherworld. What she heard instead was more frightening.*

It was her voice.

Speaking to her through the still silence was her own voice. It echoed through the receiver and buffeted against her crumbling psyche. "Hello? Ma?"

The cordless telephone fell from Ricki's fingers and tumbled to the floor, shattering into several pieces.

She was no longer in a strange room, lying in a strange bed, listening on a strange phone to someone with her voice ask for their mother. She stood in the hallway of her house, in front of a small table that had been knocked over. Batteries from the fallen phone rolled past her foot and stopped at a pile of mail strewn across the floor. The door to her bedroom was open. The lights were off, but the glow from her computer monitor illuminated the room. Books had been knocked from their shelves and littered the floor. Beanbags were thrown into the corners, with stuffed animals scattered everywhere. It was a domestic disaster area.

Her body began to shiver. She didn't know what to think, or even where to start in figuring out how she had gotten from point A (lying on her beanbag, reading a book) to point B (standing in the hallway over a broken telephone she'd apparently just been talking into). A yawning hole in her sanity had opened up before her, and she teetered on the edge of falling in.

Ten minutes later, when Mike came out of his bedroom to get a midnight snack, Ricki was still kneeling over the overturned table. It took five minutes for him to get a coherent response from her regarding why the hallway was a mess. It took another five minutes for him to reorganize the mail, pick up the table, and fix the broken phone. And convincing her to go back into her room took most of the night.

She eventually was too tired to put up a fight and allowed herself to be herded into the bedroom. After coercing her into bed, he tucked her in and watched over her until she fell asleep.

Maybe having an overprotective big brother with a god complex wasn't so bad after all.

"Spinach or coleslaw. It's not that hard of a decision."

"What?" Ricki snapped out of the brooding funk she was drowning in and turned to the girl beside her in the cafeteria line.

The girl looked like she had sucked on one lemon wedge too many and had a few permanently stuck in her plump cheeks, making her lips pucker in a fixed expression of disapproval. Her pinched scowl of condemnation was now directed at Ricki. She impatiently tapped her foot and balanced a plastic tray loaded with French fries and a salad on one well-rounded hip. "Make up your mind. You're holding up the line."

"Right. Sorry." Ricki grabbed a bowl of congealed green vegetables—she was gambling on spinach—and moved down the lunch line to the cashier.

She was almost to the register when the dreaded sensation of being watched made its first unwelcome appearance of the day. In a flash, the blind hysteria she'd worked so hard to bury the previous night came bubbling to the surface. She fought to tamp it down.

Get a grip. Nobody is behind you. It's all in your head. She set her tray on the counter and whirled around to confront the empty air.

Except the air wasn't so empty. This time when she looked to see who was watching her, somebody was actually there. Damian stood several feet away, holding a plate of onion rings and studying her. He looked as tired as she felt. Dark circles shadowed his eyes, and his usual proud shoulders sagged under an invisible weight.

She raised an eyebrow at him, but he just stared at her, his questioning eyes giving away nothing as they probed her own.

She crossed her arms. "What?"

His eyes narrowed.

"What are you looking at?" she demanded.

The unspoken question faded away, replaced by a wicked glint. Slowly looking her up and down, he shrugged. "Nothing," he drawled. "Nothing at all." Throwing his signature sneer of contempt her way, he dismissed her with a nod and strolled away.

"Freak," she muttered, turning back to the line.

Everyone had almost finished eating by the time she made it to the table. She plopped her tray onto the engraved slab of cement and slid into her designated seat beside Yolanda. She was pleased to see Reggie had joined their lunch crew, but she could've done without the four extra bodies filling up space at the other end of the table. Grunting a dour greeting in their direction, she dove into her bowl of leafy mush.

The stone table in the eastern corner of Kirby's outside eating area, the Lunchyard, was the spot where the five sophomore princesses held court. It was an enviable honor to be welcomed into the domain of the undergrad elite, and the five seats where Reggie and Co. sat was a constantly revolving door of lunch guests. Most days, Ricki didn't mind having the extra people around, but on days like this one when she needed privacy to tell her friends about the weirdness she was going through, they were just nuisances.

Sighing to herself, she poked at the green mush with her fork and moved on to a crumbling, brown lump of beef.

"Word in the halls is Aaron likes you," Denise whispered.

Unfortunately, her whisper was about as soft as a vibrating sledgehammer. The entire table went silent, and nine pairs of eyes centered on Ricki.

She choked on her first bite of meatloaf.

Not to be deterred by a fit of wheezing and chest-wrenching coughs, Denise pressed onward. "You're gonna go talk to him, right?" She jerked her head toward the center of the courtyard, where a group of soccer players filled a table almost twice the size of their own.

Aaron sat in the middle of the group, munching on onion rings.

Ricki dislodged the lump of dry meat from her throat with a gulp of soda. "Hadn't planned on it, no," she mumbled. She glared at Denise over the soda can and hoped her eyes properly conveyed the message "shut up, everyone is listening, you idiot."

If they did, Denise chose to ignore them. "Why not? He invited you to go eat with him yesterday, didn't he?"

If the ears at the table strained any harder to hear their conversation, they'd fall right onto their plates.

She picked up a fruit cup and shoveled a large spoonful of jelled peaches into her mouth. She hated peaches. "Mmm," she replied.

"Exactly. Now it's your move."

Feeling a nice, healthy panic attack coming on, she said, "Denise, I can't talk to him right now. He's in the middle of eating."

And the fact that he was surrounded by half the soccer team, including Damian, didn't help, either.

"You've got to strike while the iron's hot," Denise insisted. "Girls are lining up to get with him, so you can't be caught slipping." She looked around the table. "I mean, am I right? Or am I right?"

With the exception of a few people—namely Reggie, Yolanda, and Teresa—everyone jumped enthusiastically onto Denise's matchmaking bandwagon.

A cold sweat washed over Ricki's body.

Denise forged ahead. "Look, I didn't want to scare you, but Chervanna told me in gym class that she heard a couple of girls saying their friend was going to ask Aaron out after lunch. Isn't that right, Cheri?"

The petite brunette sitting beside Reggie nodded.

"If you don't get to him before she does, it'll be too late." Denise shoved a napkin and pen into her hand. "Just shove your boobs in his face, smile, and give him your phone number. That's it."

Everything was moving way too fast, and Ricki's sleep-deprived mind was nowhere near quick enough to keep up with it. The cold sweat became a freezing shower.

Yolanda, ever the champion of the underdog, dove into the madness. "Y'all need to chill," she said. "Ricki's too shy to imitate your fast little behind, Denise. Leave her alone until she's ready."

Teresa waved a fork in agreement and shouted, "Amen," while Reggie grimly picked at the tuna fish sandwich in front of him, saying nothing.

Shooting Yolanda an annoyed looked, Denise said, "Ricki, this is what you've been gunning for all year. Give him your number, and you'll be another step closer to reaching that dream. Just do it."

Yolanda threw her hand up. "This ain't Nike," she argued. "Did Michael Jordan run by, and I missed it? Are there shoelaces strapped across the girl's forehead? This is her life, not some old YouTube commercial. And if she's not ready to talk to him, then she is not ready. No further discussion needed."

Teresa broke into applause.

Cheri politely cleared her throat. "Just an FYI, that blonde chick by the fountain has been checking him out all lunch, and it looks like she's about to step to him."

"C'mon, Ricki," Lindsey said, extending a hand. "I'll go with you. I'll say hi to Damian, and you don't have to say anything to Aaron if you don't want to."

It was now or never. Trying not to think, Ricki clasped Lindsey's hand. As she walked away from the safety of the lunch table, Teresa grabbed her arm and started to speak. She stopped, appearing to have second thoughts.

"Never mind," Teresa said. A shadow of sadness crossed her face, disappearing quickly into a smile. "Good luck."

<hr />

"If you don't call me tonight, I won't give you my number." *Okay, that doesn't sound right. Why'd it sound so much better when Denise said it?* Ricki ran the line through her head and gave it one more try. "So you'd better call me, or I won't be able to talk to you."

Crash and burn.

Several girls at the table, including the blonde Ricki needed to watch out for, snickered.

She was making a complete fool of herself. From the moment she'd arrived at the table, she had fumbled through every sentence (she would never, never live down saying "howdy"). And the attempt to thrust her chest in Aaron's face had resulted in an unfortunate brown stain on his khaki pants, courtesy of the soda she'd knocked onto his lap. If it weren't for the driving desire to wipe the smirk off Damian's face, she probably would've slunk away to a deserted corner and commenced thumb-sucking.

"How does Decker's Drive-In sound?" Lindsey asked Damian.

He broke his unblinking gaze on Ricki long enough to

reply, "Would love to but can't. Rain check?" Kissing her hand, he resumed his stare-down efforts.

Lindsey beamed and snuggled against his side. "Of course."

Irked by Damian's look, Ricki resolved to turn things around. Employing every skill available to her as an actress, she blocked him out and zoned in on Aaron's face. Everyone else at the table became the audience, fading to nonexistence beyond the borders of stage. The only people who existed in the world were her and Aaron.

She was a seductress.

She smiled in what she hoped was an alluring manner. "I really enjoyed talking to you yesterday."

Aaron returned her smile. "So did I."

Going good, so far. "We'll to have to do it again."

"I agree."

"I guess you'll have to call me, so we can make that happen." She gave herself an imaginary pat on the back. Denise would be so proud.

"Most definitely," he said. "What's your number?"

Score!

She scribbled her telephone number onto a napkin, twisted her lips into what was meant to be a sexy pout, and demurely folded the napkin into his palm. With a wink at Aaron and a victorious glance at Damian, she sashayed away.

Take that, Damian Marquez, and choke on it.

———— ❦ ————

He still hadn't called.

After waiting up all night and guarding the telephone like a bulldog each time Mike even looked at it sideways, Ricki still hadn't heard from Aaron. Denise, Teresa, Yolanda, and Lindsey—yes. But never Aaron. After four consecutive conversations of repeating how he hadn't called, yet, and hearing that he'd probably misplaced her number (but not to lose faith), she was beyond depressed and beyond ready to call it a night. It was hard to go to bed, though, when she was afraid of what sleep might bring. Last night's trauma had kept her awake in school, and it had taken most of the day to successfully lock the nightmare away in the back of her mind. It now shared a padded cell with the imaginary stalker who, thankfully, hadn't bothered her all day. But the moment she entered her bedroom, the anxiety came rushing back.

Delaying the inevitable, she grabbed the television remote and flipped through the channels. A young couple kissing in the rain caught her attention. Intrigued, she settled in to watch the rest of the movie.

Her eyelids drooped.

They sprang open. She shifted against her pillow, blinking awake.

The picture on the screen blurred. Her eyes crossed behind their closing lids. The man in the movie became a fuzzy mass of dots, barely visible through each narrow slit. He disappeared as her eyes shut and she drifted away...

"Hey, Boo. Wake up; you're missing the good part."

Her eyes slowly opened and stared into the generous cleavage of the girl on whose shoulder her head rested. She tried to lift her head but felt too groggy to move. Instead, she was held captive by the broad expanse of double-D breasts laid out under her chin as the girl with the dangerously low-cut peasant blouse stroked Ricki's head with one hand and rubbed her inner thigh with the other.

What the...? Summoning every ounce of strength she could muster, Ricki lifted her head from the girl's shoulder and looked around in dismay.

She sat in the driver's seat of an SUV in the middle of a large parking lot. Cars filled with necking teenagers surrounded her, and a giant movie screen lit up the area. The healthy physique and even healthier libido pressed against her belonged to the junior class vice president, Delilah Richards. And the reflection looking back at Ricki from the rearview mirror was not her own.

It was Damian's.

The hole leading into the world of insanity had just grown bigger, and she had tumbled right in.

CHAPTER SEVEN

IT WAS A DREAM....IT WAS *a dream...it was a dream...*

The more Ricki repeated those four words to herself, the less she believed them. It was the same as the day on the soccer field or the night she woke up in a stranger's bed: there was too much clarity in her surroundings.

Dreams were usually like a jumble of images and sounds blending together to create a sort of psychedelic movie—pictures of life flashing on the border of consciousness long enough to snatch a glimpse of the passing scenery but not enough to focus on any one detail. A slideshow of colors, scents, and feelings teasing the mind with suggestions of sensation without offering any true substance—that's what dreams were made of.

So why were the smells of popcorn and heavy perfume so pungent in her nose? Why was she able to taste corn from the small bits of nacho chips stuck in her back teeth? Why could she count every pimple on Delilah Richards's left cheek, and why was the sound of her breathing so harsh in Ricki's ears?

She tore Delilah's hand from her thigh and pushed her face closer to the rearview mirror. The face of her enemy gaped back at her, and the expression he wore mimicked the emotion that had dropped on her like a ton of soggy blankets: horror.

Delilah's hands snaked back onto Ricki's inner thigh and squeezed. "Babe, what's wrong?"

"Leave me alone," Ricki choked out. She gasped upon hearing

the unmistakable deep tones of Damian's voice coming from her mouth.

Shoving Delilah away, she held a hand up to her cheek, almost screaming as thick, masculine fingers reached for her face. Balling the alien hand into a fist, she thrust it under one trembling leg.

No way. There was absolutely no way she could be in Damian's body. It wasn't physically or scientifically possible. Sure, people wrote books and movies about it, but she had yet to actually see a documented case where one person woke up wearing someone else's skin. She had to be dreaming.

Okay, no, she had no earthly idea why she would dream about being Damian. And, yes, she would have to do some deep soul searching into why her dream also involved making out with another girl at Decker's Drive-In. But she'd worry about it all when she woke up. If she could wake up.

Why wasn't she waking up?

Squeezing her eyes shut, she searched for the trigger to snap out of this bizarre nightmare and back to her own bed—and her own body. But she could tell from the cloying scent of Delilah's ginger spice perfume that nothing would be different when her eyes opened. No unicorns would be there to greet her, and the darkness would come from an unlit parking lot, not the black paint coating her bedroom walls. There'd be no relief from the fantasy—just more of the twisted version of reality she'd plunged into.

Of course, never being one to accept reality when delusion was so much more comforting, she opened her eyes and stubbornly waited for the dream to end.

The movie playing on the giant screen at the front of the lot had just hit the theaters. It was the newest installment to the Monkey Burn *series, an unending saga about crazed simians that escaped from a New England zoo. Infected with a scientifically*

engineered virus, the pack rampaged through the country,
terrorizing unsuspecting towns and turning their victims into
zombie servants.

Ricki had never been able to stomach the nonstop gore fest.
She just wasn't evolved enough to appreciate the fine art of mass
butchering by rabid zoo creatures. So, if she wouldn't even watch
the film in her waking hours, why would she dream about it in
her sleeping ones? And how in the world would she know any of
the scientific lingo being spouted by the two lab assistants about
to be attacked by a butter-knife-wielding baby orangutan?

Quite simple—she wouldn't.

Her eyes jumped away as the knife swung through the air
toward the unsuspecting scientists. Their shrieks of terror ripped
through her senses, shrill in her ears and causing her heart to thump
brutally against her chest. As the victims were unceremoniously
slaughtered on the movie screen, she covered her ears against their
dying wails and moaned softly.

It was a dream. It was—

A light rustle from a popcorn bag falling to the floor was the
only warning given before Delilah crawled across the seat and
wiggled onto her lap. "My Boo isn't scared of those nasty monkeys,
is he?" Delilah purred, her warm breath tickling Ricki's face.

The ginger fumes wafting from Delilah's body invaded her
nostrils, putting a stranglehold on her sense of smell. Her skin
protested the girl's intrusive fingers pressing against her temples.
She wanted to respond, but the words got caught behind a
lump blocking her throat. Her mind screamed out at Delilah's
moistened lips sliding from her ear down the side of her neck in
a trail of light kisses.

She would never dream something like this.

The wet trail made its way up her chin. Her muscles kicked
into action before it landed on her mouth. She wrenched Delilah
off her and violently shoved her back into the passenger seat.

Grabbing a handful of napkins, she wiped at her neck in frantic swipes. No matter how hard she pressed, the feel of lipstick-laced saliva drying against her throat couldn't be wiped away.

"What's wrong with you?" Delilah whined. "Damian, you're scaring me."

"Don't call me that!" Ricki cried. Damian's husky voice echoed back to her, a final nail in the coffin of her delusions. The tattered napkins dropped from her fingers, joining the heap of popcorn kernels on the floor.

The first slap was a light tap. Coarse fingers brushed across her cheek. Chin stubble scratched against her palm, inflaming the panic bubbling at the surface of her emotions. The second slap was harder, desperation driving her hand against her jaw. The bubble of panic burst into a stream of tears when the real sensation of pain erupted on the right side of her face. And the realization that she still hadn't left the confines of the Jeep turned the stream into a raging current, running unchecked down her cheeks to pool into the dark fuzz of hair that now covered her jaw.

By the fifth hit, the only thing she felt was terror.

"Wake up!" she shouted at the reflection in the windshield. "Wake up!" The tears continued to flow as her hands slapped relentlessly against her face. Between her own choked sobs, she vaguely heard Delilah's screams for her to stop. "Please wake up! Wake up!

"Wake..."

"...up!"

"Ricki, I mean it! That's enough!" Mike yelled.

The shouts died in her throat. She stared at her brother, slowly registering that she was back in her own bedroom. The parking lot had disappeared, its concrete borders and headlights replaced with ebony walls and drama masks. The scattered popcorn and napkins were now fragments of trampled ballerinas and books fallen from overturned bookshelves.

She was on her back, on the floor beside her bed. Mike had her pinned down with both of her wrists shackled in his hands and her legs locked between his knees. A line of scratches ran across the side of his face, and his eyes were wide with an emotion she had never seen in him before: fear.

She didn't know what had happened to put that shadow of fright in his eyes, or why her room again looked like a tropical storm had struck in the middle of the night. She no longer knew dreams from reality or sanity from the insane, but in that one moment, she knew one thing: she had never in her life been so happy to see her brother's face.

And as soon as she was able to stop crying, she might even tell him so.

"So...um...I guess it's gonna be kind of embarrassing explaining how your little sister busted your lip, huh?"

Mike lowered the ice pack from his mouth. "You're assuming anyone will ever find out."

"I'm sorry I beat you up," Ricki meekly offered.

He groaned. "Please don't ever say those words to me again in this lifetime. You did not 'beat me up.' I just wasn't expecting..." He stopped. "Whatever. Let's stay focused, okay? You said you were someone else in your dream." Wincing, he gingerly fingered the row of scratches on his cheek. "Must've been a heavyweight boxer."

"Soccer player," she mumbled under her breath.

"And you've been having a lot of these kinds of dreams lately?"

"I'm not sure they're dreams anymore," she said. "When I'm in them, I know things I shouldn't know, and I'm doing things I'd never..." She shook off the image of Delilah's mouth closing in on hers. "Just, everything feels really real."

"Most dreams do, Ricki. Then you wake up, and that's how you know it was a dream."

"Do most people have their eyes open while they're dreaming?"

He looked uneasy. "When they're sleepwalking, yeah, I'm sure they do. How else would you move around without knocking everything over?" He looked around the landfill once known as her bedroom and chuckled nervously.

"Do sleeping people also attack you and accuse you of doing something to them when you come to check on them?" She tried to catch his eyes, but they had shifted to the opposite side of the room. "Doesn't really sound like sleepwalking, Mike."

"Of course it does," he said a little too quickly. "You see it in the news all the time—people being found innocent of all kinds of charges because they were sleepwalking when the crime was committed. At least you didn't kill someone. Did you?" He punched her playfully on the shoulder.

"But look at my room, Mike. Look at your face. How could I have done all this?" Her voice broke. "*Why* would I do this?"

He enveloped her in a bear hug. "Hey, Smurf, they're just dreams. Twisted, destructive dreams," he joked, "but dreams any way you look at it. And dreams can't hurt you—just me."

He hadn't called her Smurf since she was six. He had to be more scared than she thought.

"I feel like I'm going crazy," she murmured.

"Crazier than usual?" he teased. "I already had a straightjacket hanging in the closet, waiting for this very moment. Guess I'll have to break out the meds too."

"You really might," she whispered.

His embrace tightened. "You're fine, little girl. It's just stress. *A lot* of stress. But nothing that a hot, greasy pizza and one of your stupid chick flicks won't solve." With a light tickle under her arms, he headed into the hallway to call in pepperoni reinforcements.

Ricki took stock of her bedroom. Every bookshelf had been knocked over. The contents of her purse were scattered under the bed, and a glance into the bathroom revealed a mess of spilled makeup and lotion bottles. Even the collection of porcelain ballerinas that once enjoyed permanent residence over her bed were now piles of chalky fragments on the floor. She knelt down to finger their remains. The figurines had been a present from her father after taking her and Yolanda to see *The Nutcracker*. It was an evening that had defined her seven-year-old destiny to become the world's greatest prima ballerina. That destiny had lasted a good two weeks—the amount of time it took for her to take three ballet lessons, sprain her ankle, and retire her ruffled pink tutu to the nether regions of her closet where it now shared a corner with her discarded bathing suit and a pair of dusty tap shoes. But even though the dream of becoming a world-renowned ballerina had died at the tender age of seven, her love of the shiny, little dancers immortalized in clay and glaze never did.

She would *never* be so reckless with them, even in her sleep. Would she?

"Pizza'll be here in fifteen minutes," Mike announced from the doorway.

She jumped. "Don't scare me like that!"

"You talkin' to me?" he asked. "You go psycho sleep commando on me, nearly take out a couple of my good teeth before I'm even half awake, and then say *I* scared *you*? You're lucky I don't throw on a hockey mask and chase you around with Dad's power drill. *Then* you can talk about being scared."

She snorted, allowing herself to relax. "You would've had me if you'd threatened to use his electric toothbrush. What's a power drill going to do to me that two weeks' worth of Daddy's plaque buildup can't?"

He stretched, scratching his belly. "Nah, didn't want to pull out the big guns too soon. I'll save the toothbrush for the next time you drink up my Powerade. Now, go pull out one of your girly 'why-doesn't-he-love-me-the-way-I-programmed-him-to?' movies so we can finish up the night in style."

"Mike, you can go back to sleep. I'll be okay."

"No, you won't," he said. "You'll sit up all night, spooked by your own shadow, snuffling your way through a box of tissues. So I'm going to sit up with you and help you see that sometimes a dream is just a dream. And if that means I have to stuff myself with pepperoni pizza, a side of cheese sticks, and some chicken wings in order to make it happen, so be it." Nudging several books aside, he settled onto the floor in front of the television. "'Cause that's what a good brother I am."

＊－＋◊＋－＊

When the doorbell rang ten times, followed by a round of booming knocks, it wasn't Vick from Giovanni's Pizza Palace standing on the other side of the door, greasy cardboard boxes and a two-liter Coke in hand.

It was Damian.

"Man, do you know what time it is?" Mike demanded. His face morphed from annoyance to concern. "You alright?"

Damian leaned into the light of the doorway. He looked like death warmed over if Death had just run a twenty-mile marathon after an all-night insomniac keg party. His clothes were drenched in sweat, his eyes were bloodshot, and his hair was plastered to his scalp like an inky helmet.

"I need to speak to Rocky," he wheezed, rubbing at his eyes with a grubby palm.

Mike looked over his shoulder at Ricki. He slowly turned back to Damian, his body shifting to block the door. "Huh?"

"I really, really need to speak to Rocky." Damian's eyes darted over Mike's head, briefly connecting with hers before Mike stepped onto the porch and closed the door to a crack behind him.

She tiptoed to the door.

"I heard you the first time," Mike said. "I just thought I might've missed something since it's almost midnight and you're standing on my doorstep, looking like you just rolled out of the gutter, *telling* me you want to talk to my little sister. No explanation? Have you bumped your head or something, D?"

"I wish I could explain, man, but it's been a really bad night, and—"

"What would Ricki have to do with that? She's been here all night."

"I don't know, Mike. That's why I need to talk to her."

"What do you mean you don't know? You're over here in the middle of the night, looking crazy, and you don't know why?" Mike's voice dropped. "Are you high?"

"What? No! It's not even like that—"

"Drunk?"

"No!"

"Then why're your eyes red, D? Why are you in a cold sweat? Do I need to call your mom?"

"Mike...Mikey. You know me better than that. Man, c'mon."

"Then you need to start telling me something that makes sense. What happened to you?"

Damian's voice was a low mumble.

"She did what?"

"I said she maced me!"

Ricki tried to open the door, but Mike had a tight grip on the handle.

"Why would your date mace you? What did you do to her?"

"I didn't do anything to her," Damian protested.

"She sprayed you with mace, but you didn't do anything? Then why'd she do it?"

"I don't know why she did it!" he shouted. Catching himself, he lowered his voice. "I don't mean you any disrespect, man, but a lot of crazy stuff went down tonight that I don't understand. That's why I need to talk to Rocky."

"Okay, you're not getting anywhere near my sister tonight. She's already had a rough night."

"Rough like how?"

An edge crept into Mike's voice. "I don't think that's your concern, is it? But I do think it's time for you to go home and sleep off whatever's swimming around in your system. Anything you have to say to Ricki can wait 'til you see her at school tomorrow."

"No, it can't," Damian pressed. "I think she could know something about what happened to me. The same way I might have an idea of why she had a rough night. I don't know, though, man, that's why—"

"You got something to do with what's been freaking her out?" Mike interrupted.

"I'm not...I mean, I don't..." he stuttered.

Ricki had never heard Damian so flustered before. It had to be scary going up against Mike while he was in father-bear mode. She almost felt sorry for him. Almost. But enjoying his torment would have to take a back seat to finding out what had happened to him. She yanked on the door, attempting to catch Mike off guard, but he had it in a hold that her 105-

pound frame couldn't break. The crack only widened by an inch. She pulled on it again.

"Ricki, let go of the door," he barked. "You need to go upstairs."

"I want to hear what he has to say," she pleaded. "Let me talk to him."

"Upstairs, *now*, Racquel!"

Biting her tongue, she ducked to the other side of the door and cautiously pressed her ear against its side.

"Damian," Mike said, "your mom and my folks have been tight for a long time. You're family. Yeah, you've done some dirt against Ricki, but I know she gets pretty low-down too, so I usually let her reap what she sows."

She wrinkled her nose.

"But I've seen her breaking down the past couple of days in a way that I've never seen before. And now I have to wonder how much of that has to do with you."

"I can't speak to that. I haven't—"

"You don't speak to anything. You listen." His words fell like a hammer. "I will protect my sister from whatever or *whoever* it is that's trying to break her. That girl is not going through another night like this one."

"But I had a bad night too!" Damian objected. "What if she's got a foot in what's happening to me?"

"Turn around and go home," Mike said. "Sleep it off, and maybe we'll talk about things tomorrow when you don't smell like funk and alcohol. 'Cause if you keep pushing things tonight, then all conversation is coming to an end. You feel me?"

The air crackled with aggression.

After a lengthy pause, Damian backed away. "I understand. I have nothing but respect for you, man, so I wouldn't even take it to that level. I'll let it go. For tonight."

She heard his footsteps shuffle unevenly across the porch and stop.

"But I really didn't have anything to do with Rocky's bad night," he said. "I want to you to know that." The steps resumed their movement toward the street and then were gone.

And with them went any answers to the mystery of Ricki's dreams.

———◆———

"Looks like our resident pranksters are at it again," Lindsey said.

Ricki sat with her friends across the street from her school, surrounded by several hundred other Kirby High sophomores. The ringing of a fire alarm trilled in the air. First period had barely begun when a massive cloud of dark smoke had erupted in the Junction and spread through the halls, seeping into every crevice of the school and turning Wednesday morning classes into pitch-black chaos.

She shared a bag of cheese popcorn with Denise and Yolanda while watching two firemen administer oxygen to the sooty face of Dougie Carmine. Dougie had picked the wrong morning to duck out on gym class—he was walking through the lobby on the way back from the snack machines when the first round of smoke bombs went off. A squished Baby Ruth was still clutched in one blackened fist.

"You think it was them?" Teresa asked. "I thought they pulled the fire alarm a couple of months ago. They don't usually do the same trick twice."

"But there was an actual fire that time," Lindsey replied.

"Maybe next time they'll get it right and burn this whole mother down," Yolanda muttered.

Denise grabbed the bag of popcorn from Ricki and dumped a handful into her mouth. "Don't let Dearling hear you say that. He'll think you're one of them and chain you to a pipe in the basement until you confess your sins."

The "them" under discussion was Kirby's infamous society of practical jokers, the Loki Seven. They'd first arrived on the scene almost fifteen years ago, announcing their presence with a circulated flyer declaring their mission statement: "Keeping our school officials honest. One humiliation at a time." Since that day, they had haunted the halls of RJK—a champion of the school's student body and the curse of its faculty and staff. Little was known about the group's members. Their identities were secret, even to them; it was rumored that each member operated under a code name, and pranks were planned through internet chats and phone conferences using voice-disguising synthesizers. When a member graduated, he or she found a replacement to induct into the club, and the legacy of terrorizing the Establishment continued.

Their biggest coup in Ricki's time at the school had taken place the previous year, when a recording of the school's librarian having extramarital relations with the former principal found its way into the morning announcements. It aired on every classroom television, playing on a continuous loop for three hours while the school's technicians scrambled to locate the source of the broadcast and unjam the circuits that prevented the TV monitors from turning off.

More recently, they'd set fire to the AP English teacher's hidden supply of marijuana, setting it ablaze in a roaring bonfire outside of the principal's office. And the fact that a few flames *happened* to mysteriously jump from the hallway into an open cabinet drawer containing student records was an added bonus for every student a pink slip away from probation. Rather than face the embarrassment of admitting to one of his best teachers engaging in minor drug trafficking right under his nose, Principal Dearling instead claimed to have accidentally set off a box of confiscated cigarette lighters and discreetly forced Professor Hoffsteader into early retirement. After that incident, the "Dearling Inquisition" had been in full effect, as Kirby's newest principal strengthened his crusade to track down each member of the Loki Seven and bring them to justice. He'd even held an assembly in the school auditorium and publicly declared war on them, claiming their days of wreaking havoc on the Willow County educational system were coming to an end.

Judging by the amount of smoke pouring into the street, the Seven still hadn't gotten the memo.

Ricki wiped cheese from her fingers onto the grass. She was exhausted from staying up all night. Mike had done his best to keep her company, but there was only so much girlie drama he could take before he fell asleep with a slice of thin crust pizza dangling from his mouth. After laying a blanket over his face to muffle the snores, she had watched movies and munched on pizza until the sun came up.

Fighting off dizziness, she focused on the developing tussle between Dougie and the not-so-bright fireman who'd just tried to remove the Baby Ruth from his fingers. "Oxygen may come and go, but chocolate and peanuts are forever," she giggled deliriously to herself.

"What'd you say?" Teresa asked.

"Nothing," she mumbled, searching for a coherent thought in the pile of confusion currently passing for her brain. "Just singing to myself."

"What're seniors doing over here?" someone asked.

She glanced in the direction of the voice and saw four boys cutting through the crowd. A determined Damian led the procession.

"I'm surprised he's even at school today," a voice whispered. "You heard what happened with him last night, didn't you?"

Watching his approach, Ricki was secretly glad he'd found her. She had been anxious to speak with him all morning, but Mike had driven her to school, almost escorting her to class himself when he saw Damian waiting for her at the front doors. And trying to track him down before homeroom had been a bust.

He broke away from the pack. She caught a glimpse of Lindsey's frowning face before he crouched down and obstructed her view. Outwardly, he looked much better than when he'd shown up on her doorstep, but the queer gleam in his eye made Ricki question whether his mental state had caught up with the rest of him.

Damian studied her intently before declaring, "I've been thinking about it all night, and I finally figured it out. You set me up."

She looked around, bemused. "Come again?"

"You slipped something in my drink at lunch yesterday."

"Huh?"

"Y'know, payback for the party. You've been working some kind of head trick on me since then." He leaned in. "I couldn't figure out how you'd been doing it, but you got sloppy yesterday coming by my table for no reason."

His manic intensity made her nervous. She scooted back. "I didn't come by for no reason. I came to give Aaron my number."

"Yeah, right," he scoffed. "'Cause you actually believe he'd use it?"

Ouch. "You can leave now, Junior," she said between gritted teeth. "You sound paranoid. You must still be high, and the drugs obviously fried your brain."

"So you admit it!"

"Admit what? That you're a delusional freak? Yep, one hundred percent." Uncrossing her legs, she started to stand up.

Damian yanked her back to the ground. "Why so quick to run off? Didn't think I'd catch on to what you've been doing?"

Ricki pried his fingers from her arm. "Speak English. I haven't done anything to you *yet*, so why don't you rewind and tell me what exactly you're talking about."

"Mind trips, Rocky," he said. "Seeing and hearing things that shouldn't be happening. Sound familiar?"

A chill ran down her spine. Images from the past few days flashed through her mind. The boys' locker room. A soccer ball flying toward her face. Delilah Richards.

"Yeah, kinda," she acknowledged.

"It should, since you've pulled this crap before."

"I've what?"

"It's your classic MO. Just like that time you put some recording with my dead grandma's voice in my bedroom and set it off any time I had a girl over. As soon as the chick left the room to go to the bathroom or something, Abuela would start talking to me from beyond the grave." His fists clenched. "My mom already had me going to a shrink by the time I found that stupid transmitter taped behind a trophy."

She suppressed a grin. That trick had been one of her crowning achievements.

"I still don't follow what you're getting at," she said. "And I'm really too tired to try, so please go away." She tried again to stand up.

Damian's hand shot out and clamped like a steel vise onto her knee. "Then there was that time I kept getting a bunch of strange calls on my cell every night. Three AM on the dot. And when I'd answer the phone, it'd be my own voice on the other end, telling me to repent my sins. For two weeks straight, I'm getting calls from myself, and the caller ID says they're coming from inside my own house."

She almost laughed but didn't want to give herself away.

The calls had never been traced back to her, and she'd paid good money to the guys in the Technology Today club to make sure it stayed that way.

"Do you have a point?" she asked, pulling at his fingers. Her head was starting to buzz from an unhealthy mix of fatigue and irritation.

"My point is I'd almost forgotten what a warped little brain you have. And how good you can be at mind games." He placed his other hand on her free knee and slid in closer. "So I'm putting you on warning that it all ends today. If I even see a fly on the wall someplace where it shouldn't be, I'm bringing a new level of suffering down on you."

Enough was enough.

In one swift motion, her thumbs jabbed into his throat. His hands flew from her knees to clutch at his neck. Knocking him onto his side with her elbow, she stood up and brushed the dirt from her pants.

"Is this why you came by my house?" she yelled at his gagging figure. "To accuse me of drugging you? Here I thought you'd actually have something useful to say, and you come at me with this nonsense! I was having the night from hell, and you—" Her eyes narrowed. "But maybe you already knew what kind of night I was having, huh? Maybe *you've* been the one drugging *me*, and you really just came by to get a good laugh."

He glared up at her wordlessly, his hands still clutching his throat.

"I don't know why I didn't think of it sooner. This is exactly like something you'd pull." Ignoring the attention she'd drawn from the other students, she paced back and forth. "Last year, you broke into my locker and kept changing my picture on the door with those age-progression ones. Every time I went to my locker, my picture would look older and older. And when I asked people if they noticed the difference, they told me I was imagining things. I got so weirded out, thinking I was losing my mind." She stopped pacing and frowned down at him. "And you always *happened* to be passing by in time to see my reaction."

Conversations stopped as more people turned to watch her.

Her pacing resumed. "Sixth grade, you convinced my entire homeroom class to act like I'd been killed by a head-on collision with a Mack truck. On my birthday!" She kicked a cloud of dirt at him. "I go to school expecting a party, and they're holding a wake in my honor. The whole class pretended like they couldn't see or hear me."

"Ooh, I remember that," Denise whispered.

"There was even a newspaper on my desk, opened to my obituary. I freaked out so bad, thinking maybe I'd really died and was a ghost...until you walked into the room. Supposedly to give the teacher a note from the principal." The buzzing in her head had gotten so loud, she almost expected a swarm of bees to fly out of her ears. "I'm so stupid! Trying to make me go crazy is your 'thing'—you pull something to screw with my head, then come around to admire your handiwork. But you've taken it too far this time, Spawn."

He lumbered to his feet. "Stop acting innocent," he rasped. "It doesn't look right on you." He moved in front of her, blocking her from taking another step. "Playtime is over, and things are going to get ten kinds of ugly for you if you don't stop the games."

"Well, they can't get much uglier than you are now," she retorted, eyeing him with disdain. "Or any uglier than you're going to look when I tell Mike what you've been doing to me. The beatdown he gave you over selling naked pictures of me is nothing compared to what you're going to get."

Despite Mike's long-standing policy to stay out of his

sister's battles, discovering that she'd been made into an unwilling centerfold pinup had been enough to earn Damian a painful one-time exception to the rule.

"If you even think of pulling Mike into this," he warned, "it'll just go worse for you."

"You're actually threatening me?" she said. "You've been tormenting me all week, and now you have the nerve to *threaten* me? I'd laugh if you weren't too pathetic to be taken seriously. You're not going to touch me."

"Rocky, I'll do more than touch you." His dark complexion grew darker by the second. "Keep playing with me, and I'll show you exactly what I can do."

Denise stepped forward, placing a hand on Ricki's shoulder. "Okay, guys, I think that's enough."

Knocking the hand away, she advanced on Damian. "Ooh, big tough guy. Drugging and threatening a female half your size. Mommy must be so proud."

His face took on an odd purplish color. If steam could actually come out of his ears, she knew the blast would incinerate her, but she couldn't seem to get her thoughts together enough to care. "Stop being such a punk and man up, you little bi—"

"You don't want to finish that sentence," he rumbled. "And you're the last person to be judging someone's manhood." He leaned back, examining her from head to toe. "Considering you don't even know what it means to be a woman."

The crowd collectively inhaled.

"It must suck for you," he said, "still looking like a third grader. Especially when you've got friends who look like that." He gestured appreciatively at Denise. Looking back at Ricki, he sneered. "I didn't hit a nerve, did I? Nah, you must be used to it, knowing you'll never measure up to girls like her. That you'll always be the second-string leftover some wasted reject settles for when he can't get the main dish."

Crack!

She would never recall at what point her hand left her side and connected with Damian's face, but the red imprint of her palm on his cheek and promise of retribution in his eyes made Ricki think things might just have taken a nasty turn.

"I-I didn't mean..." she stammered, taking a step back.

Denise and Teresa rushed to stand between them.

"Denise," he growled, "you would want to keep your girl away from me." His stormy glare turned to Ricki. "You are going to regret pushing me. I promise you this." He muscled his way through the crowd, returning to the other side of the school and leaving her to wonder how many days she'd just taken off her life.

She looked in mortification at the faces of her fellow sophomores, all of whom stared at her as if she was a fiery train wreck, horrified by the unfolding disaster but too fascinated to look away.

Teresa grabbed her hand and thrust it high into the air. "And the winner of Ricki versus Damian, round one thousand goes to our own Racquel Nichols. Defeating her opponent with the time-honored pimp slap. Okay, show's over, folks!"

As if on cue, the school bell rang.

⊷ ⬥ ⊶

The altercation with Damian left more on Ricki's mind than the embarrassment of having lost control. She spent all day thinking about things that had been said...or not. She spent her lunch break in the library, staring sightlessly at the pages of random books, her thoughts consumed with that morning's conversation. His words ricocheted through her mind. She couldn't pay attention in class. She constantly envisioned the look in Damian's eyes when he'd sat down in front of her. Wasn't it the same one she'd seen on her own face when she first looked at herself in the mirror that morning?

She had little to say to anyone. She heard even less when anyone spoke to her.

And when she fell asleep during rehearsal and woke up in the Marquez living room holding an Xbox controller and lying on a pair of dirty soccer cleats, she somehow managed to hold her panic at bay until she snapped back into the school auditorium minutes later. Since it was only a drug-induced hallucination, there no reason for panic.

Right?

He really *was* like a cockroach—always popping up in your face when you least expected it but impossible to find once the can of Raid is in hand and you're on the hunt.

"Was Damian at practice today?" Ricki shouted to the soccer player jogging by on his way to the parking lot.

He shook his head.

Sighing, she resumed her post at the school entrance.

A tall boy in a junior varsity uniform exited the building, fiddling with his iPod's headphones.

"Did Damian go home after school?" she asked loudly.

He jumped back, looking around wildly. Politely tugging at the hem of his jacket, she waited for him to catch his breath and repeated the question. With a shrug, he carefully stepped around her and hurried down the sidewalk. She yelled her thanks at his retreating back.

Two more players, two more occasions to be looked at like a deranged stalker. "Where is he?" she said aloud.

"Right behind you."

Whipping around, she saw Reggie leaning beside the school bulletin board, observing her with a grin. "You *were* looking for me, right?" He sauntered up to her. "What's the word, Rick?"

Her eyes made one last desperate sweep around the parking lot. She gave him a thin smile. "The word is *strike*," she said, her mind making an unwilling trip to the latest rehearsal disaster. "As in, one more and I can kiss my part in the play goodbye." *And my sanity.*

"Nah, I think you're safe," Reggie said, "Q can't get any madder than he was today. His meds won't let him."

"Then maybe I need to take whatever he's using so I can stop spazzing out on stage." She touched his arm. "I am so, so sorry about throwing you into Mr. Lonnie's trash cart."

Grimacing, he pulled at his shoulder. "I told you: it's cool. That bag of spoiled pudding cups broke my fall."

She didn't laugh. Nothing was cool about any of this—not falling asleep in the middle of her own scene, not chucking her friend off the stage in the middle of another sleepwalking rage, and not getting evicted from rehearsal for the second time that week.

"I'm sorry," she mumbled again.

"Would you cut it out?" He took her hand, his fingers closing around hers. "I know you didn't mean to do it. It's not in you to hurt someone."

Her thoughts flashed to the moment she slapped Damian and continued a backward journey over sunlight reflections in the eyes, falsified STD tests, homemade poisons made from fermented potatoes...

"You said you were sleepwalking," he said, stopping her thoughts before they got to the bag of needles she'd emptied into Damian's sneakers in the fifth grade, "but what were you dreaming about? You kept shouting out your name and yelling about the game being over and stuff. Were you a WWF wrestler or something?"

Soccer player. "Reg, I really want to tell you about it, but I couldn't make you believe it if I tried." Because it was impossible. *But maybe not as impossible as it should be.*

His other hand captured hers. He stepped in closer, lowering his head to look into her eyes. "Try," he said softly.

A cough stopped her from speaking. "Am I interrupting something?"

Startled, Ricki stepped back, her foot slipping off the sidewalk curb. Reggie's hold on her hands was the only thing that kept her from falling. She looked toward the voice, almost choking to discover Aaron standing by the school entrance.

"No," she said, her voice strangled. Her hands pulled out of Reggie's grip so quickly they almost caused second-degree burns. "You're not interrupting anything."

"Too bad," Aaron said smoothly, eyeing Reggie. "That would've been fun."

Reggie's face burned. His lips tightened into a scowl.

Aaron walked up to them, his presence filling Ricki's world until nothing existed beyond his hazel eyes. They simmered warmly at her, melting her spine on contact. "If I'd known you'd be out here, I would've made Coach end practice a lot earlier."

She rummaged through her murky thoughts for a witty response. "My brother's picking me up." *That's the best you come up with?*

"I'll take you home, Rick," Reggie volunteered. "You can help me work on lines for the pep rally."

"That's okay, dude," Aaron replied. "I'm here now. I got this."

Reggie's face grew darker, his lips a thin, disgruntled line across his face.

Ricki smiled gently at him. "Thanks for talking to me, Reg. I'll be okay, now."

His eyes dropped. "Any time, Rick. See you in practice tomorrow." Shoving a fistful of curls out of his face, he stiffly walked away.

"Nice kid," Aaron said, watching him. Once Reggie was out of sight, he turned back to Ricki. "Why aren't you riding home with your girls?"

Not wanting him to know she'd been kicked out of rehearsal, she went for the next best excuse. "Because Teresa is driving. She just got her license, and we're all afraid she'll use it." She let out a nervous giggle.

His head cocked to the side.

Maybe it'd go over better with a drum roll. "She's a terrible driver, so keeping her off the road is our way of saving the world. One pedestrian at a time." Another giggle.

His eyes went glassy.

Time for a quick subject change. "Did you have a good practice?" she asked.

The blank look disappeared. "Yeah, it was pretty good. D didn't show up, so I got a chance to shine for once." He winked at her. "Thank you."

"For what?"

"Because I heard about you single-handedly taking out my boy with one slap. He dipped out of school right after that." He hugged her. "So, thank you."

She stumbled, her head a merry-go-round of sensations. "Anytime," she croaked.

"Hey, I'm sorry I didn't call you last night. Something came up."

Still unable to articulate a full sentence, she waved a hand in dismissal.

"I promise I can make it up to you if you'll let me." He gave her a lazy grin. "Go out with me tonight."

If the screams of joy in her head got any louder, she might

end up the first person in history to ever go deaf from her own thoughts. She forced her vocal cords into action. "I can't go out on school nights. Lame, I know." *But not as lame as you knowing I can't even date until my parents have grilled you a few hundred times.*

"Isn't that what bedroom windows are for?" he asked.

"What do you mean?"

"Sneak out."

Her eyes widened. "My brother would kill me."

"He'd have to catch you first."

"Oh, there's no way," she protested. *Is there? No...*

"How about Saturday, then?"

She looked into his eyes, drowning in a sea of hazel lava. "Saturday's perfect," she breathed. She'd figure out how to get around Mike later. At the moment, she was flying higher than a jet plane and had no plans of coming back down to earth.

"Cool," he said. He looked over her shoulder and frowned.

Turning around, Ricki saw Delilah Richards leaving the school, chatting with a few student council members. She glanced up from her conversation and locked gazes with Aaron. The light disappeared from her face. Her step quickening, she said goodbye to her friends and hurried to her car.

"She was stupid to show her face around here this week," Aaron said, glowering after Delilah's car.

"Why?" Ricki asked.

"You hadn't heard? That chick got it in her head to attack D last night at Decker's. She maced him."

Unease washed over her.

"They were kickin' it, and she went ballistic on him. She's trying to say it was the other way around—that D was the one acting crazy—but we all know better." He started rifling through his gym bag. His lowered head almost masked the resentful expression on his face. "It's D we're talking about. He doesn't know *how* to lose his cool. Unless it comes to you."

She was no longer listening. The mention of Decker's Drive-In had brought all activity in her brain to a slamming halt. Finding her voice, she asked, "Do you happen to know what movie they went to see?"

He looked at her strangely. "Yeah. It was *Monkey Burn*."

And the jet plane took a fiery nose dive back to earth.

CHAPTER EIGHT

"**W**HY'RE YOU WATCHING *FREAKY FRIDAY?*"

Ricki pressed pause on the remote and looked at her brother in annoyance. "Why wouldn't I?" she answered evasively. "It's a classic."

"Yeah, but it doesn't have all the melodramatic romance crap or gnashing of teeth that you love so much." Mike strolled into her bedroom and crouched down to look through the pile of DVDs in a heap on the floor.

"*Prelude to a Kiss*," he read aloud. "Okay, that one I can understand; it's more on your level." He picked up another case. "*Big.*"

She snatched the movie from his hand. "Don't you have a date to go to?"

"Not for another twenty minutes." He peered down at the last movie she was maneuvering under her leg. "*The Hot Chick?*"

"Michael, you're invading my personal space," she cried in frustration. She hastily shoved the stack of movies under the bed and charged at him, trying to push him out the door. "Get out!"

He sidestepped her grasp, slid an arm around her neck, and put her in a loose choke hold. She struggled to break free as he mussed her hair in wicked glee.

"You're only sixteen," he said. "You don't have personal space." Releasing her, he inhaled deeply and puffed out his chest in mock pride. "Wow. I've been waiting four years to say that."

"Now your life is complete," she grumbled, smoothing her hair back into place. "Get out."

He brushed past her and settled onto the nearest beanbag. "I guess we're getting moody, independent Ricki today. I forget what it's like to be a teenybopper sometimes."

She frowned her displeasure at him. This was not a good time for family bonding. She glanced out the window to the bedroom facing hers. Yep, he was still there, watching her. He had avoided her phone calls all afternoon. Typical Damian—he'd rather spy on her than actually behave like a normal human being and have a civil conversation. Her gaze shifted away from the window. She knew he was plotting something. *The games we play. It always has to be tit for tat, even when I'm not responsible for the tit.* But there was no time for games. And there would be no sleep that night.

"Mike," she said, attempting to draw her brother's attention away from the DVDs, "you don't need to do this."

He studied her, his face suddenly somber.

"I'm okay, seriously. You don't need to hover and check on me every ten minutes. You're getting on my nerves, so just call your girlfriend and tell her you're on your way. What's her name again? Veronica?"

"Florence."

"Close enough. Call her and get out of here." When he didn't move, she started to walk toward the door. "I guess I'll give her a call, then. What was the name of that casino you guys went to when she was home sick with the flu?"

He leaped from the beanbag. "Whoa, whoa. There's no need for all that. We're family—we can work things out." He stretched. "Y'know, I think it might be time for me to go."

"You think?"

"Yep. But I'll be back in a few, so don't burn the place down while I'm gone." Giving her a hip bump, he sauntered out of the room.

After waiting a few minutes to make sure he didn't come back, she swept the heap of DVDs from under the bed and arranged them in viewing order. She then pulled a small notebook from her purse and a lukewarm six-pack of Coca-Cola from her backpack.

Let the researching commence.

Roaches never do sleep at night, do they?

Damian hadn't moved from his window in over an hour. The last time Ricki had peeked outside, he'd actually had the nerve to wave a half-eaten chicken wing at her. She'd been tempted to throw an empty Coke can at him but fought the impulse.

She considered closing her curtains, but that would be too much like letting him win. Let him watch her. Let him sit there all night and rot while she took the initiative to figure out a solution to their problem. As soon as she figured out what exactly their problem was.

It really would help if he talked to her.

She took another sip of warm Coke and yawned. She'd already finished *Freaky Friday* and *Big* and was halfway through *Prelude to a Kiss*. After three pages of notes, she'd become too sleepy to write, almost nodding off while trying to scribble down a barely lucid thought. She eventually traded out the pen and paper for a continuous supply of caffeine and sugar. Empty soda cans and crumpled Smarties wrappers littered the floor. Now if she could just stay awake until Mike got home from his date, she'd finish the rest of the movies tomorrow.

The skin on her neck prickled. She turned off the television and looked around. "Mike," she yelled, "are you back?"

The house was quiet.

She crawled over to the window and peeked over the windowsill at Damian's house. His silhouette was still outlined in the window. Smirking, she crawled back to her spot in front of the television.

No wonder he hadn't moved in over an hour—he had fallen asleep. Lightweight.

Brushing at her neck, she turned the TV back on and reached for another soda. Her hand froze as she felt the presence of someone standing over her. A scream in her throat, she looked up, but no one was there.

"Here we go again," she muttered.

Grabbing the can and raising it in a mock toast to the invisible phantom, she turned the volume up on the TV in an attempt to block out the stifling sense of being watched. Instead of fading, the feeling intensified. And with it came a lulling sensation of lethargy. She gulped down the rest of her Coke and reached for another, but there were none left. No more candy either. She started to get up to go to the kitchen for more supplies, but her legs were too heavy to move. The caffeine and sugar high was swiftly crashing. She sat helplessly on the floor, the drowsiness overwhelming her in one crushing sweep.

She fell asleep...

...and opened her eyes to darkness.

The room around her was dim. The only light came from an outside streetlamp and a shining LED display on the sound system in the corner of the room. Her head rested on top of her crossed arms, which were sprawled across a cool windowsill. The crick in her neck and mild cramp in her thigh told her she'd been sitting in that position for a while.

A plate of chicken bones lay on the sill by her elbow. Lifting her head, she looked out the window. She was mystified to see her own bedroom, facing her from across the yard. A square of light came from its window. Through it, she saw her own body lying on a beanbag in front of the television.

Her head felt like it was about to explode. What was happening? In one surreal moment of horror, she wondered if she had died and become a ghost.

She watched as her body stirred.

It sat up, clutching at its head. Struggling to its feet, the small figure stumbled into the bed and then tripped on a stray DVD case. Looking around, disoriented, it froze. Slowly, deliberately, the head turned toward the bookshelves. It swept the room, studying the opposite wall where a myriad of comedy and tragedy masks hung.

A scream of fear bubbled in her throat when the body spun in her direction and lurched to the window. She held her breath as it leaned into the glass and looked out at her.

It held up its hand.

Exhaling shakily, she put her own hand up to the window, feeling a numb sense of acceptance to see the thick, strong fingers of a boy raised before her. She stared across the yard into her own face, now knowing with certainty who looked back at her.

Damian.

"Bet you'll want to talk to me now, huh?" she whispered.

＊━◦✕◦━＊

Whose dog did I run over in a past life to earn the sick punishment of switching bodies with my worst enemy? Ricki looked down at her new physique. *And shouldn't there be a rule to stop it from happening across genders?*

Her small, polished hands were now large and rough, the

fingernails chewed in ragged edges down to the skin. Her once slender arms bulged with muscles. And the sixteen years it had taken for her to develop breasts had been wiped away in the seconds it took to fall asleep—her chest now flat and chiseled beneath a snug T-shirt and open robe, giving an unobstructed view all the way down to her size thirteen feet.

Wow, those are some big, ugly feet. She wiggled the toes in perverse fascination. *My feet?*

Movement behind her silk boxer shorts caught her attention. Scandalized, she realized the view down to her feet wasn't such a clear shot after all. Her eyes grew to the size of saucers before darting away, her face on fire.

"What is going on?" she squeaked. Except, with a voice several octaves deeper than usual, the sound came out more as a hoarse gurgle.

Turning back to the window, she pressed her nose against the glass. Her eyes zoned in on a rustling clump of bushes midway between the two houses. The faint outline of an arm waved to her, sending her scampering across the bed to the nearest door.

She peeked into the hall, listening for Ms. Marquez. The house was silent, with no lights showing under any of the doors. Easing into the hallway, she tiptoed through the darkness to the stairs. Fortunately, the Marquez house was like a second home to her. She knew its layout almost as well as her own, having run through its halls for as long as she could remember. The only area off-limits to her had been Damian's bedroom—made clear when she was nine-years-old and had opened the door to a BB gun leveled at her face. A shot to the tush as she beat a hasty retreat had been his parting gift to her.

Reaching the front door, she ran outside and rounded the corner of the house. As she neared the row of bushes, Damian stepped into the open. Hazy light from the nearby streetlamp illuminated his figure.

Her figure.

She skidded to a stop. That girl with her face and her body, standing there, motioning to her...

Standing barefooted on the grass, with a sheer nightgown hanging down to her knees, was a girl who should have been Ricki but wasn't. The skinny arm waving at her—her arm, but she wasn't the one controlling it. The distress in those brown eyes—her eyes, but the emotions behind them belonged to another.

She stood there, gawking, when the person inside the body she had until recently called her own said, "What've you done, and how're you gonna fix this?"

The spell was broken.

"What do you mean, me?" she snapped. "I was hoping *you* might know something. Oh, wait, that's an oxymoron—you knowing something."

Those familiar eyes narrowed into slits. "Stuff like this isn't supposed to happen, Rocky," he said. The sound of his voice—her voice—was harsh in the quiet of the night, ringing an alien tone in Ricki's ears. "I'm not supposed to be standing here in a...a girl's body. And it keeps happening, every day, every time I wake up. And I keep telling myself none of it's real, because it's not supposed to be." He took a step forward. "But it *is* real, and it is *happening*. Now, you tell me why *you* are the one it's happening with. Tell me what you did."

He advanced, attempting to intimidate her, but the light bulb went off that height and muscles were no longer on his side. His feminine shoulders slumped in defeat.

A rush of empowerment from her new vantage point twelve inches above his head surged through her. "Doesn't feel so good now that the shoe's on the other foot, does it?" she gloated.

He dropped to his knees on the dewy ground, unmindful of the grass sticking to his bare legs. "Enjoy it whiles it lasts," he mumbled.

She looked down at him. He looked so pathetic, huddled there—his enormous ego trapped inside her tiny body. She didn't even have the heart to tell him to close his legs.

She sighed. "I'm not enjoying it." She started to kneel beside him when her sense of balance suddenly shifted. She blinked and found herself sitting on the ground, back in her own body, looking up into Damian's face.

"How did we…?" Damian stared at his hands. He ran them over his body and grabbed at the front of his boxer shorts in ecstasy. "It's back!" he whooped.

"You are so vile." She stood up, pulling the soggy gown from her rear end.

"And loving every inch of it," he replied.

So was she. She hugged herself, reveling in the feel of being in her own skin, even if it was prickled with goose bumps from the chill in the night air. She'd been in Damian's body for less than ten minutes, but it had felt like an eternity.

"I didn't do this."

He stopped inspecting himself and looked at her skeptically.

"I almost wish I did, though," she said. "At least then I'd understand why this stuff keeps happening to us, and I'd know how to end it." She rubbed at her arms for warmth. "I just need you to understand that whatever *is* going on, I didn't do it."

He pulled off his robe and handed it to her. He walked toward her house, not waiting to see if she would follow. "I believe you," he said over his shoulder. "I just don't want to."

Wrapping herself in the warm flannel, she padded through

the grass behind him. He'd already settled onto her front porch by the time she arrived. The pavement was too cold for her bare feet, so she was forced to sit beside him, bundling her toes in the robe's folds.

"I needed this to be your fault," he said, "because that's the only thing I can comprehend. Everything else is too crazy." He cracked his knuckles, a sign of his unsettled nerves. "Rocky, we're switching places with each other."

She rested her head against her knees, the enormity of the situation sinking in. Every time she'd woken up in a strange place, she had actually been waking up in Damian's body. Damian's bed, Damian's car, Damian's soccer practice. While at the same time, he'd been in her body, attacking Mike and ransacking her bedroom. Nuzzling Denise's chest...

She frowned at him.

Not noticing her irritation, he kept talking. "And since I'm about as clueless as you on why it's happening, we're in trouble. *You* being clueless about anything is pretty much a given on a good day, but for me...man, this is insane."

The frown intensified to a nasty glare.

"It's been like one bad dream after another all week, except they kept getting weirder and longer. And it never made sense to me why I'd dream I was the scrawny chick from next door."

She geared up to blast him when a beam of headlights coming up the driveway wiped the words away.

Mike was home.

She took stock of the scene greeting her big brother. Her: barely dressed, snuggled in Damian's robe. Damian: wearing only boxer shorts and a T-shirt. Both of them: alone together, in the middle of the night.

"Oh no," she groaned.

She wasn't even sure if Mike let the car come to a complete stop before jumping out of it. All she saw was a blur charging up the driveway, grabbing Damian by the throat and slamming him against the front door so hard the windows on the house rattled.

"What are you doing over here with my sister?" he thundered.

Damian tried to speak, but Mike's hold on his neck choked off the response.

"Mike!" Ricki shouted, leaping onto his shoulder. "Please, please stop it. You don't understand what's going on." She pulled in vain at the arms pinning Damian to the door.

He shook her off, tightening his hold on Damian's neck. "You are really testing me, D. You sneak over here the second I leave Ricki alone, and do what?" He glanced at her, taking in the filmy nightgown revealed through the loosened robe. The sight enraged him even more. "Did you touch her?"

"Michael!" she exclaimed, appalled.

Damian sputtered ineffectively.

"Michael, cut it out," she yelled, punching him on the back. "Think about it—it's Demon Spawn. Would I really be doing anything with *him*? I'm crazy, not brain dead, remember?"

It took a few seconds for the fury to recede from his face. His grip loosened. Damian swiftly moved to a safe distance on the other side of the porch, rubbing his throat.

Mike studied them. He yanked Damian's robe off her and replaced it with his jacket. "Talk," he ordered, throwing the robe at Damian.

Ricki knew he'd never believe their story. If she told him that she and Damian had just flipped out of each other's body, he would accuse them of coming up with the lamest lie in history and proceed to beat Damian to a bloody pulp. Or he would assume she'd lost her mind, accuse Damian of taking advantage of his little sister's break in sanity, and then proceed to beat him to a bloody pulp. Either way, Damian would get beaten to a bloody pulp—a concept that usually brought her great joy, but right now, he was of more use to her in one piece.

"I was sleepwalking again," she said, spitting out the first thing that came to mind. "I guess I made it out of the house somehow, and Damian saw me. He came outside and brought me back home." She glanced at Damian, willing him to stay silent.

Time crawled as Mike looked back and forth between them. They stared back at him, breaths held. Appearing to make up his mind, he walked over to Ricki, who did her best not to cringe.

He hugged her.

"I'm sorry, Smurf," he said. "You could've got hit by a car or something, and I wasn't even here." He turned to Damian. "Man, my bad for jumping on you. Thanks for looking out for her. Much appreciated."

"Anytime, Mikey," Damian replied, carefully keeping his eyes away from Ricki. "It's all good."

"Well, you don't have to worry about this happening again. I've got my eye on her from now on." His arm tightened around her shoulder. "I'll make sure you *never* need to look after her again." He gave them a smile that didn't quite reach his eyes. "'Cause that's what big brothers are for."

She shivered. The chill in the air had just gotten a whole lot colder.

"Why aren't you in the library?"

Ricki dropped her lunch tray onto the salad bar counter and spun around. Damian stood over her, glowering.

"Why aren't you in the library?" he repeated, inching closer. He leaned in, resting his hand on the counter beside her. "You were supposed to meet me there."

She peeked around the lunchroom. She wasn't positive, but she thought she saw Lindsey lurking at the soft serve station. "What are you talking about?" she hissed, nudging him back. "I've been running around all morning, trying to catch up to *you*."

"I left a note in your locker to meet me in the library."

"But I never went to my—"

"Do you even want to figure out what's happening to us? Or are you just waiting on me to fix everything?"

"Excuse you? Who the hell—"

"Save it. Let's go."

Grabbing her arm, Damian half-led, half-dragged Ricki out of the cafeteria. She caught a glimpse of Lindsey at Ice Cream Island with her mouth gaped open in a wide O before being pulled through the doors into the Lunchyard. A flash of blue from Teresa's newly dyed hair danced in her peripheral vision as she was paraded past a dumbfounded lunch crew to the other side of the courtyard. Her final view was of Aaron staring after them with a puzzled frown before being hauled out of the sunlight and into the dusky corridors of the library. Damian hustled her to a secluded table in the farthest corner of the room, pushed a stack of books aside, and dumped her into a chair.

"You just announced to the entire school that something is going on with us," she said, rubbing her arm. "What am I supposed to tell Lindsey? Or Aaron?"

"Something's always going on with us," he said dismissively. "Why should today be any different?"

"Well, I don't appreciate you putting your hands on me. Next time you need me to go somewhere with you, you fix your mouth to ask."

He sat across from her. "I didn't want to waste time with you putting up a fuss just to be arbitrary."

She was about to ask if he could even spell *arbitrary* when the school librarian, Mrs. Braum, poked her head around the corner and motioned for them to lower their voices.

Leaning into the table, he whispered, "I saw you last night."

"So what? I saw you too."

"No, I *saw* you. While I was asleep. In my dreams, I saw what you were doing." He cracked his thumb knuckle. "I fell asleep again after I went home. You'd have thought sleep would be the last thing on my mind, but..." He shrugged. "Next thing I knew, I was knocked out."

She understood. Had it not been for Mike keeping her stress level at maximum capacity all night, she probably would've fallen asleep too. She couldn't so much as go to the bathroom without him knocking on the door, asking if she needed more toilet paper. If she went downstairs to get a snack, he was right behind her getting a drink. And if she lingered too long beside a window, he was there to close the curtains "to keep a draft from getting in." There was no way she could go to sleep—she was too scared of him climbing into the bed with her to make sure the sheets were warm.

"I saw you and Mike sitting at your kitchen table," Damian said. "You were holding this big book open, asking him questions, and you were still wearing that nightie thing."

"That was you?" She'd been in the middle of helping Mike go over chapter review questions and had felt phantom-stalker's presence hovering over her shoulder. Good to finally know who the stalker was.

"It's been happening all week," he said. "While I'm asleep, somehow I'm watching you. And I think you've been watching me." He searched her eyes for confirmation. "It was you at the party, wasn't it?"

She rubbed her temples. "Yeah. I saw you playing pool, but I thought I was dreaming."

See the reality, not the dream...

"You were passed out in Teresa's room," he said. "I went to play pool after I—" He stopped. "You were asleep at the party while I was awake, but you saw what I was doing."

Once in a blue moon...

"And last night, I was asleep while you were awake, but I saw what you were doing."

Not the dream...

"So when only one of us is asleep, I guess we watch the other person through our dreams. Does that mean we change bodies when we're both asleep at the same?" Damian leaned back in his chair, staring at the ceiling. "What's making this happen?"

...the dream...

"I think I know the answer," Ricki blurted. She dropped her head onto the table and groaned. "We've been cursed."

Mrs. Braum again appeared beside the table to shush them before vanishing back into the library's shadows.

Ricki buried her head under her arms. "And I think it really *is* my fault."

She relayed her meeting with Madame Dupre to Damian, keeping her gaze fixed on the scarred wood of the library table, too embarrassed to meet his eyes. She glossed over the riddle's words, instead focusing on the vial found by Calvin Ma and his terror squad. Her throat almost closed when she got to the part about putting the potion in Aaron's drink, but she forged ahead, staunchly ignoring the muffled sounds of laughter coming from the seat across from her.

"Let me get this straight," he drawled. "You believe some crazy gypsy woman put a curse on us? What, did you cuss out her spirit guide or look in her crystal ball the wrong way or something?"

"I didn't say that." Ricki rolled her eyes in annoyance. "I

said Madame Dupre predicted something big would happen to me at the party, and it had to do with dreams not being reality. Like how after the party we started dreaming of each other. But then, in reality, we *become* each other. Do you follow me this time, or do I need to draw pictures?"

"Only if they show a map to your brain." Damian tilted farther back in his chair, tempting Ricki to kick it out from beneath him. He snickered. "I can't believe you went to a fortune-teller to get a man. Has dating life really been that hard for you?"

"Wow," she breathed. "I don't think I'll ever get used to how much I can't stand you." Her toe inched toward his chair.

"Yeah, back atcha. I hate you, you hate me, and God obviously hates both of us 'cause He just stuck us together in the world's worst joke on mankind I can think of." He sighed. "Next. Can this gypsy lady predict how to fix this mess?"

Her shoe stopped its trek across the floor. "I don't know. And the fair doesn't come back in town for about two more weeks, so I don't think we have time to wait and find out." She toyed with the cover of a paperback and murmured to herself, "When I found the potion, I was so sure that my life was about to change for the better, not change genders." She looked at Damian. "What did you end up doing with that potion after you took it from me?"

He cracked a knuckle. "What potion?"

"The vial you stole and wouldn't give back. What did you do with it?"

"Oh, that. I dumped it down the toilet, then tossed the bottle. What'd you say it was, by the way?"

"Well, I'd thought it was a love potion Madame Dupre had led me to." She leaned forward. "What did you do with it?"

Crack went another knuckle. "I said I dumped it down the toilet. You didn't hear me the first time?"

"I heard you. I just don't know if I believe you."

His chair thudded against the ground. "Then listen harder, so you will. I dumped it. I figured it was some stupid drug you were gonna use to make me sick, so I tossed it as soon as you left and didn't give it another thought."

His eyes were a bit too jumpy, but she decided not to pursue it. Even if he had held onto the potion, she hadn't seen him again for the rest of the party, so it couldn't be the cause of their troubles. She would let it go...

"You're full of it," she declared.

His mouth tightened.

"But, since it doesn't really pertain to the matter at hand, I'll let it slide."

"Pertain to the matter at hand?" he huffed. "What, are you channeling your inner grandma right now? What girl your age talks like that?"

"I'm just saying that you're lying, and I know you're lying, but I don't care. You don't have to get nasty about it."

"You're calling me a liar, and I don't have to get nasty about it?"

Mrs. Braum stomped up to the table and rapped on it with a marker. They looked up guiltily. Pointing a warning at them, she pivoted on her heels and stomped away.

"Why are you being so difficult?" Ricki whispered heatedly. "I'm just trying to figure out what went wrong at the party to put us in this mess. The potion probably didn't have anything to do with it, but at least I'm putting some thought into it and not making fun of the way people talk. But I don't know why I'd expect anything better from *you*. I mean, consider who I'm talking to—"

"Whoa." He held up a hand. "Save the speeches for the stage. I got bigger things on my mind than getting caught up over some stupid drink you found to finally get a guy to look at you." His lips wrinkled in distaste. "Every time I fall asleep, I'm waking up as my worst nightmare. My body, gone. My muscles, my voice, my 'pride and joy'…gone. I'm nothing but a nagging, washed out version of a throwback Cheetah Girl wannabe."

"Oh, please," she spat. "Like it's really my biggest wish in life to be trapped in the body of a…a 'roid-ridden waste of male flesh with the intellect of a squashed frog. It's what I've always aspired to be, right? But at least I'm not hiding things."

"Not hiding things?" he countered. "Tell me everything. Everything that gypsy chick told you."

Her jaw clenched. There was no way she would share the full prophecy with him. It was still precious to her, even if it *had* momentarily ruined her life.

"Exactly," he stated. "So don't talk to me about hiding things when you've got your own secrets. It's all good to get high and mighty on me, but when the shoe's on the other foot, you don't know how to handle it. You've always been that way."

Her head snapped back. "You think you know me?"

"Know you? I could write a book about you."

"Yeah? Well, wouldn't that require you actually knowing how to read? Or write?"

"Are you calling me stupid now?"

"I'm not *calling* you anything. If that's what you *are*—"

"Enough!" Mrs. Baum loomed over the table, the marker clenched in a bloodless hand. "The both of you, out!" She glared after them as they shamefacedly gathered their belongings and slunk toward the exit.

"I can't believe I actually thought you'd be any help," Ricki grumbled through the corner of her mouth.

"That was your first mistake," Damian murmured back. "Thinking."

They reached the library's door, leaving its fluorescent

domain to enter the sunny world of the courtyard. Lunch period was nearing its end, with only a few kids still left in the quad. Unfortunately for Ricki, those kids happened to be her own lunch crew and half the soccer team, all staring at her and Damian in varying degrees of curiosity, with Aaron and Lindsey's being the strongest.

She turned her head just enough to whisper, "I don't need you, Devil Boy. I'll find a way to fix this without you. Just stay out of my way." Discreetly elbowing him in the ribs, she lifted her nose into the air and marched across the quad to the school's lobby, blocking out the eyes that followed her.

Her conversation with Damian had been next to useless, but at least there was one valuable thing she'd gotten out of it: she had to find Madame Dupre.

"What do you mean it's policy not to release personal info on your participants?" Ricki yelled into the phone. "You guys have been bouncing me around and putting me on hold for over an hour, and *now* you're telling me?"

The call waiting alert beeped.

Ignoring it, she said, "I really need to get in touch with this woman. She doesn't have a website, and I don't know what city she lives in or even what state. I don't even know if Celeste Dupre is her real name. You guys are kind of my last hope." She listened grimly to the county fair associate on the other end of the phone. "Could I at least give you *my* name and number, and you could pass it on to her?"

The phone beeped in her ear for the sixth time.

Ricki rubbed her forehead in aggravation. How many times was Lindsey going to call? She'd already told everyone that Damian had pulled her out of the lunchroom to apologize for their fire drill fight, which had then led to another argument that took up the rest of the lunch period. Denise and Teresa had immediately accepted her story, and Yolanda had eventually come around, but Lindsey was apparently still skeptical. She hated to keep lying to everyone, but the lies were so much more believable than the truth. And as soon as she located Madame Dupre and fixed the whole situation with Damian, she would go back to her honest, bland life with no one the wiser.

She tried to focus on the conversation. "You mean there's absolutely no way to contact her until the fair comes back?" A pit opened in the bottom of her stomach. "Okay, well, thanks for your help."

Hanging up, she threw herself onto the bed and moaned into the pillows. From the moment she'd opened her eyes and seen Damian waking up in her body, she had accepted with absolute certainty that her life no longer followed a path of logic or common sense. Her world was now upside down and skipping to the beat of broken drums. She didn't like it, she hadn't had a full night of sleep in almost a week because of it, and she would probably end up in a nuthouse by the time it was all said and done.

Fine, whatever.

It was what it was, and she was doing everything in her power to find a way to fix it. But after an entire afternoon of trying to track down Madame Dupre, she was no closer to finding that stupid gypsy than when she started. She'd always suspected life hated her—now she had proof.

Maybe she'd been too quick to dismiss Damian.

Rolling onto her side, she grabbed a stuffed unicorn to snuggle. *Why do I always let him get to me?* They'd barely exchanged any useful information before going for each other's throats. She looked at her watch. Mike had been called in to work the evening shift. Maybe she could swallow her pride and try to talk to Satan Jr. before he got home.

A picture of Damian's smug face flashed through her mind. Her hands involuntarily crushed the unicorn. "Let me search the internet again," she muttered. "How many Celeste Dupres could there be in the entire United States?"

As she reached for the telephone, a dark figure materialized in her window. She let out a small scream before recognizing Damian's face peering at her through the glass. He gestured for her to let him inside.

She unlocked the window, allowing him to crawl into the room. Sticking her head out, she looked down at the trellis that traveled up the side of the house to her room. "So that's how you did it," she mumbled.

A few years back, Damian had stolen several pages from her diary—the most humiliating ones, of course. He then made mass copies and distributed them to the entire school. She had always wondered how he'd made it into her room, past the security system known as "Mike's bedroom." Now she knew.

He studied the room's black walls. "Let me guess. We're standing inside your brain."

"How could you possibly know that? You bugged my room again, didn't you?" She rushed over to her bureau and began rifling through the drawers.

He flopped onto her bed and tossed the flattened unicorn into the air. "Nah, I just know how your warped little mind works." Catching the unicorn in one hand, he squinted at the ceiling. "I always wondered what color the sky was in your world. So...it's gray."

She snatched the stuffed animal away and shoved him off the bed. "What do you want?"

"I want to have a full night's sleep and not wake up in your body." He picked himself up from the floor. "I want to have a dream with somebody other than you as the starring attraction. I want my life back the way it was."

She raised an eyebrow, waiting for the punch line.

Damian sighed. "I've been hustling all afternoon, trying to find a way to get us back to normal. But—and I really hate to say this—I'm realizing I can't do it on my own."

She fell back onto the bed and frowned, reflecting on her own failure.

"So I've been thinking," he said. "The way I see it, there's no way we're going to end this body-swapping stuff if we don't work together. But we've got a lot of obstacles to get around." He dragged the desk chair over to sit in front of her. "Mikey wants to break my neck every time I get within five feet of you. And I *do not* want anyone to find out what's been going down—my cred would be worth next to nothing if people find out I'm parading around as a girl. Plus, if we try to tell anybody any of this, they'll think we're crazy as hell. But I really think our biggest obstacle is *us*. And we're going to have to get over that hurdle if we want any chance of ever getting our lives back to normal."

Ricki was thrown. His lips were moving, but he didn't sound like a blithering idiot. Intelligent and logical weren't two adjectives she'd typically use to describe Damian Marquez. Ignorant and loser were more like it.

Shaking off the unexpected moment of appreciation, she asked, "What are you saying?"

"That we need to squash our differences. For now, anyways. Table the attitude; try to get along until we get our bodies and dreams back. And I think the first step is to lay all our cards on the table, so I'll go first." He took a deep breath. "I have an idea of what might've caused this whole thing."

He pressed on his thumb and rolled his head from side to side, stretching the muscles of his neck until she heard a faint pop. His hands braced against his knees. "See, I think it's really *my* fault."

CHAPTER NINE

"How was I supposed to know you were running around with some voodoo drink you'd snaked off an old hack?" Damian protested.

His hands rubbed together in agitation, occasionally reaching down to scratch at his ankles. His eyes darted everywhere in the room but Ricki's face. "You were being so shady about that bottle, getting all worked up and acting like it was this huge secret. It struck me the wrong way. So I figured maybe it was something you planned on putting in someone's drink. And since you'd just said I 'owed,' the obvious drink in question was mine." He shrugged. "I returned the favor."

Ricki's fingers itched to wrap around his neck and squeeze the stupid out of him. "But I told you the vial was none of your business," she said. "That meant it didn't have anything to do with you!"

"Yeah, I know. I didn't believe you."

"How'd you even get it open?" she asked, somehow keeping her temper in check. "What did you do, use the Jaws of Life or something?"

An eyebrow lifted. "What're you talking about? The stopper pretty much fell out by itself."

She considered this information. Eight sets of hands, including her own, hadn't been able to pull the cork out. *How did it open so easily for him?*

"But how'd you get it into my drink?" she asked, setting the thought aside. Her breath caught. "Did Aaron help you?"

For a moment, he didn't speak. "If I told you he did, would you believe me?"

She recoiled, her throat tightening until she remembered the prank phone call Damian had made to her the day after the party. She relaxed. "No."

His eyes dropped to his lap. "Nah, he didn't know," he said, rubbing his ankle. "I heard he was going to talk to you, so I slipped the stuff into your cup when he wasn't looking."

"Then what?"

"Then nothing. I tossed the bottle and sat back to watch the fun begin. I gotta say, Rocky, you falling asleep on the dance floor was just anticlimactic."

"I'm so sorry to disappoint." Her voice dripped acid.

"Hey, no offense intended. All I'm saying is, nothing big happened to make me think I needed to get the bottle back."

"My passing out didn't set off alarms?" she asked in disbelief. "Me being laid out in the middle of the floor—that's kind of big, don't you think?"

"Not really. I just figured it was a sleeping drug or something, and that you'd probably planned on knocking me out so you could take blackmail pics. You getting caught up in your own drama was just poetic justice."

"I said none…of…your…*business,*" she bit out, the urge to throttle him intensifying. "How would you think that meant I was going to drug you and take pervy pictures of you?"

He scratched his chin. "I gave you too much credit?"

The battle for calm was lost.

"How deluded are you?" she shrieked. "You spent the whole night trying to overthrow some stupid, imaginary plot against you, and all you did was ruin our lives!" She vaulted across the bed, grabbed a unicorn, and hurled it at his face.

As he ducked, a second stuffed animal bounced off the side of his head, almost toppling him from his chair.

She blindly grabbed for another one. "That night was supposed to be wonderful and beautiful and perfect, and *you* shouldn't have been in it at all! Now, because of you, my life is something I wouldn't wish on my worst enemy...who *is* you!"

"We don't know this is totally my fault," he protested, ducking the next round of fluffy artillery.

"It doesn't *need* to be totally your fault. If you'd just left me alone like I told you to, none of this would've happened!"

"Okay, maybe," he conceded, shielding his head. "Yeah, I spiked your drink, but *I* didn't drink any of that stuff, did I? Rocky, if you keep blowing up at every little thing I say, we'll never get anywhere. You need to chill."

She grudgingly lowered the hand holding her favorite plushy, Peppercorn. Relaxing, Damian brought his arms down from his head. With a quick flick of the wrist, she chucked the unicorn at him, beaning him in the face. Satisfied, she settled back onto the bed.

"Proceed," she stated tartly.

He kept a wary eye on her. "I didn't see you again after you were taken to Teresa's room. Your girls stayed with you, and they said you were okay. I didn't see any reason to think different."

He held onto the unicorn, pressing it between his palms. Tension coursed through his fingers as he withdrew into his thoughts of the night that had changed their lives. "I hung around after that, playing pool. And everything was all good up until my last game with Jonas. I was just about to make a shot when I got this creepy feeling someone was standing at the other end of the table, watching me. It's like all I felt was these eyes watching every move I made. At first, I thought I was buzzing too hard, but the feeling just kept getting more intense. To the point where I almost couldn't breathe. I was right on the verge of losing it, and then the feeling went away. Like that." He snapped, making Ricki jump.

"The whole thing freaked me out so bad, I figured I'd drank too much and it was time to call it a night. But then the same thing happened the next day. I was getting ready to take a shower, and all of a sudden, I'm being watched again. The feeling went away after a couple minutes, so I let the whole thing go.

"But when I went to bed that night, the dreams started. Crazy dreams where I'd either be watching you like some stalker or waking up in weird places. And they kept coming, getting longer and crazier, until it got to where I didn't even want to sleep anymore. I'd even wake up with bruises, or people would treat me funny and tell me about stuff I'd supposedly done while I was asleep.

"Like that one time with Delilah. We were at the movies, and I was tired, so I closed my eyes. Just for a second. But when I opened them, I was laid up in a bedroom. At first, I thought it was another dream, but the longer I laid there, I could tell something was off. I'm not sure what it was."

"Too much clarity?" Ricki offered.

"Clarity?" Damian nodded. "Yeah, I guess that's a good word for it. I think I tripped on every stupid toy in this room, trying to get out. I couldn't find a light switch, and it seemed like every time I turned around, I was knocking a bookshelf over. Then I heard someone coming down the hall and ended up in a bathroom, hiding until I could sort everything out in my head. The last thing I expected to see when I turned on the light was your face looking at me in the mirror. Then Mike showed up and called me by your name, and I broke. I don't even know what happened from then on. I just lost it." He stared at the floor, caught up in his memories.

Ricki felt the strangest urge to comfort him. All the times she'd been scared and confused, Damian had been going through the same thing. How odd to see him as an actual human being experiencing emotions identical to her own. But there he was, sitting in front of her without his usual battle gear—the cocky sneer he wore as armor and the arsenal of insults he wielded as dangerously as any weapon. Just a boy, trying to make sense of the inexplicable.

She sat on her hands to stop herself from reaching out to him and waited for the uncomfortable feeling of compassion for the enemy to pass.

He resumed speaking. "Then all of a sudden, I'm back at the movies, and Lilah is screaming in my ear, crying and calling me psycho. I'm freaking out 'cause I don't know what the hell is happening. She's freaking out. Before I can put two thoughts together, I'm getting beer thrown at me, and she's spraying me with mace. And while I'm literally trying to claw my eyes out of my head, the girl shoves me out of my own car, locks the door, and refuses to let me back in. Then she threatens to call the police and tell them I tried to rape her. I was so messed up; I didn't know *what* I'd tried to do, so I left. I walked home."

"Why didn't you call one of your boys to come get you?" Ricki asked.

"And say what? That I may or may not have attacked my date while I really thought I was attacking your brother on the other side of town? How do you explain something like that? Besides, I didn't want the fellas coming down on Lilah for what she did."

"Too late," she said, recalling her conversation with Aaron.

"Yeah, I know. Word got out, and they've been giving her a hard time about it. We look out for our own."

Ricki thought of the countless temporarily scarring things

she'd done to Damian since coming to Kirby. Not once had anyone on the soccer team ever tried to retaliate against *her.* Maybe she needed to stop cursing the legend of Mikey Rae Jr. and be thankful for it.

"But the twisted dream drama started for me right after I drank the spiked punch," she said. "I'm still not seeing how you entered the mix."

"I don't know. I slept good when I got home from the party. But the next night..." He shuddered. "Sunday night is when things got real funky."

"You started getting the dreams a whole day after I'd already been having them? Why? Something's got to be missing."

A minute passed as he sat thinking, his fingers scratching around the hem of his jeans. His hand stilled. "It was the water."

"What water?"

"Right before I left the party, a serving guy gave me a bottle of water. He said it was a complimentary parting gift for guests to make sure we stayed hydrated." He frowned. "Or some crap like that."

"You got water. So what?"

"So I didn't see anyone else with water bottles. And I didn't drink it until *the next day.* Sunday night, after I got home from hanging out with my boys and was about to go to bed. That's when all the weird dreams started happening."

She was about to scoff, when the series of events leading up to Sunday night flashed through her mind. The dream about Damian playing pool—that happened Saturday night. Watching Damian get undressed—Sunday afternoon. Actually waking up in Damian's bedroom...*Sunday night.*

"It really *was* the water," she marveled. "Before you drank it, I only dreamed about you. But after you drank it, I actually started switching with you. But how did the potion get into that bottle? Who would want to slip you a spiked drink?"

He eyed her. "Only person I can think of is you."

"Move beyond the obvious, okay? I didn't do it, so who did? Did anything out of the norm happen during the party?"

"Besides having a drugged-up chick spy on me in her psychic dreams?"

She rolled her eyes. "Work with me."

Standing up, he strolled around the bedroom, deep in thought. On his second lap around the room, he stopped in front of an old comedy-and-tragedy mask hanging above her bureau. It was the first mask she'd ever bought and was so worn that its pearly glaze had peeled away from the edges of each frozen grimace, exposing the red clay beneath its surface. He stared at it.

"Red," he announced. "When you were trying to get that bottle from me, some dust from the vents fell on me. When I looked up, I saw red."

"Red what?"

"I don't know," he said testily. "Just red. You asked if anything weird happened. I thought it was weird that plaster was falling on my head and red things were running around in the air vents."

"Red things running around in the air vents," she repeated to herself. On a hunch, she asked, "Was it maybe red like a baseball cap? Or...red hair?"

He looked confused. "I don't know. I guess it could've been hair."

Teresa's words broke through the wall of her memory: "... wanted me to tell you, 'the treasure is back in safe hands.'"

Ricki marched to the telephone and snatched it from its cradle. "Calvin," she growled softly. "And his little goon, Tom."

"I'm sorry, sweetie," Teresa said. "As soon as Calvin saw the car drive up, him and his little rat pack scurried off."

Ricki looked up at the Ma residence, examining it from one sprawling end to the other. It seemed to go on for miles. "But why would he run? He knew I was coming, right?"

"Yeah," she replied. "I just don't think he knew you were coming with *him*." Teresa pointed at Damian, who stood at the bottom of the steps with desire to inflict violence clearly stamped across his face.

During their drive to Teresa's house, Ricki had filled Damian in on her dealings with Calvin and Company. Given that Calvin had first contacted her via the home's ventilation systems, it led to reason that he and his bunch must've been hiding in them when Damian had stolen the vial from her in the hallway. Concealed in the air vents, they'd probably followed him throughout the party and caught him in the act of pouring the potion into her cup. They'd apparently decided to retaliate on her behalf. One spiked drink for another.

Damian was livid to learn a pack of sixth graders had taken him down. It had never occurred to him that while he was busy plotting Ricki's downfall, a group of little kids had been plotting *his*. And his anger was made worse by the fact that the miniature marauders had also sabotaged him earlier in the day, when he'd stopped by the Ma estate after school.

According to a fuming Damian, he'd intended to ask Teresa if he could talk to the staff, hoping one of them may have found the bottle during the post-party cleanup. But he'd barely made it up the steps when the door was opened by "the little moppy-headed Ma boy and his Chuckie sidekick" who promptly stuck a Solicitors Not Welcome sign on the front porch and slammed the door in his face. Ignoring the sign, he'd rung the doorbell and was almost barbecued by an electrical shock through the arm. He then knocked on the door and triggered a sensor in the antisolicitors sign that shot a stream of steaming honey all over his brand-new sneakers. Thinking to steer clear of any other booby traps, he then ventured into the yard to knock on a window and stepped smack into an angry swarm of fire ants conveniently nesting just beyond the porch. But it was when he saw the little boy with a jar of wasps skipping around the corner of the house that he recognized maybe the time had come to explore other options for tracking down the vial. He'd retreated home to slather his legs in hydrocortisone cream and call a temporary cease-fire with Ricki, never understanding why the band of preteen vigilantes had declared war on him.

Score: Middle School Mafioso—two. Damian—zero.

"Teresa," Ricki said, looking back at her friend, "did Calvin tell you where he put the treasure he mentioned?"

"Okay, you're asking me that like Calvin and I actually talk or something." Teresa flipped her blue Mohawk to the side. "The last thing that boy ever said to me was 'stop, it hurts when you twist it that way.'"

"Terry, I'm serious."

"So am I! He pissed me off." She ran a hand across the side of her head, smoothing the stray hairs into place with her sapphire-tipped French manicure. "Sweetie, I don't know what to tell you. He poofed out of here as soon as he caught a whiff of Damian. And trust me: I don't call the little snot a rat for nothing; when he goes into hiding, you need an exterminator to smoke him out."

"So we're screwed," Damian grumbled.

"I didn't want to say it, but yeah. Look, if it really means that much to you guys, you're welcome to try and find him," Teresa offered, a picture of benevolence. "I just don't think—"

Not waiting for her to finish, Damian stomped up the steps and marched into the house. Pausing for a second to glare around the foyer, he disappeared. Teresa, mouth still open, stared after him. "Okay, that was rude."

"I'm sorry," Ricki said. "We just really, really need to find Calvin."

"I'm starting to see that." She pulled out her cell phone. "Why don't you go ahead and check the grounds, and I'll put the staff on alert and even call in a missing person's report if he doesn't show up in the next thirty minutes. Sound good?"

Ricki pulled her into a bear hug. "You're the best."

Laughing, Teresa pushed her away. "Oh, hon, that's a given. Now go."

Ricki started down the steps, but then turned back. "Aren't you going to ask me what I'm looking for? Or why I rode here with Damian? Or why we're even breathing the same air?"

Teresa shook her head. "No way, that's against my religion. It's under the book of *Nunya*. Chapter 'Don't Ask,' verse 'Don't Tell.' Ask not other people about *their* secrets lest they actually want to start knowing about *mine*." Bursting into giggles, she spun around and danced into the house.

Grinning, Ricki hopped down the steps and made her way along the side of the house to the gardens. She had just passed a forest of rosebushes when a noise stopped her.

"Psst!"

She whipped around. *It could've been the wind.* She took a few more steps.

"I *said*, Psst!"

"Hello?" she called out, looking around.

"Over here!" a small voice hissed.

She inspected the wall of rosebushes bordering the house, but nothing looked out of the ordinary. She turned to walk away, when a beam of light from the setting sun illuminated the leafy jungle and reflected off what appeared to be a pair of wire-rimmed glasses. Leaning in closer, she realized that what she'd mistaken for a misshapen rose was actually a lock of stringy red hair falling out of a green baseball cap. She reached inside the tangle of thorns and carefully nudged a clump of roses to the side. Two small faces looked back at her.

Calvin and Tom.

Surprised, she asked, "What are you guys doing in there? *How* did you guys get in there?"

"Don't look at us!" Calvin ordered. "Act like you're doing something else."

She stared at them, bewildered. Before she could ask another question, a freckled hand reached out and slammed a thorny stem against her wrist.

"Yeouch!" She released the bush and jumped away, rubbing at her stinging hand.

"Don't say anything," the bush instructed. "Just listen. Sasquatch is on the prowl. We don't want any trouble, so tell him we're sorry for what we did, but if he keeps trying to get at us, there will be repercussions. Tell him that Tom…knows people."

Tom grunted.

Seething, she wiped a drop of blood from her wrist. How much trouble would she get into for strangling an eleven-year-old with a rose stem? "Sasquatch?" she asked through gritted teeth.

"The big dude."

She sighed. "Calvin, Damian isn't looking for you. He's looking for the vial."

The sound of hushed whispers between the two boys spanned several seconds, and then Calvin's small voice responded, "He told you to say that."

"No," she said, irritated, "he didn't. We just really need the vial because the stuff in it had some…unexpected side effects. We think if we drink some of it a second time, it might cancel out the bad effects."

More whispers.

"We got back at him for you," he said. "So if you're trying to sell us out, that'd be really foul."

Her irritation dissolved. "You guys poured some stuff from that bottle into his drink, didn't you?"

"Um…"

The low murmur of a heated argument reached her ears. It went on for several minutes before eventually being resolved with a loud thump and muffled cry.

Calvin spoke up. "Yeah. After we saw him do it to you, we figured payback would be sweet." The bush rustled. "Now he's after us."

"He's not after you. Okay, he's a little mad," she slipped in, "but he'll be alright. Do you still have the vial?"

"Uh-huh."

She wanted to weep with relief. "Do you think I can have it?"

He conferred with his partner before responding, "It might be doable. But only if you promise to keep Sasquatch away from us. And you have to give it back by the end of the week."

She was torn. If those kids ever found out what the potion could do, there would be trouble. To let a future criminal mastermind like Calvin loose on the world with a body-switching potion could quite possibly mean an open door to Armageddon.

"Well," she hedged, "if you want it back, sure. But ever since me and…Sasquatch drank it, we've started having these really gushy feelings for each other. We kind of think it may actually be a love—"

"Keep it," Calvin barked.

Tom mumbled in agreement.

"Great! I'll wait here while you get it."

He snorted. "You'll be waiting a long time."

"Like what, an hour?"

"Try longer. We don't have it."

She yanked the rosebushes apart. "What do you mean, you don't have it?"

"Nope. It's Omar's turn to hold onto it."

The desire to maim reemerged. "Then call Omar and tell him to bring it over."

"No can do. He went out of town."

Tom reached out and prodded her numb hands away from the bush. The leaves closed over their faces, enclosing the two boys back into their hidden lair of twigs and rose petals.

Calvin's disjointed voice drifted through the foliage. "And he won't be back 'til next week."

They took turns sleeping that night.

Ricki pulled the first shift, sleeping five hours until two in the morning. It was the most sleep she'd had all week. By the time the alarm clock rang, she was already stirring into consciousness and feeling more clear-headed than she'd been in days. She spent the rest of the night watching movies.

And worrying.

One drink to begin the merry-go-round of body leaps, another to end it. Such an obvious solution. Even in the movies, the characters almost always went back to normal by recreating the same action that had dumped them in the wrong body in the first place. But what if too much time passed before she and Damian finally got the potion back from Calvin and his merry band of juvenile delinquents? What if the potion's effects had become permanent by then? A week might be too late.

The thought festered in her mind, keeping her company through the night along with Damian's invisible presence popping in every so often to hover over her shoulder. And with every hour that passed, her anxiety grew.

She waited for the sun to come up.

And she popped another movie into the DVD player.

And she worried.

The last thing she expected to find the next day when she reached into the brown paper sack containing her lunch was the vial. It sat on top of her roast beef on rye, wedged between an apple and Snickers bar. The shiny cut of its glass twinkled merrily at her. It took Ricki's mind several seconds to accept what she was seeing.

"What's wrong?" Yolanda asked, peeking over her shoulder.

"Nothing." She quickly clamped the bag shut. "I, um, just remembered that I forgot to make my sandwich."

How did the vial get into her lunch bag? She'd packed the lunch herself, and it had remained in her locker all morning. Her *locked* locker.

She jumped up. "I'd better go buy something from the hot bar."

Fleeing the table, she rushed across the quad. Her steps slowed as she passed Damian's table. Catching his eye, she discreetly jerked her head toward the cafeteria.

"Hey, Ricki," a voice said from the middle of the table.

She stumbled to a halt. Turning around, she sought out the voice's owner.

Aaron sat in the midst of the other soccer players, watching her.

Her skin became clammy. "Hi," she said, her throat oddly dry in contrast to her damp skin.

"We're still on for tomorrow night, right?" he asked.

Her mouth opened to respond, but she suddenly found her view blocked by Damian's chest. A hand closed around her elbow.

"Aaron," Damian said over his shoulder, "I need to borrow your girl for a sec. I'll bring her right back."

As he pulled her toward the school doors, Ricki experienced a sickening sense of déjà vu. She looked over her shoulder and saw the faces of Aaron and Lindsey staring after her. Only, what had previously been confusion on Lindsey's face now veered toward rage. Aaron's expression remained blank, which was almost worse.

Damian led her to the back of the cafeteria and dropped her down at a deserted table.

"I'm getting sick and tired of you doing that," she said, rubbing her elbow. "Touch me again, and you'll only be hitting high notes for the rest of your days."

He waved an indifferent hand. "Whatever. I'm trying to keep you focused."

"No, you're trying to keep yourself on my hit list is what you're trying to do." Shaking the aggravation out of her system, she plopped the sack on the table and pulled out the vial.

"How'd you get that?" he demanded.

"It was in my lunch. Which has been in my locker all day. So, basically, I have no idea."

Attached to the vial was a note. "We have our ways of getting what we want, where we want, when we want it," she read aloud. "Remember that. Your friend, Cal."

They looked at each other in apprehension.

"That kid scares me," she muttered under her breath.

"How'd a middle schooler get into your locker unnoticed, in the middle of the day?" Damian asked.

She wished she knew the answer to that question, then

settled on, "Tom knows people," and pushed the vial to the center of the table.

They stared at it in wonder as the cafeteria lights reflected from its surface, creating a dazzling rainbow of colors in the air.

Ricki was the first to speak. "Me first."

She picked up the vial. It simmered in her palm. Poking cautiously at the stopper, she was surprised at how easily it fell from the top of the bottle. She sniffed its contents, intoxicated by the sweet scent of vanilla and peppermint. She touched it to her lips and prepared to swallow.

"You know this means our truce is over, right?" Damian asked.

She flashed him an evil grin. "And I wouldn't have it any other way." Tilting her head back, she let several drops flow down her throat. It tickled its way down her chest and settled gently in the bottom of her stomach.

Snatching the vial from her, he held it to his mouth and swallowed.

The air between them crackled with anticipation.

Ricki felt a sudden rush of dizziness, almost sending her from her seat. It quickly passed.

Damian held his hands up to his head, his body swaying. After a few breathless seconds, his eyes opened, and he smiled.

"It's over," she crowed.

Handing the vial to her, he winked. "And it's back on." He stood and saluted her, then sauntered across the cafeteria and back into the Lunchyard.

She slipped the vial into her pocket. After a quick stop at the hot bar, she almost skipped back to her table, pausing just long enough to wave at Aaron and mouth, "See you Saturday." She was filled with such joy that she almost missed the dark storm looming on Lindsey's face.

"What was all that about?" Yolanda asked, full of suspicion.

"Nothing big," she lied. "Spawn just wanted to make sure everything was okay between him and Mike."

Lindsey frowned and turned away.

Yolanda looked back and forth between the two girls. "You sure that's all it was?"

"Of course." Ricki focused on her food. "It would never be anything else." She held her breath, waiting for Teresa to mention their trip to her house. She was relieved to hear silence.

Sensing the tension, Denise jumped in. "Ricki, we were talking about going to the mall tonight. You in?"

She looked up and smiled. "Nope, not tonight."

"You too?" Teresa whined. "Lindsey already said she's got to take her sisters to the movies. What're you doing tonight that's so major?"

"Sleep," Ricki replied, reveling in the thrill the word gave her. "I am going to sleep."

"You couldn't stay awake long enough for me to change?"

The words played at the border of Ricki's mind, beckoning to her from the deep sleep in which she currently wallowed.

"I know you said you were tired, but I wasn't gone that long."

She let out a loud snore. Her thoughts tried to follow the sound back into the waking world, but the lure of blissful oblivion was too seductive to ignore. She dived off the trail to consciousness and drifted back into nothingness.

A finger snapped in her ear. "Wake up."

Rolling onto her side, she swatted at the pestering voice. "Lemme lone," she mumbled.

"I promise you it'll be worth it if you wake up," the voice cajoled.

Her head burrowed into the crook of her arm. "Pssrzhhh…"

"Damian, stop playing."

Ricki's eyes flew open and focused on Lindsey standing seductively in front of her, framed against the backdrop of the Callahan living room. A powder blue nightie dripped from her body, flowing down the curves of her willowy frame and stopping just above her knees. Light from the television shined boldly through the sheer material, illuminating areas of her body where even the shadows were too prudish to tread. Her golden mane flowed loosely over her shoulders, strategically covering her breasts in places where the see-through lingerie failed.

She blushed furiously and twirled in a circle. "You like?" Lips pursed, she eased onto the sofa and moved in for a kiss.

Ricki shot up, touched her face, and almost burst into tears. The tickle of beard stubble against her fingers told her everything she needed to know.

Drinking the potion a second time hadn't worked. She and Damian were back to square one. And now one of her best friends was slithering across the sofa toward her, intent on seduction.

"Oh dear," she squeaked.

CHAPTER TEN

I T WILL BE OVER IN *a few minutes.*

At least, that's what Ricki kept telling herself. Her mind was a schizophrenic battlefield, warring between devastation over finding herself back in Damian's body and anxiety over how to avoid Lindsey's advances. She couldn't decide whether to cry or play dead. She opted to scoot down the sofa, away from an oncoming assault.

Strawberry-glossed lips missed her cheek by inches, leaving the scent of sugary fruit lingering in the air.

"Hey," Ricki objected, flinching at the sound of Damian's voice. "What're you…uh…whatcha doing?"

Lindsey oozed onto the sofa beside her. "If you can't tell, I must be doing it wrong."

Huddling against the armrest, Ricki risked a glance at the clock above the television. 8:41 PM. *How much longer before I return to my own body? A minute? Two?* Throwing herself forward, she grabbed at her shoelaces just as Lindsey leaned in to nuzzle her cheek.

"Is everything okay?" Lindsey begged.

"My shoes are pinching my feet. Give me a sec." She slowly untied the right shoelace, easing the string through each hole while her mind clicked off the passing seconds. After a minute, she moved on to the next shoe.

Lindsey's head rested on her shoulder. "Might as well take them off," she murmured. Her fingers slithered up to caress Ricki's neck, sending the skin crawling beneath their touch. "Once we're done, they'll be sharing the floor with my nightie anyway."

The shoelaces folded to the floor.

"They'll do *what*?" Ricki blurted, staring at Lindsey aghast. When had the "sweet as sunshine" angel of the crew decided to take a leisurely stroll on the hoochie side?

Lindsey pulled back. "What's wrong? I thought you'd like my surprise," the fallen angel sulked. "I bought it just for you. But if you don't like it, I guess I could take it off." She leaned in, allowing the straps to tumble down her shoulders. "What do you want me to do?"

How about something along the lines of putting some freakin' clothes on? danced on the tip of Ricki's tongue. "That's a good question," she said instead, nudging Lindsey back with a long-reaching stretch. "Why don't you give me a call when you and your sisters get back from the movies, and we'll talk about it?"

Dodging a flying elbow, Lindsey frowned. "I didn't tell you I was going to the movies with my sisters."

"Yeah, you did. At lunch."

"No, I didn't. You didn't even talk to me at lunch."

She felt a tickle of unease. "Then maybe it was after lunch."

"Why would I tell you I was going to the movies with my sisters when my whole family is at an awards assembly? I had to fake sick just so they wouldn't make me go too." Lindsey's arms crossed. "Who told you I was taking my sisters to the movies?"

Ricki's eyes shot to the clock. 8:46 PM. *Still no flippage?*

"Ricki told you, didn't she?" Lindsey pressed.

Her head whipped around. "What?"

"You and her have been talking a lot lately," Lindsey said peevishly. "Is she reporting on me to you or something?"

"You know I'd never do that to you! I mean, *Ricki* wouldn't do that," she hastily amended. "How could you even fix your mouth to say something like that?"

"What am I supposed to think?" Lindsey protested. "You're always sneaking off to be together. You guys act like you're enemies, but I've never seen two people who hate each other try to be around each other so much. And now you're even repeating stuff I told her." Her eyes misted with tears. "I thought you liked me."

Kill me. Just kill me now. "Hey," Ricki soothed, awkwardly patting Lindsey's knee. "Of course I"—she closed her eyes—"like you."

"You don't act like it. You didn't even look at me once today at lunch. But as soon as Ricki walked by, you were all over her." Lindsey pouted. "If I'm competing with her, you need to let me know."

"No," she insisted, pinching the bridge of her nose. "You will never, *ever* be in competition with Ricki for Dam—" She caught herself. "For me. I promise you that."

The weight on the sofa shifted. Her eyes opened in time to see the nightie's straps sliding farther down Lindsey's arms. The silky material peeled away from her pale skin and slid, inch by inch, down to her waist.

Ricki was frozen in horror. Only her eyes could move, and they darted desperately to the wall clock. 8:50 PM.

"I'm glad you said that," Lindsey said in a shaky whisper. "Because I really care about you, Damian. More than Ricki ever could." She edged closer, nudging the straps out of the crook of her elbows and guiding their descent to the sofa. "Let me show you." Licking her lips, she leaned in for the kill.

"Whoa!" Ricki erupted from the sofa and skittered across the living room. "Whoa, whoa! What are you *doing*?"

Lindsey clutched a pillow against her chest. "I don't

understand. You said you like me. Why are you acting like this?"

"Why are *you*?" Ricki shouted. "Lindsey, you hardly know him, and you're trying to have sex with him already?"

"Him *who*?" Lindsey's face flamed. "I'm not seeing anyone else, I swear. Did Ricki tell you I was?"

"I didn't tell him anything! Seriously, what kind of friend do you think I am?" Turning away, she covered her eyes with a trembling hand. "Okay, I can't talk to you until you get dressed. This whole thing is making me ill."

She waited for the tremors in her hand to stop before removing it from her face. The clock loomed on the wall in front of her. Three more minutes had passed.

A muffled sob came from the sofa.

Ricki turned around, finding Lindsey huddled in a ball, shoulders shaking as she cried silently into a pillow. Blonde hair stuck to her wet face in stringy wisps. Ricki silently cursed herself. *Brilliant move, genius. Going with the double whammy—rejection and humiliation—all in one blow.* She sighed. *Guess I can't make it any worse, can I? Damian, I'm sorry.*

She walked down the hall to the coat closet and pulled one of Mr. Callahan's trench coats from a hanger. Mentally bracing herself for the Pandora's box she was about to open, she returned to the living room and draped the coat over Lindsey's sobbing figure.

Gently pulling damp strands of hair from Lindsey's cheeks, she whispered, "Hey."

Lindsey whimpered, turning her face away.

"Please look at me."

Her head lifted from the pillow. Looking at Ricki with bleary eyes, she uncurled and sat up.

"I've got something to tell you," Ricki started. "I probably should've told you as soon as I woke up, but I guess I thought it would do more harm than good. Now I don't think it's possible to do more harm, so I'm hoping this'll do some good."

"What is it?" Lindsey asked dully.

Time to pull you into the deep end with me, Lindz. I hope you can swim. "It's just that...well, you shouldn't feel bad about Damian turning you down, because he didn't. It was me. Ricki."

Lindsey swiped at the tears on her cheeks. "I don't get it."

"I don't either. It's crazy and illogical and unbelievable, but somehow"—the words squeezed past the lump in her throat into the open air—"somehow, we keep ending up inside each other. And we have absolutely no idea how to stop it."

There. She'd said it.

The pillow dropped from Lindsey's lap. "Ricki is inside you," she said, her voice flat.

"Yes! It's been going on ever since Teresa's party. And the effects keep getting stronger. We've been trying to figure out how to make it stop, but..." She gestured meaningfully at her body.

Lindsey's eyes narrowed. "Effects? You mean, like a connection between you guys or something?"

"I guess you could say there's some kind of magical bond thing going on," Ricki said. "And I couldn't tell anyone about it because Damian's reputation is some huge deal, and I didn't want people thinking I'm crazy. But now you know, and you're not freaking out, so I guess I was worried about nothing after all, huh?" She exhaled, her heart feeling light. She'd just told someone that she and Damian were switching places, and the world hadn't stopped. Better yet, Lindsey didn't even look like she was about to call the men in the little white coats.

In fact, she looked eerily calm.

"So this *is* about Ricki." Lindsey said.

Her head cocked in confusion. "Of course it is. I'm the

one stuck in this body. Like I said, I have no idea how it even happened, but—"

"But somehow you caught feelings for Ricki, and now you can't get her out of your system," Lindsey interrupted. "She's in your blood, and the bond's getting too strong to break. Or something cheesy like that, right?"

The world tilted. "Did you completely ignore everything I said? It's Ricki. Not Damian. *Ricki*."

"Of course it's Ricki," she said bitterly. "When isn't it? When you're with me, you're staring at Ricki. When she's not around, you're looking for Ricki. And now you can't even bring yourself to be with me tonight because of her?"

"Lindz," Ricki said, the world spinning around her, "I don't think you're understanding me. I *am* Ricki."

Lindsey rolled her eyes. "Just save it, Damian. If you didn't want to be with me, you could've said it the second I invited you over."

"I am not Damian," she stressed. "I am Ricki. Something beyond the realm of human possibility happened at Teresa's party, and now we keep switching places."

Lindsey stood up. "Is this a joke? Do you actually think anyone would buy that crap, or is this special brand of stupid only for me?" Her next words came out in a broken whisper. "Because you know how bad I like you that you could tell me anything and I'd lap it up. Maybe that means I'm the joke."

"I'm telling the truth," she insisted. "Please believe me." The heaviness in her heart reemerged. "If *you* don't, who will?"

Lindsey turned away, her head shaking in disgust.

"Wait, listen to me." The words came tumbling from Ricki's mouth. "Remember last year, when your pad got knocked loose during gym class? Remember how Cheryl Rivers stepped on it when she got out of the shower, and it stuck to the bottom of her foot? Nobody could ever figure out whose pad it was. Who else but me would know that?"

Lindsey spun around, her eyes the size of saucers. "I can't believe Ricki told you!"

Ricki's mouth flapped like a dying fish. Every time she spoke, the night went from bad to horrendous. Did she want to try for cataclysmic?

The cell phone in her pocket vibrated. She pulled it out and tried to swipe it open with Damian's meaty fingers, but maneuvering his body was too much like operating foreign machinery. The phone fell from her clumsy fingers and bounced across the floor.

Lindsey snatched it up. "Like I thought," she said, staring at the screen. "It's Ricki. Hope you guys have a good laugh on me."

"No, wait. I'm trying to explain—"

"Save it. Just save it. And get out!" She spun on her heels, marched to the front door, and lifted the cell phone over her head, then hefted it across the driveway.

Ricki winced at the sharp jangle of metal cracking against asphalt. What could she say to make things right? Looking at Lindsey's face, she realized there was nothing. Not that night, anyway. Maybe never.

The sound of the door slamming behind her unlocked the chest of fears she'd believed for one misguided moment would never have to be opened. No one would believe her. Her friends would turn away from her. She would be trapped in Damian's body forever.

The faint echo of bugles from the nearby military base broke the grim silence of the night. She listened to the haunting notes ring across the city, calling its wayward youth back into the base's secured border in time for the weeknight curfew.

It was nine o'clock. Twenty minutes of the new and

undisputed worst night of her life had just passed. *How many more to go?*

When she stuck the key to Damian's Rubicon into the ignition, the answer to that question became painfully clear. A lot more minutes of misery were about to be added to an already miserable night. Because she had no idea how to drive a stick shift.

Trekking through the city in the body of a sweaty, oversized boy hadn't been on Ricki's top ten list of things to do when settling down for the night.

It could've been worse, she supposed. At least he was in shape. And she wouldn't have to worry about being abducted by some homicidal perv on the prowl for his next body count. Only a fool with a death wish would try harassing the near two-hundred-pound mass of solid muscle she was hauling down Berkley Ave.

But what she wouldn't give for some hips.

After fifteen years of lumbering through life with nothing to swivel and even less to shake, her body had gone into shock when those strange things resembling curves first bullied their way out to the surface. Her legs, suddenly at the mercy of uncoordinated hips, hadn't known what to do with themselves. For most of freshman year, she couldn't make it down the hallway without them locking up on her, making her walk look less "sassy vixen" and more "dying robot." It took several sessions with Denise and months of practicing in front of a mirror before she was able to walk like she didn't need either a set of crutches or a good pair of orthopedic shoes. But at that moment, as she lurched gracelessly down the street, she was painfully aware that the dying robot had come back home to roost.

She tripped over her third soda can of the night.

They never should've taken that second drink. *One to begin it all, and one to end it? More like one to begin it and one to lock it in forever.* Her fist thumped against her temple, driving the thought from her head. *No!*

A passing car slowed long enough for the driver to peer fearfully at her before gunning the accelerator and racing away.

I'm not crazy! she wanted to shout at the retreating tail lights. *I'm just navigating through a crazy life, and my compass is cracked.*

She collapsed onto the sidewalk, drained of the will to go on. Go where? To a home that no longer belonged to her and to friends that wouldn't even recognize her? She looked down the hill, gazing across a city peppered with neon store signs and brightly lit streetlamps. In the distance, tiny figures traveled from shop to shop, oblivious to the forlorn figure watching them from miles away.

If that was her future, she'd really rather not go to it.

A set of blinding headlights crested the hill, cutting the town from view. She shielded her eyes and squinted against the glare. A white Kia Sorento sped toward her, shaking the ground with a rumbling thunder of rap music. Heads poked from the car, shouting, "Yo, D!"

Ricki barely had enough time to dive away from the curb before the car came to a screeching halt inches from the spot where she'd just been.

"You alright, D?"

Carefully lowering her arms from her head, she uncurled from the sidewalk.

Guillermo Espinoza gazed down at her from the car window. The Greene twins peeped over his shoulder. "Whassup?" he said.

She stood up, brushing dirt from her hair. "My ride left me," she muttered, avoiding eye contact.

Guillermo gave her a skeptical once-over. He exchanged a knowing look with Marcus Greene—almost sending Ricki into a panic—and commented back to her in Spanish.

She didn't know what he'd just said—nothing from Guillermo's foul mouth would ever make its way into Señora Torres's lesson plan—but the howling laughter from the driver's seat indicated it was a joke. At her expense, no doubt.

She forced an obligatory chuckle. "Yeah, whatever, Willie. You guys giving me a ride home, or what?"

The door swung open.

First test passed. Preparing to act out the most important scene of her life, she slid into the car and shut the door, closing herself in with a group of boys she'd never talked to for more than five minutes at a time. They were Damian's crowd, not hers, and she had a fifteen-minute ride home to convince them that she was one of them.

Loud, smelly, and obnoxious. The role of a lifetime.

The driver, Javier Ortega, twisted around to look at her. Pointing at the rip on her dirt-smeared shirt, he quipped, "Stop, drop, and roll, huh?" Everyone burst into laughter as the car pulled away from the curb and coasted up the street.

Let the opening act begin.

With an occasional grunt and well-timed belch in the appropriate places, Ricki's first foray into the world of boyhood went off without a hitch. Conversation stayed on girls, sports, and what each boy would eat if a bag with a million dollars fell from the sky. As long as she limited her responses to words of no more than two syllables, she was wholeheartedly embraced as the leader of the pack. If only her talk with Lindsey could've gone as smoothly.

After they dropped her off at Damian's house, she dashed over to her own yard and crawled up the trellis, hefting what felt like a ton of extra flesh up the side of the house. When she reached the window, she saw her body sitting at her desk, typing on the computer. She closed her eyes, blocking out the image. Seeing her body move without her in it would take some time getting used to.

Good thing you'll have all the time in the world.

Pulling herself together, she rapped on the glass.

Damian gaped at her. Glancing cautiously at the bedroom door, he hurried to let her in.

"Why didn't you answer the phone?" he hissed.

She rolled across the windowsill and tumbled onto the floor. "Couldn't. Lindsey took it. Where's Mike?"

"Either studying or trying to fake me out. Dude bum rushes me every time I leave the room." He shuddered. "The last time he caught me by the stairs, he tackled me and wouldn't let me go until I let him rub his foot in my hair." He ambled over to a beanbag and flopped down. "How do you live like this?"

"With a little blackmail and a whole lot of Gold Bond." She grabbed another beanbag and dragged it over to sit beside him. Keeping her voice low, she recounted her experiences of the evening, starting with waking up in Lindsey's house and ending with the unexpected ride home with Willie and Friends. By the end of her story, Damian looked overwhelmed.

"You left my car on the other side of town?"

"It was that or your transmission."

"You broke my phone?"

"No, Lindsey broke your phone. Get it straight."

"And you told her you were me?"

"Junior, would you calm down? Yeah, I told her, but she didn't believe me. Your supposed manliness is still intact."

"And you better make sure it stays that way," he grumbled. "I can't have folks finding out I'm running around as a girl, so you better keep it shut down from here on out. I mean it."

"Seriously, can you focus? On the totem pole of importance, don't you think we've got higher priorities than what 'folks' think? Like why we haven't switched back yet?"

"That's obvious," he replied. "We screwed up. Drinking that crap a second time either made these body flips permanent or made them last longer. Problem is, only time's going to tell us which one it is."

"I guess if I still have the urge to pass gas and scratch my crotch twenty-four hours from now, the answer will be pretty obvious, won't it?" she said.

"You've had it rough tonight, so I'm gonna let that one slide." He produced a notebook. "Since I've been stuck in here, I've been searching the net. Looking up stuff on body-switching potions and—"

"Hold up," she cut in. "How'd you get the password to my computer?"

"Seriously, can you focus?" he mimicked. He ignored her glare. "Anyway, I thought I might even find some info on that bottle, at least a picture or something. But there's nothing legit out there that'll help us."

"Of course not," she grumbled. "That would be too much like right."

"Exactly. So I started writing down details about every time our bodies switched. Where we were, what time, everything. It's always the same pattern: we fall asleep at the same time; we wake up and ride it out in each other's skin for a few minutes; we switch back. And the switches seem to last about a minute longer each time."

"Not this time."

"No, but except for the length of time, the whole pattern has been the same," he said. "It's making me think that these effects might not be permanent—they might just be *longer*. Because if drinking more of that stuff was going to scramble the formula and lock us in each other's body for good, I'm guessing it would've happened as soon as we took the drink. Maybe all we need to do is just wait for the effect to run its course."

"How long will that take?"

"No idea. The switches lasted an extra minute at a time before, but who knows what time frame we're working with now. Hours? Days? Weeks?"

"Weeks?" she said in a small voice. "But it was only a sip. How could a little sip have such a strong effect?"

"I'm hoping it can't, because sooner or later, there's got to be a point of no return."

Ricki frowned in confusion.

"A point where our spirit's been disconnected from our body so long that it won't go back," he explained.

Shivers frosted her spine. "Let's pray we're operating on hours."

Damian glanced at the clock. "If we are, we should flip back in another ten to fifteen minutes or so. And if it really *is* temporary, we've got to figure out a way to break the pattern before it becomes permanent. If we can throw things out of whack one good time, it might stop happening." He awkwardly brushed a piece of hair behind his ear and shuddered. "How do you deal with this mess every day?"

She gave him an unsympathetic shrug. "If we can't stop this thing, it'll be *your* hair, Junior. Figure it out. Now *focus*."

Glowering, he shoved the notebook at Ricki. "Here. I made a list of everything that might work."

She looked at the paper. A string of ideas flowed down the page, covering everything from the scientific (chemical neutralization) to the whimsical (wish ourselves back). "These are pretty good," she said, wondering if being in her body had raised his IQ an extra hundred points. "I'm impressed."

"Yeah, it's what happens when you live outside of Rocky World," he replied. "You get a mind that's actually grounded in reality."

"I'll give you a freebie and let that one slide," she sniffed. "You've earned it."

He cut his eyes at her and smiled.

If it hadn't come from her own face, she might've appreciated the gesture. Instead, it made her queasy. Her attention returned to the list. "What should we try first?"

"How about the first one—electric shock?"

"Huh-uh, I am not electrocuting myself. I'd suggest you go stick *your* finger in a light socket, but my body would be the one to get fried. So, next."

"You were born to be difficult, weren't you? I'm not talking about full-on electrocution. Just jolting our systems a little to make our minds wake up and get back home."

"Oh. Well, how're we going to do it?"

"Like this."

Before she could protest, Damian touched her arm. A sharp sting crackled, making her yell out in a mixture of pain and surprise and causing her arm to whip out and crack Damian across the bridge of his nose. His head flew back and struck the windowsill. A howl of agony escaped from him before Ricki shoved a pillow over his face to muffle the sound.

"It was just static shock," he groaned through the feathery barrier. "Why do you always have to be so dramatic?"

"You should've warned me," she said. "Well? Did it wake your mind up?"

"If I still have breasts, the answer is no."

She wanted to suggest they try the next item on the list, but the sound of her bedroom door slamming against the wall was the last thing Ricki heard before she was hefted to her feet and thrown across the room. Her stomach slammed into the edge of the computer desk. Doubled over, she landed on the floor and slid halfway under the bed. She felt as though her limbs had shattered into a dozen pieces. Resisting the urge to throw up, she weakly pushed up to her elbows.

A pair of hands grabbed the back of her shirt and dragged her across the room.

In a daze, she tried to speak, but the collar of her shirt pulled tautly against her windpipe, cutting off the ability to make a sound or even breathe. All she could see was the beige expanse of carpet sliding beneath her face. The edge of a passing DVD case scraped her cheek.

She gagged, digging her fingernails into the carpet.

Suddenly, she stopped moving. The grip on her shirt loosened, releasing the tension against her throat. She quickly scrambled in the opposite direction of the hands and made a beeline for the bedroom door, ignoring the screaming pain shooting through her sides. Once she reached the border of safety, she risked turning around.

Mike stood near her bed, a pillowcase pulled over his head. He stumbled blindly across the room, his body wrenching violently from side to side.

Damian clung to Mike's neck, his legs wrapped in a pretzel around Mike's shoulders. With the end of the pillowcase gripped tightly in both hands, he held on valiantly, twisting and weaving away from Mike's grasp. When Mike reached to the left, he dipped to the right, never relaxing his hold.

Ricki watched the odd rodeo dance in horrified fascination.

Damian locked eyes with her. "Run!"

It was enough to get her feet moving. She fled from the room, raced through the house, and left Damian to fend off the enraged bull once known as Mikey Ray.

There she was, exiled from her own house by a deranged brother having an identity crisis—*her* identity. And adding to Ricki's rotten string of luck was the fact that Damian's house key had fallen out of her pocket during the scuffle with Mike. There was no way she was going back for it. She valued her life.

With no place to go, she ended up in the backyard, sharing a cozy yet dirty spot with Domino in the back of his doghouse. After a short growl and a few tense sniffs, recognition had kicked in, and he'd welcomed her into his doggy domain with frenetic gusto, almost smothering her beneath his mop of a tongue. Huddled against his side, Ricki thought about Damian's list.

It was thorough but focused on ways for them to snap out of the switches, not how to stop the switching from happening altogether. Could it be stopped? She glanced at the watch on her wrist, snidely noting that Damian was the only boy she knew who needed three dials on a watch to tell time. Snuggling into Domino, she stared at the stars, her thoughts lost in a glimmering sea of lights as vast and unfathomable as the problem she faced.

Almost ten minutes passed, and Ricki finally blinked and opened her eyes to Mike's face. It was inches away from her own, distorted in anger and yelling nonsense about "lockdown" and her not seeing daylight until her grandkids were on Social Security. She let his voice become a hum in her ears, recognizing she had more important things to think about. The switch might not be permanent, but it was still happening, and it was lasting longer than before.

So whose turn is it to sleep first?

CHAPTER ELEVEN

"WOULD SOMEONE MIND PULLING THIS dagger out of my back?"

The four girls walking through Kirby's abandoned halls turned to Lindsey.

"What's in your back?" Yolanda asked, craning her neck. "I don't see anything."

"She said price tag," Teresa answered. "Check her collar—looks like something's sticking up."

Ricki hunched her shoulders and remained mute. The walk to rehearsal had gone so well, without the pesky little details of last night's melodrama coming out. *Keep your mouth shut, and she might let it drop.*

"I think she said dagger," Denise chimed in. "You said dagger, didn't you, Lindz?"

Everyone stopped walking except Ricki, whose legs couldn't seem to stop moving. The neon exit sign at the end of the hallway beckoned like a glowing angel of mercy calling her home from the gallows of death.

"Ricki, hold up!" Denise shouted.

She willed her feet to stop and reluctantly circled around, the soft swoosh of a guillotine playing through her mind. When she heard Yolanda demand, "Who stabbed you in the back?" it took every ounce of willpower not to make a final break for freedom.

"Ask Ricki," Lindsey said. "I'm guessing she's missing a knife or two."

All eyes swiveled her way. A breeze from the imaginary blade swished by her ear.

"I don't know what you mean," she offered lamely.

"Sure you do. The knife you left in my back last night when Damian told me about the feelings you guys have for each other."

The hall erupted.

"The *what*?" Yolanda and Denise screeched in unison.

Teresa staggered away, flinging her purse to the ground and collapsing onto a trash can. "It's over!" she cried. "Damian and Ricki are feeling each other up! Armageddon has come! Saint and sinner united. Man and beast as one. Dogs and cats living—"

Yolanda pulled a comb from her purse and hurled it at Teresa's head. "Would you hush?" she hissed. Pulling Lindsey and Ricki aside, she sat them against the wall. "Explain."

"She called Damian while he was at my house," Lindsey said. Her eyes shot venom at Ricki. "Right after he told me how he couldn't be with me because you guys have been messing around since Terry's party."

The air pressure in the hall dropped as Yolanda, Denise, and Teresa collectively sucked in their breaths.

"That's a lie," Ricki exclaimed.

"I know what I heard."

"You heard wrong! You're just twisting everything that was said around."

"So he did run back and report to you," Lindsey said, triumphant. "I knew it."

"Are you on something?" Ricki sputtered. "I've hated that boy my whole life. How could you think I'd all of a sudden be making out with him behind your back? Don't you even know me?" Her voice grew bitter. "Do I even know you?"

"What's that supposed to mean?"

"For one, how could Damian have been at your house last night when you were supposed to be at the movies with your sisters?" She looked at the other girls, hoping to shift the focus of their condemning eyes to Lindsey. "You mean you *lied* to us?"

"Oh...my...*word*, this is getting good," Teresa breathed. Raising her voice, she called out, "Lindsey, you mean to tell me you passed on a seventy-five percent off red clearance sale at Basement Barney's just so you could get your freak on with D-Dog? My dear, have you no priorities?"

"Will you get serious?" Yolanda snapped.

"I will when there's something to get serious about," Teresa retorted. "Ricki would never get down with Damian. Wires obviously got crossed somewhere. Case closed, pass the Haagen-Dazs."

"Yeah, Lindz, you know Ricki would never scam on you like that," Denise said. "Especially not with Damian."

"Except he also happened to think I was going to the movies with my sisters," Lindsey said. "Did any of you tell him that?"

Each girl shook her head.

"Which means Ricki's the one who told him. Plus, he recited the most embarrassing moment of my life that only she knows. Verbatim."

Rick saw a field of doubt blossom in Yolanda's eyes.

"And why'd her number show up on his cell?" Lindsey asked.

Panicking, Ricki blurted, "Michael called him." Her voice quivered.

Denise's brow wrinkled. The playful smirk dropped from Teresa's face. She slid from her trash can perch to stand beside Yolanda. The three girls gazed soberly down at Ricki.

"See?" Lindsey trumpeted. "She's been doing this all week.

Lying about calling him. Sneaking off to be with him during lunch, then having some lame excuse for what they were doing. Haven't they been spending a lot of time together lately?"

Teresa appeared thoughtful.

Ricki's heart thumped. She stared at Teresa, silently begging her to stay quiet about the trip with Damian to her house. Teresa stared back in question, and then looked away, a hurt expression on her face.

"And if he supposedly hates her so much, why would he claim they're dating?" Lindsey persisted. "Isn't that kind of strange?"

Their answering silence hung heavy in the hallway.

Ricki lowered her head, giving the guillotine a nice, clear path to her neck.

Denise broke the silence. "Nope. It's not."

Ricki's head shot up.

"It's no stranger than any of the stuff that goes on with them," Denise said. "You've only been in the mix for a couple of years, Lindz, so I can kind of understand you getting things twisted, but the rest of us are card-carrying survivors of the Ricki-Damian Chronicles. And *anything* you *ever* see between them is usually a setup for the next round of vicious, nasty, low-down cruelty they're about to inflict on each other. It's just their way; trust me."

Lindsey frowned. "But you didn't—"

"Look, Ricki would more likely eat a dead frog squished under a garbage truck than put her lips anywhere near Damian's body. And she'd never willingly spend time with him. If he says otherwise, you'd best believe he's lying."

Teresa nodded in agreement, but her eyes remained fixed on a distant spot across the hall.

Yolanda's gaze remained glued to Ricki.

"I know what I've been seeing," Lindsey said. "And I don't

care what she says, I know something's not right. I'm not as naïve as you guys think I am."

"Ain't that the truth," Ricki mumbled.

Lindsey's flush grew deeper. "Excuse me?"

"What'd you mean earlier, when you said Damian couldn't 'be' with you?" Ricki asked slyly. "What exactly was he doing at your house last night?" *Pass the chopping block.* "You couldn't possibly be talking about *sex*, could you? I mean, you haven't even been on one date, so there's *no way* you'd be taking it there with him, right?"

Lindsey looked trapped.

Ricki almost felt sorry for putting her business on blast, but turnabout was fair play.

Teresa nudged Lindsey's knee. "Hey, I was just joking about you getting your freak on with Damian. But, were you...uh, seriously trying to get your freak on? Like, already?"

Lindsey's eyes skipped around the circle, seeking escape. Finding no opening, they dropped. "How else can I compete?"

"Compete with who?"

"Her," she spat, jerking her head at Ricki. "And Kayleigh and Olivia and Evelyn and Aisha." She gave a humorless laugh. "Do we have an hour? Because that's about how long it'd take for me to list every single girl I'm up against. And that's just in this school. And they're all short and skinny, and he could get with any one of them he wants. How do I compete with that?"

Ricki stared in disbelief. "Have you seen you? There is no competition."

"Then why didn't he want to be with me last night?"

"I don't know. Maybe he wanted to take it slow? Having sex this early in the"—Ricki paused, gagging on the next word—"relationship would just mess everything up. He probably knew it was too soon."

"He's a guy," Lindsey said. "There's no such thing as too soon."

"True," Denise muttered.

"But if you give it up, what incentive does he have to stick around to get to know you?" Ricki asked.

Lindsey shook her head. "What incentive does he have now?"

"Gee, I don't know, your personality?"

"Not enough," Lindsey declared, standing up. "He said he's not looking for a girlfriend, so if I want to change his mind, now's the time to step it up."

"But you've only been talking to him for, like, a week," Ricki said, appalled.

"Exactly, and he's already losing interest. How pathetic is that?"

"So you think sexing him up will change his mind?" Ricki's lip curled. "What's the motto—spread your legs; keep a boy?"

Lindsey whipped around, almost knocking Denise over.

Yolanda stepped in, placing a protective hand on Lindsey's shoulder and frowning down at Ricki. "You need to pull it back."

Teresa let out a nervous cough. "Yeah, um, I think our time is way up."

Eager to release the words that had been building in her since the previous night, Ricki stood up. "Don't talk to me— talk to her," she told Yolanda, pointing at Lindsey. "She's the one who throws herself at every boy who gives her the teensiest bit of attention, but *I'm* in the wrong? How about instead of checking *me,* you tell *her* that she doesn't have to sacrifice her body just to get a boy to pay attention to her for more than two hours. How about that?"

"Here comes the self-righteous," Yolanda said in exasperation. "Just save it."

"Right," Lindsey said, "because we all know your tune will be different when Aaron starts losing interest. If he hasn't already."

"My tune would never change," Ricki said, arms crossing. "You know I'm not having sex until I get married."

"Of course you're not," Yolanda replied. "It's always easy to 'just say no' when no one ever asks you."

Teresa gasped.

Denise slid to Ricki's side. "Not cool, Yolanda."

"I'm just being real," Yolanda said. "How's she going to judge folks when she ain't even been alone with a boy before?"

"Isn't that kind of funny?" Lindsey added, leeching courage from Yolanda. "Lecturing me about keeping my legs closed when no one's ever tried to open hers?" She tossed her head. "What're you going to do, Ricki, when Aaron gets restless?"

Ricki looked down, hurt but unable to deny the raw truth behind their words. "I don't know what you mean," she replied weakly.

"Restless," Lindsey repeated. "Bored. Aaron's a big boy just like Damian, and he'll want to do more than just gaze into your eyes and give butterfly kisses. You knew that, right?"

She had no response.

Lindsey strolled away. "Just remember, there are a lot of girls that want to be with him. And they'll give up whatever, whenever, to make it happen. So maybe instead of making nasty comments about my choices, you should start taking notes." With those words lingering behind her, she disappeared through the exit.

"That went well," Teresa mumbled. Handing Yolanda her comb, she peered sideways at Ricki. "Is there maybe something you want to say to clear everything up? 'Cause now would be a pretty good time to trust us."

You wouldn't believe me, Terry. No more than Lindsey did.
Swimming in misery, Ricki shook her head.

Teresa ran her fingers across her Mohawk and said in a
chilly voice, "Then there's nothing more to ask." Spinning
around, she followed Lindsey's path out of the school.

Yolanda's hawk eyes were trained on Ricki. Shaking her
head, she slipped the comb into her purse and departed, her
silence speaking more loudly than any words of rebuke.

Denise's arm slid around Ricki's shoulder. "It'll be okay,
girl. They just need a breather. Then they'll realize how silly
they're acting. But maybe it'd be a good idea to steer clear of
Damian for a little while."

She clung to Denise's hand. "I wish I could, Denny. I
really do."

"And why can't you?"

She looked over Denise's shoulder. "Because he's coming
this way."

Damian approached, bringing five soccer players, three
groupies, and the team mascot with him. And Aaron.

Aaron looked at Ricki for only a millisecond before
directing his attention to a spot two feet above her head.
She waved but might as well have been shooing a bug away.
A groupie with a layered, platinum-blonde bob grabbed his
shirt sleeve and giggled, smirking as she snaked an arm around
his waist.

Ricki's heart sank.

"Rocky, gotta talk to you," Damian announced, pulling
away from the group.

She stared at Aaron for a few more heartbroken beats,
then dragged her eyes over to Damian. She did a double take.

He limped toward her, supporting the left side of his body
with an arm covered in scratches. An ugly red whelp slashed
across his neck to a jaw tattooed with purple bruises. Ricki

was comforted to know that while she had been left to deal with the emotional fallout from last night's events, he'd at least suffered the physical one.

She poked Denise. "I know I suck for asking, but can you cover for me at practice? Just a few minutes, and I'll be right there."

Denise wrinkled her nose at Damian. "Huh-uh. No way I'm feeding the paranoia by walking up in there without you. Handle your business, and I'll go wait with the guys until you're done." Giving Damian a critical once-over, she sashayed away.

Ricki leaned back to examine Damian. "You bruise easy."

"Yeah, something about your rabid brother and even more rabid dog leaves a lasting impression, I guess."

"Domino did some of that to you?"

"About two seconds after I flipped back to my body. I didn't even have time to figure out where I was before that dumb dog tore into me."

She held in a laugh. It was poetic justice—payback for Damian trying to train his own dog to attack her on sight years back. Fortunately for her, Columbus had the body of a full-grown Rottweiler but the soul of a puppy. Instead of mauling her to the ground at the sound of his attack word, he would assault her with doggy kisses until Domino arrived to chase him off. In retaliation, she had trained Domino to pee in Damian's soccer cleats anytime they were left on his porch. She'd always considered soggy sneakers a fair exchange for a soggy face, but the sight of a mutilated Damian was so much better.

Fighting giggles, she said, "I thought I heard a scream right after we switched back, but I assumed it was my imagination. Wow. You scream like a little girl."

"When this is over, I'll make sure *you* scream like a little girl," he grumbled. "But right now, we need to talk about this whole staying-awake-for-the-rest-of-our-life thing."

Sleep deprivation. Item number one on her own list of ways to stop the body swaps, alongside divine intervention, spells, system flushes, and every other idea she could write down before Mike stormed the bedroom for one last lecture. The only thing she'd refused to put on the list was kissing—opting instead to scribble 'death,' which seemed a less painful alternative.

"Good, you got my email. I wasn't sure I had the right address." She snuck a tortured glance at Aaron. "I know you changed it a few times after that whole web subscription misunderstanding."

"I don't think I misunderstood you signing me up to every porn site on the net," he said. "I don't think my mother misunderstood it either when she signed on to my account and saw pictures of chickens—"

"Bygones," she cut in. She chanced another peek at Aaron. He leaned over the blonde, grinning as she whispered in his ear.

Ricki couldn't help but stare. *Why would he like her? That chick's two bleach jobs away from permanent hair loss. It's like she has a mop of fried straw on her head.*

Damian's body slid in front of her, cutting Aaron from view.

Blinking, she refocused on the conversation. "Okay, so why don't you think staying awake will work?"

A blurry cloud of red hair and Axe body spray raced by. It paused to heft a squealing Denise over its shoulder and took off toward the exit.

Denise, bobbing in the air and clutching a handful of Marco Downing's hair, yelled, "Five minutes, Ricki! Ten, tops!"

The doors clanged shut.

Damian scowled after them. "Would somebody go get that fool?" he barked.

Three players jumped to attention, taking off after Marco. To Ricki's dismay, Aaron wasn't one of them. His attention remained wrapped up in the bleached Bratz doll.

Damian watched her watching Aaron, then frowned. "Aaron!"

Aaron looked up. "What?"

"Go after them. Make sure nobody gets lost." His arms folded. "Matter of fact, everybody bounce. I'll catch up in a minute."

For the second time that morning, Aaron looked at Ricki.

She crashed against the thunderstorms brewing in his eyes before they went disturbingly blank.

He cocked his head at Damian. "Sure, whatever." He headed to the door, the blonde succubus still attached to his side.

You're losing him. Desperation crept into Ricki's mind. *You only got him interested in you for a second, and you're already losing him.* "Hey, Aaron!" she called out.

He slowly turned to her.

Painting a friendly smile on her face, she trotted up to him. "I wasn't sure if you're still interested in doing something tonight. Do you still have my number?"

He glanced at Damian. "Yeah. I got your number." With a dismissive nod, he walked away.

She watched him go, melting into a puddle of self-pity. It seemed all she'd done that morning was watch people she cared about walk away from her. First, her friends. Now, Aaron. Could she make them come back?

"Ready to focus now?" Damian said from behind her.

Setting her resolve, she faced him. "Junior, I'm ready for anything that'll fix this mess. Whatcha got?"

"I'm telling you, *Freaky Friday* was a movie, not a book."

Ricki groaned. "You really are illiterate, aren't you? Reading is fundamental for a reason. It was a book that was made into a movie."

"Whatever," Damian said. "I'm still not letting you turn my life into a Disney flick. No wishing."

"But it was your idea in the first place!"

"Yeah, but then I realized I've wished you out of my life at least a thousand times, and you're still here. I obviously don't have the magic touch." His finger ran down the piece of paper. "And going to a priest is dumb, so scratch that one off too."

"You can't keep shooting everything down, Junior," she argued. "You already crossed off the system flush."

"I just had the stomach flu last month. There's no way I'm making myself puke and have the runs on purpose. Why don't you try it and let me know how it turns out?"

"Only if you try getting hit by lightning," she snapped. "If you're ten feet underground, I won't have anyone to switch with and can finally sleep in peace. So, please, kill yourself. Take one for the team."

He let out an evil chuckle. "Hey, book freak, I got a good one for you. How about *He's Just Not That Into You*? Try reading it, then wishing you don't turn Aaron off every time he looks at you."

Gut punch.

She inhaled sharply, picturing Aaron cuddled up with the groupie. The sting of tears tickled her eyes. "You are such a foul toad," she mumbled, her voice thick.

Damian grew serious. "Maybe you just bring out the best in me," he said, almost apologetic. He examined the paper. "I guess we could try wishing."

She picked at her fingernails, waiting for the mist over her eyes to clear before looking up. "What about system flush?"

"Only if wishing and sleep dep don't work." He frowned. "And why should sleep dep work?"

"Because I looked up stuff on sleep and its cycles." She sat down. "I read that sleep cycles have about four or five stages, starting with drowsiness or a light sleep and ending with REM. REM's the deepest level of sleep, when we usually dream."

He joined her on the floor. "Okay, I'm following."

"Well, some cultures think a dream is actually the act of a person's spirit leaving the body and going to another realm. Kind of like how *our* spirits are leaving our bodies while we're asleep, but instead of visiting another realm, they're visiting another body. And it must be happening during the REM cycle, when dreams occur."

"So?"

"So we're switching when we both hit REM at the same time. But what if we never hit REM? Maybe if we can go more than twenty-four hours without sleep and totally bypass the dream cycle, we'd break the pattern. Or instead of the potion's effects getting stronger every time we switch, maybe it'll get weaker every time we don't."

"Could be a plan," he conceded, "but saying we're going to stay awake and actually *staying* awake are two different things. It's not getting harder for you to stay awake when I'm sleeping? 'Cause it's hell for me to stay up when you're asleep."

"That's why we have backup ideas." She stood up. "Wishing time. Hurry up before Denise gets back."

He groaned. "Rocky, this is stupid."

"You're stupid. C'mon, you said you would do it."

Grumbling, he pushed himself to his feet. "Now what?"

She pointed to the paper. "Line six."

Peering at the sheet, he read aloud, "I wish for my spirit to stay in my body for the rest of eternity or at least until death?"

"Exactly, except with more feeling. And we need to say it at the same time."

Checking to make sure they were still alone in the hall, he stood in front of her. He squinted in concentration, his face scrunched so tightly that he appeared to be under siege by the world's foulest gas bomb.

She snorted. "This is the infamous look that raises a girl's pulse and drops her panties?"

His face relaxed. A devilish glint appeared in his eyes. "Nope. This is."

Without warning, his face swooped toward hers. She tried to step back, but his hands shot out and held her in place. His gaze locked onto hers, the dark moons of his pupils intensifying on contact.

Her body began to tingle.

His eyelids drooped sensuously, his gaze deepening.

Fire stirred in Ricki's belly. With each second, she felt herself being sucked into the bottomless pits opened before her. Two small windows, leading to an infinite cavern too dangerous for her to explore.

A hypnotic rhythm pulsed between them.

Confused, she yanked her arms away and stumbled backward. Her stomach flipped in erratic somersaults, competing with the light spinning of her head.

Chuckling, Damian straightened up. His eyes became harmless once again. "Tell the difference?"

Putting more distance between them, Ricki composed herself. *What the heck was that?* "You looked constipated," she said, letting out a shaky laugh. "Maybe we need to start with the system flush after all."

He gave her a knowing smile. "Whatever you say, Rocky."

Approaching him with caution, she hesitantly returned her gaze to his eyes. "Just say line six, okay?"

They repeated the wish.

After a few seconds, Damian asked, "Feel any different?"

She really couldn't say—her head hadn't stopped spinning. "I don't know. Do you?"

He rubbed his forehead. "Nope. I guess we're going with sleep dep."

"Okay, we'll aim for as long as we can, but no less than twenty-four hours."

"Deal." He picked up his bag. "And remember: you don't tell *anybody* about what's happening. I'm not saying it again. You tell anyone, I ruin your life. And since there's a possibility I'll be back in your body, the different methods available for wrecking you are endless."

"Please," she huffed. "Like I'd want anyone knowing I've been inside *that* flesh. But we need to avoid being seen together from now on. No accosting me in the Lunchyard. No running into me on the way to practice. You don't want anyone to know you're spending time in my body, and I don't want anyone to know that I even acknowledge your existence. Agreed?"

He grinned. "Most definitely."

"Good." Ricki felt a tingle of hope. As long as she stayed away from Damian, she might be able to smooth things over with Lindsey and Aaron.

The school doors opened, admitting a tousled Denise. She brushed past Damian to give Ricki a hug. "Everything's going to be okay," she burbled. "We're having a sleepover at Terry's house tonight." She beamed at Damian. "And you're invited."

CHAPTER TWELVE

"TELL ME AGAIN HOW MANY laws you broke to make Mike let me out of the house?"

"No written ones," Denise quipped, her fingers tapping along with the beat blasting from the car stereo. "I just had Terry's good ole Granny talk to him on your behalf. You'd have to be all kinds of heartless to say no to a sweet, little old lady."

Ricki checked her makeup in the car mirror, trying not to think of the reception awaiting her at Teresa's house. If the attitudes thrown her way during rehearsal were any indication of the evening to come, it was about to be one long, lonely night.

"Stop worrying," Denise said. "I talked to the girls. Marco talked to Aaron. It's all breezy from here."

Ricki pulled out a tube of lip gloss and nervously reapplied it for the third time. Maybe it wouldn't be so bad. After all, spending the night with her friends would keep her awake a whole lot better than sitting home alone in front of the TV.

If they bother to talk to you, that is.

She applied a fourth coat.

When they arrived at the Ma estate, walking into the family room made Ricki feel like a stuffed hen tossed into a den of starving foxes. Yolanda snuggled in a love seat with Emille. Teresa presided over what looked to be an intense game of poker with Damian, Marco, and some boy Ricki assumed was her date. And Lindsey reclined on the couch, talking to Aaron. The second Ricki's foot crossed the threshold, every person in the room stopped what they were doing and turned their hungry eyes on her.

Her steps faltered.

Denise shouldered past her. "Hola, my peeps!" she sang. "The delicious divas are here. Let's get the party started!"

Teresa sprang up from the table and rushed over to hug Ricki. "I'm sorry, sweetie," she said. "We were trippin'. Blame it on hormones and indigestion. Bygones?"

Ricki released a relieved breath. "Bygones."

Teresa gave her an exaggerated kiss on the cheek, then whirled around to face the room. "Movie time!" she announced, dancing over to the entertainment center. A discreet foot shot out to kick Yolanda as she two-stepped past the snuggling couple.

Yolanda disentangled herself from Emille and approached Ricki. "You know we were stuck on stupid, right?" she offered.

Ricki hid a slight grin. "Are you ever *not*?"

"Bygones," Yolanda said, hugging her.

Lindsey waited for Yolanda to leave before coming to stand humbly in front of Ricki. A harsh flicker of resentment in her eyes contradicted her contrite demeanor. She leaned in to hug Ricki. "I'm glad Aaron's here for you," she said softly. "Just like Damian's here for me. Everything's the way it should be, and I really hope it stays that way. Bygones?"

Was that an apology or a warning? Ricki stepped back, giving her a cautious smile. "Sure."

Lindsey walked away, stopping beside Damian. She leaned over his shoulder under the pretense of looking at his cards and kissed him on the cheek. Damian, his eyes not leaving the table, gave her a pat on the head and gestured for another card. She smiled with satisfaction, peering back at Ricki.

He could set her house on fire, and she'd still forgive him as long as he gave her cookies and milk afterwards, Ricki thought sourly. She turned away and found Aaron still watching her from across the room.

He waved.

Denise appeared behind her. "Go get him," she whispered, nudging her toward Aaron with a not-so-gentle push to the back.

Ricki was halfway across the room before her brain connected with her feet. Her footsteps slowed, but a flash of Lindsey's blonde hair reminded her of how close she'd already come to losing Aaron to the competition. Blow it now, and she'd be back to scouring the net for daily horoscopes and living vicariously through historical romance novels well into her geriatric years.

Folding her arms to hide her trembling hands, she sat on the opposite end of the sofa. "Hi."

He gave her a lopsided grin. "What'd you say?"

"Hi," she repeated louder.

He shook his head, his eyes lazily drinking her in. "Nope, still can't hear you."

"The girl said hi!" Damian boomed from the poker table.

The grin fell from Aaron's face. He twisted around in his seat. "D, what game you playing?"

Damian glanced up from shuffling the cards. "You know we're playing poker, man."

"Then how 'bout playing it?"

Scowling, Damian turned back to the table.

Aaron looked at Ricki, the smile back in place. "Why're you so far away? I can't hear you from all the way over there."

Growing warm, she scooted closer to him. "Is this better?"

His arm slid around the back of the sofa until his fingers tickled the edge of her shoulder. "Nope."

Inching closer, she stopped within the border of his arm, which then dropped onto her shoulder.

"Hello," he said.

She let out a wheezing giggle.

"I'm glad we could hook up tonight." His fingers brushed lightly against her neck. "I didn't really get a chance to talk to you before practice. I thought you were mad at me."

She was astonished. "You did?"

"Yeah. You spent the whole time talking to D. I felt neglected."

"Really? But you were in pretty deep conversation yourself," she stammered.

He frowned. "Was I?"

Of course you were! With the peroxide puppet who looked like she was about to shove her tongue down your throat! "I think so," she replied tactfully.

He still appeared lost.

"Some blonde girl?" she prompted. "Over by the wall, when everyone went after Marco and Denise? It looked a little intense."

"Oh," he said, comprehension finally making an appearance. "You mean Mitzi."

Mitzi. Figures. "Yeah, I guess. She's a pretty good friend of yours?"

He shrugged. "Hardly know her. She likes one of our boys on the team, so she's trying to get in good with me to get to him. I was trying to get rid of her so you and I could maybe get to know each other a little better, but she wouldn't get the hint." His tone became injured. "But after I saw how tight things were with you and D, I figured you didn't want to talk to me anyway."

Why did his words paint a different picture than the one in her memory? Her mind replayed the entire scene from that morning. She wanted to figure out the answer, but the sensation of his fingers stroking her neck was having the craziest effect on her ability to think. Coherent thoughts rapidly jumped ship as his thumb drew circles at the base of her chin. Her eyes traveled the path from his fingers to his face and met with a hungry stare. All reason was abandoned.

"I'm sorry," she breathed.

"It's all good. I've got your attention now." His face moved closer to hers.

A pack of cards whizzed through the air and smacked Ricki across the temple.

"Damian!" Lindsey exclaimed.

"Break it up." Damian sauntered over to plop down beside Ricki and Aaron. "It's movie time, and you're hogging the good seats." Ignoring the danger sign flashing in Ricki's eyes, he settled into the sofa, spreading his legs so wide they were almost on top of hers. "Lindsey, can you bring some popcorn over here? Extra butter."

"D, we weren't done with this hand," Marco protested.

"Yeah, we were. I win."

Ricki shoved Damian's leg away and scooted as far away from him as she could without actually crawling onto Aaron's lap. "Would you go somewhere else?"

Smacking his lips in contentment, he accepted a bag of popcorn from a clearly disgruntled Lindsey. "What's on the big screen tonight, Teresa?"

Teresa, buried amid an island of Blu-ray cases, frowned. "Dunno. I think we need a vote. I know the guys won't go for romance—" She stuck out her tongue at the loud grumbles and boos from the boys in the room. "So we're left with horror or action."

"Horror," Aaron, Marco, and Lindsey called out.

"Action," Ricki and Damian answered in unison.

Ricki clenched her jaw. "I mean horror."

"You hate horror movies," Damian mumbled smugly.

"What are you even doing here?" she hissed under her breath. "Lindsey was supposed to be through with you after last night."

"We worked it out. You know I can't have a female hating on me."

"You don't seem to care that *I* hate you."

His eyes cut to her chest. "I said female."

"Ha freakin' ha. You're so funny, I may actually remember to laugh sometime next year." She turned to Aaron. "Want to sit closer to the TV?"

"I was just thinking the same thing," he said, giving Damian a satisfied smirk. Taking her hand, he led the way to an oversized papasan chair just big enough for the two of them.

Teresa finished tallying the votes. "Horror, it is!"

Ricki grimaced. She hated horror movies.

Teresa rummaged through the movie pile until her fingers closed on a random case. "Lights out!"

Damian stood up.

"Careful on the way back," Aaron remarked. "Don't trip on a piece of lint and bust a hip."

Shooting a middle finger at him, Damian crossed the room to flip the light switch. On his way back through the darkness, his footsteps were suddenly replaced by a loud thump and the sound of furniture slamming into the wall. A string of curse words followed just as the television screen lit up to illuminate his crumpled body at the base of the poker table.

Marco and Aaron erupted into laughter.

With battered dignity, he pulled himself to his feet and limped around the edge of the sofa. He slid beside Lindsey, cradling his knee.

Marco raised his voice above Aaron's laughter. "D, you've been getting hurt all week. It's like you have a death wish or something."

Ricki snorted. "And yet here he is, still breathing. Can't do anything right, huh, Junior?"

"Let me look at your face," he fired back. "That ought to get the job done."

She bristled.

"Teresa, skip the previews," Yolanda ordered. "The only scrapping I want to see is up on that plasma. I swear, y'all need to argue almost as much as you need air."

Lindsey scowled at the television.

Five minutes into the movie, Ricki felt Aaron's arm slide around her waist. He pulled her against his chest. She allowed herself to relax into the warmth of his body, his coldness of that morning easily forgotten. It didn't take long for her to lose track of what was happening on the screen, each of her senses too immersed in Aaron. Her ears zoned in on his breath over the shouts from the surround sound. Her nose filled with the scent of his cologne instead of popcorn butter. And her eyes were mesmerized by sight of his fingers resting on her arm.

It was a fantasy come true.

"What're you thinking?" he whispered in her ear.

"Nothing," she lied. "Just watching the movie."

"Want to know what I'm thinking?"

She was afraid to speak. "Hmm?"

"How sexy you look. And how good you smell." His nose traced tiny circles around the rim of her ear. "Do you know how soft your skin is?"

Her brain was almost on overload. "It is?" she croaked.

He shifted, both arms enveloping her waist. "Yeah," he murmured. "Your skin is so sexy. It's smooth and dark, like a chocolate bar. Every time I see you, all I think about is what it'd be like to unwrap you."

His lips lowered to her neck.

A popcorn bag flew across the room and collided with the side of Ricki's head, landing in her lap. Hot popcorn kernels stuck in her hair, buttery goo running down the side of her leg. She vaulted out of Aaron's lap.

"My bad," Damian called out.

"Are you crazy?" she yelled, swiping at the mess on her jeans. Pieces of popcorn rained from her hair, leaving a grease trail down her cheeks.

Teresa jumped up to turn on the lights while Yolanda and Denise ran for paper towels.

Lindsey rounded on Damian. "Why did you do that?"

"Seriously, man, what are you doing?" Aaron demanded.

"No harm meant," Damian said, a picture of unruffled innocence in the face of a hostile mob. "I thought Rocky was falling asleep."

"What do you care if she falls asleep?" Lindsey shrieked. "Let her sleep!"

"Things could go bad if she sleeps tonight," he said. "Right, Rocky?"

Accepting a handful of paper towels from Yolanda, Ricki covertly studied his face for signs of foul play. He smiled back, giving nothing away.

"Why would things go bad?" Yolanda asked.

She wiped at her jeans, unsure of how to respond.

"Ricki?" Lindsey prompted.

"She's a snorer," Damian volunteered. "Loud. So loud, I can hear her all the way across the yard. Isn't that right, Rocky?"

Her eyes widened in mortification and shifted to Aaron. Trapped, she halfheartedly nodded.

Aaron's face darkened. "D, lemme holler at you for a minute."

The two boys retreated to a far corner of the room.

Denise walked over to Ricki and Yolanda. "Yolanda, will you go hold Lindsey's hand for a sec? She looks like she's about to implode, and you're so good at talking her down."

Eyeing her and Ricki with open suspicion, Yolanda shoved the wad of paper towels at Denise and stalked away.

Pretending to focus on a stubborn grease stain, Denise whispered, "What's the deal?"

Ricki grimaced. "Smell my hair and ask me that question again."

"No need; the congealed butter highlights speak volumes," she deadpanned. "I'm talking about Damian. I busted heinie all day getting everyone on the same page about you two, and he's blown it all to hell in less than an hour. What's up with that?"

"I'm sorry, have you met Demon Spawn? It's his classic MO—ruin any chance of happiness in my life at all costs."

"Huh-uh. The vibe is different, and everyone can tell. Why do you think Lindsey looks like she's on the verge of tears?"

"Maybe because she's stuck with the Unholy Offspring as a date?" Ricki suggested. "That thought alone would make anyone cry, don't you think?"

Denise's lips pursed. "Don't even try it. Ricki, we all know you don't snore. And Damian also promised to be on good behavior tonight, but all he's done is mess with you and Aaron."

"Please," Ricki sniffed. "A dog can promise not to scratch its own butt, but it'll still take a good swipe if the itch is strong enough. It can't fight its nature, and Spawn's nature is to be a pain in *my*—"

"Movie time is back on," Damian announced, strolling

away from a sullen Aaron. Beckoning to Lindsey, he fell backward into the sofa and gave a lazy stretch. "Where'd we leave off?"

Aaron woodenly made his way back to the papasan.

Ricki squeezed onto the chair beside him, trying to wriggle into his arms, but he turned his back to her.

The rest of the evening passed in tense silence.

Ricki tried to recreate the magic of their earlier moment, but every time she spoke, Aaron responded with short answers. By the end of the movie, she wanted to scream in frustration.

What did Damian say to him?

She glanced over her shoulder to glare at the perpetrator in question but was instead caught by Lindsey watching, hawk-like, from her perch on Damian's lap. Pretending to scratch her chin on her shoulder, Ricki looked away.

After the movie ended, it was time for the boys to leave. With a stiff peck on the cheek and a stilted hug, Aaron was out the door and down the walkway, leaving Ricki with memories of a first date that started with the promise of explosive fireworks and ended with a soggy fizzle. By the time he disappeared down the driveway, she already wondered if the night had even happened.

A rustle of paper in her pocket caught her attention.

She reached inside and pulled out a small note. Unfolding it, she saw a sloppily scribbled phone number followed by the message:

> Call me so we can do things right
> next time. Without the bodyguard.

Aaron's initials at the bottom sent her heart pounding. Squealing, she ran to show the note to the other girls, swept up in a delirium of excitement.

Too bad the excitement couldn't keep her from falling asleep.

———◦⟡◦———

"You couldn't stay awake, could you?"

Ricki sat in Damian's room, experiencing the bizarre sensation of being chastised by her own voice over the telephone. "What do you mean, *me* stay awake?" she said. "You must've fell asleep too, or we wouldn't be where we are."

"Whatever," Damian said. "Fact is, now I'm stuck in your body in a house full of females. How do I pull this off?"

She glanced at the clock. "It's almost three in the morning. What's there to pull off? Just ride it out while everyone's still asleep."

"But what if someone wakes up and wants to talk about their dreams?" he whined mockingly. He chuckled—a sure sign to Ricki that his next words would be something she wouldn't like. "What dream should I say you had? Something about Aaron? Something wet and nasty?"

She knew him too well.

"Things were looking kinda smoky between you two," he prodded. "So...what should I tell them?"

"That every single time we got close, your trifling behind ruined it."

"Really? I didn't realize my timing was so off. I guess you guys were really getting to know each other, huh?" He paused. "What'd you learn?"

"Excuse me?"

"While you were getting close, what'd you learn? You got a lot in common?"

She started to respond but found herself stumped.

"No? Then I guess you were talking about how your day went."

Again, no response came to mind.

"Oh, I get it," he said cryptically. "It was *that* kind of getting close."

"What do you mean, '*that*?'"

"Y'know, the kind that doesn't need conversation beforehand." He chuckled again. "Or afterward."

"We actually had a really nice conversation," she said, annoyed. "You know, the art of conversing? That thing you can't do without someone's hand up your butt, moving your lips?"

"About what? I'm all ears."

What *did* they talk about? Her skin? "Mitzi. We talked about Mitzi."

"Sounds deep," he said dryly.

"Oh, shut up."

"Touchy, huh?" He clicked his tongue in mock admonishment. "Alright, I'll let you off the hook. On the serious tip, I think we need to go back to sleep. It might reverse things."

She relaxed. "Okay, but how're you going to fall asleep with all my friends around you?"

"I'm a man. I can sleep anywhere, anytime, with anyone."

"Or anything," she muttered.

"Obviously not," he countered. "I wouldn't 'hit' you with a baseball bat."

"Please. Like you could—" The phone went dead on the other end. "Hello? Junior?"

She stared at the receiver. Had he just hung up on her or had someone hung up for him? She lay back on Damian's bed.

Sleep, she chanted silently to herself. *Sleep*.

And, surprisingly, she did.

Ricki later awoke in a small, empty bedroom, alone but wearing the right skin. The wall clock read 5:26 AM. Almost two-and-a-half hours had passed since her talk with Damian.

When she stepped into the hallway, she almost tripped

over her overnight bag. Her things were haphazardly crammed into its pockets, spilling onto the floor. Kicking the bag aside, she walked to the other end of the hall, to the room where her friends slept.

It was locked.

She knocked, but no one answered. She knocked again, harder. Giving up, she sank to the floor and waited. After what seemed like an hour, Teresa opened the door. Mumbling a rushed greeting, she stepped over Ricki and hurried down the hall. The other girls stirred from their beds, pretending not to see her in the doorway.

She received the silent treatment for the rest of the morning.

The ride home was uncomfortable. Denise had nothing to say, and Ricki was too scared to ask why.

It wasn't until they pulled up in front of Ricki's house that Denise spoke. "We're going to talk. Not now, because I need to take care of something. But I'll be back this afternoon, so be ready to explain to me what got into you last night. And make me believe it." She then sped away, leaving Ricki with an impossible mission: find out what had happened in the three hours Damian had controlled her body and then figure out a way to explain it.

But the afternoon came, and she was still clueless. The only thing she did know was that nobody would take her calls. And Damian? Nowhere to be found. When the candy-red Mustang pulled into her driveway, she still wasn't sure what she would say. But one look at Denise, and she stopped wondering.

Ricki couldn't remember the last time her friend's skin had seen the light of day without a good barrier of foundation and powder to block out the sun, but her face was scrubbed clean. Her hair was pulled back into a tight, frizzy braid. And the body that repelled clothing like a raincoat shunned water was hidden beneath a grubby T-shirt and sweatpants. She had hit the rocky bottom of the fashion scale.

But she still looks better than me on a good day.

Ricki led the way in silence to her bedroom. Once inside, she asked, "Are you okay? You look really...tired."

Smiling thinly, Denise sat at the edge of the bed. "I feel like crap. Me and Marco broke up this morning. Just tears and drama. All the nonstop crying has given me a serious headache."

Ricki handed her a stuffed unicorn to snuggle. "He took it that bad, huh?"

"Yeah!" she huffed. "And I swear, if he calls me one more time blubbering about how our love was meant to be, I'm gonna slap a restraining order on his whiny behind. I mean, seriously, man up."

The two girls looked at each other and burst into giggles.

Reaching out, Denise grabbed Ricki's hand and pulled her onto the bed. They lay back, shoulder to shoulder, staring into the tranquil gray space overhead.

"What's going on?" she asked quietly.

Ricki gazed into the gray nothingness, gathering her thoughts. She took a deep breath, released it, and let the jumble of words swimming through her mind find their way out of her mouth. "What if I told you the bottle I found at Teresa's house wasn't a love potion?" she asked. "What if I found out it was actually a body-switching potion, and both me and Damian accidentally drank it? And now we keep switching places with each other every time we fall asleep?"

Denise's head rolled in her direction. She stared until Ricki began to squirm, then grinned. "I'd say that explains a lot."

Ricki blinked. "Huh?"

She sat up. "It totally makes sense now. You acting weird

in rehearsal. All the secrecy between you and Damian. Last night."

"You believe me? Really?"

Denise pinched her leg. "Of course I believe you. I'm your best friend. I stood in line with you for three hours just so you could get your fortune read. I even tried to hunt Aaron down for you so you could spike the boy's drink with something a bunch of middle schoolers dug out of the ground. How could you think I wouldn't believe you?"

Ricki was humbled. And ashamed. The one person she should've turned to all along was the last person she'd decided to trust. "Because no one else would?"

Denise tensed. "Oh, so you mean you've told other people, just not me?" She jumped up from the bed.

"Hey, no, it's not at all like that. It's just..."

And so Ricki told her everything. All the way back to the moment she'd drunk the spiked punch and ending with her falling asleep at Teresa's sleepover. She lost track of time as everything she'd gone through over the past week came pouring out. Denise listened, never interrupting or looking at her as though she'd lost her mind. And the more Denise listened, the more Ricki found she had to say.

By the time she finished talking, Denise was staring at her in amazement. "Wow. Just...wow. I knew something weird was going on with you, but there's no way I'd have imagined it'd be something like *this*." She nodded in sober understanding. "What can I do to help?"

A flood of emotions swept over Ricki. Gratitude. Wonder. Regret. Denise had always stood by her side, something she'd taken for granted in the good times and abandoned as soon as things got bad. But what were best friends for if not to lean on when life made you too weak to stand on your own?

"You're the best, Denny," she said thickly. "But all I need

right now is a ride over to Mildred's Curio. I need ingredients for a curse-breaking spell I found in some old book in the Ma library, but I can't reach Damian."

Denise rolled her eyes. "I'm not surprised."

"About that," she ventured, afraid to ask the question she knew had to be asked. "What exactly did *I* do last night?"

"Are you sure you want to know?"

"Not really. But hit me with it anyway."

And, boy, did she get hit. A sledgehammer would've dealt a gentler blow than finding out about Damian's nighttime escapades in her body:

He tried to make out with Lindsey.

He spied on Teresa taking a shower.

He got into a blowout fight with Yolanda.

And he broke things off with Aaron.

It took Ricki a while to absorb everything. It was almost too outrageous to accept. But accept it she did, along with one more definite, crucial fact of life: finding a cure would have to be put on hold that night. She needed one more go-round inside Damian's body. One more time to take control of his life and subject it to her every whim.

Because now it's war.

CHAPTER THIRTEEN

Let the destruction of Damian Marquez commence. It was Monday morning, and Ricki was back in Damian's body. For the first time, she was glad to be there. Now she could make his life as miserable as he'd made hers. Even more, if she did her work right.

She started with the simple things.

Cologne, aftershave, and shampoo went down the sink. A password locked his computer, and parental controls blocked every station on his DVR. She then went through his cell phone, writing down every girl's number before clearing the contact list and tossing it into the toilet. She'd just wiped his iPod clean and was about to sketch a graffiti masterpiece on his soccer trophies when a knock sounded on the bedroom door.

"*Mijo?*"

She dropped the permanent marker, panicking. Damian's mother. Ms. Marquez should still have been at the hospital, usually not getting home from the night shift until after eight o'clock. But it was only 6:33 AM. What to do?

"Um…yeah?" she replied.

"It's past time to get ready for school. You awake?"

Ricki toyed with her options. Of all the things planned for her Day of Destruction, confronting Ms. Marquez was definitely not one of them. Trying to pass for someone's son was way too risky. Her best bet would be to mumble a short response and hope she went away. Then again, she could never pass on an opportunity to get Damian grounded.

"Why're you asking stupid questions?" she said. "I wouldn't be talking if I was still asleep, would I?"

The doorknob turned. "What did you say?"

"I *said*," she shouted, "stop asking stupid questions."

The door flew open, and Ms. Marquez marched into the room. A petite woman with mousey hair, Marianna Marquez was the opposite of Damian in every way. Sweet and gentle, where he was sadistic and brutal. Soft-spoken and rational, where he was vulgar and psychotic. Ricki had often wondered how such an evil creature had come from such an angelic woman—reinforcing her third-grade theory that a hospital mix-up had stuck the Marquez family with a demon changeling in place of their own baby. But at the moment, the family resemblance was all too clear.

"Little boy, were you speaking to me?" she demanded, looking like a mad tiger about to pounce.

Ricki casually nudged the trophy aside. "Depends. What'd I say?"

"You're getting smart with me?"

She snickered. *A smart Damian? That'll be the day.*

"Damian Emmanuel Marquez, I am not playing with you. What has gotten into you this morning?"

She opened her mouth to fire off a comeback but made the mistake of looking into the face of the woman who was like a second mother to her. All the times Ms. Marquez had watched after her and Michael when their parents weren't around ran through her mind. The disrespectful retort died on her tongue, and she hung her head. "I'm sorry," she mumbled.

Marianna perched on the edge of the computer desk. "Let me guess: Racquel."

Ricki drew back. "What?"

"Isn't it always Racquel? What did she do this time? Throw your schoolbooks into the recycling bin? Sprinkle sugar around your gas tank so you'd think your car had been vandalized?" She stopped. "No, no…that was last month."

"She didn't do anything," Ricki said, inwardly cringing. When had her tricks on Damian become such public knowledge? After the potato incident in the seventh grade, she'd thought their battles had successfully remained underground.

Marianna chuckled. "Now I know something's wrong."

She scowled.

"*Pobrecito*," Marianna cooed, reaching out to rub her hair. "You don't have to tell me. You never do anyway. But when will this stop? You're a man now—in a few weeks, you'll graduate from high school and leave your poor mama behind, along with all childish things. But never Racquel, no?"

Ricki frowned at the computer desk.

Her fingers clenched Ricki's hair, pulling her head back and forcing Ricki to look into her eyes. "Year after year, I watch and I wait for this animosity festering inside both of you to end. But it only gets stronger. *Mijo*, why? Where did it come from, this venom that controls everything you are and everything you do?"

Ricki was caught in her gaze. "I don't know."

"I think you do. And you need to remember that next time you feel like smarting off to your mama." Abruptly releasing Ricki's hair with a push, she stood up and walked to the door. "Now get up and get ready for school."

———◈———

Guess you should've factored how you're getting to school into your master plan, huh? Ricki stood a few feet away from the black Rubicon. Damian's truck mocked her, daring her to move it for more than two blocks without ending up in a ditch.

"I told you I had the second shift," a voice behind her rumbled. "And I didn't say it in Spanish, so tell me how those simple words got lost in translation?"

She spun around to face Damian and recoiled. "What have you done to me?"

It was chaos on two legs. Mismatched clothes draped his body like a clearance rack explosion. His unwashed face gleamed with oily pores. And there may actually have been a ponytail hidden somewhere in the bushy jungle that Ricki once called her hair, but it was lost amid the jigsaw puzzle of barrettes splashed across his head like confetti.

He smoothed a hand over the decorative tumbleweed. "What're you talking about? Isn't this how you always look?"

"You can't let anyone see me walking around like that," she sputtered. "Don't you know anything about girls' hair?"

His lips twisted into a sneer that didn't fit his new feminine features. "Just how to mess it up."

"Well, you'd better learn how to fix it!" Ricki's eyes narrowed. "Did you even brush my teeth?"

He blew a puff of breath into the air and sniffed at it. "Nah," he answered, clearly enjoying her distress. "Seems I don't do a lot of things the way you would if you were in your own body, do I? Maybe you should've thought about that before you decided to fall asleep on the wrong shift."

She cursed herself. In her haste for revenge, she'd just handed Damian permission to run amok in her body. She'd let the dog off the leash, opened the fence, and presented him with detailed directions to the stack of meaty bones on the other side of the city. Why couldn't she ever think straight when it came to him?

"I did not *decide* anything," she said, her brain scrambling. "I was sleepy, so I fell asleep. Completely out of my control."

He gave her a measured look. "I know you, Rocky."

"You know what?"

"I know you probably heard what went down at your girl's house the other night, didn't you?"

"Something went down?"

"Fine, play stupid. It's what you do best anyway." He turned to leave.

"Denise told me everything," she blurted. "All the stuff you did to sabotage me. So whatever I do to you, you deserve."

He stopped. "You told Denise what's going on?"

"Yeah." Her chin flew up in defiance. "And what?"

"Good luck getting to school," he replied. He gestured at his car and smirked meaningfully at her. "Guess you'll finally have to learn how to handle a stick after all."

Her face grew warm.

He walked away, heading back to the Nichols house. "You're in my body for the next few hours," he said over his shoulder. "I can't change that, and I can't stop you. But get ready for what I'm about to do in yours. You're gonna be a legend."

She didn't wait for his threat to end before racing into his house. She snatched up the phone, her fingers flying over the numbers.

"Denise," she said, "it's Ricki. I need you."

⸻

"How could Mike let you out in public looking like that?" Denise asked.

Ricki glowered across the school lobby at Damian putting on his best impression of a deranged sideshow clown in heat. He held a random freshman hostage, begging to be told how pretty he was as he held the boy in a chokehold and batted his overmascaraed eyes. A crowd surrounded them, making catcalls.

"You're like a walking freak show exhibit," Denise marveled. "I mean, he is. Because that's not really you. Even though it looks like you…" She peered up at Ricki. "Because here you really are. Only you're not." She rubbed her forehead. "I'm so confused."

"How do you think I feel?" Ricki anxiously glanced at her watch. She looked on as Damian wrestled another unfortunate undergrad to the floor.

Patience.

"I'm still trying to figure out if I should be considered a girl or a boy," she said. "I mean, if I'm really a girl in a boy's body, what does that make me?"

"An actual male with a soul?" Denise replied.

Looking again at her watch, Ricki scanned the hallway. Right on schedule, Delilah Richards came around the corner.

Denise followed her gaze to Delilah and smirked. "Alrighty, let's do this." Pulling back her hand, she slapped Ricki across the face. "I told you to leave me alone!" she screeched. "You think you can treat girls any kind of way and let your buddies clean up the mess. I'm not scared of them, and I'm not scared of you! I don't care if I'm the only girl in this entire school who has the balls to stand up to you; I'm telling Principal Dearling everything you've done." Giving Ricki a sideways wink, she stormed off.

Delilah watched her walk away, a conflicted expression of empathy on her face. Her gaze dropped to the floor, then back to Denise. Seeming to come to a decision, she squared her shoulders and changed the direction of her course. It now matched Denise's trail to the principal's office.

For the first time in Kirby High history, Delilah Richards was going to be late to class.

Ricki smiled. *Phase two complete.*

Her smile turning evil, she sashayed across the lobby toward Damian. Blowing kisses to a few of his teammates, she shooed his captive away and cornered him against the wall. He glared up at her.

"I think you've made enough of a fool of yourself today," Ricky chided. "Time to put you out of your misery."

Hefting him over her shoulder, she carried his struggling body to the janitor's closet and threw him inside. His shouts echoed through the lobby.

"Guard her," she instructed two soccer players. "And don't let her out until after the bell rings."

Now, on to phase three.

She should be getting called to the principal's office any minute now.

If Denise and Delilah's sexual assault charges didn't get Damian suspended, then his forcing a girl into the janitor's closet should be enough to seal the deal. He should be looking at no less than two weeks of suspension. Ricki wondered if he would even be allowed to graduate. *You wanted to play ball. Well, catch.*

Any minute now…

But the minute turned into five minutes. And five turned into ten. Fifteen minutes passed, and the intercom remained stubbornly silent. It appeared there was nothing a soccer player could do short of jumping the principal himself to get in trouble. And Ricki wasn't quite ready to engage in full-on assault and battery. Yet. She guessed she would have to call phase two, Destroy Damian's High School Career, a bust.

Good thing she'd spent most of the morning working on phase one: Destroy Damian's Love Life.

Her ride to school with Denise had given her time to call every phone number from Damian's cell. At first, it had been funny to hear the rabid excitement of each girl getting asked out by *the* Damian Marquez. Then it veered to nauseating when their reek of desperation could literally be smelled over the phone. But when "Damian" mentioned that he wouldn't be able to get physical on the date because he suffered from impotence as a side effect of his raging case of syphilis…well, then things got funny again.

The laughs ended, however, when she walked into school and encountered Damian's one-woman circus show. Now the playing field had been leveled, and she needed to step her game up.

How do I compete with someone who can't get in trouble?

She looked across the aisle at the cluster of boys whispering and gesturing toward the front of the classroom. The homeroom teacher, Miss Jones, crouched in front of the chalkboard, emptying a hole puncher into the trash can. Her shirt had ridden up her back, inching higher with every movement. Low-rise slacks stretched tightly across her bottom, exposing the top of a red satin thong peeking over the waistband. With each shake of the hole puncher, her pants slid a tiny bit lower, revealing a bunny tattoo on her left cheek. Ricki could almost hear saliva dropping from the mouths of every boy in the room, dribbling right onto their desks.

Like this.

"Miss Jones, your butt is showing."

Chairs scraped hastily across the floor. Every boy in the room straightened up, pretending to look at a textbook.

The teacher planted her back against the wall, tugging

at her shirt and pants. "That's not embarrassing, is it?" she gasped. "Thank you so much for telling me, Damian."

Invoking her inner actress, Ricki stood up and marched to the front of the classroom. "No, Miss Jones," she declared, whipping around to face the rest of the class. "No female should *ever* have to thank a boy for not treating her like a piece of meat. Like your only value in life is to be this cheap, useless lump of flesh in a bra and old panties."

She paused to survey the room, delighted by the sea of confounded faces gawking back at her. Pumping herself full of righteous indignation, she ranted, "How could I accept your gratitude for behaving like a decent human being? Unlike Javier, over there, who just won twenty dollars off his bet on whether you wear thongs or granny panties. Or Maurice, who was taking pictures."

Javier shoved a fistful of dollar bills into his pocket.

Maurice eased a notebook over his cell phone, crossing his arms over it. The looks on their faces almost made Ricki break character and dissolve into laughter.

"What is he doing?" a girl whispered in the back aisle.

"I'll tell you what I'm doing." Ricki flung a dramatic finger at the girl who'd spoken. "I am standing up for women everywhere who are tired of being looked at as sexual playthings. I am doing what *you*, Jessica, should've done for a member of your sisterhood instead of snarking to everyone that no woman over twenty should be caught dead with a bunny tattoo." She snorted. "Who're you kidding, Jessie? You're just jealous that you're under twenty and *still* wouldn't look good with a tattoo. The poor bunny would suffocate underneath all those folds of cellulite you're sporting."

Several boys laughed and were immediately glared into silence by the girls in the room.

"He's lost it," someone muttered.

Hello, Destroy Damian's High School Reputation, Ricki rejoiced. Word would get around school within hours. The boys would brand Damian a traitor, and the girls would write him off as being too crazy to mess with. With one impromptu speech, she'd damaged four years' worth of credibility, and she hadn't even had to sacrifice her dignity to do it.

He could take a lesson.

She grabbed a pencil from the teacher's desk and jabbed it toward a lanky boy with sandy hair. "And Victor? What exactly is a 'banana split?'"

"Okay, Damian," Miss Jones cut in, her cheeks enflamed. "I think that's enough chivalry for today. Please take your seat."

Ricki strutted back to her chair, humming a victory tune under her breath.

Miss Jones fiddled with her watch. Self-consciously tugging at the back of her shirt, she announced, "We're going to make today an early day. Everyone is dismissed."

They didn't need to be told twice. The students rushed to escape the room, hurriedly grabbing up backpacks and books. A pencil set fell to the floor in one boy's haste to flee, but he kept moving, never looking back.

Stepping over the scattered pencils, Ricki was almost to the door when the teacher stopped her.

"Damian, please wait," she instructed. "I'd like to speak to you for a moment."

Ricki inwardly celebrated. *Maybe a soccer player can get in trouble after all.* Looking as solemn as a church procession on a rainy Sunday, she circled around to the chalkboard.

Miss Jones waited for the room to empty before saying, "That was quite a speech you gave. I hope you realize that you put me in quite an awkward position."

"No more awkward than flashing your goodies to every boy in here," Ricki commented, aiming for the final blow.

A tiny smirk appeared on the teacher's face. "But I thought the red ones were your favorite."

She blinked. "I'm sorry?"

"Don't be sorry, Damian. I thought your jealousy was cute. But you don't have to worry—you know anything I flash is for you and only you."

She gaped at the homeroom teacher, her mind reeling.

Miss Jones played with the top button of her blouse. "Aren't you curious to see if I'm wearing the matching bra?"

Ricki stumbled away from the chalkboard, tripping over the trash can and falling into the desk. She clutched her books in front of her like a shield. "I have to go," she stammered.

She fled the classroom, leaving behind a scandal too hot for even her to touch.

Almost three hours down with not much more time left, and Damian's life was no worse off than before she'd taken it over.

It wasn't as if Ricki hadn't given her all. Word of Damian's homeroom meltdown and the syphilis rumor should've already spread like wildfire, but girls kept throwing themselves at him. And the male masses had turned Damian into a hero, giving him mad respect for his "inspired" ploy to get in good with Miss "Mighty Jugs" Jones. Even her attempt to flunk his first period history exam had failed. The teacher had taken one look at the blank sheet she'd turned in, scribbled, "Good luck on today's game! A+," and sent her on her way.

The only thing left for her to do with the remaining time in Damian's body was damage control. And since Denise was, yet again, running interference with Lindsey, Yolanda, and Teresa, it was up to her to smooth things over with Aaron.

She immediately spotted him in the back row of the trigonometry class. He was typing into his cell phone, ignoring the cluster of boys around him. Bracing herself, she maneuvered through the maze of desks toward him. When the group saw her coming, they parted like the Red Sea.

"Hey, Aaron," she said.

He spared a brief glance. "'Sup."

"Can I…holler at you for a minute?"

His fingers stopped moving. "What about?"

She looked around. The noisy group of boys had suddenly become very quiet. "Just some stuff going on that I think you should know."

His eyes finally left the phone screen and met hers. The hostility in them hit her like a hammer. "'Bout what?"

Maybe trying to talk to him while in Damian's body wasn't such a good idea after all. She backed away. "Uh, never mind."

"Naw, man," he said, pocketing his phone. "Speak your peace. It's about your girl, right?"

She frowned. "Lindsey?"

The boys behind her laughed. "Be more specific, Aaron," one of them said. "You know D's got about twenty dangling on the line."

"I mean his main girl."

"Oh," the group harmonized. "*That* one."

"You already made your feelings real clear about where things stand," he said to Ricki. "Let it drop, alright?"

She was lost. Time to play it off and make a graceful exit. "Okay, cool." She turned to leave.

"You can't have them all," he said.

She turned back to him, confused. "I can't?"

"Just like D," someone muttered. "Greedy."

Aaron stood up.

The crowd stepped back, leaving a wide clearing around the two of them.

Apprehension crept through her.

He circled around his desk, coming to stand within inches of her. Even though she had height on her side, he was solid with muscles and evenly matched. Having him so close in her face, looking as though he wanted nothing more than to body slam her to the ground, should've made Ricki want to make a break for the nearest exit.

Instead, she wanted to kiss him. She stared into his eyes, admiring the gold flecks highlighted in their hazel depths. The last time she'd been this close to him had been at Teresa's house, on the verge of having her first kiss. And this time, there was no Damian around to interrupt.

Forgetting where—and who—she was, Ricki leaned in.

The intercom buzzer went off, bringing her to her senses. She pulled back, surprised at herself. A few more seconds and she would've been lip-locking it with Aaron while still in Damian's body. How disturbing would *that* have been?

A seed of sabotage sprouted in her mind.

The intercom sounded. "Everyone report to the gymnasium for today's pep rally. Seniors, please leave your classes now and report to your assigned section. Juniors, please leave at..."

Aaron stepped away. "Let's squash this until another time."

"Yeah, sure," she said, formulating a plan. "But wasn't the pep rally supposed to be after lunch?"

A boy beside her answered. "Loki Seven. Word got around that they had something big planned for the rally, so I guess it's getting bumped up to throw them off."

She could barely contain her pleasure. She'd just stumbled upon the perfect means of dealing the deathblow to Damian's playboy reputation. And the timing was great. Humming to herself, she followed Aaron out of the room.

Showtime.

The gymnasium was packed.

Freshmen sat on the north side of the gym, in the nosebleed section, with the sophomores directly facing them on the south side. Juniors were positioned below the freshmen, and seniors were situated underneath the sophomores. The bottom rows were for the athletes, with the front row seats reserved for the soccer team.

Ricki made sure to sit beside Aaron. She scanned the sophomore section for Damian but couldn't find him. The rest of her friends were missing too. She had a nagging feeling she should know the reason for their absence, but her brain was too preoccupied with laying out the next scene of her plan.

Too bad her friends would miss the big show.

She furtively observed Aaron. He sat engrossed in watching the Kirby High cheerleaders bounce around the court, showing off their school spirit with death-defying somersaults and backflips into the air. One of them, who looked suspiciously like Mitzi, skyrocketed across the gym, tore a papier-mâché figure of a jackrabbit into shreds, and slam-dunked the pieces into the basketball hoop.

The gym went wild.

Once the roar of the frenzied crowd died down, it was time to make her move. She tugged on Aaron's sleeve. "Aaron?"

"Yeah?"

"There's something I've been wanting to tell you."

"What's up?"

"Well, I've had these feel—" A blast of intro music stopped her midsentence. Her pulse sped up, keeping time with the ice water rushing through her veins. How could she have forgotten…

The drama troupe rushed onto the floor, replacing the cheerleaders as they cartwheeled out of view. Half of the troupe was dressed as Kirby Kangaroos, the other half as Jefferson

Jackrabbits. They took their positions across the floor, pairing one kangaroo to every rabbit. Reggie, in regular clothing, stood in the midst of the couples, holding a microphone.

Ricki didn't even hear Reggie speak. Everything was a dull hum in her ears. She focused on Damian dressed as a rabbit, having miraculously lost the ten layers of makeup previously spackled onto his face. She knew he didn't have any idea what to do in the skit, but he didn't look the least bit concerned.

He looked downright gleeful.

Her mind raced through the routine, searching for areas he could massacre. Reggie was the only person with lines—everyone else just had to follow basic choreography. At the worst, Damian might try to take the microphone and say something stupid, but Denise could probably tackle him before he got far. Even if he messed up the blocking, it wouldn't be life-shattering. Deciding there wasn't anything too terrible for him to do, she relaxed.

Why is he unbuttoning his costume?

She sat paralyzed, watching his fingers nimbly skip down the front of the costume. The furry pelt fell from his shoulders, revealing a blue-and-gold T-shirt underneath. Reggie continued to talk into the microphone, oblivious to the striptease taking place behind him. Denise broke away from her kangaroo counterpart and hurried toward Damian. He scurried out of reach.

The pelt was now down to his knees.

Denise chased him around the gym floor, snatching in vain at the tail of his rabbit costume. The rest of the drama crew watched helplessly. Damian lifted the T-shirt over his head.

"Is this part of the act?" Aaron asked.

Ricki bolted from her seat and started to rush after Damian but realized she would be too late to stop him. He'd already kicked off the costume and was fumbling with the bra. Thankfully, he couldn't get a good grip on the hooks, and his hands kept slipping off the clasps. More members of the troupe had joined in the chase to stop him, but his soccer skills came in handy as he dodged and weaved his way through them.

The crowd was in an uproar. "This is the best pep rally we've had all year!" a voice in the stands shouted. "Take it off!"

In a flash of desperation, she dropped onto one knee in front of Aaron. He leaned back, alarmed. Ignoring the chaos behind her, she grabbed his hand. "Aaron, there's something I've been wanting to tell you for a long time."

The stampede of footsteps slowed.

"You're a really great guy." She clenched his hand tighter, struggling against him as he tried to pull it from her.

"Dude, what are you doing?" he demanded.

"I feel like I've been waiting all my life to meet someone who fits all the qualities I'm looking for," she said in a rush. "You're handsome and sweet and nice."

The rest of the soccer players now stared at her and Aaron, their mouths hanging open. The sound of mayhem had quieted on the floor.

"Aaron, what I'm trying to say is that I'm in lo—"

"*No!*" a voice behind her roared.

The weight of a small body slammed into her back, knocking her to the ground. She tried to roll over but was entangled in folds of fuzzy cloth. Hands pressed the garment against her face, suffocating her in the smell of mothballs. Her own hands waved helplessly, clutching at what felt like hair until they worked their way down the sides of a face to a throat.

She squeezed.

The hands loosened, giving her the opportunity to push the body away and yank the furry material from her face. She threw what ended up being a jackrabbit costume to the side and pushed herself onto her knees. Rubbing strands of faux fur out of her eyes, she looked up.

Principal Dearling stood over her. In one hand, he held the back of Damian's neck. In the other, he held the discarded rabbit costume, which he used to cover Damian's exposed body. His face was the picture of pure fury.

"Both of you," he growled, "in my office."

Ricki looked at Damian. When her eyes touched his, she became lightheaded. In a blink, she was back in her own body, almost naked and about to face the expulsion she'd tried so hard to get for Damian.

Great timing.

CHAPTER FOURTEEN

"YOU DON'T OWN ME!"

Ricki was on a ranting high and showed no signs of slowing. She waved her finger at Damian. "If I want to go to sleep, I'll *go* to sleep, and I'd like to see you stop me."

"Then you'd better say a good prayer first," Damian fired back. "How does it go? 'If I should die before I wake?'"

"Was that a threat? Principal Dearling, you heard him just threaten me?"

Lawrence Dearling massaged his temples. "Of all the weeks for my dear wife to go on a holistic medicine kick," he muttered. "I'd kill for a Vicodin." Wincing, he slammed a paperweight onto the desk. "Enough! You two. Always you two..."

He pushed the paperweight aside, replacing it with two files. *Nichols, R. A.* and *Marquez, D. E.* were stamped across the tops. He drummed his fingers on the files, smiling into Ricki and Damian's alarmed faces. "Funny how the threat of cold discipline garners respect where patience and understanding fail," he said with satisfaction. He began to open one of the files, when the telephone intercom buzzed.

"Principal Dearling," a woman's voice said, "there was an incident during the pep rally."

"I know, Velma." He eyed Ricki and Damian. "They're sitting in front of me."

"No, sir, this is a Seven incident. The cafeteria was left

unattended during the rally, and the entire lunch supply was stolen and replaced with…well, with bunnies."

"Bunnies?"

"They're hopping around all over the place."

Dearling dropped his head into his hands and groaned.

The intercom crackled. "They also spray-painted a message across the east wall. It says, 'Since our cooking staff doesn't know what real meat looks like, here's a hint. Go ahead, Kangaroos, get *these* jackrabbits.' Sir, quite a few of the rabbits have escaped into the school. We're not sure what to do."

"Thank you, Velma," he mumbled through his fingers. "I'm on my way." Covering his eyes, he counted to ten between clenched teeth, then stood up and marched out of the office.

Five minutes passed before either of them spoke.

"Are we supposed to wait for him to come back?" Damian asked.

"Why don't you leave and find out?" Ricki replied. "If he suspends you, you'll know the right answer."

"Then you'll think you won, huh?"

"I don't know what you're talking about," she sniffed. "As usual."

"You don't know a lot of things, but what I'm talking about isn't one of them. What you and Denise tried to do was low-down, even for you. Mess up my chance at graduating? Cost me my scholarships and going to college?"

A pang of guilt hit her. Maybe she had taken things a *little* too far.

"Blame yourself," she stubbornly responded, brushing the inconvenient thought aside. "You could've gone back to sleep at Teresa's house like you were supposed to, but you thought it'd be more fun to ruin my life. If you don't like payback, oh well. Suck it up and deal with it."

"And here's Rocky's Get Out of Jail Free victim card," he said with a dry laugh. "Usable for every time she doesn't want to take responsibility for overreacting. Which is all the time, so I'm surprised it hasn't expired yet."

"Overreacting? You messed things up with Aaron and molested my friends. They won't even speak to me anymore because of what you did. Me wanting you to know what it feels like to lose everything is called 'what goes around comes around.'"

"Step outside of Rocky World, would you? Reality is calling. Did it ever occur to your simple mind for one second that we could've ended up stuck inside each other for good this time?"

Biting off a nasty comment, she paused to consider his question.

"Every time we switch could be the *last* time we switch," he said. "And you took that risk, all because you popped off, thinking I'd done you wrong, and wanted to get back at me." He shook his head and snorted. "Classic Rocky."

She frowned at the ground, simmering impotently.

"If I didn't know any better, I'd think you like being me," he said, turning up the flame. "Maybe it's the only time you actually have a life."

The anger churned.

"Must be why you came up with such lame ideas for getting us back to normal," he continued. "Going to a priest? Next thing I know, you'll have us singing hymnals in the rain, waving pigeon feathers under our butts."

She slapped a hand against her forehead. "That's right. I forgot you're not allowed in a church."

"Don't be stupid. You know I go to mass every week."

"And your hand doesn't burn off the second you touch the door?"

"Whatever," he muttered. He crossed his arms over his face and leaned his chair against the wall, dismissing her.

She slyly cut her eyes his way, not willing to let him retreat. "I think when Principal Dearling comes back, I'm telling him all about you and your homeroom teacher."

"Not a clue what you're talking about," he mumbled.

"Y'know, what's going on between you and Miss Jones."

He twisted around to face her. "Nothing's going on between me and Miss Jones besides a little healthy flirting between a cougar and her prey. She likes to show me what she's working with. I like to admire it. Don't hate."

Her mouth curled in disgust. "You get your rocks off ogling old women's underwear? Figures."

"She's twenty-four. That's not old; that's just right. Maybe one day, when you grow up, you'll actually have a little something to fill out those old women's underwear." He chuckled. "Oops, never mind."

Her face grew hot. "Never mind what?"

"Well, you know," he said meaningfully. "After being in your body, let's just say I've gotten real familiar with everything *you're* working with."

She lunged at him.

"Whoa!" He laughed as she tried to wrap her arms around his throat. Swatting her hands away, he pushed her toward to her chair. "Would you stop?"

She collapsed into the chair. "I hate you! My body is not a joke. It's not something for you to play with or show the whole school."

"Why so shy?" he taunted. "Everyone's already seen you naked, remember? Those old nudie shots of you were a top-seller. I bought one whole movie ticket off the money they made."

She again flew out of her seat. His knees kicked into the

air, blocking her left-handed punch at his stomach—leaving him open to the right-handed swing at his face. Her fist connected with his skull and exploded in pain. Tears sprung to her eyes as she pressed her teeth against her hand to keep from crying out.

Groaning, he firmly shoved her away with his foot. "Would you chill? You're really gonna get us suspended."

"I'm so sick of you," she hissed, slapping his foot away. She ambled back to her chair, nursing her hand. "I've never taken *your* clothes off. I don't even go to the bathroom in your body!"

"And I wish you would," he said. "My bladder's about to bust every time we flip back."

"No, because I'm a decent human being, unlike you. It must be nice to do whatever you want and never have to pay for it. Screwing around with teachers—"

"Didn't I tell you we are *not*—"

"Screwing around with teachers," she repeated, talking over him. "Bullying girls—"

"When did I bully—"

"Spreading STDs—"

"I did *what*?"

"And I doubt you've earned an honest grade in your whole four years here. That varsity soccer jacket is better than a Get Out of Jail Free card; it's a free ticket through life. No one can ever bring you down." She rubbed her sore fist and looked at him bitterly. "No matter how hard they try." *And I'm getting tired of trying.*

Even now, with a physical attack, he appeared none the worse for wear, but her hand felt as if it had cracked in half. The best she could ever get against him was a stalemate, and the price of achieving that hollow status didn't seem to be worth it anymore.

"You seem to be doing a good job of it," Damian mumbled.

"Yeah, right. I don't know why you were even worried about your cred hitting zero if people found out about us. You could dress up in Victoria's Secret angel wings and dance on a Lunchyard table singing Disney show tunes and everyone would still think you're the coolest thing since dry ice."

He grinned. "I wouldn't go that far."

"I would," she grumbled.

"I bet you would if I let you back in my body, wouldn't you?" he said. "But maybe you're right. Maybe all it takes is one shutout game, and every person in this school will forgive me for anything." He tenderly touched his temple and winced. "Everyone but you."

She sucked on her hand and glared at him.

He turned away from her to gaze out the window overlooking the soccer field. They sat quietly, lost in their thoughts, the silence occasionally broken by shouts and pounding footsteps. A pair of brown rabbits hopped past the window, oblivious to the subdued battlefield only a few feet away.

They were still in those positions when Principal Dearling returned to the office, ten minutes later. He studied them before wearily shuffling over to his desk and collapsing into his seat.

"I'm letting you both off with a warning," he announced, returning their folders to his desk drawer.

They glanced at each other in surprise.

"I have seven bigger fish to catch and fry and simply do not have the mental resources to deal with the two of you right now. When a group of vigilante delinquents like the Loki Seven are on the loose, the wheels of justice sometimes have to be prioritized." He massaged his temples. "It also doesn't help that we've got a critical game against Jefferson this afternoon and cannot afford to have our star goalie sitting on the sidelines."

Ricki glared at the floor, fuming. *Devil Boy gets a free pass again.*

"And you, Miss Nichols. Sexual assault is a serious matter. It is neither a joke nor a tool for you to use in your game of one-upping Mr. Marquez." He directed a shrewd eye at Ricki. "Do not believe for one second it escaped my notice that it was *your* best friend who issued those harassment charges. I don't know how you managed to rope in Delilah Richards, but you had better thank your lucky stars that I owe your father a favor. When he returns from his trip, you tell him that I said we're even."

She meekly nodded. Maybe free passes came in shapes and sizes beyond a blue-and-gold letter jacket.

"Now before I let you two go, I have something to say." He stood up and walked to the front of the desk. Settling on its edge, he pointed a finger at Ricki and Damian. "This must end."

They stared up at him, eyes wide with confusion.

"Don't give me that look. Just because this is the first time I've had you both in front of me, don't think that it's the first time I've been aware of your activities."

The confusion dimmed, replaced with dismayed under-standing. How much did he know?

Reading their expressions, he chortled softly. "Since the day I stepped foot in this school, your antics have reached my ears on an almost weekly basis. And I'm not proud to admit it, but your ongoing saga has become something of a highlight to my day."

Damian shifted in his seat, clearly uncomfortable.

"I can't say I wasn't warned. Your parents prepared me for the drama. And as long as no physical harm took place, I simply updated them and let them determine our course of action for dealing with your behavior. They seemed to feel that, in due time, you both would find a way to work through your differences and reach a more mature level of interaction. After today, however, I'm beginning to strongly doubt that time will ever come."

Ricki hung her head in embarrassment. Her parents knew every nasty trick she'd played? She'd done so many underhanded things to Damian she should've been on punishment for the rest of her days. *Why didn't they ever say anything?*

"Your parents are under the impression there is a lesson for you to learn," Dearling said as if reading her mind. "They believe if you both can find your own way to put an end to these destructive games without our interference, your insight into yourselves and each other will be enriched."

Ricki peeked over at Damian and saw he was similarly puzzled.

"Children," the principal sighed. He motioned for them to come closer.

Uncertain, they inched forward.

"Believe me when I say I once was your age," he said, his already weary face growing more worn. "And like you, there was someone I grew up with. Russell, but everyone called him Rascal. Almost from the womb, wherever you saw me, you saw Rascal. Cookouts, church, yard sales—our families did everything together. And since our parents were best friends, they expected us to be as well. We even ended up in the same class every year, up to the eighth grade. People took to calling us the 'shadow twins.'"

He paused to wipe a hand over his eyes. When his fingers lowered, a slight sheen of moisture glistened off their tips.

Ricki's heart went out to him. Rascal must've been a pretty special friend.

"We despised each other," he declared. "If I had a toy, he had to have a nicer one. If I had a girlfriend, he had to have a prettier one, or steal mine. I cannot think of a single time that one of us did not sport a busted lip or broken nose. And the more our parents tried to force us to play nice, the more we resented each other.

"By the time we reached high school, our only mission in life was to make one another miserable. And my goodness, did we get creative with it. There was nothing too low that we wouldn't do to each other. The sad thing, however, is that if we'd taken even a third of the passion we put into battling each other and focused it on our studies, we would've been straight-A students and probably even graduated early." He looked pointedly at Ricki and Damian. "Sound familiar?"

Their sheepish faces dropped.

"Yes," he murmured, "the hate Rascal and I had for one another is what drove us forward." Standing up, he walked over to the window. He stood in front of it, his back to them.

"It was the spring break of our junior year," he said. "Cherry Lake was still the hangout spot, although there wasn't as much there—no barbecue pits and volleyball nets, or things of that sort. Just a lot of wide open field surrounding the lake. Dirt roads. The older kids would sometimes drag race along the edge of the lake, showing off their rides and hoping to impress the young ladies.

"One evening, I learned that Rascal had driven one of his father's cars down to the lake. So, of course, I had to beg my dad to lend me one of his. He almost wouldn't do it, but I wore him down until he gave me the keys to an old, beat-up Chevy Impala. It was far from a beauty, but I didn't care—if Rascal had a car, I had to have one too. I even upped the ante by getting my girlfriend and her friends to ride with me. I knew Rascal had just been dumped, so I wanted to make a show of arriving at the lake with a car full of girls to rub in his face." He continued to stare out the window, lost in his memories.

Ricki wondered if he remembered they were still in the room.

"He had just won the last race when I arrived, and he was still bragging about it," Dearling said. "When he saw me driving my dad's oldest car, he joked that the girls I'd brought were probably just there to help me push it to the lake. We instantly devolved into our usual chorus of 'who's better than whom.' I said my car was better than his—substance over flash. He challenged me to prove it. I said I didn't need to prove it, so he said I was scared. Called me chicken.

"Chicken. That was all it took. I jumped on that word and did the dumbest and most destructive thing I have ever done in my life: I challenged him to it. I don't know if you children are familiar with the game of chicken, but it's a contest where two people drive their cars on a collision course—usually toward a cliff or each other—and whoever hits their brakes first is crowned the chicken. And since Cherry Lake has no cliff, our version involved driving toward each other. Whoever was the first to break would have to return to school covered in chicken feathers.

"I could tell Rascal didn't want to do it. He didn't say anything, and his face never changed, but for a split second, there was something in his eyes. I later recognized it as common sense trying to prevail. At the time, however, I mistook it for fear. And it forever haunts me, because in that second, I could have turned everything around and changed the challenge to a race. But I didn't. I clucked at him."

His hands pressed against the windowsill.

"We drove to opposite ends of the lake. Everyone cheered us on, flashing their headlights and waving jackets in the air.

I vaguely recall my girlfriend trying to give me a good-luck kiss, but it was all a blur. I didn't see anything beyond the image of Rascal: covered in chicken feathers, walking into school with everyone laughing at him. Inferior. Defeated.

"When his car's lights got closer, I was still caught up in the dream of victory, finally winning and putting him in his place. I saw him getting pulled into the principal's office and his parents coming to the school. Him possibly even getting suspended. Me holding the door open for him as he was marched out of the school in disgrace...

"It wasn't until his headlights were shining directly through the windshield and into my eyes that 'daydream Rascal' disappeared, and I saw the real one staring back at me from his car seat. Shocked and scared. Realizing it was too late for either of us to avoid collision."

He stopped speaking. Straightening his shoulders, he left the window. His face was aged with the burden of sadness and regret he'd carried for so many years.

Ricki rubbed at the goose bumps forming on her arms, unable to look into his haunted eyes.

"I woke up some months later," he said, his voice husky. "I had been in a coma. Apparently, substance *did* win out over flash, because Rascal was not so lucky. He was dead."

She gasped.

"The front of his car crumpled like paper on impact, and he died almost instantly from the injury to his chest. They told me that he never even made it to the hospital."

Damian spoke up. "Mr. Dearling, I—"

"No," Dearling said, motioning for silence, "there's nothing for you to say. I just want you to listen. It took a long time for my body to heal after the accident, which gave me a lot of time to reflect on life and where my actions had taken me. I eventually got out of the hospital and reentered 'normal' life. Physically, I was better. I could walk and talk, and I returned to school the following year. But mentally, I remained broken. Not only was I left to struggle with the guilt over Rascal's death, but the one thing I never would have expected crept up on me—I missed him.

"My life became strangely empty without Rascal. Growing up, I'd believed him to be my worst enemy, but once he was gone, it hit me that he was actually the driving force who made me into who I was. Competing with him was what got me out of bed each morning. He made me want to be better, stronger, smarter. With him no longer around, it was as though I had lost my purpose. He was the quintessential yin to my yang, and it took losing him for me to recognize it."

Ricki resisted the urge to look at Damian. As crazy as he drove her, would she feel a void if he were to suddenly disappear?

"He also knew me better than anyone," Dearling said, interrupting her thoughts. "Just as I knew him. Only someone who really understands how you tick can know which buttons to push to get you going. It's amazing how much we had in common, but we misused our knowledge of each other as ammunition, instead of using it to build one of the strongest friendships we might've ever had. Perhaps if we could have found a way to put our egos aside just once, our brief time could have resulted in something lasting and positive instead of destructive."

Ricki noticed Damian's eyes flicker in her direction.

Principal Dearling shook his head, clearing the pain of old memories from his mind. Standing up, he brushed off his pants. "I suppose we'll never know what could have developed between Rascal and myself had he lived, will we?" he said. "Whatever demon resided in me that night at Cherry Lake made sure of it. And it's a demon I have had to wrestle with every day of my life since."

The intercom buzzed. "Sir, animal control is here. They don't think they brought enough traps."

"On my way, Velma," Dearling said. He peered sternly at Ricki and Damian. "All right, you two are dismissed to return to your classes. I trust I will not be seeing either of you in my office again?"

They nodded.

"Good." He stood up to leave. As he passed their chairs, he said softly, "Every night for more years than I care to count, I would see Rascal's face whenever I closed my eyes. I would see the look in his eyes as he stared back at me through the windshield, realizing he was about to die. There was a question in his eyes that tormented me well into my dreams. Why?"

He stopped at the door, his hand resting on the doorknob. "To this day, it is all I can ever ask myself. Why? What made us so determined to win that we would not back down no matter the cost? I wonder if it's not time for both of you to ask yourselves that question."

Opening the door, he walked out of the office, leaving Ricki and Damian alone to wonder the same thing.

"You haven't talked to him since?" Denise asked, munching on a bag of potato chips.

Ricki sat with Denise in the back of the auditorium, conspicuously separated from the rest of the troupe. Her scenes had been cut as punishment for her R-rated rough-and-tumble production at the rally. She was disheartened, but at least Quincy hadn't replaced her with Yolanda. His meds were obviously keeping him on the mellow and compassionate side that day. She wished the same could be said for everyone else.

Arriving at rehearsal had been like stepping into a war zone with her on the losing side. She was pretty certain lepers got warmer welcomes. Unspoken resentment coated the air, with almost everyone going out of their way to avoid her. Getting the not-so-subtle hint, she'd slunk away to the most secluded spot she could find and spent rehearsal brooding over Principal Dearling's speech. Each time she replayed his story in her mind, she got chills. His relationship with Rascal was almost a mirror image of the one she shared with Damian. Even the lengths they went to, to beat each other were the same. Hadn't she been willing to sacrifice her own body just to get a chance at wrecking Damian's life? And the only reason they were switching bodies in the first place was because of a trick he'd pulled on her in retaliation for a trick he'd thought she was pulling on him. How far would things have to go before they stopped the tricks and learned to coexist?

Would it take death?

"No," she said to Denise. "I haven't spoken to him. I don't even know what shift to take for sleep or if we're trying anything else to stop the switches. I'd like to do that spell, but I never picked up the ingredients. I was too busy thinking up ways to get back at Damian. Nice to know I have my priorities straight, huh?"

"You were mad," Denise reasoned.

"I'm always mad. At him, anyway." She picked at her nails, still pensive. "What do you think of Damian?"

"I don't," Denise answered briskly. "I mean, it used to piss me off how he treats you, but I figured out a long time ago it's just a thing between you two. It's how you guys relate to each other: maim and destroy."

Ricki gave her a small smile. "Did you know every single person in this school thinks he hung the moon?"

"Yeah, the twenty-man entourage trailing him around the halls kinda gave me that impression."

"No, seriously. In the few hours I was in his body today,

I felt like I ruled this place. It's like to everyone else, he can do no wrong. He's some sort of great guy." Her forehead wrinkled. "What am I not seeing? Is he that great, or am I the only person with any common sense and everyone else is a brainless sheep?"

"Maybe you're just the only person he treats the way he does," Denise offered. She popped a chip in her mouth and chewed thoughtfully. "Sometimes it's like he works overtime to make sure you hate him."

"Well, he's succeeded."

Denise shrewdly observed her, then glanced down the aisle. Her demeanor abruptly changed. Grabbing Ricki's shoulder, she whispered in her ear, "You accidentally took your mom's Ambien instead of Advil, and it made you get all loopy and trip out at the rally. You barely remember anything."

"Huh?" Ricki asked, lost.

"Ambien," Denise stressed. She faced forward, looking determinedly innocent.

A figure materialized at the end of the aisle, startling Ricki.

"Rick," Reggie greeted, scooting into the seat beside her. "Rick, Rick, Rick. What is the word, man?"

"Ambien," Denise stated, speaking before Ricki opened her mouth. "You didn't hear?"

"Yeah, I heard you telling Q about it before my scene started." He patted Ricki's leg. "I'm sorry that happened, Rick. One time, my uncle took a sleeping pill and woke up at a liquor store in nothing but a pair of flip-flops and tighty-whities. And it was the middle of winter." His hand rested on her knee. "How're you feeling now?"

"Still groggy," Denise answered quickly. "I've been keeping her hopped up on Mountain Dew. She'll live once the embarrassment wears off. Right, Ricki?"

Reggie studied her intently, his face pinched in concern.

Ricki tried to meet his gaze, but the burden of constantly
lying to such a trusting friend dragged her eyes to the ground.
She nodded, feeling wretched.

"Hey, don't even sweat it," he said. "Once word gets
around that you were under the influence and weren't really
responsible for what you did, the sticks will fall out of
everyone's butts. It won't even be a memory by next week."

She looked up. "What if I *was* responsible?"

A sharp elbow from Denise jabbed into her side. Grunting,
she forged ahead. "I mean, so what if a substance controlled
my actions? I put everything into play by taking the substance
in the first place, right?"

"But you took the wrong pill. That's not your fault."

"Even though I knowingly did the thing that set events
into motion that caused me to get humiliated at the rally
and end up in Principal Dearling's office? And now I might
even get kicked out of the play. Whether or not I *intended* for
those things to happen shouldn't matter. I should've thought
through the consequences of my actions before falling
asleep—" She caught herself. "I mean, before taking a pill
that would put me to sleep."

"But you had a headache," he pointed out.

"So I get to blame the headache for everything?" she said,
frustrated. "Something made me feel bad, so everything I do
to get back at it is justified no matter how reckless it is?" She
bowed her head, allowing herself to accept a truth that had
been gnawing at her all afternoon. She murmured to herself,
"I think it's time for me to tear up my victim card."

Reggie looked over her head at Denise, his eyebrows raised
in question.

Denise shrugged and went back to rustling through her
bag of chips.

"Stop beating yourself up over things you had no control

over," he said, rubbing Ricki's leg. "You didn't mean for the stuff at the pep rally to happen. Rick, you'd never intentionally hurt anyone. You don't have a mean bone in your body."

Denise exploded into a fit of coughing. "Sorry," she wheezed, waving the potato chip bag at them. "Ignore me."

Ricki glared at her, then took Reggie's hand, giving him a smile. *Maybe one more little lie will be okay.* "I feel a whole lot better now," she said. "Thanks, Reg."

"My job here is done," he said, his face breaking into a wide grin. "Now I need to get back up front before Q sends the dogs after me. Stay sweet." Giving her hand a lingering squeeze, he got up and jogged down the aisle.

Denise stared after him, a chip dangling from her mouth. She shook her head. "So naïve." Her purse buzzed. She reached inside and pulled out her cell phone. "Interesting. It's a text from Damian."

Ricki almost snatched the phone from her hands.

"He wants me to drop you off at St. Jude's after the game." Denise dropped the phone back into her purse. "Looks like he's willing to talk to a priest after all."

"Feel any different?"

Ricki closed her eyes. The swirling in her head might have been from the potion leaving her system, but she wasn't sure. It could have just been exhaustion.

She handed the Bible to Damian and answered, "Don't know. Do you?"

"Does stupid count?" he replied. "I think Father Fitzgerald was lit. It's the only reason he didn't laugh in our face and kick us out of the church."

"His office *did* smell like alcohol," she said, wrinkling her nose. "But I thought he was pouring wine for communion or something."

"More like Jack Daniels. And the only thing he was communing with was the flask under his robe."

Her voice lowered. "Teresa said her Granny Han sees him at the casinos sometimes. He says he's there to save lost souls in their own territory. The money chips in his pockets are supposed to be bait to lure the souls back to the path of redemption."

"Then the dollar bills he carries at the strip clubs must be the reward for when they get there," he joked. They laughed quietly, not wanting to disturb the other parishioners in the church.

She looked at her lap, suddenly feeling nervous. "What made you change your mind? I thought you hated the priest idea."

"I did," he said. "But it was the least I could do." He absently flipped through the pages of the Bible. "About that night at Teresa's...look, I didn't mean for a lot of the stuff that happened to happen. I just kept forgetting who I was supposed to be, and things kept getting to me."

"Things like what?"

"I'm a dude, Rocky. Surrounded by a bunch of sexy, available girls snuggling up on me and running around with no clothes on. Figure it out."

"You couldn't control yourself?"

"Normally, but I wasn't really in a normal position," he said. "Like, me and Lindsey were sharing a bed, and she rolled over on me. I'm half-asleep, so I don't even realize I'm rubbing on her until she freaks out. Then I try to escape to the bathroom, and there's Teresa, naked in the shower. Who takes a shower at four in the morning? It caught me off guard, and I can't help it—I see a naked girl, I'm gonna look. But it wasn't even for a second, and I was about to turn around when she saw me." He laid his right hand on the Bible and held the other in the air. "On the real, Rocky, I was not trying to get your friends to think you were pushing up on them."

She chewed over his story, doing her best to keep an open mind. The logic was twisted, but in a male dog sort of way, she supposed it made sense.

Except...

"What about Yolanda?" she asked. "You picked a fight with her."

"I don't like the way she talks to you," he stated. "So I told her what she could do with her attitude. She didn't like it."

"Why didn't you tell me any of this? I called you all day, but you kept avoiding me."

"Yesterday was crazy." He rubbed a hand across his face. "My mom had a car accident, and I had to go get her from the hospital. Her back got a little messed up, so she's out of work for the next few days. After I picked her up, we had a lot of stuff to do with insurance and putting the car in the shop. But when I called to let you know I needed to sleep the second shift, you didn't say anything about what had happened, so I thought everything was all good."

"I didn't know," she said lamely. "But what about Aaron? Why'd you tell him I didn't want to see him anymore?"

His mouth puckered into a small frown. Not looking at her, he asked, "Why don't you want me to be with Lindsey?"

His question threw her. "I don't want to see her hurt," she answered.

"And you think I would hurt her?"

"Wouldn't you? You've never been serious with any one girl since I've known you. For some reason, I don't see that changing for Lindsey."

"So you're looking out for a friend?"

"Yes. I am."

"Well, maybe I'm doing the same thing."

She frowned at him, puzzled. "I would never hurt Aaron."

Sighing, he turned to her. "I don't want to argue with you anymore, Rocky," he said softly. "I'm tired of fighting."

She stared into his eyes, surprised to see her own inner turmoil reflected back to her. She gave a shy smile. "So am I."

He handed her the Bible. "Ready to go home?"

"Yeah. Let me borrow your phone for a sec, so I can call Denise to come get me."

He shook his head. "I'll take you home." Standing up, he reached out a hand to her. "Matter of fact, you'll drive. I think it's time you finally learn how to drive stick."

She looked up at him, wondering if he was mocking her. Amazingly, he wasn't.

Taking his hand, she pulled herself up. They walked side by side to the church's exit, leaving old hurts and a lifetime of grudges at the altar. It was time, Ricki knew, to put their old history to bed. From that day forward, a new story would be written between them.

And for some reason she couldn't fathom, the thought terrified her.

CHAPTER FIFTEEN

INSTRUCTIONS TO HELP YOU THROUGH
THE DAY IN CASE WE DIDN'T MAKE
IT THROUGH THE NIGHT.

RICKI READ THE NOTE A third time, its significance
made clear by the hand holding it. Damian's hand. They
had failed.

Last night's ride home from church had gone well. If
cornered, she might even describe it as...*fun*. Damian could
be halfway human when he wanted to be. He was patient
when she couldn't figure how to put the car into reverse. He
was reassuring when she almost blew out his transmission for
the fifth time. And he even kept his cool when she nearly ran
them into a ditch after a bug flew through the window and
landed in her hair. It wasn't until she confused the accelerator
with the brakes, almost wrapping them around the back of
an RV, that he chose life and limb over tolerant teaching and
commandeered the wheel away from her.

In between driving lessons, they'd discussed their next
move. Since they had little faith that Father Fitzgerald's
prayers would be inspiring any divine intervention on their
behalf, they considered taking the potion to Ricki's chemistry
teacher for analysis. Unfortunately, he was on vacation until
Wednesday, so they decided to go with Ricki's spell.

Too bad she'd never taken the time to read the whole thing.

After scouring Mildred's Curio Shop for everything from black salt to mandrake juice, they hit the last ingredient and the one thing to bring their plan to a grinding halt: a cat's eye. Damian hadn't seen the roadblock, but Ricki put her foot down at mutilating kitties, alive or dead. End of discussion and end of spell. And that, to Damian's displeasure, had left them at system flush. With a quick stop at the drugstore for the necessary arsenal—laxatives and a case of Powerade—and a hasty drop-off before Mike got home from work, the cleanse began. By the time Ricki's shift came around, she was so physically drained that it took only seconds to fall asleep.

Her spiritual eyes had opened to Damian sitting in front of his TV, watching a movie. She thought she recognized it as a foreign romance, but before she could be sure, he sensed her presence and flipped to a boxing match. She continued to visit him throughout the night, each time finding him engaged in different activities to stay awake—playing on the Xbox, lifting weights, plunging his face into a sink full of ice. Her final visit had found him in the kitchen, slumped over a steaming cup of coffee, his hands trembling as they lifted it to his lips. Helpless, she watched him try to slap himself awake. Setting the cup aside, he picked up a pen and pad of paper. He began to write, his head dipping lower, bobbing with each stroke of the pen. Before he'd reached the bottom of the sheet, he was gone—the low rumble of a snore emanating from the back of his throat.

Their switch had been almost instantaneous.

And here was the note he'd written for her with his last bit of energy. A few sentences ran off the page and coffee stains blurred some of the words, but it appeared to be instructions on how to successfully masquerade as him for the next several hours.

She stared blindly at the note. Why wouldn't the potion

let them go one whole night without switching? The longer it stayed in their systems, the stronger the compulsion became. Why?

She looked at the calendar on the refrigerator. It was Tuesday—ten days since the craziness had started. The fair wouldn't return to Willow for another ten days, meaning their switches would last an additional ten hours on top of today's five, if they couldn't get things under control. Throw in about five hours for actual sleeping, and it would be almost an entire twenty-four hours outside of their own bodies by the time they got to the gypsy. Might as well be permanent.

Her eyes returned to the paper, now crumpled in a trembling fist. She skimmed it, realizing the note might not be a guide for only that day, but for the rest of her life. Slipping it into the pocket of her jeans, she whispered silent words of gratitude to Damian. One, for writing the note. And two, for thinking to dress himself before falling asleep.

Too bad she hadn't thought to do the same.

"I think Mikey is coming around."

Ricki looked askance at Damian as they walked into the school. "In what world?" she asked. "He tried to run me over, thinking I was you."

"Yeah, but he hit the brakes, didn't he?" Damian held the door open for her and Denise.

Noticing the strange looks a few students were giving them, Ricki quickly took the door from Damian and let him walk ahead of her. "How about getting him to also unlock the car door next time, so I can actually get in?" she said. "Denise lives on the other side of town. She can't keep driving me to school."

"I told you; it's not a problem," Denise said. "You guys

need me around, anyway, while you're all switched up. I'm like your chaperone or something. And who else could get Damian looking so presentable?"

Ricki gave an appreciative once-over to the work Denise had done to her body. In less than five minutes, she'd managed to turn Damian into a creation worthy of *Teen Vogue*. A sleek side bun, eclectic assortment of jewelry around his neck and wrists, and Bohemian print scarf wrapped around his waist for "dramatic flair" had him looking more stylish and trendy in Ricki's body than Ricki herself ever had.

Wow. I actually look…not so bad. "I should let you dress me more often," she said.

Damian rolled his eyes.

"Junior," Ricki said, shooing away a couple of undergrad cheerleaders who kept sidling up to her, "I'm doing what I can to get you back in good with Mike. But while *you* are in my body, you've got to do better. We can't cure ourselves if we can't be around each other. And in order to be around each other, Mike needs to not want to kill you."

"So tell him to stop trying to kill me," he responded. "You're not doing anything wrong, right? Stop letting him treat you like you are."

"Preach it," Denise muttered under her breath.

Ricki ignored her. "A lot easier said than done. You guys know Mike doesn't listen to me."

"I never understand why you give him so much control." He stopped in front of her homeroom class. "He's your brother, not your father, and we got enough stuff getting in our way without Mikey Ray being one of them. Handle it." Pointing a finger at her, he backed into the classroom.

Denise shrugged. "The boy speaks some sense." She turned to follow him.

"Hold up," Ricki said, grabbing her hand. "I will keep working on Mike, but how's it going with everyone else?"

"Let's just say I'm running into walls," she replied carefully. "Lindsey throws a drama fit whenever I bring you up. Yolanda can't stop arguing every frickin' point long enough for me to get your side of the story out. And Teresa claims she's not mad at you. She says it's a trust issue that only you can fix." Looking around, she whispered, "She also said something about you asking her and Lindsey for a threesome yesterday. I'm guessing Damian had control over that one, so I'm not even touching it."

Ricki's face fell. "It's like that, huh?"

"For now, yeah. But not for always. Just worry about how to get your body back, and let me worry about the rest, 'kay?" She squeezed Ricki's hand. "Good luck."

Ricki turned to face the group of kids who'd been discreetly trailing her through the school. A mishmash collection of jocks, popular elite, and the obligatory female groupies hung back, waiting for a signal to approach. Holding in a groan, she forced a welcoming smile on her face and beckoned to them. Within seconds, she was surrounded.

Good luck, indeed.

By lunchtime, the switch still hadn't ended.

Ricki walked with a group of Damian's friends to the cafeteria, her nerves frayed to their ends. The past few hours had taken her to new heights of stress and dangled her dangerously over the edge—struggling to remember names and faces, not knowing how to respond to certain questions, continually forgetting who she was and trying to hold conversations with the wrong people. When one of her friends from Spanish class almost went into convulsive shock after *the* D Marquez approached her at the water fountain, Ricki realized she needed to be more careful with the body she wielded. Apparently, Damian's flesh was deadlier than a weapon of mass destruction.

And having to muddle through Damian's third period gym class *and* survive the boys' locker room without going blind or sick to her stomach? The sights she had seen. The odors she had smelled. There were no words.

She squirmed. Plus, she *really* needed to use the bathroom.

"The sculpture is coming out pretty well," a short, wiry boy with glasses and a borderline mullet said to her. "Are you still coming to my house tomorrow to help me finish the head?"

She frowned down at him. "Tomorrow?" she echoed.

"Or the day after," he hastily amended. "It's no biggie."

She studied him from the corner of her eye. He carried a backpack overflowing with books and paperwork, forcing him into a lopsided hunch. His stringy hair—already styled in a blatant crime against all things fashion—glistened with oil, and his pants were an inch away from declaring impending disaster by flood. He was all but missing a pocket protector and D&D handbook. He certainly didn't seem like someone who would be allowed anywhere near Damian's inner circle.

"Right," she said in a noncommittal tone.

"Great, dude," he said, his face lighting up. "See you in class." Shifting his backpack's weight to the other shoulder, he marched away, knocking into students as he bumbled down the corridor.

"You and your pet projects," one of the boys beside Ricki mumbled. When she looked his way in question, he coughed nervously. "Nothing, man. My bad."

She faced forward, pensive. It had been that way all morning—different people coming up to her, asking about all kinds of things Damian had promised to help them with. And if they didn't want his help, they wanted his opinion. Her brain had been picked about everything from what she thought of yesterday's game against Jefferson to what she thought they should eat for lunch that would be "low in carbs but high in soluble fiber." She didn't even know what soluble fiber *was*, let alone where to find it in their lunch menu.

If asked a few weeks ago, she would've insisted Damian's life consisted of playing soccer, picking his nose, and making out with random girls. In no particular order. The idea of him actually lending some tangible value to society never would've been a thought in her mind. But people looked up to him, and the burden of their faith in his opinions was becoming a little too heavy for her to carry.

As she entered the cafeteria, a slender arm slipped around her waist. "Hey, Boo."

Flinching, she stopped herself from flinging it away. Instead, she gritted her teeth and smiled down at the short, raven-haired beauty in skintight jeans.

"We're still going out tonight, right?" the girl crooned.

Ricki was slow to answer, wondering if the girl was a recipient of yesterday's crank calls. Should she ask if syphilis had been mentioned at any point in their conversation? "Tonight, huh?"

The girl pouted, twisting a finger through her lustrous black hair. "I knew you forgot. Damian, if you didn't want to come to my sister's party, why didn't you say so?"

"My mistake?"

"It will be if you don't come." The girl poked a curvaceous blonde who had just joined them at the Entrée line. "Hey, maybe we can double with you and Aaron."

Mitzi. Ricki felt as though she'd been doused with ice. She opened her mouth to speak, when the world suddenly swam…

...and deposited her back into her body.

She looked around, wild-eyed. She sat at a Lunchyard table, surrounded by a group of gawking faces. Denise was the only familiar one in the crowd.

"Are you okay?" someone asked.

"Low blood sugar," Denise said, stepping in. She tossed an apple at Ricki, almost smacking her in the face. "Eat up."

Ricki bit into the apple, chewing slowly as she collected her thoughts. She looked at her watch. As expected, the switch had lasted an hour longer than yesterday. If they weren't able to stay awake tonight, she'd be spending the whole lunch period as Damian tomorrow.

She stared wistfully across the courtyard at her old table. A couple of drama troupe members now occupied her and Denise's seats. The table seemed strangely quiet, void of its usual laughter and rowdiness, but Ricki's heart still ached at how quickly she'd been replaced.

Her gaze traveled to the soccer table where Damian was back in action, holding court as though everything was normal. He looked her way and offered a small wave. She gave a short nod in return, aware of Lindsey probably cataloging their every move.

Her attention shifted to Aaron.

Mitzi sat at his side, giggling and poking him in the shoulder with her fork. Each time she jabbed him, he swatted her away in annoyance. Shifting away, he noticed Damian's attention on Ricki. He looked across the Yard, his eyes locking with Ricki's.

He smiled.

Air rushed from her chest. That twitch of the lips told her everything she needed to know. Despite Damian's interference and her pep rally disgrace, she still had a chance. And if she still had a chance with him after all that craziness, there was no way she'd let him slip away to someone else. Someone who hadn't waited as long for him. Someone who hadn't gone through as much. Someone who wasn't bright enough to stop sticking him with a freakin' fork while he was trying to eat.

Standing up, she gave her feet free rein and obediently followed them across the Yard.

"Where're you going?" Denise hissed.

She didn't answer. If she allowed herself to think of the words to respond, then she would think of all the reasons she shouldn't do what she was about to do. Thinking was overrated. Action was in order.

"Hi, Aaron," she said, sliding into an empty slot on the bench across from him and Mitzi. Blocking out Damian's disapproving frown, she smiled politely at Mitzi. "Hi."

A meticulously tweezed eyebrow arched in disdain. "Do I know you?"

Ricki held the smile in place. Cutting her eyes back to Aaron, she allowed the words "Do you want to go out tonight?" to flow from her mouth.

Talking at the table stopped.

An agitated Damian reappeared in her peripheral view.

"I heard some good movies are coming out at Decker's," she said. "Since I owe you a rain check for Teresa's movie night, I thought you might want to collect."

Aaron's mouth spread into a satisfied grin. He took in Damian's dark scowl, and the grin grew wider. "Sounds good to me."

Her insides glowed. The urge to shoot a victorious smile at Mitzi was strong, but she instead contented herself with the dumb expression printed across the girl's face. *Classic.*

"No can do," Damian cut in. "She can't go out."

The glow dimmed. "Excuse you?"

"There's no way Mikey's letting you out of the house."

"He's my brother not my dad, remember?" she snapped. "And neither are you, so how about staying out of my business?"

"Yeah, D," Aaron said. "The lady wants to kick it with me tonight. Something you can't control. Imagine that?"

Disregarding him, Damian said to Ricki, "But don't you already have something important you're supposed to be doing tonight? Something about a *spell*ing bee you're watching on TV?"

She glared at him. "The *spell*ing bee was last night. And it didn't last long because the kids got stumped on the word *feline*. And *ocular*. So they decided to move on to something else. Why don't you do the same?"

He held his hands up. "Hey, it's straight. Do your thing." He turned away and began talking to the boys next to him. Taking his cue, conversation at the table resumed.

She eyed him suspiciously. That was too easy. She turned back to Aaron, considering postponing their date, when she caught Mitzi openly looking her up and down like she was an insect needing to be squashed.

She smiled brightly at Aaron. "How about dinner before the movie?"

He was watching her.

Ricki sensed Damian's presence in the car not long after the movie began. It had been hovering near her shoulder for the past five minutes.

She bit her cheek to keep from cursing, unable to believe he had deliberately fallen asleep and dream-projected into the middle of her date with Aaron. No wonder he hadn't put up a fight during lunch.

"Something wrong?" Aaron asked. "You've gotten all tense on me."

"No, everything's fine," she said, forcing herself to relax. She snuggled into the crook of his arm, trying to ignore Damian's presence. "I must be spooking myself out before the movie can get to me."

Monkey Burn V played on the drive-in screen. The first murder scene was underway with a homicidal chimpanzee stalking two garbagemen through a city park. She watched through her lashes as the animal bashed one of the men across the skull with a trash can lid and gutted the other with a broken recycling sign. Her stomach twisted as the man's intestines poured into a patch of daisies, magnified to twenty times its normal gross-out factor on the big screen.

This definitely was not the movie she'd had in mind for their date.

They were supposed to be on the other side of the lot watching *An Unusual Way*, the new romantic comedy she'd been waiting on all year to hit the theaters. Seeing the movie had given her almost as much incentive to get out of the house as being alone with Aaron. Cuddling over a bag of popcorn, watching a tale of young love unfold on the screen as it simultaneously unfolded between her and Aaron? *So* worth lying to Mike about running lines at Denise's house.

She never would've imagined that her tale of blossoming love would instead be one of bludgeoning massacres. Or that the popcorn bag was two dry heaves away from becoming a vomit bag. It was a good thing she couldn't hear Phantom Damian—he was probably rolling all over the back seat, belting out a good laugh at her dream date gone wrong.

Aaron didn't like romances. And he wasn't too hot on comedies either. He wasn't big on much of anything that didn't include killing, car chases, or a minimum of three gratuitous sex scenes per hour. It was a disappointing discovery for Ricki, but she'd been willing to put her own interests aside for the bigger picture. One stupid movie or a future as Aaron Miller's girlfriend? Not a tough choice.

But it was the kind of choice she seemed to be making a lot that night.

She had wanted Italian for dinner. Aaron decided they'd have more fun at a cheesy Mexican dive where the highlight entertainment included a pair of eighty-year-old men in sombreros, shaking maracas while balancing bowls of plastic tacos on their heads. She had wanted to stop at the lake to feed ducks before going to the movie. He opted for a joyride through downtown Willow, scaring homeless people awake with a blaring car horn and pretending to offer them cash before driving off when they reached the car. Not exactly Ricki's idea of a rip-roaring good time, but she'd chalked it up to possibly being a male thing.

She risked a peek at the movie screen just in time to see the lab assistant who'd later be disemboweled by a butter knife fight off two rampaging monkeys and escape into a Porta Potty. Groaning came from the other cars as the monkeys pushed the mobile bathroom onto its side and a week's worth of human filth spilled all over the trapped assistant.

Aaron laughed.

She guessed tasteless bathroom mishaps also fell under the category of "male things."

"Why did he run into that tiny, little toilet when there was an empty warehouse just a few feet away?" she whispered.

He looked at her as though she'd just asked the world's dumbest question. "Because the john was right beside him."

"But now he's trapped." She glanced at the screen. "And rolling down a hill in a portable toilet. Isn't that kind of silly?"

Grunting in response, he continued watching the movie.

She stared down at her hands, unhappy. Nothing about this

date was going the way she'd fantasized it would, even without Damian's unwelcome appearance. *What am I doing wrong?*

His arm tightened around her shoulder. "What's up? You're not having a good time?"

"It's okay," she replied. It had to be her imagination, but she could swear she heard a snort come from the back seat. "All the blood and stuff is making me a little nauseous, that's all."

"It *is* kind of gross," he sympathized. He looked at the screen, then looked at her thoughtfully. "Do you want to go somewhere else?"

"In the middle of the movie?"

"Sure. I can't enjoy myself if you're not enjoying yourself."

It hasn't stopped you this whole evening. Why start now? She caught herself, wondering where that traitorous thought had come from.

"Where can we go?" she asked.

He checked his watch. "The lake should be empty around now. Want to ride by?"

The air around them changed. It grew heavier as though another person had joined them in the car. Ricki turned her head, almost expecting to see a flesh-and-blood Damian behind her, eating the rest of her popcorn. The seat remained empty. She shivered. His presence had never been this strong before. This substantial. Like it was actually trying to materialize and make physical contact with her. How could Aaron not notice it? Then, in an instant, he was gone. She closed her eyes, trying to feel if he still lurked nearby. There was nothing. His dream cycle must have ended.

And the next one could start at any time.

"Ready to go?" she asked anxiously. "I mean, we don't really have much time before I have to get back home."

Aaron flashed a lopsided grin. "Your wish is my command."

Throwing the car into reverse, he backed out of the parking spot and pealed out of the lot.

The ride to the park was short, fast, and near lethal. Aaron seemed on a mission to prove he'd never met a red light he couldn't run or a speed limit he wouldn't break. Ricki had hoped to get some type of conversation going but was too focused on not screaming every time the car almost flipped over. The lake was almost deserted when they arrived. Aaron pulled into a spot near the bank, close to a small group of ducks padding along its edges. Several geese nested nearby, watching the car's approach with hostile curiosity. Ricki gazed across the peaceful expanse of water, illuminated by the arriving moon. It was beautiful. She looked at Aaron.

It was perfect.

He cut the engine off. "Happy?"

"Very," she sighed. Eyeing the ducks, she shook the bag of popcorn. "Want to help me get rid of this?"

"Sure thing." Grabbing the bag, he flung it out the car window. The flock of geese let out a splitting honk and stormed the fallen kernels. "Anything else?"

She sat dumbfounded, her hands still gripping the air where the bag had been. "Um, I kind of meant if you wanted to help me feed the ducks with it."

He pointed to the geese battling it out over the empty bag. "They're fed." He fell back laughing as one of the geese flapped its wings and charged the rest of the group. "Look at 'em go."

"Yeah," she said in a strangled voice, "look at 'em."

"My money's on the runt. Short but feisty." Stretching, he snaked an arm around her shoulder, pulling her close. "What now?"

Well, definitely not duck feeding. "How about talking?"

A deep crease wrinkled his brow. "About what?"

"Maybe us?" she offered.

His arm eased back to his side.

"I mean about *ourselves*. Like, I tell you about me, you tell me about you."

"I dunno," he hedged, sliding his arm back into place. "It's hard for me to talk to someone when I really like them. The way I like you." Rubbing her shoulder, he looked into her eyes. "I try to hide it, but I'm kinda shy. A lot of people don't know that about me. But I know I can tell you 'cause you won't judge me for not being this cool, got-it-together player everyone thinks I am. You're different."

His gaze dropped awkwardly to his lap and then lifted. It melded openly with hers, hiding nothing. Sliding his thumb along the side of her chin, he lowered his lashes and gave her the sweetest smile she'd ever seen pass across a boy's face.

She melted. All reservations about their date evaporated and floated away, sucked into the sincerity of his sherry eyes. Her heart warmed. She had been right. He was The One.

His thumb traced tiny circles along her jaw, inching leisurely toward her mouth until it paused at her bottom lip. "Has anyone ever told you that you have the most perfect mouth?" he murmured.

She thought her head might be shaking no, but her brain didn't seem to be in sync. She was captivated by his eyes, by the roughness of his thumbs brushing across her lips, by the scent of his cologne. Crisp and clean like an ocean breeze with a hint of earthy musk. A scent she'd become achingly familiar with over the months, recognizing it whenever she passed him in the school halls. She inhaled, imprinting his aroma into her senses.

Her eyes swept across his face, dreamily relaxed and drawing nearer. Her limbs began to tremble, the realization of what was about to happen bringing on a sudden burst of fear. She had never been this close to a boy before. Alone. His face was mere centimeters away. The warmth of his breath caressed her lips. The faint smell of hot sauce from their Mexican dinner wafted from his mouth, intermingling with the fresh linen undertones of his cologne. His hand left her face and slid to the back of her head. Fingers twined through her hair, drawing her close.

Her eyes closed.

Is this really happening? I'm about to kiss Aaron Miller. I'm about to kiss Aaron Miller! Oh God, where do my teeth go?

Their lips gently touched and pulled apart. They touched again. Opened. Something warm and soft invaded her mouth. Withdrew. It reappeared, firmly colliding with her tongue and twirling around in urgent, forceful circles. Not knowing what to do, she held her mouth open and gave him full rein. His tongue delved deeper, sliding across the walls of her cheeks and tickling the roof of her mouth. The sour essence of salsa and butter-flavored popcorn grease coated her taste buds.

She wanted to gag.

Was a kiss supposed to feel this messy and…gross? As his tongue darted possessively toward the back of her throat, his teeth mashing against her lips, her mind raced through every book she'd read with the heroine experiencing her first kiss. It had all been cotton candy and rainbows, comets bursting from the sky and fireworks announcing the arrival of new love. She couldn't remember anything about a thin film of saliva coating the perimeter of the heroine's mouth or queasiness developing in the pit of her stomach. She couldn't even breathe with her nose squashed against the side of his face. And the pressure of his chin smashing against her mouth bruised her jaw.

He moaned.

Her eyes flew open. The kiss intensified, any thought of coming up for air obviously not on Aaron's itinerary. The hand in her hair held her in place while his other hand journeyed up the side of her waist. She clamped her elbows tightly against her side, blocking further access.

"Don't be scared," he mumbled, his teeth tugging against her bottom lip. "It's okay."

Was it? What happened next if she let his hands go where she knew they wanted to? Lindsey's voice whispered in her memory, *"Aaron's a big boy…"*

She'd come so far to get to this point. If she stopped him now, would he lose interest in her? Go back to Mitzi? Her elbows relaxed slightly.

His hands pushed against the opening, widening the gap between her arm and stomach. They crawled up her torso, dragging the hem of her shirt with them. A breeze from the open window blew against her bare skin.

The air around them shifted and thickened. Damian was back.

Her senses came rushing back to her. She shoved Aaron away. "I have to go home!" she blurted.

He sat back, visibly irritated. "Now?"

She jammed the bottom of her shirt back into her jeans. "It's past curfew, and Mike will come looking for me if I don't get home." She touched her bruised lips, on the verge of tears but not understanding why. "I told him we might come here, so he'll probably be showing up any minute."

A glint of unease passed across his face. "It's okay. I understand, baby." He removed her hand from her lips and softly kissed each finger. "We'll have another time to keep getting to know each other."

She swallowed the lump in her throat and nodded. The comprehension of where she was about to let things go frightened her. Would she really have gone all the way? She liked to believe she wouldn't, but—she looked into the hazel eyes gazing gently at her—it was Aaron…

He again kissed the inside of her hand and held it in his

lap as he started up the car. "Y'know, a girl like you is hard to come by. I think I could fall in love with you."

Her ears delivered the message to her unbelieving mind. *Love.* Not like. *Love.*

Shaking, she shoved her free hand under her hip. Aaron Miller had just said he could love her. She should be pole vaulting to cloud nine and setting up permanent camp. But all she could think about was how grateful she was to Damian for showing up when he did.

Go figure.

He sat waiting for her on the front porch when Denise dropped her off at home.

"Nice date?" Damian asked as Ricki waved goodbye to Denise.

"You would know," she wearily replied, easing down beside him. She eyeballed the small box on his lap. "What's that?"

He handed the package to her. A blue ribbon tied it shut, with a ragged piece of paper taped to its side. Looking at him suspiciously, she unfolded the note.

> Thought you might need this.
> Calvin

Afraid to see what was inside, she cautiously pulled at the ribbon. The lid fell off, revealing a small stone set in the center of a velvet cushion. It was lemon yellow in color with an almost translucent line running through its center, giving the appearance of a cat's eye. As she turned the rock from side to side, the line shifted.

"It's called a cat's eye stone," Damian said. "Found it on my front porch when I got home from practice."

She gaped at the rock. "How in the world did Calvin know we were looking for a cat's eye?"

Damian shrugged. "I guess he knows people."

She shook her head, trying to clear her thoughts. "Um, wow. A rock, not an actual eyeball. But we still can't do the spell tonight. It has to be under clouds, and the sky is completely clear."

"Rain's in the forecast tomorrow."

She couldn't tear her eyes away from the stone. *That Calvin...*

"Okay," she said. "We'll do it tomorrow."

"Deal," he said, standing up. "I'd better get going before Mikey gets home."

"Weren't you supposed to be on a date tonight yourself?"

"Was I?" He scratched his chin. "I canceled it. Thought I might be able to get a little sleep in while you were doing your thing with Aaron. Figured you'd be so hopped up, there's no way you'd fall asleep too."

"So you didn't take a nap just to spy on me?"

"Why would I do that?" he said. "You're a big girl. Why, what'd you think?"

"Maybe that you weren't ready to give up messing with me just yet." Her head tilted. "Are you?"

Chuckling, he reclaimed his seat on the porch. "Rocky, do you know why I always picked on you?"

"Because you're evil?" she half-joked.

"Because you needed it," he said. "You're so self-conscious it's painful. You think about every single move you make, every word that comes out of your mouth. Like you think everyone's waiting to judge you or something. Even when you're just sitting down, you're thinking about how to do it perfect instead of just plopping down on a chair and having a good time." He grinned sheepishly. "So I kick the chair out from under you."

She stared at him. "You're twisted."

He nodded. "Maybe. But after you fall, don't you have a good time coming after me?"

She couldn't help but grin.

"There's only two times I ever see you drop your guard and just let go. One, when you're onstage. And two, when you're trying to kill me."

Without meaning to, she burst into laughter. "Well, trying to kill you *is* fun."

"Must be why you made it a lifetime hobby," he teased, nudging her with his knee.

"I could say the same about you, y'know."

"Me?" He shook his head. "No way."

"Yeah, you're Mr. Cool all the time. Walks right, talks right, dresses right. But the only time you drop *your* guard is after I take that chair and try to beat you over the head with it." She giggled. "Then, Mr. Cool has left the building!"

"Hey, I guess you just have that effect on me," he conceded. "But only you. Anyone else tries coming at me with that chair, they'll find it wrapped around their neck." He looked thoughtful. "To be honest, though, nobody else but you would ever try."

"Guess it's a good thing we retired the chair, huh?" she asked wistfully.

He gave her a lazy smile and stood up, stretching. "Ah, Rocky. We'll always have that chair. It ain't going nowhere."

She met his smile. "Goodnight, Junior. I get the next shift?"

"For all the good it'll do, sure." Starting to walk away, he stopped. "And Rocky? Next time you're in my body, would you *please* use the bathroom? I about wet myself today when I flipped back. I know you got the modest thing going, but you can't hold it in forever."

She smirked. "Watch me."

CHAPTER SIXTEEN

A NOTHER DAY AS A BOY...ANOTHER day closer to losing her mind.

Ricki pushed the lunch tray away, unable to summon an appetite. Her head hurt, her bladder was on the verge of exploding, and her skin still itched from the cologne she'd doused herself with that morning. She rubbed her chin against her shoulder, taking a discreet sniff to see if the Acqua Di Gio/Creed/Polo concoction was still holding up under five hours of crowded hallways, bad nerves, and the ever-dreaded gym class.

So far, so good.

She turned an exasperated eye to the mane of silky black hair beside her. Damian's latest toy. The girl's mouth hadn't stopped moving for the past ten minutes, and her voice was about as pleasant as screeching tires before a ten-car pileup. "Chloe," Ricki broke in, too tired to be civil, "don't you want to put some food in that mouth sometime before lunch ends? Seriously, anytime you're ready." Cutting the girl's astonished face from view, she stabbed at a wilted stalk of broccoli.

Aaron scooted down the bench to put his arm around Chloe. "Dang, homey," he chided Ricki, "why're you so cold?" He nuzzled the girl's neck, making her giggle. "There you go, baby. Did I make it better?"

Smiling coyly, she nodded.

Ricki's eyes narrowed.

One of the boys nearest her whispered, "Don't even sweat it, D. You know Aaron always wants what you have."

She crammed a forkful of broccoli into her mouth, glaring.

"Hey, people." A petite, dark-skinned girl hefting a tray of food stood at the table. Smiling graciously, she muscled her way onto the bench, positioning herself firmly between Aaron and Chloe.

"Mikey Ray told me to tell everyone hi," the girl said. Having cemented her undisputed right to a spot at their table, she rubbed her belly. "Man, I'm hungry," she declared, tearing into a stuffed pita pocket. Mushrooms and lettuce rained down onto the table.

Ricki gaped at herself. What did Damian think he was doing, coming to the jock table while still in her body? She watched him finish off the last bite of pita with gusto before attacking a pile of onion rings. A giant smear of grease ran across his chin, but his napkin lay untouched on the tray.

She cringed as he snatched a pickle from Aaron's plate and introduced it to the rest of the half-chewed food in his mouth. "I can't eat all that," she uttered in dismay, before realizing she'd spoken aloud. "I mean, um, *Ricki*, you have something on your chin."

Aaron's head jerked. "Since when is she 'Ricki?'" he mumbled.

Damian swiped the back of his hand across his chin. "Thanks, *Satan's Seed*," he quipped. "What would I do without you?" Stuffing another onion ring into his mouth, his gaze swept the table. "Maybe finally get some," he said, his eyes dancing as he nudged Aaron.

All talking died. A hoot sounded from the other end of the table, and everyone dissolved into laughter—everyone except a perturbed Aaron.

Ricki looked around, lost. Damian winked at her, plucking

another pickle from Aaron's plate. As soon as the laughter died down, he started talking to the boys next to him, asking about their strategy for the upcoming soccer match. He soon had everyone caught up in conversation, his attention spread equally among the athletes, groupies, and "other." He talked sports with one group and switched gears midbreath to ask another about the best stores for shopping. Before Ricki knew it was happening, he'd dominated the entire table.

How did he do that?

In only minutes, Damian had entered the exclusive kingdom of athletic royalty and wrapped it around his little pinkie. Without even breaking a sweat or bothering to wipe the crumbs off his face. And he hadn't done it as himself—he had done it as *her*.

Plain, boring, unimpressive her.

She observed him, smiling and laughing with ease. How could he be so comfortable in her skin? She wasn't even comfortable there. Reserved and fidgety were polite words to describe her on a good day. *So this is how a king rules, even when he's in the body of a servant girl.*

"Dude, she's hot," she heard someone whisper.

Disbelief burned her ears. A boy had just called her hot, and it hadn't been the punch line of a joke? She took a hard look at Damian, noticing that Denise had done another impressive job dressing him. The burnt-orange tank top hanging loosely from his shoulders complemented the chocolate coloring of her skin. A high ponytail sat at the crown of his head, cascading down to the nape of his neck and exposing delicate cheekbones and ears. And Denise must've used a different makeup, because her skin seemed smoother than usual. Even her eyes were more striking than Ricki had realized. Their dark pupils caught the sunlight and twinkled every time Damian smiled.

She sat quietly, scrutinizing herself through the eyes of someone else. Why did she look so different from the outside? She'd looked at that person in the mirror every day for sixteen years, yet she felt as though she was seeing herself for the first time.

And what she saw wasn't so bad.

As she studied herself, every word Denise had said over the years flooded her head. In more ways than Ricki could count, her friend had told her that beauty came from within. And Damian, of all people, had somehow tapped into the beauty within her. It showed in his confidence and every smile he flashed. In spite of an onion-grease smear on his chin and a face that obviously hadn't been touched by a blotting sheet all morning, he put every other girl at the table to shame.

She looked down at the pile of napkins stacked in front of her and thought of the collection of compact mirrors stashed in each of her purses. Useless crutches. What good were those things to her if she never felt any better about herself after using them? Maybe the next time she looked in the mirror, she needed to do it through other eyes. Ones that weren't quite so critical and didn't pinpoint every imagined flaw. Ones that didn't compare the reflection in the glass to her friends. Maybe she needed to reintroduce herself to the girl in the mirror and get to know the *real* her.

It was time to get her body back. She had a lot of reacquainting to do.

As if the urgency of her wish had been heard, an answer was given. The world around her spun, depositing her two seats over on the lunch bench, between Chloe and Aaron. Her hands lifted to her face, thrilled to feel the nose she'd once scorned under their fingertips. They paused over a greasy smudge, tempted to wipe it off but deciding to leave it there.

Damian also rubbed his hands across his face. He breathed

a sigh of relief. "Finally," he muttered. Louder, he said, "Who saw that racing movie on TV last night?"

And like that, the crowd was again under his rule. Only this time, he was on his rightful throne and wearing the proper robes.

She stared at him in wonder. *He really is something else.*

"Do I have you all to myself again?" Aaron murmured in her ear.

She reluctantly pulled her attention away from Damian. "I don't know," she said, her voice frosty. "Am I the one you want?"

"Of course you are," he said. "Don't you know you're the *only* one I want?" He blew on her neck and kissed it.

She softened, giggling. "In that case, sure. I'm yours." She turned away, and her eyes locked with Damian's. They lingered longer than intended, and an unusual warmth grew in her belly. The giggles died in her throat.

"Sure," she repeated, dragging her gaze back to Aaron. "I'm all yours."

"Something's different about you."

Ricki wrinkled her nose at Reggie. "What, am I more tired and haggard than usual?" she joked.

He squinted at her through the dimness of the auditorium. "Can't tell," he said, straight-faced. "It's too dark in here for the light to really capture the gray hairs and bags under your eyes. I'm seeing ash, but I can't tell if it's wrinkles or if you just need some lotion."

She bumped his shoulder, smothering a laugh. Lindsey and Denise were in the middle of their scene, and she didn't want to give Lindsey yet another reason to hate her. Her lunchtime presence at the soccer table had done a well enough job of stirring the pot as it was. Teresa wouldn't stop staring at her, and Lindsey's death glares had become a bit too scary.

She and Reggie were relaxing after their last scene of the day. For once, she had gotten through practice with no forgotten lines or missed blocking. If she could somehow keep it together until opening night, she wouldn't have to worry about Quincy dropkicking her into theatrical exile.

It was a shame Damian would soon be taking her place on the stage.

Their big plan to have her chemistry teacher analyze the potion had been a big bomb. Mr. Cartwell had been on board, placing the entire science wing at their disposal, but they ran into one unexpected complication: the bottle refused to open. Again.

They'd pulled. They'd pried. They'd yanked with every tool they could get their hands on, but the stopper wouldn't budge. After an hour of getting nowhere, Ricki and Damian finally gave up, knowing no way would be found to get it open. The potion wouldn't allow it.

Now all they had left was the spell. And if it didn't work…

Ricki laid her head on Reggie's shoulder and sighed, not wanting to think about it. In a few more days, Damian would be bumbling his way through her scenes, and she'd be tripping her way down a soccer field. It would take a miracle for them to pull it off.

"Tell me," she said. "How am I different?"

Reggie laid his head on top of hers. One stray curl fell across her temple. "I dunno. I guess you're more like yourself today."

"One little rehearsal where I'm not knocking props off the stage or body slamming someone into furniture, and all of a sudden I'm back to normal, huh?" She tugged on the curl and smiled. "Shows what you know."

"You seemed pretty normal during lunch."

She stilled. "Did I?"

She felt his head shake. "No, you didn't. You were better than normal." Sadness crept into his voice. "You were really happy."

"As opposed to the dark cloud over my head and wet blanket covering my shoulders every other day?" she said, half-joking.

He didn't answer.

She gave a self-conscious laugh. "You're right. Who am I kidding? I'm the poster child for teen angst." She glanced up at him. "Reggie?"

He remained quiet for a moment, then abruptly said, "You like that Aaron guy a lot, don't you?"

Her head lifted. "Where did that come from?"

"Nowhere," he said, looking away. "Just seemed like you were having a lot of fun with him at lunch, that's all. And... you just seemed different around him. That's all."

"Yeah," she said hesitantly, "I like him."

"Why?"

"Why what?"

"Why do you like him?"

She shrugged, uncomfortable. "Why wouldn't I? He's cute and nice. And he likes me too."

"And?"

"Isn't that enough?"

"What do you know about him?" he asked, his expression serious. "What does he know about you?"

She leaned against her chair, putting space between them. "Enough. What's up with all this questioning? I feel like I'm on trial or something."

"I don't know," he said, agitated. "Alright, yeah, I do. I'm trying to understand why someone like you would even give him the time of day."

Her eyes widened. "Don't you mean that the other way around?"

"Are you kidding?" His voice grew louder.

Teresa twisted around in her seat, several rows up, and peered back at them.

His eyes blazed. "That guy is lucky you even waste breath on him. And the only reason you do is because he's cute and likes you? Sad, Rick, really sad."

"I think we need to change the sub—"

"Guys like him get by on looks, with absolutely nothing else to back them up," he said, his voice continuing to rise. A girl at the other end of the aisle scowled at him, holding a finger to her lips. "They don't have to be smart. They don't have to have a personality. They don't even have to be decent human beings. They're just useless, good-looking blots on society that suck up air and styling products and don't give anything back to the world but STDs and greenhouse emissions."

She couldn't speak. The words wouldn't come to her brain fast enough. Where was her Reggie? Someone else had to be inhabiting his body because *her* Reggie would never speak to her like this or look so...so angry.

Shoving a fistful of hair out of his face, he continued. "And they get to treat good, innocent girls like yesterday's trash and move on to the next one and the next one, until all they've got is a bunch of damaged chicks for guys like me to clean up after. And you want to know why they get away with it? Because girls like you don't make them step up and be better than what they are just because they're *cute* and *they like you!*"

By the time he finished speaking, the entire front row had turned around to glare at them. Teresa looked on, with concern.

Okay, time to go. Grabbing her purse, Ricki dashed out of the auditorium.

Footsteps pursued her. "Rick, wait," Reggie's voice called.

A hand shot out and caught her arm. She spun around.

"What the hell, Reggie?" she demanded, throwing his hand from her arm.

He stepped back, holding both hands in the air. The happy-go-lucky Reggie she'd known since freshman year was nowhere to be seen in the broken boy before her. His shoulders slumped, and his face was heavy with warring emotions. His emerald eyes, usually vibrant and twinkling with humorous light, had dulled. Even his curls drooped around his head like a wilted mop.

"I'm sorry," he said. "I'm very, very sorry."

"What just happened?" she asked. "I don't want to be mad at you, but you've got to help me understand what's going on here."

Without warning, he pulled her to him. His lips collided with hers.

Too shocked to move, she stood paralyzed as his mouth moved across hers. Gently, then more insistent, an unspoken question passed from his lips to hers.

He drew away slowly. "I've always wanted to do that. But when I saw you at lunch, I realized I might never get the chance."

"Why?" she said, choking up. "With all the girls who like you, why would you even *want* to kiss me?"

"Rick, I've been wanting to kiss you since that first time you did your monologue last year in Dr. Thorpe's class." He touched her hand. "There's nobody else like you in this whole school. You're so sweet and beautiful, and you're kind. You're perfect—the Mia to my Darius in every way."

"Who's this girl you're talking about?" she breathed. "It sure doesn't sound like me."

His fingers wrapped around hers. "It could only ever be you. Don't you know how special you are?"

"Reg, I'm so screwed up it's ridiculous," she protested. "I'm a brat. I'm moody. I'm nowhere near perfect."

"You are to me. It's why I love you." He placed her hand on his heart. "You don't ever need to be anyone other than who you are. Racquel Amanda Nichols. If you were someone else, I wouldn't think about you so much every day. My heart wouldn't race every time I'm around you." His pressure on her hand increased. "Can you feel it pounding right now?"

Ricki stared at his hand, her own heart breaking. It was like a scene from a play. In Reggie's mind, he was the handsome bachelor professing his love to the blossoming spinster. Cue music, falling flowers, and closing curtain. Except the bachelor didn't realize the spinster he'd fallen in love with wasn't the person he'd created in his head.

"So," he said, tilting her head up until her eyes met his, "what's the word, Rick?"

The longing in his voice made her want to cry. "The word is *no*," she answered thickly, dying a little inside to see pain replacing the hope in his eyes. "As in, you are the best, most wonderful guy I know, but we'd never work. Let's be real—I'm kind of a head case. And I don't want the side of me that isn't so nice to come out around you sooner or later and ruin what we've got. I don't ever want anything to do that. You mean way too much to me." She kissed his cheek, tucking a curl behind his ear. "I'd kind of like you to always think of me as this sweet, perfect girl. I want to always be your Mia."

"I guess Aaron knows this other side of you?" he asked bitterly. "And that's why you like him so much?"

She had no response. Nothing that came to mind sounded

right, even to herself. No, Aaron didn't know the other side of her. To be honest, he didn't know *any* side of her yet.

Hypocrisy, thy name is Racquel, she thought miserably.

The truth was, only one boy had ever seen her at her worst. Her ugliest. Her lowest…

She shut off the rest of the thought. "No, that's not why I like Aaron."

"Then why do you?"

Her eyes dropped to the ground. "It's hard to explain," she mumbled. *Even to myself.*

———⚬⟡⚬———

"Can you at least wait for us to do this spell thing before you kill yourself?"

Ricki ignored Damian, her eyes fixed on the golf club above her head. Rain poured over her upturned face, blinding her to anything but the long metal pole pointing toward the sky. A streak of lightning flashed through the dark clouds.

"Gimme that," he ordered, marching up to her and pulling at the club.

Shrugging him away, she stumbled deeper into the backyard. Domino barked at her from his doghouse, too afraid of the storm to venture out and interfere with her ill-designed suicide attempt. She blinked against the torrent of water splashing into her eyes, not knowing or caring where the rain ended and her tears began.

"I can't do this anymore," she wailed, her voice almost drowned out by a rumble of thunder.

"Oh, please. Save the performance for the Oscars." Damian planted his feet on the muddy ground and pried her fingers, one by one, from the pole. Maneuvering it out of her hand, he tossed it aside where it landed in front of the doghouse. Domino poked his head out, snapped at the club's handle, and dragged it through the opening of his doggy door to become his new chew toy.

"You've always got to be such a drama queen," Damian grumbled, dragging Ricki to the front of her house. He pushed the front door open. "Inside."

Sniffling, she shuffled into the house and collapsed on the living room floor. He walked into the kitchen, coming out a few minutes later with an armful of towels and napkins. He dumped the napkins onto her lap and began drying her head with the towels.

"Why do you do these things?" he huffed. "Never mind. Why am I asking a stupid question?"

She brushed his hands away. Taking one of the towels, she dried her face. "You should be happy," she said. "Once I'm dead, you won't have to worry about ever waking up in my body again. Because you know that's the only way this is ever going to stop, don't you?" She flung the towel away and threw herself backward against the sofa, arms spread wide. "The stupid sleep shifts aren't working. The spell's not going to work. Madame Dupre won't be able to help us. We're just going to keep changing bodies over and over until we finally become each other. And that might as well be death, so why not end it now, on our own terms?"

He stared at her, unsympathetic. "Are you done?"

A tear ran down her cheek. "I broke my friend's heart today," she said, her voice cracking.

He frowned. "Denise?"

"Reggie."

"Who?"

"*Reggie*. From my acting troupe."

"Oh," he drawled, recognition dawning, "your toy soldier boy." He picked up another towel and handed it to her. "He'll be alright. Now cover your head—you're getting the sofa all wet."

She draped the towel over her head. "He told me he loved me," she said softly.

Damian snorted.

"He's the first guy who's ever said that to me, and I stomped all over him."

"So you decided to come home, stand outside in a storm with a golf club, and get struck by lightning? Doesn't that seem a little extreme, even to you?"

She hugged her legs. "It's not just that."

"Then what?"

Closing her eyes, she rolled her forehead across her knees. The towel blocked out the light, secluding her in her own world. A fresh round of tears bubbled at the back of her throat. She hiccupped.

"Hey." He pulled the towel off her head. "Look at me."

She peeped blearily at him.

"You know until this switching stuff ends, you're stuck with me, right?" He settled in front of her, crossing his legs with his knees touching hers. "So, release. What's wrong?"

She wiped a hand across her face and sniffed. He handed her a damp napkin. Taking it, she looked into his eyes and was caught off guard by the earnest concern in them. They drew her in, offering a safe haven for her to confide her troubles.

She decided to accept the invitation. "I'm losing everyone. I have Denise, and I guess I have"—she vaguely waved a hand toward him and rolled her eyes—"*you*. But everyone else is gone, and I feel so alone. My parents won't be back for another two weeks. Mike's too busy being my bodyguard to be my friend. Lindsey, Yolanda, and Teresa hate me. And now I've lost Reggie because things aren't ever going to be the same between us, I know."

He looked as though he wanted to speak but wisely chose to keep his words to himself.

"It's like, for the longest time, I had this cool, incredible bunch of friends who let me be part of them. Now I don't." Her thumb caught a falling tear before it rolled down her cheek. "They don't want anything to do with me anymore."

"They're just being females," he said. "Arbitrary and vindictive. Give it a week, and they'll be back to being your bestest of friends. Little soldier boy too."

"I don't think so. Reggie couldn't even look at me for the rest of rehearsal. And I wish Lindsey would *stop* looking at me. It's like she's trying to hex me with her mind or something. I just wish everything could go back to the way it was before that stupid party." Blowing her nose, she mumbled, "I knew I should've stayed home."

"And I should've left you alone when you bumped into me in the hall, but I didn't," he said. "Instead, I thought it'd be funny to spike your drink. Big laughs from that one, huh?"

"But you wouldn't have spiked my drink if I hadn't shined the sun in your eyes."

"But you wouldn't have shined the sun at me if I hadn't—" He put a hand over his eyes. "You know we could go on like this all night, don't you?"

She allowed a tiny smile. "All night? Try all week."

"All month."

"All year."

"All decade."

"All our natural born lives…"

"Touché." Pulling her legs out to rest on his, he removed her shoes and began drying her feet with a discarded towel. "Your friends are mad at you. So what? They'll get over it."

"Easy for you to say. You have ten truckloads of friends, so who cares if a couple fall off your radar? I can count mine on one hand. And they made me feel like I was somebody." She brushed away the remaining tears. "I know you can't relate, so let's just move on."

"Rocky, all those people following behind me aren't my friends. They're just fans. And yeah, there's a difference. They don't know the first thing about me, and to be honest, they don't *want* to. D Marquez, captain of the soccer team. Bam, that's all they want to know. Anything else would just mess up the image." He held up his hand. "My real friends can only be counted on these five fingers too. But what I'm not getting is why you think you *were* somebody with them. Like you're not somebody now?"

She stared at the ceiling. "I don't know who I am," she whispered. "Just that I feel alone. Their lives have gone on like I was never even a part of it. They replaced me at lunch. They walk past me in the hall like I'm not there. It's like I've been exiled from my own life."

"Give 'em time. See how things shake out. Sometimes people just need a cooling-off period before they can get it together."

"You might be right," she allowed.

"And while they're cooling off, maybe you need to ask yourself why you think your life is defined by your friendships and not by who you are."

She looked down her nose at him. "How profound. Do you know who *you* are?"

"I'm D Marquez, baby!" he replied, grinning wickedly. He flexed both arms and struck a pose. "Strong, sexy, and sinful. What you see is what you get."

Holding in a laugh, she shook her head. No, what she'd seen for the past ten years was definitely *not* what she was getting now. And maybe he was right about her making peace with her own identity, independent of her friends. She couldn't be the social reject shining off the light from other people's stars forever. Who was she underneath all the insecurity and fear?

Pretty ironic for her to take that first step on the path to finding herself just as she was on the verge of becoming somebody else.

"You realize we're only a few days away from becoming each other for good, don't you?" she asked.

His smile drooped. "Yeah, I do. But I don't need to get freaked out over stuff I can't control."

"I wish I could be so Zen," she said. "Instead, I'm hyperventilating every ten minutes, thinking about what it's going to be like when the switch becomes permanent. Remember not wanting your life to turn into a Disney movie? Well, how do you like it now that it's turned into *Nightmare on Elm Street*? Don't go to sleep or you'll wake up in your worst nightmare."

"I'm still your worst nightmare?" he asked, pretending to be hurt.

"You used to be." She laughed. "Now you're more like a gas-induced bad dream."

He laughed along with her. "Nice to see I'm taking a step up in the world."

"Talk to me in a couple of weeks when my period starts. Then you'll *really* be in your worst nightmare."

His eyes shot to her face, horrified. "No. Oh, no..."

"Oh yes," she said smugly. "How do you like your Zen world now?"

He groaned. "Please let the spell work."

She stopped laughing, the gloom returning to her face. "Why should it? Nothing else has, and we've done about everything. We even drank holy water the other night, and *that* didn't even do anything."

"Stop it," he said. "We're gonna do this spell, try to stick to the sleep shifts, and find that stupid gypsy the second the fair hits town. Anything else is just stress."

"And I definitely don't need any more of that." Lifting her feet from his lap, she stood up. "Let me put on some dry clothes and get the stuff for the spell."

When she returned to the living room, she found Damian sprawled across the floor, his head resting on a mound of wet towels, eyes closed. She paused, her arms loaded down with an assortment of candles, herbs, and mysterious bottles with gray symbols engraved on black labels.

He looked so peaceful. So harmless.

She looked at the rain splattering against the windows. Less than an hour ago, she'd wanted nothing more than to drown her troubles away in that rain. Now, after talking with him, she felt like maybe she had a fighting chance. Everything didn't have to be so black and white; maybe there was a gray balance of tranquility that could extend beyond the four corners of her bedroom ceiling.

She wasn't sure how long she stood in the doorway staring at him, but she almost jumped when one of his eyes opened to look at her. Her cheeks filled with heat. She looked away, unnerved.

"Are we doing this thing or what?" he groused.

Composing herself, she walked over to him and dumped the contents of her arms onto his stomach. With a loud "Ooph," he sat up and glared at her.

"Okay," she said, rubbing her hands together, "let's do this."

Thursday morning, 7:02 AM, and Ricki stood in the bathroom staring at the toilet. *I'll never be able to do this. Not in a million years.*

She opened the medicine cabinet and looked at the assortment of razors and shaving creams sitting on its shelves. Her hand skimmed the shelves, searching for the toothpaste. *Why does he always put it in a different place every time?* The toothbrush was still in her mouth, foam dribbling down her chin when the doorbell rang. Quickly rinsing her mouth and running a washcloth over her face, she dashed downstairs to answer it before Ms. Marquez woke up.

She was unprepared for the visitors awaiting her at the door.

Teresa stood on the porch, one fist wrapped around the frilly collar of a struggling Damian and the other clutching the hair of a sullen Calvin. A piece of paper peeked out of his hands. Ricki caught the word "curse" printed across the top of the sheet before his fingers closed over it.

It was a copy of her spell.

"Okay," Teresa wheezed, breathless. "I've given you time to come clean with me, but you insist on being difficult. I'm tired of waiting. So, *Ricki*, why don't you tell me what's going on?"

And with a deep breath, she did.

CHAPTER SEVENTEEN

ONLY TERESA COULD SOLVE IN twenty minutes what had taken Ricki almost a week to accept.

Ten minutes of ransacking her little brother's bedroom to uncover Ricki's spell; five minutes of interrogation, breaking Calvin down to a full confession about the potion and party events; two minutes of creative paperclip usage to "encourage" further details on an unnamed security guard he'd blackmailed into trailing Ricki around town; and a final three minutes of tripping up Damian with questions she knew he couldn't answer had brought her to the incredible conclusion that Ricki and Damian were swapping bodies. And all before the top coat of her pedicure even had time to dry.

When Ricki asked why she'd gone to so much trouble to uncover the secret, she answered, "Sweetie, I said I mind my own business. But when you start acting a straight fool on your friends and break up our happy home, *you* become my business. Plus, I knew there's no way you'd be caught dead with a face shinier than groundskeeper Jay's bald spot in July, but that's a whole 'nother story."

Classic Teresa, and Ricki couldn't have loved her more for it.

With no further questions asked, she and Calvin jumped on board with the hunt to track down Madame Dupre. If there was a rock somewhere out there that the gypsy was hiding under, they made it their mission to find it, obliterate it, and scatter its dust to the four winds in remembrance. Private investigators were hired. Undisclosed sums of money were dropped on the desks of Commissions Board officials. Notices were posted on websites and in newspapers across the country.

When four days had passed, Madame Dupre still hadn't been found. After the fair departed Willow to move on to the next town, Madame Celeste Dupre had not moved with it. Instead, she'd vanished with no clues left behind. She simply ceased to exist. With all avenues exhausted, a disheartened Ricki and Damian admitted defeat and accepted that nothing was left for them but to wait until Friday for the fair to return. Another week of body swaps and more hours lost to wearing each other's skin. But they'd at least managed one small victory against the potion.

Abandoning the sleep shifts, they instead chose to fall sleep at an earlier time, forcing the switches to happen much sooner in the night. When done early enough, they had time to fall back asleep and spend the majority of the swap unconscious. The past three days had been spent in their correct bodies and nights were a mere inconvenience.

Until last night.

An all-night shouting match between Mike and his girlfriend had Ricki crawling into bed well after midnight… and crawling out of Damian's bed Monday morning. With the switch now lasting almost eleven hours, it had taken them through the entire school day, leaving Damian to survive drama rehearsal and Ricki to navigate the dangerous world of high school soccer practice. Athletically challenged, sports-illiterate her.

Getting dressed in the locker room was traumatic enough—she spent the whole time with her eyes closed, doing her best not to touch anything on her body or off. But getting on the field and being subjected to an exercise routine that would put the average human being in a coma was downright inhumane. Practice started with running four laps around the field. Yeah, right. She barely made it one whole lap before the novelty wore off and she was ready to comfort herself with a bag of Doritos and a Coke. She tried faking a twisted ankle, but two teammates thought they'd be helpful by propping her up for the remaining three laps. They were no doubt surprised when all they got for their troubles was a mumbled "bite it."

Next came footwork: kicking a ball around the field and bouncing it off various body parts. The kicking part, she could handle. It was when she actually had to move with the ball that problems arose. *Coordination* was a word she usually associated with dancers and fashion designers. It was something her body had never quite gotten the hang of, and she'd long ago stopped trying to push the issue.

Run? Fine.

Kick? Cool.

Do both? She didn't think so.

After tripping, fumbling, and outright bulldozing her way through the field, she was ready to give up. And after seeing the wake of destruction she'd left behind, the coach should've let her. Instead, he ignored her complaints of a pulled hamstring, smacked her on the bottom, barked, "Suck it up!" and shoved her toward the goal.

When she found herself staring down the path of a fifteen-man lineup—all holding soccer balls aimed in her direction—she knew it was beyond time to call it a day. There was a nice bench on the sidelines waiting for her butt to warm, and she was ready to make its acquaintance. Only, by the time she took her first step away from the goal, it was too late.

It began with a whistle and ended in a whimper.

They came flying. Innocent soccer balls suddenly turned

into deadly projectile missiles with direct launching orders to
her gut. They slammed into her, ricocheting off her arms and
head and driving her to her knees. Her hands flew up in a futile
attempt to stop the onslaught, but the balls kept coming.

It was a massacre.

The beating didn't stop until she was on her face, eating
grass. The blessed sound of Coach Jackson yelling, "Enough!"
broke through the humming in her ears. Pushing herself up
on quivering arms, she struggled to her feet.

The team stood rooted in place, mouths open.

Swaying to her left, she limped to the goalpost. Her mind
raced for an explanation to save Damian from ridicule. *When
in doubt, pass out.*

"Vertigo," she croaked, folding to the ground.

It was enough to save her. For the rest of practice, she
reclined on a bench, sipping water with a wet towel over her
head. She stayed in that spot after practice ended, not ready
to brave another visit to the locker room. Basking in the feel
of the sun warming her face, she lost track of time.

A girl's voice shouting her name brought her back to
consciousness. She looked across the field to see Damian
jogging toward her, clutching his sides.

"Are you alright?" she asked.

"I...can't breathe," he panted. "Only...few yards...feels
like steamroller."

"Exercise isn't really my thing," she said in apology.

"I can...feel that." Damian fell to his knees, trying to
catch his breath.

It took Ricki a minute to readjust to seeing him in her
body. She'd gotten so used to having control of herself the past
few days that she'd almost started to believe everything had
been a dream. But there was her reality staring her in the face,
crumpled on the ground and panting like a wounded dog.

SEALED WITH A TWIST

"How did you know I was out here?" she asked.

He grabbed her water bottle from the bench and drained it. He belched. "Wasn't hard. Half the team is up in the halls, making noise about my big practice show out." Cradling his head, he laughed to himself. "What're you doing to me, girl? Didn't I tell you to fake an injury?"

"I tried! Your ankles are like miniature tree trunks. I'd need a saw to get any real damage done."

He shook the water bottle at her, showering her with the few remaining drops. "Fake, Rocky. *Fake.*"

She squealed and pushed him away with her foot. "Semantics. Anyway, how'd rehearsal go?"

"Just like you planned. Every time I had to get on stage, Teresa started up a temper tantrum, or Denise had a wardrobe emergency. That teacher was about to pop a vessel before he shut my scenes down. Why does he even put up with them?"

"Because Teresa's dad basically funds the department, and nobody else can play Polly but Denise," Ricki said. "Queen of the Amazons, the walking incarnation of beauty. Mr. Q had to beg her to take the part instead of doing hair and makeup, so there's no way he's kicking her out."

"Well, good looking out. But I noticed the other two still aren't talking to you."

She looked away. "It kind of gets that way when your friends think you're a cheating liar and you can't tell them truth."

"Hey, I appreciate you keeping things quiet for me until this is over," he said, reaching out to grab her hand. The moment he touched her, a dizziness engulfed Ricki, and she returned to her body.

He winced, massaging his arms. "Why do I feel like I just got beat down with a baseball bat?"

"Oh, man up." She let him pull her to her feet. "You ready to head out?"

"Depends. Think you can make it the whole way home this time?"

She grinned. "Get your keys, and we'll find out."

"If you go any faster, we might actually make it home by sometime next week."

Ricki squinted at the speedometer. "I'm going the speed limit."

"No, you're going the *minimum* speed," Damian said. "Now act like you know how to go faster than my Abuelo Jorge in his wheelchair, or I'm taking over."

Pouting, she pressed on the accelerator. The needle crawled to forty-five mph. "Happy?"

"Pull over."

The car sped up.

"Better." Gazing out of the window, he said, "I forgot to tell you. I'm hanging with Lindsey later."

The car slowed back down.

"Why?" Ricki asked. "I mean, how late are you staying out?"

"Not too late. She's been having some trouble with math, so I told her yesterday I'd help her."

"Help her do what? Fail?" Her foot edged back onto the gas pedal.

"Cute. How 'bout I help you out of my car and leave you begging for rides on the side of the road?"

"Like you could." Her fingers dug into the steering wheel. "You're seriously pushing back our bedtime so you can hook up with Lindsey?"

"Look, I'll be back by eight o'clock. There's nothing for you to be getting worked up over."

"Who's worked up?" she said, her voice hitting a pitch audible only to dogs and large rodents. "Have a great time.

Be careful what you eat, though. I heard there's a salmonella thing going around, and I'm not trying to be in your body for almost twelve hours if it's going to be glued to the toilet the whole time."

"Did you see that cop you just passed?" he asked.

"Yeah, so?"

"So slow down! You're going almost seventy!"

She eased the car down to fifty-five mph. "Why's she asking *you* for help, anyway? Does she need to know how many yards are in a soccer field? Or if player A leaves his goal at four thirty, and player B leaves his at four thirty-five, what time will they figure out they're missing the other half of their brain and get hit by a train?"

"Oh, I don't know. Maybe my three-point-eight GPA with straight As in every math class I've taken might've made her think I could do a little something for her." He smirked. "That's right; pick your face up. I saw it roll under the brakes a few seconds ago."

She recovered. "You're a soccer player. Of course you have great grades. I turned in a blank test in your history class, and you still got an A."

"My little Rocky," he chided, "clueless as usual. That test was a makeup exam to replace the lowest score. Since my lowest score was a ninety-six, I didn't *need* to take the test."

"Oh," she said, deflated.

"Don't get it twisted. Every grade I've gotten, I've gotten legit. There's brains behind this beauty."

"And yet when I look at you, I see neither."

"Keep telling yourself that, and one day you might believe it." His eyes returned to the passing scenery. "How do you think I'm getting the money to go to UC? A soccer scholarship won't give me a full ride, but my academic one covers almost everything."

"I thought your dad would pay for everything." Although Ricki had only seen Damian's father a few times, she knew quite a bit about him. A former army officer, he had come to Willow with a wife and small child and left with divorce papers, a thriving technology company, and a new bride to help him spend his budding fortune. Growing up, she'd eavesdropped on more than a few conversations between her parents and Ms. Marquez, most of them centering around the different excuses Raul Marquez gave for why he couldn't show up for holidays or his son's birthday. But he always made sure to send huge presents to Damian to make up for his absence— the hugest one being the SUV she was currently driving.

"I don't want him paying for jack," Damian said gruffly. "The only thing he needs to do with his money is take care of my mother and stay the hell away from me."

Recognizing she'd touched a hot topic with the potential to become explosive, she switched to cooler grounds. "Books over brawn, huh? You're giving up dreams of being the next Pelé to be the next Bill Gates?"

"I wouldn't say soccer is my dream," he said, turning away from the window. "It's just something I saw Mikey playing, so I wanted to play too. Don't get me wrong; I love playing, but I don't know if I want to make a life out of it."

"At least you know you could if you wanted to," she said, wistful.

"What do you mean?"

"Nothing. Just, it's nice that you have a choice between what you love and what makes sense. It's kind of different for me." She sighed. "Passion or practical? Pounding the streets for an acting gig or getting a steady job—which one's going to put food in my stomach and a roof over my head? At least, that's the way my dad says it."

"Don't sell yourself short," he said quietly. "You've got a lot of passion."

Her eyes turned to meet his. Bad move. A flutter began in her chest, flitting its way down to her stomach. Her gaze swung back to the road in time to avoid rear-ending a Hyundai Tucson that had switched into their lane.

"I mean, in your plays," he amended. "You're really good."

The butterflies settled down, leaving a warm tingling in their place. "Thanks."

"And at least we can understand half of what you say now, without all that metal in your mouth," he joked.

She suppressed a laugh. Exiting the highway, she pulled onto the main road leading to their neighborhood. "Do you know they wanted to keep those braces on my teeth for another year?"

"Yeah, my mom told me about it. She said something about you threatening not to eat, or something like that."

"No, the hunger strike was to get rid of the glasses."

"Yeah, that's right. The braces came off around Halloween, and the glasses were about a month after that."

She glanced at him. "Aren't you observant."

"Only to things worth paying attention to."

Electricity crackled through the air, sucking the oxygen out of the truck's cabin. The warmth in her belly spread. Confused, she gripped the steering wheel for support. "So, um...you and Lindsey, huh?"

"Rewind on that one. There is no me and Lindsey. We're just friends."

"Does *she* know that?"

"She should. I've made it clear from the jump that I'm not looking for anything more."

Hating herself for wanting to know but unable to stop herself, she asked, "What exactly are you looking for?"

He stared at her, not responding. Seconds ticked by. "Nothing," he finally said. "Not right now anyway. Better for me to keep things simple than start something up that won't get finished."

"Sounds pretty lonely." She looked sideways at him. "Don't you ever want to fall in love?"

"You read too many books," he scoffed. "My mother and father were each other's first love, and look how they ended up. They got married too young, he couldn't keep it in his pants, and she got stuck raising me while he took off with a trophy wife and started a new family. What good is trying to get serious with somebody at my age when it's going to fall apart in a couple of years? I'll wait 'til I'm older to deal with all that mess."

"Love isn't a mess," she said. "It's a beautiful connection between two people who understand each other and look out for each other. A joining of spirits."

He studied her, a smile tugging at his lips. "Did your unicorns tell you that?"

She punched his leg. "I'm serious!"

"Okay, look. Do I believe in love? Yes. Do I believe in it for me, *right now*? No, because I'm too young. Right now, the only thing I'm looking to handle are three of my four ABCs."

"You actually know your alphabet?" she teased. "I'm impressed. And what are they?"

He held up a finger. "Okay, first, there's my 'Buddy.' It's the person who doesn't have any potential to be more than just a friend. Like your little drama boy toy, Randy."

"Reggie."

"Whatever. Second, there's what other guys refer to as the 'Chickenhead,' but I call her my 'Cupcake.' She's the one you get a sweet tooth for every once in a while, then put back on the shelf after you've had your fill. And she's always there to hit the spot next time you get a craving."

She made a face. "Careful, your snout is showing. Next."

"The third one is the girl I like to think of as my 'Deputy.' She's the special friend you kick it with for a while, and you both know what time it really is. You have fun together, and once it's run its course, a new Deputy is elected to fill the vacancy."

"So, kinda, sorta like a girlfriend, but not really?"

"Exactly."

"That's stupid. Why not go ahead and call her a girlfriend instead of trying to make a loophole out of it?" She turned into their neighborhood, feeling strangely bummed that the ride was coming to an end.

It never felt this natural with Aaron. She ate lunch with him every day and talked on the phone with him every afternoon, but their conversations were so disconnected. Okay, superficial. Soccer, his body fat percentage, and whatever he watched on TV that day were the highlights of discussion. And whenever they got around to talking about her, it always seemed to be at the exact moment he had to get off the phone. Maybe things would get better when they finally had a second date, but she wasn't so sure.

The car slowed to a crawl.

"How can you put girls in these dumb categories like they're objects?" she asked. "You really are a dog, aren't you?"

"Correction, I'm a boy. And believe it or not, I'm one of the nice ones. I'm just schooling you on what every guy thinks, but without the colorful wording and anatomy descriptions." He eyed the speedometer. "And I'm always straight up with every girl before anything gets started. If she still wants to keep it going with me, that's on her."

"Technicality, but whatever lets you sleep at night, right?" Going through each category in her head, she said, "You covered B, C, and D. So, what's A?"

He cracked a knuckle. "The 'Ace.' My 'A Thang.'" He pressed on the other thumb. "My lady when the time's right."

"And when will that be?"

"When she falls out of the sky and knocks me unconscious," he glibly replied. "I'll take that as a sign."

"Could Lindsey ever be your lady?"

He looked horrified. "Not in this lifetime. She's a great girl and all, but let's be real—she's about as challenging as hopscotch. If I wanted something following me around and worshipping me all day, I'd bring Columbus to school."

Guiltily wishing his response didn't make her feel quite so pleased, Ricki asked, "So, what exactly is she?"

"At the moment?" He pointed through the windshield. "Standing outside your house, looking like she's brought all hell with her and it's about to break loose."

Following his finger, Ricki saw Lindsey, arms crossed, foot tapping, and eyes blazing as she watched the car's approach.

Oh, yeah. The day of reckoning had arrived.

———————◦✧◦———————

"Lindsey, I promise you, if you stick your finger in my face one more time, you'll be tasting it!"

Backing away to a safe distance, Lindsey jammed the offending hand against her hip. "I knew you were after him!" she shrieked at Ricki. "You're nothing but a two-faced, backstabbing, scandalous—"

"Keep going," Ricki warned. "Please, so I won't feel bad when I snatch that hair off your head and strangle you with it."

Empty threats, but diplomacy had flown out the window five minutes ago with her patience. From the moment the car had stopped, Lindsey had been in her face, accusing her of using every underhanded trick in the book to steal Damian away. And the more Ricki tried to pacify her, the more she twisted things around, interpreting reason as mind games and silence as an unofficial admission of guilt.

Ricki risked taking her eyes off Lindsey to sneak a glance at Damian. He was leaning against his car, watching them with an expression that seemed a bit too self-satisfied for her liking. Did he just wink at her?

Bristling, she looked back to Lindsey. "Pull the psycho in for a second and listen, because I am not saying this again. I don't want him. I've never wanted him. But if he means so much to you that you'll stomp any dignity you have into pieces just to get him, by all means, *take him!*"

"I guess I don't have a say in the matter," Damian mumbled.

"Only if it's to tell yourself to shut up," she snapped.

He grinned.

Lindsey pointed at her. "There it is. Right there. You guys act like an old married couple, so don't you tell me there's nothing going on when it only takes two eyes to see that there *is*."

"Then those eyes must need glasses because they have no idea what they're talking about."

"Eyes can't talk," Damian cheekily commented.

"Junior, *shut up!*"

"Don't you speak to him like that."

"Or what?" Ricki yelled. "I'll keep speaking to him the way I've *been* speaking to him since way before he ever knew you were a blip on this earth."

Lindsey tossed her head. "Just because you knew him first, you think you own him? Is that why you couldn't stand it when he started liking me over you?"

Ricki's head buzzed. The point had been reached. Irrationality had won out over common sense. She visualized herself grabbing Lindsey by the hair and dragging her across the yard. Her fingers twitched.

Before she could act, a gold Cayenne zoomed around the corner and whizzed into the Marquez driveway. She was relieved to see Denise and Teresa jump out of the car. The feeling quickly morphed into dread when the driver's door opened and Yolanda emerged.

Surveying the battle scene, the three girls rushed into the fray. Denise came to stand at Ricki's side, Yolanda at Lindsey's, and Teresa positioned herself in the center of the group.

"What're you guys doing here?" Ricki mumbled to Denise.

"Lindsey saw you leaving school with Damian and called Yolanda. Then Yolanda called us so we could get over here." Denise frowned at Damian, who smiled benignly back at her.

"She's out of control, Denise."

"Yeah, we figured it'd be a bloodbath. That's why Yolanda drove Terry's car, so we'd actually get here in time, alive. Oh, and be warned—I think Lindsey might've called Aaron too."

As if on cue, a gray Nissan Pathfinder rolled onto the street. Everyone's head turned to watch the truck pull up to the curb. An irate Aaron stepped out.

The amusement dropped from Damian's face.

Aaron slammed the car door and stalked up the driveway, heading straight for Ricki. Yolanda hurried out of his path, pulling a smug Lindsey with her. Damian moved to stop him but was shouldered aside.

He loomed in front of Ricki. "We need to talk."

The strength drained from her legs. She leaned into Denise for support. "About what?" she asked, unsuccessful at keeping the quiver out of her voice.

"Are you stepping out on me with D?"

"Of course she is," Lindsey answered for her. "You see how guilty she looks, don't you?"

"Stay out of this," Ricki spat. "It doesn't concern you, so keep your input to yourself."

SEALED WITH A TWIST just kidding

"I think it does concern her," Yolanda said, "considering she's the one you've been lying to this whole time."

"No one asked you what you think, though, did they?" Damian replied.

Yolanda's cheeks puffed up.

Muttering, "Dangerous turbulence ahead," Teresa eased her way into the street.

"So, what's up?" Aaron asked Ricki, ignoring the verbal skirmish behind him. "Are you with him or with me?"

"Neither," Ricki blurted. "Okay, that didn't come out right. I mean it's not that simple."

His face darkened. "Make it simple."

She gnawed on her lower lip, peering over his shoulder at Damian. "I can't."

Denise nudged her. "Yeah, you can. Or at least say *something*."

"Me and Damian aren't doing anything wrong," she offered, reaching for him. "That's the only thing I can say. Everything else is just a bunch of confusion that I can't really get into right now."

He shook her off. "When I offered to take you home after practice, you said you were catching a ride with your girl. Then I find out you're riding around in some other dude's car?"

"*Driving* his car," Lindsey added.

His face grew darker. "And that BS about you being sick, so you couldn't hang with me over the weekend—you trying to make me look like a punk?"

"Believe me," Ricki pleaded, "I'm with you."

"Not anymore." He turned his back to her. "You and D want each other, you got it. I'm done."

Tears sprung to her eyes. "It was just a ride home."

Shaking his head, he walked away.

She watched her world crumble behind him. This whole

debacle had started because of her quest to snag Aaron Miller's heart, and it was now the very thing causing her to lose him. She choked on the irony.

Damian's voice rang out. "We're switching places."

Aaron stopped. He slowly turned around.

"Me and Rocky accidentally drank some weird stuff that was buried in Teresa's backyard during that party, and it's been making our bodies act crazy. If we don't find a fix for it soon, it'll become permanent, and we'll be screwed." He shrugged. "That's it in a nutshell. Us trying to find a cure is the only reason we've been around each other."

"'Bout frickin' time," Teresa mumbled.

"I'm confused," Lindsey said.

Ricki rolled her eyes. *What else is new?*

"What do you mean, you guys are switching places?"

Denise stepped in. "Don't you remember what happened at your house a couple of weeks ago?"

Lindsey frowned, still not connecting the pieces.

"The whole story Damian gave you about him and Ricki being *inside of each other*? Y'know, before you accused him of lying, broke his phone, and kicked him out, into the street?"

She blanched. Her eyes darted to Damian and then Ricki. "Teresa?" she said weakly.

Teresa nodded. "Yep, it's true."

Lindsey's hand shot to her mouth. She looked dismayed.

"Hold up," Yolanda demanded. "Y'all need to back it up a little, 'cause none of this is making any kind of sense to me."

Aaron, similarly puzzled, put his car keys back into his pocket and rejoined the group. Ricki moved to stand beside him, but he turned his shoulder to her.

Sighing, Damian motioned for everyone to follow him into his house. Once inside, he pulled the vial from his pocket and placed it on the living room table. Even in the room's dimness, it sparkled and looked as mystical as it had when it was first discovered. Yolanda and Lindsey leaned forward, enthralled.

He spoke. "It all started on the night of Teresa's party..."

The fair had come to Willow.

Again.

And children of every age poured from each corner of the city to flock to its entrance.

Tin Pin Bowling Alley was deserted.

Willow Square Mall remained empty.

All was as it should be because the fair was in town.

Except, this time, Madame Celeste Dupre had not come with it.

CHAPTER EIGHTEEN

THEY WERE, IN NO UNCERTAIN terms, screwed. Teresa folded a stack of bills into her Gucci wallet and faced the group of anxious faces waiting outside the Willow County Fair administrative tent. "Madame Dupre's not coming," she announced. "She couldn't make it this year because of unforeseen circumstances."

"How does a fortune-teller have unforeseen circumstances?" Damian demanded. "Isn't it her *job* to see the future?"

"Apparently not tonight," Teresa replied, "'cause she's officially MIA with no forwarding address."

Ricki pulled away from Aaron, deaf to everything but the roar of the world crashing around her. She staggered over to the nearest curb. Denise sat next to her, wrapping an arm around her shoulder. It was over. The potion had won. They'd run out of ways to stop it, and in ten more days, it would have twenty-four-hour control over their bodies. No Madame Dupre, no hope.

She looked at the group of people surrounding her, their faces set in worry. Everyone who mattered to her most: Denise, Yolanda, Aaron. Even Reggie was there, standing between Teresa and Calvin, looking equal parts concerned and confused. Teresa had bullied him into riding with her to the fair, telling him nothing more than that Ricki was in trouble. She numbly wondered if he'd still want to kiss her after she turned into "Golden Boy."

Lindsey nibbled on a thumbnail, her fretful gaze shifting between Ricki and Damian. "What happens now?"

Any answers were drowned out by a crowd of middle schoolers stampeding down the pathway. Squeezing past the roadblock of dejected teenagers, they ran screaming toward the giant pavilion at the end of the block where a flashing sign announced the newest fair attraction: the Hall of Mirrors.

Calvin studied their retreating backs, then turned to whisper into the ear of the dour redhead next to him. He reached into his backpack and pulled out a paper sack and small walkie-talkie and handed them to the boy.

Somberly accepting the bundle, Tom tipped his baseball cap and took off toward the neon tent.

"We have to do something," Damian declared. "It can't just go down like this."

"But if Madame Dupre's always on the move, there's no way we'll find her," Yolanda said. "We might as well hang it up."

Ricki's remaining hold on her composure cracked. She slumped against Denise, burying her face in her hands.

"Maybe we could ask the other people who work the shows?" Denise said. "If they travel together every year, someone would have to know *something* about Madame Dupre, right?"

A flicker of hope sparked. Ricki lifted her head. "How would we do it?"

"How 'bout we split up and ask around?" Teresa said. She patted her purse. "And I've got plenty of dinero if we need to light a fire under some tongues."

Discussion was quickly underway, figuring out the logistics of who should go where. As they talked, Calvin slipped away. Eventually, they agreed on a game plan. Ricki and Aaron would take the north side of the fair, which included the Hall of Mirrors and most of the game booths. Damian and Lindsey got the south end, which—to Ricki's displeasure—had the Tunnel of Love. Teresa and Yolanda had the east side, and Denise and Reggie got the west.

As the group dispersed, Ricki looked around. "Where'd your brother go?" she asked Teresa.

She fluffed her green Mohawk and shrugged. "Who knows? Maybe I lucked out and he's buried under a Ferris wheel somewhere." Brushing aside their reproachful looks, she said, "What? He came with my parents, so let them worry about finding him."

"Cold, girl," Yolanda said, grabbing her arm and dragging her down the walkway. "That's really cold."

Ricki smiled as she watched the two girls march to the other side of the fairgrounds, bickering the whole way. She'd almost forgotten what it felt like to have all her friends on her side. It was nice to know she could face life on her own, but maybe it was a little nicer knowing she'd never have to.

"When do you think they'll realize they're going the wrong way?" Reggie stood a few feet away, hands in his pockets and feet shuffling against the curb. He stared at her, appearing to want to say more.

The sound of his voice encouraged her. He hadn't spoken to her in over a week, avoiding her after rehearsals and walking in the opposite direction whenever he saw her in the halls. "What's the word, Reg?" she asked gently.

"The word is *sorry*," he said, an uncertain smile flitting across his face. "As in, it takes a really sorry individual to stop being cool with someone just because she doesn't have the same feelings for him that he has for her." He held out his hand. "I'm sorry in every sense of the word. Can we be cool again, Rick?"

"Icy," she said, knocking his hand aside to embrace him.

His face glowed a brilliant red. He cleared his throat. "Now that we got all that good stuff out of the way, mind telling me what's going on?"

She noticed Aaron and Damian watching them from the street corner, identical frowns on both faces.

"Why don't I give you the abbreviated version?" she said, taking his hand. "Walk with me."

"Nobody in this whole freakin' homemade playground knew anything?" Teresa huffed. "How is that even possible?"

"I guess money can't buy everything," Yolanda groused, plopping onto a bench.

"Stop with the crazy talk. The sugar rush from that cotton candy must've gone to your head."

"At least some of us had time to enjoy the festivities," Ricki said sourly, eyeing the fresh hickey exposed over Damian's collar. "Nice to see we're not letting a Friday night go to waste."

He plucked a stuffed animal from her arms and waved it under her nose. "Guess not."

She started to fire off a comeback but decided to let it ride. It wasn't her fault that while she was busy grilling every tent owner in the area, Aaron was off playing carnival games. About the only help he'd given for the past two hours was getting them lost in the Hall of Mirrors and filling her arms with cheap dolls. Thinking of how useless he'd been during their search just made her irritated.

But not quite as irritated as seeing that red mark on Damian's neck.

She snatched the gorilla away and unloaded it onto the bench with the rest of the stuffed animals. "What are we supposed to do?" she moaned, collapsing onto the cushiony pile. "We can't find that stupid woman, and we're never going to stop flip-flopping bodies." Covering her face with her hands, she let out a muffled sob. "I wish I'd never found that stupid bottle."

Everyone rushed forward to comfort her, Teresa reaching her first. "It's not your fault, sweetie," she cooed. "Technically, you weren't the one who actually found it."

Yolanda threw a miniature dolphin at her.

"Hey, silver lining, okay?" She shook the dolphin from the moussed folds of her Mohawk. "I'm just saying, if you want to blame someone, blame Calvin. I always do."

Ricki wished she could, but the only person responsible for her life being officially over was her. And Damian. She peered at him through tear-drenched fingers.

Guilt was written heavily across his face. Sensing her eyes on him, he turned his head to Lindsey.

Her heart twisted.

Ever since that stormy afternoon, he'd been her biggest support system. He listened to her. He kept her from having more breakdowns. He taught her how to drive stick. And now?

Now he had a hickey.

A fresh round of tears began.

"It'll be okay," Denise said, rubbing her shoulders. "Maybe a really, really good doctor can fix you guys."

"Try a mad scientist," she blubbered. "Better yet, the Tooth Fairy. Or maybe Santa Claus because that's about as much chance as we have of finding somebody who'll be able to stop this."

Everyone looked at one another, helpless.

A small voice intruded on their thoughts. "We got it."

Calvin and Tom materialized through an opening between two tents, leaning against each other for support. Dirt stained both faces, and their clothes were rumpled. Tom's baseball cap was missing, exposing fiery red hair matted to his forehead.

Limping away from Tom, Calvin approached Ricki. He laid a tattered piece of paper in her lap. The paper was yellowed and brittle with age, the letters on it almost faded away. Only two things were written on the note in delicate, spidery handwriting: the name C. Dupre and...

She gasped. "Her address. Where did you get this?"

"Let me guess," Damian said. "They know people."

"Yeah, we know people," Calvin replied sarcastically, pulling two black T-shirts from his backpack and tossing one to Tom. "We know people good enough to know they're not giving out someone's personal business to a bunch of kids just because you ask for it. *Duh*."

Tom snickered.

Calvin shrugged into the oversized shirt and shook two camouflage masks out of the bag. "My guys are good at getting in and out of places without being seen—even have a few lock experts. The right tent, the right chest, the right lock..." He looked around. "Get the picture?"

All heads nodded dumbly.

"Our job here is done," he said, handing the mask and a tin of black greasepaint to Tom. "You don't owe us anything. Consider it a freebie."

Tom whispered in his ear.

"Roger that." He jerked his thumb at Ricki. "Tom wants a hug."

The redhead blushed and ducked his head.

About to burst from happiness, Ricki leaped from the bench and glided over to Tom. Sweeping him into her arms, she planted a noisy kiss on his cheek. "Thank you so much," she gushed. She kissed him on the other cheek.

Cheeks flaming to match his hair, Tom mumbled

something under his breath. He then shuffled away to begin smearing the black makeup on his face.

"You've been like my own personal hero," she said to Calvin. "I don't think there's anything I can ever do to thank you."

Glancing at Tom, he replied, "You already did," and slipped the mask over his face. "Ricki, it's been real." He turned to Damian, dipping his head in acknowledgement. "Sasquatch."

With a dramatic solute, the two boys sprinted into the field, heading to the outer border of the fairground. Keeping their shoulders hunched, they stayed low to the ground, nimbly avoiding crowds and slipping by unnoticed. As they passed a clump of bushes, a trio of matching figures detached from the shadows to join them. They soon merged into the darkness of the night and disappeared.

"That boy is going to be king of the state pen one day," Damian observed.

"Only if he gets caught," Denise said, watching a herd of frazzled rent-a-cops race by.

Teresa rubbed her hands together. "Alright, what're we waiting for? Let's go get our gypsy!"

"No can do," Yolanda said, punching the address into her phone. "This place isn't even in this state. It'd take us tonight and most of tomorrow morning to get there."

A moment of silence passed before everyone shouted in unison, "Road trip!"

Ricki waved them down. "We can't go on a road trip," she protested. "What if we drive all that way and she's not even there? We'll be right back at square one."

"Wrong," Damian said. "We'll be at square two because we'll have an address to come back to."

She shook her head. "There's no way Mike would let me go."

"Mikey only *lets* you do things because you *let* him get away with telling you what to do," he argued. "It's not like you're trying to go on some sort of sex-and-drugs crime spree across the country. Your life is at stake." He pointed to himself. "Hell, *my* life is at stake."

"But what about practice tomorrow?" Ricki asked, feeling cornered. "Mr. Q will shut the whole play down if we don't show up."

Reggie chimed in. "Practice is canceled because of the fair, remember? It's tradition."

Teresa sighed. Taking Ricki's arm, she led her over to the bench. "What's the deal? Why're you coming up with excuses not to go?"

Her head dropped to her chest. "It's too much risk," she whispered. "What if it's just an abandoned building? If we get there, and she's not there, I'm…I'm not going to be able to handle it."

"But, sweetie, that's life. And I always say life is like fashion: it's hit or miss." She swept a hand across the green-and-blue polka-dot cargo shorts and green summer vest to match her grassy Mohawk. "And you'll never hit if you let yourself be held back by the fear of missing."

"That actually made sense," Yolanda muttered.

Yeah, it did, no matter how much Ricki wished it didn't. She closed her eyes, summoning the strength to say her next words. "Denise, call Mike. Tell him to meet me over here."

"No need," Denise said. She pointed across the street to the cotton candy stand where he stood in line with his girlfriend. "Still want me to call him?"

"Funny." Willing strength into her legs, Ricki began the difficult walk to the concession stand. "Wish me luck."

Her legs grew heavier the closer her brother's back got to her, and when she took the final step to arrive at his side, the weight from her legs mysteriously traveled up to her tongue, cementing it to the roof of her mouth.

A choked gurgle alerted Mike's girlfriend to her presence. She nudged Mike.

"Oh, hey," he said, yanking his hand out of Florence's back pocket. "What's up?"

Her tongue loosened. "I have to go."

"Okay, I'll see you at home." His brow wrinkled. "You feeling okay?"

"No. I mean, yeah, I'm feeling fine." Her body tensed for battle. "But I have to go…somewhere that's not home."

"You going to Denise's house?"

"No. I'm going here." Forcing herself to look in his eyes, she handed him the piece of paper with Madame Dupre's address. "Tonight. Because I have to."

The crease in his forehead deepened. "You have to do what?"

"I have to find the woman on that paper. Madame Dupre. She didn't come to the fair this year, and it's *really* important that I see her. Like, right now. It absolutely can't wait."

"I see." His face said otherwise. "And why can't it?"

"I wish I could explain everything, but it would take too long," she said. "Just, please, please believe that it's life or death, and I have to go. Tonight. But I'll be back by tomorrow night, I swear."

"Sure you will," he scoffed. "And who exactly do you think you're going with?"

"Them." She gestured over her shoulder. When her friends saw Mike look in their direction, they turned away and pretended to be engaged in a gripping debate. Except no sound actually came from anybody's mouth.

Her eyes lowered in disgust. *Most of you call yourselves actors and you can't even fake a conversation?*

Mike chuckled. "Yeah, I don't think so. I'll see you at home." He turned back to Florence.

"Michael, listen to me," she shouted, surprising herself. "I am telling you that I *need* to go to that address. That I need you to trust me, even though I can't give you the exact reasons right now. And I need you to start acting like my brother, not my zookeeper. I've never, ever given you any reason not to trust me, have I?"

"It's got nothing to do with you," he said, taken aback. "What I don't trust is the situation you're asking me to allow you to put yourself in. So you're not going, and that's that."

"I'm not *asking* you anything." A rush of newfound courage pumped through her. "I am telling you. Why can't you talk to me about it instead of immediately issuing orders?"

"What's there to talk about? You can't tell me anything more than that you want to hop in a car with a bunch of teenage boys and go out of state, and I'm supposed to be okay with it?"

"I go out of state with teenage boys all the time when we have our play competitions," she countered. "And what goes on, on those trips is a whole lot wilder than anything you could ever imagine would happen tonight."

"But you have adult supervision."

"If you want to call it that, sure. A drama teacher who's passed out from overdosing on meds and a bus driver who's too busy making beer runs to notice half the kids sleeping in our hotel rooms aren't even from our school. If you want to get upset about me traveling out of town with guys, at least do it on the right occasion."

He deflated, his case rapidly losing steam.

She softened. "But I never let myself get involved with any of the craziness. Mom and Daddy raised me right, Mike. So did you. Now you have to trust me."

"But—"

"Let me rephrase that. You *have* to trust me because I'm going whether you like it or not. So you might as well program Denise's number in your speed dial and accept it. Anything else is just unnecessary drama."

"Then I'll take you," he feebly offered.

"And who'll answer the phone when Mom makes her midnight house call? You know she'll set the whole Willow police force on us if nobody answers."

"Like last time," he said, mournful.

She nodded. "Like last time."

He stared down at her, his left eye twitching.

"Everything okay?" Damian's voice asked from behind her.

"Everything's fine," she answered, not turning around.

Mike pocketed the paper. "You going too?" he asked Damian.

"Yeah, Mikey."

He rubbed on his neck and gazed into the sky, a low rumble coming from the back of his throat. His right hand clenched and unclenched. After a few moments of tense silence, he looked at Damian.

"Watch out for her, man."

Damian's body relaxed. He held out his hand. "Wouldn't do anything else."

Mike took his hand and pulled him in to pat him on the shoulder. They gave each other a brotherly slap on the back. Ricki watched the familiar scene, one she'd seen so many times over the years. It used to piss her off. Now it had the opposite effect.

Giving her brother a hug, she walked back to her group. She grinned and flashed the thumbs-up sign.

"Woo-hoo!" Teresa whooped, pulling out her car keys. "Okay, the boys ride with Damian. Girls ride with me. Let's roll out!"

Yolanda stepped in front of her. "Teresa, you can't drive."

"What're you talking about? How do you think I got here?" She twirled the keys in the air. "Have driver's license, will travel."

Yolanda yanked them out of her hand. "Yeah, well, my cat chewed up my library card last week, but that don't make him a scholar." She tossed the keys to Denise. "You. Can't. Drive. You're like the Grim Reaper with a new paint job, and I value my life. Denise, take the wheel."

Teresa's mouth popped open in indignation. Ricki gave her a sympathetic smile before turning away to mouth a silent thank-you to Yolanda. She gently took Teresa's arm and escorted her to the car while Denise and Lindsey gave each other a discreet high-five in the background.

Let the road trip begin.

<hr />

"Do I even want to know why you're shopping for condoms?"

Lindsey returned the silver box to the drugstore shelf and picked up a purple one. "Didn't they cover that topic in phys ed?" she airily replied.

Yolanda clapped her hands over her eyes. "Please tell me you're not trying to get down with Damian tonight. Lindsey, girl, you know it ain't that kind of party."

"I think he might be coming around to the idea of me being his girlfriend," she murmured, comparing the purple label against a black package in her shopping basket. "I need to seal the deal before he changes his mind." She glanced at Ricki out of the corner of her eye. "I don't want *something* to come up that might make him break things off."

Teresa poked her head over Lindsey's shoulder and filtered through the basket. Holding up a bottle of clear fluid, she wrinkled her nose. "Is it still called 'breaking things off' when two people aren't actually together? And never have been?"

Lindsey snatched the bottle away. "You can call it whatever you want because, after tonight, I'll be calling Damian all mine." She continued browsing the shelf, humming to herself.

The back of Ricki's neck burned.

If I knock her unconscious with this bottle, would that throw her plans off? She fingered the soda bottle in her hand. *Nah, that's insane.* She watched Lindsey grab another pack of condoms and dump them in her basket. *I'd need a bigger bottle.*

Lindsey flashed a broad smile her way. "Guess you'll get your man tonight, and I'll get mine."

"We're stopping at a hotel to get some sleep, not have an orgy," Ricki snapped, her voice angrier than she'd intended.

Lindsey smirked. She handed Ricki a silver box and strolled away. "Have to hook the fish before he gets hungry for other bait. Think about it."

"This is going to be a long night," Yolanda groaned. Her head jerked toward the opposite aisle. "Denise!" she hissed loudly. "What is in your hands?"

Denise held up a six-pack of Mike's Hard Lemonade. "What, this?" she asked. "I said we needed to stop for overnight stuff, didn't I?"

"I thought you meant a toothbrush and some soap. Liquor does *not* constitute emergency supplies."

"Run, Denise!" Teresa trilled. Giggling, the two girls dashed down the aisle.

Yolanda stomped off after them.

Ricki shook her head. About to follow, she remembered the small box still in her hand. The silver packaging shimmered seductively at her, its crimson words promising new, scandalous experiences. She studied it, wondering if such a small scrap of material could live up to all the hype. *I wonder if Damian's ever opened a silver box like this one?*

His voice intruded on her thoughts. "Stuffed animals not enough for you? Need new toys to play with?"

Nearly dropping the box, she hastily shoved it back onto the shelf.

Damian stood over her, the old familiar sneer back at home on his face. "Get away from Mikey for one night, and you let it all hang loose, don't you?"

"I don't have to explain anything to you," she said primly. Her eyes again fell on his hickey, her body temperature inexplicably climbing. "And you're not exactly someone to talk about *loose* things, are you?"

"The only things loose around here are your brains floating around in that tiny skull." He plucked the box from the shelf. "A little ambitious, aren't you? Going for the home run when you still don't know how to pick up first base?"

"It figures you'd equate making love to sports," she retorted. "Because all sex is to you is a game with dumb alphabet titles. You don't even care about the girls you do it with just as long as you can get some." She moved to shoulder past him, but he blocked her way.

"Does Aaron care about you?" he asked gruffly.

"Of course he does."

He moved in closer, forcing her back against the shelves. Placing a hand on either side of her, he leaned in. "What does he know about you?"

"Enough," she said, not liking the sense of déjà vu his question evoked.

"Does he know your middle name?"

"Do *you* know my middle name?"

"Amanda. Does he know your favorite food?" Without waiting for a response, he answered, "Spaghetti. Does he know your favorite movie?"

"We've only been dating—"

"*Titanic*. Does he know you go through a new book a week, and you've probably reread the old ones twenty times? Does he know you can't swim, but you'd risk drowning just to throw a cracker at a stupid duck?" His fist pounded against the shelf, rattling the bottles and threatening to knock them onto the floor. "Does he know *anything* about you?"

She stood dumbfounded. Raw emotion raged in Damian's eyes, revealing a whirlpool of unexpressed feelings. She tried to maintain eye contact with him, but the intensity of his gaze scorched her senses. Her eyes fell to the floor.

He waved the condoms under her nose. "But you're still putting yourself out there to be nothing more than his piece. What the hell is wrong with you?"

Twisting her head away, she slapped the box from his hands. She tried to push his arm out of her way, but he grabbed her chin and forced her to look at him. Their eyes again collided.

The heat of anger coursing through her body was suddenly replaced with fire of a different kind. "I'm nobody's piece," she weakly protested.

His breathing was harsh. "Then stop acting like one."

The flame died. "You don't know a thing about me either, do you?"

His hand reached up to touch her cheek, but she turned her face. The hand hovered for a second, then fell to his side. "I guess not." He stepped back. "Maybe we should keep it that way from now on."

A knife ripped through her gut. "Maybe we should."

Bowing mockingly, he turned to leave but stopped. "Y'know, you really should be thanking me."

She glared at him. "For what?"

"For giving you the hook up to your Mr. Right Now. If it weren't for me sending Aaron over to you with that drink, you'd probably still be dried up and lonely." He scratched his chin. "He wasn't too interested in getting you drunk, though, until I told him about your little crush on him. Then he was *really* down with the game plan."

She went numb.

"After all," Damian glibly continued, strutting away, "he's always said the sleeping ones are the best kind."

CHAPTER NINETEEN

D AMIAN WAS LYING.
Ricki sat on the edge of the bed, her nerves tense as she watched Aaron close the hotel door, shutting the two of them away from the adjoining room where the rest of their group was settling in.

He had to be lying. There was no way Aaron would've deliberately given her that spiked drink, so he could take advantage of her. Only Damian's deranged mind could come up with such a twisted story.

Aaron walked over to shut the curtains.

He was jealous. He was incapable of experiencing any true human feelings of his own, so he wanted to ruin the one good thing she had going. Because Aaron would never do anything close to what Damian said he did.

Would he?

Aaron sat beside her. "Are you ready to listen to me now?"

She stiffened. "I've been ready since we left the store. You just haven't said anything."

"You kind of threw me off guard," he said.

"I only asked you a simple question—did you know Damian had slipped something in my drink? All you had to say was yes or no. Not get mad and stop speaking to me."

"I handled it wrong, I know." He took her hand. "But let me fix it right now by saying that it's a straight-up lie. I did *not* know D had drugged your drink, or I *never* would've gave it to you. I swear on my mother's grave."

She pulled away. "Aaron, what made you approach me at Teresa's party?"

"What're you talking about?"

"I mean, you'd never paid any attention to me before. I didn't even think you knew I existed. Then, all of a sudden, you were asking me to dance and acting like you liked me."

His eyes jumped away. "I've always liked you. I just didn't know how to step to you before, because you're *the* Mikey Ray's little sister."

"But I was still Mike's little sister at the party," she reasoned. "And just like that, you stopped being intimidated? Why?"

"I don't know," he said, looking uncomfortable. "I guess it felt like magic or something when I saw you. I didn't want to miss out on the chance to get to know you, so I made a move."

Magic on the night of the blue moon. She closed her eyes, trying to get her thoughts together.

The bed shifted. "Look at me."

She opened her eyes to Aaron kneeling on the floor in front her. A single red rose was in his hand. He placed it in hers. "I'd never hurt you, Ricki," he said. "You're special to me."

She stared at it, dazed. No one had ever given her flowers before. As her hand closed around the stem, a thorn pricked her finger. She yelped and stuck the finger in her mouth.

"Here." He took the finger from her and kissed it. "Better?"

She offered a small nod. Smiling, he kissed it again. Before she could stop him, his lips closed around the finger, pulling it into his mouth and slowly sucking on it.

She jerked her hand away.

He looked up at her, wounded. "You're still mad at me?"

"No," she answered. Feeling closed in, she glanced

longingly at the closed room door. "I just thought we were supposed to be talking. Not doing…stuff."

"Ricki, you know how hard it is for me to talk when I'm around you." His hands pressed into her thighs, his gaze intensifying. "I love you."

Time slowed to a near halt.

His hands moved up her legs. "I knew it that first time we danced together," he murmured, kissing her neck. "We were meant to be together."

Aaron loved her. Something Ricki had dreamed of since the day she'd first seen him. It meant everything.

It changed everything.

His hands massaged her waist. The chilled air from the room's air conditioner hit the bare skin of her stomach. "I've been waiting for a girl like you all my life," he said against her neck. "Don't make me keep waiting."

His fingers unintentionally tickled her ribs, making her giggle. Feeling childish, she tried to relax and surrender herself to his flow. Her mind withdrew from her body, leaving it on the bed with Aaron…

He's my soul mate. He loves me, and this is what two people do when they love each other. It's just the next logical step in our relationship. Why else have I been chasing after him all school year if it wasn't for us to be together?

The weight of his body leaned against hers, pressing her back onto the bed. His hips settled between hers.

Okay, so maybe holding a conversation with him is about as comfortable as getting teeth pulled. He doesn't get my sense of humor, and frankly, I'm not sure he even has one. And we don't like the same movies. Or the same TV shows. Or the same books.

"Let me show you how much you mean to me."

Does he read?

One by one, the buttons of her shirt opened.

But he's the one I'm supposed to be with. All the riddle's signs pointed to him. It was destiny for us to be together, and now everything is how it should be. How it was meant to be. So why do I feel like throwing up?

The cotton material slid down her arms, exposing her bra.

Maybe love isn't what all the books and movies made it out to be. Maybe the soap operas got it wrong. It's not all warm and fuzzy feelings and wanting to be around the other person all the time because they make you feel whole, like the other side of your coin. Talking about your dreams and what you want from life. And even when you two don't agree on the same thing, you still blow each other's minds.

His lips traveled down the crook of her throat to skim the bra's lacy red trim.

It's not knowing that he's seen you at your absolute worst and wouldn't want you to be any different than how you are. Or thinking about him every minute of the day from the moment you wake up to the minute your head hits the pillow. Because he affects you, whether it's from driving you so crazy you want to kill him or making you so comfortable that whenever he's around, you feel like you're home.

One hand fiddled clumsily with the hooks behind her back as the other disappeared under the bed.

Be honest with yourself, Ricki. For once. Aaron doesn't make you feel any of those things. And something is telling you that no matter how much time you spend with him, he never will. The same something that's saying you didn't get the definition of love wrong. You got the person wrong.

The button on her jeans unsnapped.

You didn't even know Aaron before you decided you were in love with him. You just saw him, decided you wanted him, and then made it your mission in life to get him. You didn't care that he was more interested in getting physical with you than getting to know you. You brushed off his flirting with other girls. You ignored the fact that he's not the brightest star in the sky and probably has the IQ of roadkill. You refused to see anything beyond making him yours. Well, now that you've got him, are you happy?

The zipper slid down.

Do you even like what you got? Does he fulfill you emotionally? Challenge you in any way? Or are you so fixated on your misguided notions of soul mates that you'll hold onto him for dear life no matter what you're stuck with…or what you have to give up?

He tugged at the rim of her pants, pulling them down her hips.

Anything, rather than admit that, Racquel, you messed up…

Her hands shot out. Pushing with all her strength, she heaved Aaron's body off hers. Falling backward, he got tangled up in the legs of his pants and landed on his butt.

Ricki jumped to her feet, zipped her pants, and slid into her shirt. Buttoning her blouse, she gazed triumphantly down at him and said, "Aaron, before we take this any further, I've got one question for you."

He gaped up at her, confused. "Of course. You can ask me anything."

"What's my middle name?"

⊷⬦⬦⊶

"And then you threw the rose at him, kicked him in the balls, and ejected his sorry tail from the room?"

Ricki laughed, tossing a pillow at Teresa. "No, I told him if he doesn't even know my middle name, there's no way we know each other well enough to be having sex."

"How'd he take it?" Denise asked.

"He tried to change my mind. Then he got mad and said if I wouldn't take the next step to prove I wanted to be with him, I could forget about us ever taking any other steps. That's when I told him amnesia had already set in, threw the rose at him, and ejected his sorry tail from the room."

Yolanda grinned. "I'm impressed."

"I know, right? It's like I was finally seeing this guy for who he is, and he's *not* all that." Ricki looked around the hotel room. Realizing it had almost been the burial ground for her virginity, she shivered. "Have you guys seen him since he left?"

"Nope. He never came back to the other room," Yolanda said.

"Good," she mumbled, hugging another pillow.

Denise dumped the rose in the trash can, brushing her hands together in satisfaction. "I am *so* proud of you, girlie."

"So am I," Teresa agreed. "I couldn't stand his fake behind."

Ricki looked up in surprise. "Why not?"

"Besides the obvious? That he's a posing, second-rate manwhore who runs through girls like it's a marathon and he's going for platinum? Or that he's a self-absorbed prick who's so insecure about being a low-rent version of Damian that he'd go Oedipus on his own mother just to say he got to her first?" Teresa shrugged. "You pick."

"Dang, girl," Yolanda teased, "tell us how you really feel."

"Gladly. It's about time I finally can." Teresa flopped onto the bed beside Ricki. "Remember the 'play room' at my party? The one with the scarf on the door?"

Ricki searched her memory. "Sort of. What about it?"

"I didn't have the heart to tell you, but Aaron had been at the party way before you showed up. Need three guesses for why you couldn't find him?"

Denise gasped, apparently reaching the question's destination well ahead of Ricki's naïve mind.

"He was in that room," Teresa declared.

Yolanda's hand flew to her mouth. "He's a straight freak."

"In every sense of the word," Teresa agreed.

Ricki stared in astonishment at Teresa. "I don't know why I'm surprised," she finally admitted. "It's always been about sex for him, and I guess he gets it however he can. But why didn't you tell me?"

"I didn't want to hurt you," Teresa said. "As far as you were concerned, Aaron could do no wrong. I didn't want to risk you getting upset, so I hoped you'd either figure out what a douche he is on your own or he'd prove me wrong and end up being worthy of walking upright on two legs."

"But you could've said or done *something*. Even a little hint would've been better than nothing."

"Did Damian ever try to give you little hints?"

Ricki wanted to deny it, but her memories answered for her: Damian constantly interrupting her and Aaron at Teresa's sleepover; Damian trying to break her and Aaron up when he had control of her body; Damian deliberately going to sleep during her date with Aaron....Damian protecting a friend.

"But he never bothered to explain," she said, mentally kicking herself.

"We all know you, sweetie. You wouldn't have listened."

"If he cared so much about me getting hurt, why'd he sick Aaron on me in the first place?" A spark of anger burned away her self-rebuke. "He basically put me on a silver platter and offered me up to the shark."

"Not following," Teresa said.

"He convinced Aaron to give me the spiked drink by telling him about my crush on him. If Damian knew Aaron was slime, then he never should've put me on his radar. Period."

"But there's no way he could've known Aaron would keep pursuing you after the party was over," Denise reasoned. "He just needed someone you'd accept a drink from. He was only trying to ruin your night, not your life."

"I could've been raped," Ricki said, indignant.

"Nothing would've happened to you. Trust."

"How do you know?" She left the bed to pace around the room. "Damian drugged me and left me with a boy who thinks 'sleeping ones are the best kind.' After I passed out, Aaron could've hauled me off somewhere and done whatever to me before anyone even knew I was missing."

"Doubtful, unless he moves at the speed of light," Teresa said.

Ricki stared at her, puzzled.

"Who do you think was right there to pick you up and carry you to my bedroom?"

Yolanda put a hand on her shoulder. "I'll give you a hint. It wasn't Aaron."

"Damian?"

"Bingo," Denise said. "And *nobody* is stupid enough to mess with you. Not then, not now, not ever. Not if they value their lives."

"What does that mean?" Ricki asked.

Teresa sat her back on the bed. "You've done a lot of foul stuff to Damian since we got to high school. You never wondered why none of the soccer team ever came down on you in retaliation? Not even once?"

"Of course they wouldn't. I'm Mike's little sister."

"Oh, hon, Mikey Ray's been gone for two years. There's been a new Kanga King in town for a while, and his name is D Marquez. And everyone knows that D Marquez will bring down *the Wrath* if anyone ever touches you."

"Remember Dobbs Henley?" Denise asked.

Ricki frowned. "The boy they found tied up naked in the girl's bathroom last year?"

"You mean the senior who dumped you in a trash can during Haze Week," Teresa corrected. "Make the connection?"

Her eyes grew wide.

"Aaron grew a big set by even *thinking* about messing with you. I guess his wanting to stick it to Damian overrode his sense of self-preservation."

Yolanda sucked her teeth. "After the mess he just pulled, all bets are off. That boy better go into the witness protection program while he can."

Ricki tried to process the information they'd just dumped on her. Damian had been looking out for her all this time? With all his posturing and threats, he'd actually had her under his protection? "Why didn't anyone tell me?" she whispered.

"He didn't want you to know," Denise replied. "He said you'd probably start causing drama with people on purpose just to get him into fights."

"He knows you well," Yolanda cracked.

"Then why tell me now?"

Denise keenly studied her. "Because I get the feeling that now you might actually care."

She avoided responding, instead asking, "Does Lindsey know?"

"Duh. Why do you think she's so paranoid about you?"

Ricki realized for the first time that one of their crew was missing. "Where is she anyway?"

Silence.

"Oh." Her heart dropped. "She's with Damian."

Denise's eyes skipped away. "He tried to follow you and Aaron in here, but she stopped him with some story about a huge emergency."

"I saw her go back to the front desk after we checked in," Teresa added, examining an emerald-green fingernail. "She had her fake ID with her. I think she got another room on the sly."

Ricki dug her nails into her palms, wondering why her

world had suddenly gone a few shades darker. "Do you think he'll sleep with her?"

"He's a guy," Teresa got out before Yolanda yanked on her Mohawk.

She bit down on the inside of her lip to keep the tears from falling. *No more crying. Not over a boy. Never again.*

She stood up. "Good for her," she said briskly, walking to the door. "She'll finally be getting what she wants."

Reaching for the handle, she almost shrieked when the door flew open and narrowly missed her face.

Reggie stood in the doorway, breathless. "You girls better come with me." The words came out in short bursts. "Now."

Looking apprehensively at one another, the four girls followed him from the room to the other end of the hallway. They turned the corner and stumbled to a halt. Damian stood outside of an open door, glaring murder into the room. Seeing Ricki, his demeanor morphed from fury into concern. She started to smile, feeling an inexplicable joy at finding him without Lindsey and with all of his clothes on, but his expression replaced her joy with dread. She pushed past him to see what was on the other side of the door.

She wasn't prepared.

Lindsey cowered in the middle of the king-sized bed, clutching a sheet over her naked body. The black box from the drugstore sat open on the nightstand beside the bed. Her clothes were scattered across the floor along with someone else's.

Ricki's eyes followed the trail of discarded clothing to the other side of the room where a boy hopped madly on one leg, haphazardly shoving the other into a pair of rumpled pants. He bumped into the wall and spun around, falling to the floor.

Aaron.

Yolanda peeked over Ricki's shoulder. "Oh my." She let

out a low whistle. "Bet that witness protection program is looking mighty good right about now."

———————⊷⊛⊷———————

"You're actually throwing me out?" Lindsey's shrill voice bounced off the walls of the hotel room.

Ricki held out a gold earring she'd found near the foot of the bed and dropped it into Lindsey's hand. She proceeded to carry the rest of her belongings into the hallway and deposited them at Aaron's feet.

"Can't we at least talk about what happened?" Lindsey pleaded.

"What's there to talk about?" Denise asked coldly. "You did the deed with Ricki's man, got busted, and now you gotta go." She turned to Teresa and Yolanda, who sat at a table watching Lindsey and Aaron's banishment with identical expressions of disappointment. "Wouldn't you agree?"

Conflicted, they turned their heads.

"We didn't do anything wrong!" Lindsey stomped her foot. "Why're you acting like we just cheated on Ricki and Damian or something?"

Ricki's eyes cut to Damian.

He stood on the other side of the room with Reggie, leaning against an armoire. He hadn't spoken since discovering Lindsey and Aaron together. Even when Lindsey threw herself on his back, begging forgiveness, he'd merely shaken her off as nothing more than an annoyance. Scanning his blank expression, Ricki wondered if his withdrawal was a cover to mask his rage…or his pain?

Meeting her gaze, he winked.

Her heart skipped. She looked at Teresa and Yolanda. They were staring at the table, deliberately removing themselves from the confrontation. Even Reggie remained quiet, looking out the window. In their own way, it seemed each of them was telling her the same thing.

It was her fight.

She walked over to Denise, motioning for her to join the other girls at the table. She then turned to Lindsey, who stood guardedly in the middle of the room like an injured animal ready to lash out.

"You don't think you did anything wrong?" Ricki asked, her voice calm.

Lindsey glanced back at Aaron, tossing her hair behind her shoulder. "No, I don't. Aaron said it was over between you guys. He said you dumped him."

"And you thought it'd be okay to pick him up? Without even seeing how I felt?"

"What difference would it have made? You'd already broke things off with him, hadn't you?"

"So as long as you can justify stabbing me in the back, it's all good, I guess."

"I wasn't trying to hurt you," she protested.

"No, you just didn't think about me at all. And that's the problem." Ricki moved in closer, getting a small bit of satisfaction from the fear in Lindsey's eyes. "After me and Aaron fell out, everyone else checked on me to see how I was doing. Where were you?"

Guilt flashed across Lindsey's face.

"Exactly. Y'know, Lindz, most friends have the decency to get the okay before hooking up with an ex. Most friends even wait more than five minutes before lapping up sloppy seconds. Thank you for finally showing me exactly what kind of friend you really are."

Lindsey's chin jutted forward. "And what kind is that?"

"The kind that only looks out for number one, especially

when a boy is involved." She waved a hand toward the table. "Which puts us pretty low on the list for loyalty, correct?"

"That is so not true!"

"I think it is. We just get so blinded by your little sweetness act, that we couldn't ever see it." Venom filled her voice. "You're insecure and ruthless, and that's a really dangerous combination. Insecurity, I can get behind, but when it makes you so desperate for a guy that you'll jack over your own friend, then you have a serious problem."

Lindsey's hands balled into fists. "The only problem I have is that I got caught up in the middle of you and Damian's foreplay!"

The silence in the room was deafening.

"Be honest," she hissed. "Aren't you just happy that it wasn't *Damian* I had sex with? It's always been you and him, even before all this weird body-swapping stuff happened. Me and Aaron were just casualties who got in the way of your obsession with each other."

Ricki's face warmed. "If you thought that was the case," she said evenly, "why'd you put yourself there in the first place?"

Lindsey's mouth opened, offering no reply.

"If you really believed me and Damian had some sort of fixation with each other, wouldn't common sense have told you not to get involved with him? He said you were cute one time, and you were on him like a dog on a bone. So, no, I'm not about to let you blame me or him for your self-esteem issues."

Lindsey's eyes darted around the room, landing on Yolanda and silently begging for support. For the first time in their friendship, Yolanda declined.

Ricki continued. "Ever since I've known you, you've been chasing down guys for the wrong reasons. You used me to get next to Mike, who didn't want you. You latched onto Damian, who didn't want you. And now, it's that one." She pointed with disgust at Aaron, who was busy trying to melt into the doorframe. "And the only person *he* really wants is himself. But wasn't your whole mission tonight to get with Damian? So, how do you go from trying to screw one guy to screwing a totally different one in the same night? What does that make you?"

Lindsey's creamy cheeks exploded into crimson patches. Her eyes fixed longingly on Damian before dropping to the floor. "I didn't plan for it," she said, her voice cracking. "I got the room for me and Damian, but he wouldn't go in. He said he didn't think of me 'that way.' That I should get my money back while I could. And then he just left me. Alone."

The fight drained from her body. Whimpering, she collapsed on the bed like a broken doll. Tears rolled unchecked down her cheeks.

A small wave of pity broke through the wall of Ricki's anger.

"I was still crying when Aaron came by," Lindsey whispered. "I guess he'd just left from being with you. The door was open, so he came in to see what was wrong. I told him about Damian, and he told me about you. And stuff happened. I didn't mean for it to." She covered her face and wailed, "Why can't anyone understand that I was hurt! You don't know what it's like to keep getting rejected. Every boy here is for you. Nobody ever wants me. I just needed…even if it was only for a few minutes, I just wanted to feel wanted…" She broke down, sobbing into clenched fists.

Ricki's wall crumbled. She sat down on the bed and put an arm around Lindsey's shoulder, holding her until her cries subsided. "Oh, Lindz," she said softly, closing her eyes. She absorbed the familiar pain of Lindsey's tears into her spirit. "I know it better than anybody. I was so close to being where you are right now, it scares me."

Lying passively against Ricki, Lindsey remained quiet, her

sniffs and occasional hiccup the only signs of life still flowing in her body.

"It sucks so bad feeling like you're never good enough or pretty enough," Ricki murmured. "Making a list of all these stupid things you need to change about yourself just so you can feel like you're half as good as any other girl. But y'know, those feelings...they don't go away just because a boy pays attention to you for a few minutes. Nothing really gets better until you figure out how to like yourself just the way you are. It took me forever to get that."

"But what if I can't?" Lindsey said, her voice barely audible.

"Then I guess that emptiness you're trying to fill up is coming right back as soon as the guy stops paying attention to you. And then you'll need more attention to make you feel whole, and you end up doing stupid stuff to get it. But all you're really doing is running after a temporary fix instead of working on the permanent solution."

"My little girl has grown up," Denise crowed.

Yolanda gave Denise a playful slap on the arm.

"You're beautiful," Ricki insisted. "You're smart. Your body is insane, and you make most of the girls at school look like deformed spider monkeys."

"She better not be talking about us," Yolanda muttered to Teresa.

"But even with all that," Ricki said, "did having sex with Aaron make you feel better about yourself?"

"No," Lindsey whispered.

"And I don't think having sex with Damian would've either because I don't think you're really looking for his love. Or Aaron's, or my brother's, or any other boy's. You're looking for your own, Lindz. But until you take a step back and realize that for yourself, you're not ever going to be happy." She smiled. "And I want you to know, no matter what's happened, you *are* worth being happy."

Lindsey wiped her nose on her sleeve, her eyes squeezed shut and tiny droplets of tears glistening on their pale lashes. They opened to look at Ricki, apology shining in their crystal blue depths. "I'm so sorry, Ricki," she rasped. She looked pointedly at Damian. "For everything." Choking on one last sob, she fell into Ricki's arms.

Ricki rubbed her back. "It's okay," she said, meaning it.

No, their friendship would never be the same. But maybe it didn't need to be. She had a better understanding of Lindsey, and Lindsey now had a better understanding of herself. And, maybe that's all they'd ever be able to ask for.

She lifted her head to see Damian and Reggie huddled at the table, whispering with the girls. Appearing to come to an agreement, everyone stood up and walked over to the bed.

"We think you and Damian should go it alone from here," Yolanda announced, leaning over to kiss Ricki's cheek and tenderly detach Lindsey from her side. "Y'all need to focus on finding that gypsy, and things have gotten a little too... sidetracked up in here."

Teresa hugged her. "The ride home might be a little tight, but it'd be a whole lot more uncomfortable if we stayed, y'know?"

Ricki nodded against Teresa's neck, gently squeezing her in return.

One by one they filtered from the room, grabbing their things and wishing her and Damian luck. Everyone except Aaron, and Ricki was more than happy to never hear his voice again. She watched with mixed emotions as they left—sadness that they wouldn't be with her to finish the journey, but joy that they'd be at home waiting for her when it finally ended.

As the group walked off, Reggie called out, "Wait! We can't go yet."

"Why not?" Teresa demanded, rifling through her purse. "Did someone take my keys again?"

Marching up to Aaron, Reggie pulled his fist back, swung, and knocked him to the floor. Aaron writhed on the ground at his feet, hands cupped over a bloody nose. Stepping over his fallen body, Reggie brushed a fallen curl out of his eyes. "Now we can go," he announced, striding down the hall.

The rest of the group dutifully followed behind him.

Aaron dragged himself to his feet and staggered after them.

When the last person had rounded the corner, Teresa's voice echoed through the hall. "Shotgun!"

CHAPTER TWENTY

S HE HAD NO IDEA WHAT to say.

For the first time in her life, Ricki was nervous around Damian. And it wasn't the kind of nervous feeling she'd get when sensing the hammer of his newest prank about to descend on her head, or when she knew the next words from his mouth would inflict maximum humiliation but there was no way to stop him. It was something she'd never experienced around him before, and she didn't know what to make of it.

She felt shy.

There she was, sitting on the bed next to a boy she'd known almost her entire life, and she may as well have been sitting beside a total stranger. She remembered how old he was when his voice first changed and a mustache appeared over his top lip. She knew every food he was allergic to, and which ones he pretended to be allergic to so his mother wouldn't force him to eat them. She even remembered the only time she saw him cry while he watched his father drive away with a car full of suitcases. She knew all those things, but her mind still couldn't come up with a single thing to say to him. And each time her eyes accidentally met his, a swarm of butterflies took flight in her stomach. She wistfully thought back to the old days when the two of them being alone in a room was instant grounds for practicing a Tae Bo kick to his groin. Now it had her heart racing so fast, she was about to go into cardiac arrest.

She *had* to say something.

"Why didn't you sleep with her?" *Okay, I wish I'd known that question was going to come out of my mouth.*

Damian's eyebrow rose. "Why would I?"

"Because she offered," she said weakly, wishing she'd stuck to saying nothing.

"Just because a girl throws it out doesn't mean every man has to catch it." He lay back on a pile of pillows.

"Aaron did."

"I said *man.*"

She relaxed, feeling a little of her old self returning. "Whatever," she sniffed. "Boy or man, you're all operating with the same parts. And every girl knows guys like sex. It's almost your main reason for existing."

"Hell yeah, we like sex," he agreed. "Any dude who tells you different is probably in the middle of trying to get it from *you.* But just because we like it doesn't mean we have to have it with every single thing in a skirt. Until a guy figures that out, he's still a boy."

"So what are you? A boy or a man?"

He peered down the bed at her, his eyes hooded. "You don't know?"

Her heart pounded. "Apparently not. I thought you'd sleep with Lindsey after you made out in the Tunnel of Love, but you didn't."

He sat up, waving his hands. "Whoa! Rewind. We did *what?*"

"Your hickey…" Perplexed, she pointed at his neck.

He gawked at her for several seconds, and then burst into whooping laughter. "Priceless," he hooted. "You mean you can't even tell the difference between a mosquito bite and a hickey?"

She buried her head in a pillow. *Lame, lame, lame…*

Quieting, he scooted toward her. Tugging at a corner of the pillow, he pulled it away from her face. "Tell me something. How can you be so wicked and so innocent at the same time?"

She gave him a tiny smile. "Who're you calling wicked?"

"The only girl in Willow who's ever been able to keep me on my toes. And knock me off of them. Literally. Shoot, the only girl I'm afraid of." He matched her smile. "You asked me a question; now I'm gonna ask you one. Why didn't you have sex with Aaron?"

"I wasn't ready." Her fingers twiddled the pillow fringe. "We didn't know each other well enough. And I've also kind of always dreamed about my first time being on my wedding night." She laughed self-consciously. "I know that sounds stupid and old school."

"No, it doesn't," he said. "There's not a thing wrong with waiting until you're ready."

"Yeah, well, you might be the only guy who thinks so. It seems like most guys won't stay interested for long without a little incentive." She sighed. "Pretty hard to get to the honeymoon if I can't even get past the second date."

"That's not true," he said. "If a guy wants you for you, not just your body, he'll wait."

She looked at him skeptically. "For how long?"

Laying his head on the pillow in her lap, he looked up at her. "Ricki, the right one will wait forever for you if he really loves you."

Her heart slammed to a halt. "You called me Ricki."

"Did I?" He rubbed his jaw. "Must be all of tonight's excitement messing with my head." His eyes searched hers. "Do you mind?"

She thought for a moment before saying, "Yeah, I do."

"Oh." His gaze withdrew, leaving a trace of hurt feelings behind.

"You're the only person who calls me Rocky," she quickly explained. "It's something that's kind of unique to us. If you started calling me by my name, it would feel too weird. Does that make sense...Damian?"

He flinched. "I see what you mean." He began to play with her fingers. "Do you know why I started calling you Rocky?"

"Because my face had more bumps on it than a Braille instructional guide?"

He chuckled. "Nah, that's just what I told you. The real reason is because you're a fighter, even when you think you're not. And you proved it tonight." His hand wrapped around hers, holding it tightly. "I'm proud of you."

Her insides glowed. She didn't understand what was happening, but if she could freeze a moment in time and keep it locked forever in her memory, it would be that second: her hand in Damian's, her heart on fire, and a peace she'd never felt before enveloping her from within. She stared down at him as though seeing him for the first time, cataloging the contrast between his tan skin and jet-black hair, the thickness of his lashes that curled slightly at the tips, the light shadow of stubble across his square jaw.

The strong curve of his lips...

"Want to know why I named you Satan Jr.?" she asked, redirecting her attention back to the conversation.

"Yeah, why?"

"Because you're evil."

He laughed.

She laughed along with him, struck with wonder at how it was possible to hate someone for so long and now feel like nobody else in the world could ever fit her as well as he did. She risked putting her free hand on his head, twining her fingers through his hair.

His cheek nuzzled her palm.

She slowly traced a path down the side of his jaw, along his neck, stopping at the rim of his collarbone. Her thumb rubbed against the corner of his tattoo, its dark imprint poking out above his shirt. "Junior," she murmured, "why do you have a compass tattooed over your heart?"

"To remind me to never lose my way no matter what happens in my life," he said. "People come and go, and changes are always gonna be constant, but as long as I remember to stay true to who I am, I'll never get lost."

"Is that why you never went crazy all this time we've been switching, the way I did? Because you remembered who you were even when the reflection in the mirror told you different?"

"Our souls never changed, Rocky, just the package they were in."

His response brought another question to mind. "Do you believe in soul mates?"

"Why? Did you think Aaron was yours?"

"I made myself believe he was. Then my eyes opened, and I saw that he wasn't anything more than a naïve dream of love I tried to force into reality."

Madame Dupre's words danced in her mind. *"See the reality, not the dream…"*

"I do think there's one person out there for everyone," he said carefully. "But if you meet that person at the wrong time, it won't work out."

"How do you know if it's the wrong time?"

"If two people are too young, like what happened with my folks. I mean, you could meet your soul mate when you're still a little kid, but if you're not ready for her, then it's best to keep her as far away from you as possible until the time becomes right. Otherwise, you'll just screw everything up."

"And how exactly do you keep her away?" she teased. "By shoving her into trees and making her cry?"

He didn't respond.

She grew serious, the realization dawning that there may have been a method to Damian's madness all these years. She swallowed. "Have you ever considered that maybe your mother was never your dad's soul mate?"

His body stiffened.

"What if his second wife was the one he was always supposed to be with, but he got things mixed up because he met your mother first? Isn't it possible that if he'd met your stepmom when he was a little kid, they'd still be together today because *they* were the ones who were meant to be together?"

The air in the room chilled. He pulled his hand out of hers, mumbling, "I think you should take the first sleep shift."

"We don't do shifts anymore," she objected.

"We should tonight." He left the bed, walked into the bathroom, and shut the door, not giving her the chance to say anything more.

She stared at the closed door. If only she could go back in time and stop her big mouth from opening. But the potion only worked on body shifts, not time travel. *Too bad.*

Curling into a ball, she laid her head on the pillow. It still smelled like Damian. Inhaling his scent and storing it away in her memory, she began to doze off. Right before sleep took her, her eyes fluttered open to see him lying by her side, watching her.

With a contented smile, she drifted away.

It really was an abandoned building.

Ricki stood with Damian in front of a decrepit warehouse. Graffiti decorated its graying exterior and busted windows. The parking lot around them was a literal concrete jungle with forests of weeds shooting up through the minefield of cracks zigzagging across its cement surface.

"I knew it," Ricki moaned, clutching her head. "We're never going to find her."

Damian pulled her to his side. "Remember what I said last night. We're still going to be okay no matter what happens."

She leaned against him, careful not to let her weight knock him over since she was back in his body as of that morning. He hadn't been able to last through his shift, falling asleep less than an hour after her.

Releasing her, he walked toward the warehouse. "Maybe there's a camper or something around, where she stays. Go back to the car, and I'll check it out." He broke into a jog and disappeared around the corner of the building.

She waited a few minutes for his return, then began a disheartened trek back to the car. Maybe Damian was right. Maybe it wouldn't be so horrible living as each other. As long as they went through it together, they'd find a way to make things work. She looked in the car window at her reflection. Her fingers traveled over the contours of her soon-to-be permanent face. *And there are definitely worse faces you could have.*

She reached for the door handle just as a voice behind her said, "Looking for someone?"

Its rich, raspy tone was familiar, even after all the time that had passed. Afraid to believe her ears, she slowly turned around.

Madame Celeste Dupre stood only a few feet away, the folds of her blazing red muumuu rustling lightly against her body although no wind blew. She smiled, her face cracking into a delicate web of lines. "You found your path, I see." She studied Ricki with a critical eye. "Looks like it got a little crooked."

Ricki rubbed her eyes, making sure the gypsy's image was not a figment of wishful thinking. "You know who I am?"

"Of course," Madame replied indignantly. "You may not be in the body I remember, but eyes are windows into a person's soul. Through them, I see not only who you are but who you wish to be." She gestured at Ricki's figure. "And I find it hard to believe you wish to be this."

Dazed, Ricki looked over Madame's shoulder. She saw Damian reappear around the corner. Waving her hands wildly, she pointed to the gypsy.

He broke into a limping run, skidding to a halt before he slammed into the car. "Are you her?" he panted, clutching his side and wheezing.

Madame Dupre reached out a wrinkled hand and placed it on his face. He started to pull away, but Ricki slapped him on the arm and forced him to stand still.

Madame's eyes closed, her fingers exploring the features beneath them. She frowned. "Now I see what has happened." Her eyes opened and zoomed in on Ricki. "Tell me, child: why do you still deny the path given to you?"

"I haven't denied anything," Ricki said, baffled.

"The potion of which I foretold—the path which would lead your soul to its other half. Did you not drink it?"

"Yes, I did…"

"And after doing so, what did you see?"

"The ground," Damian snorted.

Ricki pinched him. "I didn't see anything. It knocked me unconscious."

Madame nodded. "As it was supposed to."

"It was?"

"Of course. Only when you release your conscious bonds to the world can your soul be free. The potion broke the bond of your soul to your body and guided it on the spiritual path to your heart's wish, to find your one true love. It enabled your soul to visit the owner of its other half—its mate—each time you were unconscious."

Ricki's eyes shot to Damian.

"But you never accepted the answer shown to you, did

you? And because you didn't, your wish could not be fulfilled, and your soul could not rest. Then something went wrong." She tapped a crooked finger on Damian's nose. "You. You must have drunk the potion as well."

"Not on purpose," he said.

"And what did *you* see?"

He glanced at Ricki, then at the ground.

"Children," the gypsy groaned to herself. "From the boy's silence, I gather that he too was guided to a mate he refused to accept. And given that both of you are standing here in one another's body, I venture to guess that the mate was *you*."

Ricki's thoughts reeled.

"A living soul must always have a body in which to reside," Madame Dupre explained. "If it leaves its own body to go to the body of its mate and finds that vessel vacant, it will inhabit the empty space. Had only one of you drunk the potion, this phenomenon would never have occurred—your soul would have simply visited its other half, then returned to its owner after a period of time. But because *both of you* drank the potion, both of your bodies were left empty when each soul came to visit. Finding no one home, they simply took up residence."

"But why does it keep happening?" Ricki asked.

"The longer you deny the reality that your souls reveal to you—the identity of your soul's mate—the more insistent your souls become. They have been trying to show both of you what your hearts already know but your heads continue to fight. Perhaps it is time to accept the answer to your wish and lay your souls to rest."

"You're crazy," Damian declared. "This whole thing's crazy. Rocky might've been looking for love when she drank that stuff, but I wasn't."

Madame smiled knowingly. "No, you weren't looking for

love, were you? You were too busy running from it. And it caught up to you in the end." She put a finger under his chin, turning his face toward Ricki. "The nature of love is not what you think you want, but what you actually need."

He scowled.

"You were fated to find your soul mate," she said. "And that fate was sealed the moment you touched the bottle and it read the desire of your heart."

"If that's the case, why'd it get so twisted?"

"The path was always straight, my boy. It was your own hard head that made it difficult to travel."

"But how did Aaron fit into all of this?" Ricki asked. "He was at the party too."

"Party?" An extra crease appeared across Madame's forehead. "I said nothing of a party."

"You said I'd have to wade through a gathering of hearts on the night of a blue moon. A gathering of hearts is a party, right?"

"No, a gathering of hearts is precisely that—a gathering of hearts. A number of people whose feelings for one another have become intertwined. You needed to sort through those feelings to the one that was true to you. Work with me, child. This is not rocket science."

"But I found the potion at the party," she stammered. "And it was a blue moon. And then Aaron came to me. I thought they were all tied together…"

"Never mistake coincidence for destiny," Madame replied. "The potion would have come to you, party or no party. Because it was meant only for you. You…and your other half."

Ricki was a certified fool. Not a party, but a maze of feelings she needed to navigate in order to get to her soul mate: her obsessive feelings for Aaron, Reggie's blind feelings for her, and the unexplored feelings she had stubbornly denied for Damian. And through that maze, she had taken constant wrong turn after wrong turn, almost ending up with Aaron, which would have brought her nothing but misery.

The riddle's words swept through her mind. *"See the reality, not the dream, or all you will find at the end of the path is a crushed spirit that will never be whole..."*

Peace filled Ricki's spirit.

How simple it had all been. Damian was her reality. Her soul mate. And every beat of her heart confirmed it to be true. But she'd never allowed herself to believe her soul mate could be anyone but Aaron. Even though Damian had always been a significant force in her life and knew her almost better than she knew herself, she'd never once considered him to be anything but the enemy. He had his villainous role in her fairy-tale story, and she would never let him be anything other than what she determined him to be. She had allowed her preconceived notions of what love *should* be blind her to what it really *was* for so long that she'd almost missed it.

Love wasn't designed to fit a certain list of specifications. It didn't come in a neat, preapproved package. And it wasn't about forcing the wrong person into a role and trying to make him fit. It was unpredictable and sometimes messy. It challenged you and knocked you out of your comfort zone. It was never the way you expected it to be, but it was exactly what was meant for you. And when it came to you, you had to accept it, warts and all. The way it accepted you.

"But how do we make things right?" she asked Madame Dupre. "How do we get back into our own bodies for good?"

"First, fulfill the terms of your heart's wish," Madame said, stepping away. "Be true to your feelings. Then, create a path for your souls to return to their correct owner."

"And how do we do that?" Damian grumbled.

"By making a physical connection."

He lifted an eyebrow, smirking meaningfully.

"I'm not having sex with you," Ricki blurted.

Madame pinched the bridge of her nose in exasperation. "A kiss would suffice." Gathering the folds of her dress in her hands, she stepped over a pile of rocks and walked toward the warehouse. "I will now leave you children to work the rest of this matter out between yourselves. My tolerance for teenage angst has worn thin of late, and frankly, I'm off the clock."

"Hold up," Damian said. "Something's still bugging me."

She stopped and turned to face him.

"You talked about the potion and how it was meant for just me and Rocky, right? But that bottle was buried underneath an old tree and had been there for a *long* time. Most likely before we were even born. How'd you know about it?"

"Oh, child." A mischievous twinkle played in her eyes. "Who do you think put it there?"

Ricki and Damian looked at each other, their faces identical pictures of disbelief. They turned back to Madame Dupre, a new round of questions forming on their tongues.

The gypsy was gone.

"Creepy," Damian muttered. He faced Ricki, who now gazed at him with open adoration shining in her eyes. "Why're you staring at me like that?" he asked. "What are you thinking?"

"How good it feels to finally wake up," she replied. "Junior," she said, cautious, "tell me again what you think of soul mates?"

He sighed in resignation. Dropping to the curb, he pulled her down to sit beside him. "Okay, here's the deal. I think you can meet your soul mate when you're eight-years-old. And she can be stupid enough to be wearing a pink dress on the playground, *knowing* she's gonna get it dirty. And then get mad at you when it does. And then she gets her big brother to beat you up."

She grinned impishly.

"But she's so cute, you can't help watching her every time she's around. And you do everything you can to get her to notice you, even if it means dumping spiders down her shirt or sticking gum in her hair. And when she does notice you, it's like an adrenaline rush. So you keep doing more and more stuff to make sure she's always watching you as much as you're watching her.

"And every year, she gets more in your system, and there's nothing you can do about it. She excites you because she's smarter than any other girl you've ever met and keeps you on top of your game. But she also scares the crap out of you because you never want any female to have that much control over you. So you do everything you can to push her away. Whatever it takes to stop thinking about her every day, all the time. But you can't help it. You want her."

She stared at him, helpless to do anything but listen.

He took her hand. "I've tried running away from my feelings, and look where it got me—sitting in a girl's body. So maybe I need to stop running from what I've always wanted and enjoy what I can get for however long I can have it."

A gentle song began to resonate in her heart.

"It's always been you, Rocky," he murmured, tenderly pulling her close. "I love you." His lips closed over hers, prodding her mouth open with a sweet kiss.

The world spun.

Ricki sat back. She blinked, jubilant to see Damian's dark eyes drinking her in.

He smiled, rubbing his nose against hers. "It worked," he said, caressing her face. "Do you think it's finally over now?"

"I don't know." She smiled coyly, sliding into his lap and moving in for another kiss. "Let's try again just to make sure."

And the song of her heart swelled, expanding beyond all thought and reason to encompass the lovers in a melody heard only by their souls.

THE END

Thank you for reading *Sealed with a Twist*. I hope you enjoyed taking this journey with Ricki and Damian as they traveled a rocky path to true love. Please share your thoughts by writing a review where you purchased your copy.

Come on by to www.vagivens.com to:
Stay up to date on upcoming projects and events,
Keep up with my ticklish tales about life
and totally random thoughts,
Just say hi!

ABOUT THE AUTHOR

V. A. Givens is a devourer of books and disciple of all things romance. Growing up as a military brat, she lived with a book permanently attached to each hand. Her imagination was shaped by a diverse spectrum of authors, from the fantasy of Lloyd Alexander and J. R. R. Tolkien to the suspense of Lois Duncan and V. C. Andrews. Inspired by their words, she now crafts the stories that captivated her youth: tales of ordinary people learning about life and love through extraordinary circumstances. *Sealed with a Twist* is the first in a series of books set in the fictional town of Willow, where everyone has a lesson to learn and reality is often subject to interpretation.

ACKNOWLEDGEMENTS

A flowery note of thanks, showering of love, and apples of appreciation to:

- A father who read, re-read, and re-re-read every version of this book I threw at him; who could never finish a TV show or movie without being interrupted by phone calls or texts asking, "Which way sounds better?"; and who counseled me through many an emotional breakdown as I fought my way through the creative process to put words on paper and bring imagination to life;

- A mother who has unwavering faith in my success and waits patiently for that mansion on the lake I owe her;

- A sister who gently browbeat and lovingly harassed me into getting my tush in gear and officially becoming the author I claimed to be;

- Another sister who started the dream with me and inspired me to finish it;

- Nephews who drew on command, advised on demand, and cheered me up as needed;

- Nieces who showed me how to stay hip, motivated me to stay young, and caused me to keep it real;

- A best friend who stayed in the trenches with me, encouraging me to fight through the mundane and keeping hope alive as we wait for the day we finally hit the lottery;

- An editor, Debra L. Hartmann, who stayed true to my vision, offered valuable advice, and confirmed that readers come first, rules can sometimes be broken, and being a comma commando isn't always the best way to approach punctuation in a sentence; and

- A God who keeps me grounded and stirs up my gift every day, so that I can hopefully bring a bit of laughter, hope, and inspiration to others with the words instilled in me.

Thank you.